"So. What you bettin' on the gun?" Detective Asa Hobbs looked a little like a toad, all sunken into the softly decrepit, earth-brown easy chair in Garrett's office. Garrett shuffled his feet under his desk, moved his chew, and gave Hobbs a knowing grin. "You're the expert. You've already made your prediction, so what is it? What we gonna find ...?"

McCracken, passing by the door with an armload of paperwork, poked her head in. "We won't find it. They'll find it—all those people pokin' around that place. They'll find it and dump it down somebody's outhouse hole, and that'll be the end of that—ashes to ashes and shit to shit."*

* (Author's Note: Alma, of course, would not approve of McCracken's language; she would, however, appreciate her sentiment.)

* * * * * * * *

"A great mystery doesn't always involve a mansion, high society and the butler. At some point you will realize that the enjoyment of *this* story lies not just in getting to the heart of the matter, but in being swept along on the ride ... You are absolutely guaranteed to be guessing right up until the end."

Nathan R. Sponseller
Raven Rumours Press, LLC
Publisher: *North Fork Merchant Herald*

All the Bad Stuff Comes in Threes

Karen Weinant Gallob

Earth Star Publications

Map illustration by Roxanne Smith
Cover design by Ann Ulrich Miller
Cover photo by Connie Willett

All the Bad Stuff
Comes in Threes

Karen Weinant Gallob

Earth Star Publications
www.earthstarpublications.com

FIRST EDITION
First Printing October 2006
Second Printing March 2009
Third Printing March 2014

Library of Congress Control Number: 2006934995

ISBN 978-0-944851-27-2

Printed in the United States of America

A Note of Thanks from the Author

The Delta County Sheriff's Department got me started in my life of crime. Sheriff Fred McKee, Detective Dave Duncan, and Detective Duane Morton patiently answered my questions about what happens first, second, and on and on, when law enforcement is notified that a body has been found. Aaron Clay helped me with legal questions. Dr. Thomas Canfield, Chief of Pathology at Montrose Memorial Hospital, gave me invaluable information concerning the findings of autopsy on the victims of particular types of crime. I am very grateful to these people for their assistance and I beg you to attribute any factual errors in the corpse department of this book to me, the author, only.

I also want to thank my editor, Marion Stewart, and my publisher, Ann Ulrich Miller. You got me across many a rough patch on the road!

Thank you, very special Ruth Meek, for allowing your picture to be used on the cover. Thanks to my Aunt Ula. Both Ula and Ruth are models around which I could pattern the stalwart and wonderful Hallie Flute, and I love you both.

Sara read it; Erin read it; Doug, Judy, Tanya, Amanda ... all read it. The result was dozens of useful comments which stuck to my manuscript like fertilizer on a wet spring alfalfa field. Furthermore, Erin went with me to the sheriff's office; Roxanne drew the map; Miles was there as a cheering section. I am especially grateful to Tanya, who has been here as a steady, patient sounding board for every cockamamie concern that crossed my mind. She helped with everything from verbs to the color for the cover. Thank you, thank you, Family, one and all. You rock!

When Dave reads anything I write, he always says, "Yup, sounds just fine." And that's it. Well, let's face it. Everyone knows there would BE no cozy mystery without Dave's cozy, mysterious support. Sometimes "Yup, just fine," is exactly the right thing for a wife to hear.

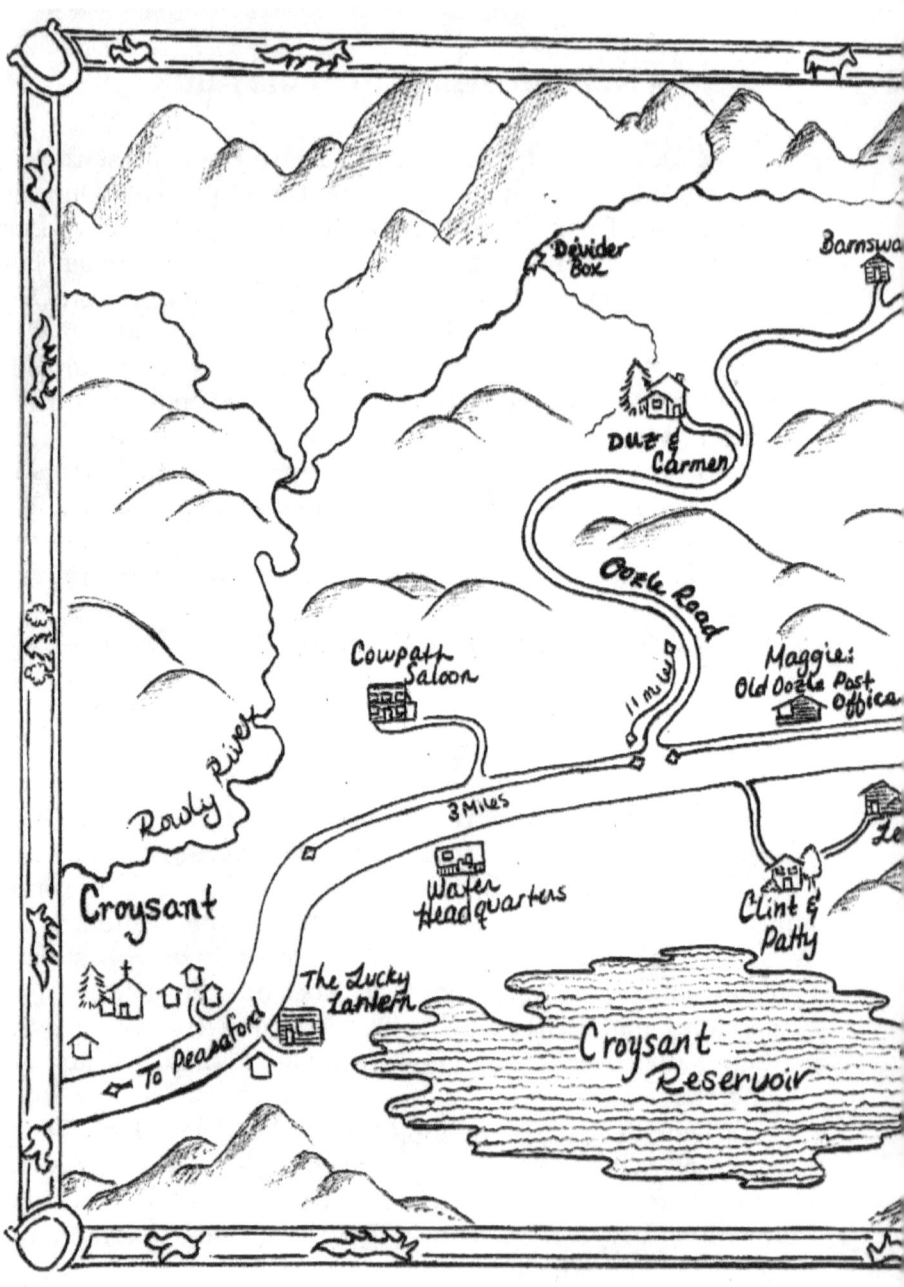

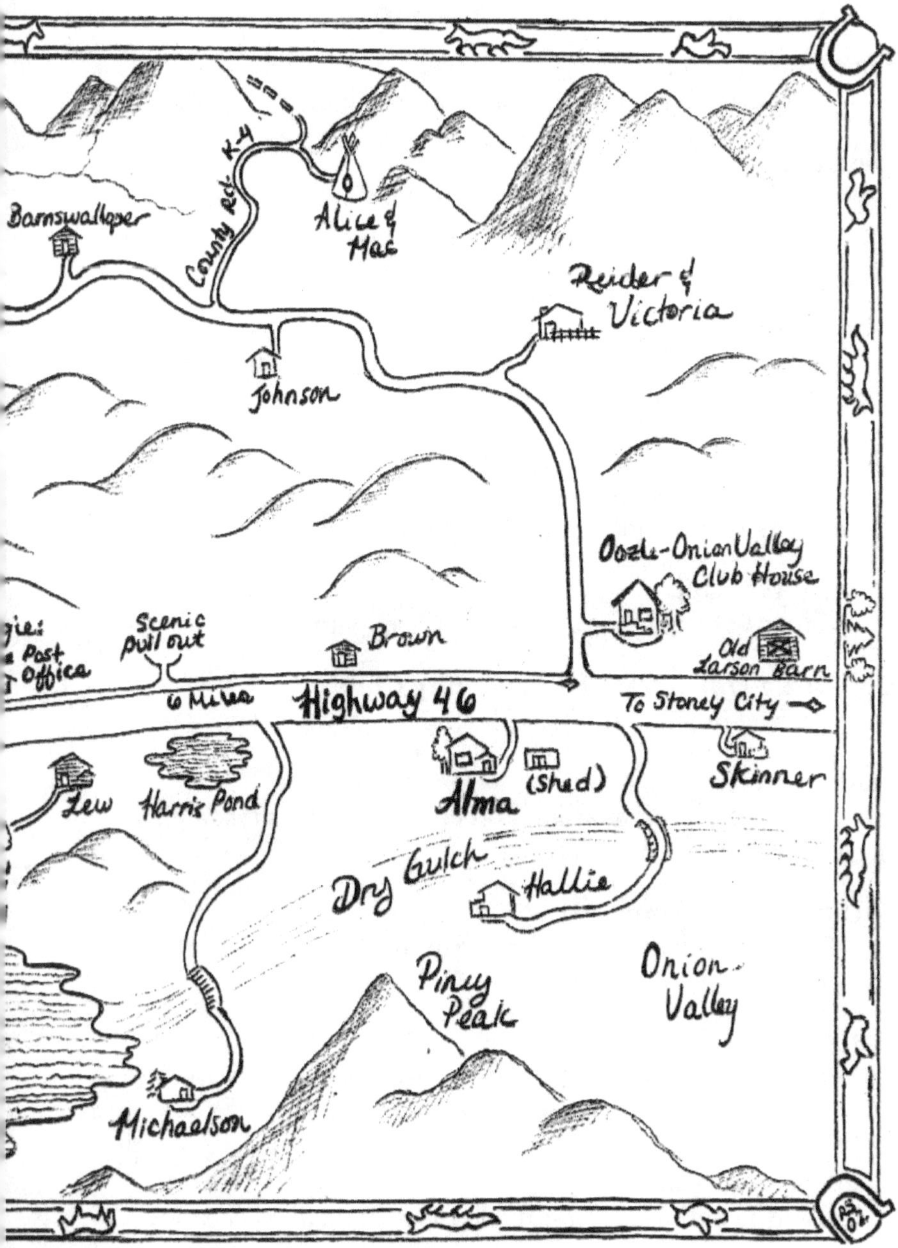

Barnswallower
County Rd. K-4
Alice & Mac
Reider & Victoria
Johnson
Oozle-Onion Valley Club House
Scenic pull out
Brown
Old Larson Barn
6 Miles
Highway 46
To Stoney City
Lew
Harris Pond
Alma
(Shed)
Skinner
Dry Gulch
Hallie
Piney Peak
Onion Valley
Michaelson

Cast of Characters

Sheriff Pat Garrett
His most frequent line: "No, I ain't that one."

Deputy Leigh McCracken
A chunky little redhead with freckles on her freckles, she figures the sheriff supplies the brains, so it's her job to provide the brawn.

Alma Weinant
She did mean to tell Duz about that body in the chicken shed, but he was late, as usual.

Douglas Ulysses Zane (Duz) Weinant
Alma's son. He just wishes the women — and the sheriff — would leave him alone. He's got irrigatin' to do.

Carmen Weinant
Duz's wife. She has a nose for a fishy situation.

The Oozle-Onion Valley Community Club
These women know *fowl* play when they see it.

Hallie Flute
Alma's boon companion and confidant, she's just a tetch hard a' hearin'.

Victoria Biedermann
She faithfully attends every club meeting, and she always pays her dues.

Reider Biedermann
Victoria's husband. He's known for his tendency to be in the wrong place at the wrong time.

'Mac' Beidermann
Victoria and Reider's son. He finds that talk is cheap.

Alice Beidermann
    Mac's wife, proving that there's no accountin' for taste.

Christa Beidermann Carr
    She knows it takes more than love to raise a child. Money helps.

Patty Harris
    It ain't for nothin' that her husband calls her "my hair trigger honey from Hartsville."

Clint Harris
    Patty's husband. He speaks best when spoken to.

Lewis (Lew) Harris
    Clint's granddad. The older he gets, the more he has to say and the louder he says it.

Lucky Harris
    She's dead.

Betsy Lee Zakely
    Alma sure has heard the name, but she can't place the face.

Lindy Zakely
    When you've been through a lot, it helps to share it.

Maggie Merimeister
    One of those California immigrants. Would she do just about anything to fit in?

Jenny Threewinds
    An old hippie gal with a sweet guitar and a long memory.

Greta Amelia Anderson
    Her brother used to call her 'Shitty Gritty' until their mom straightened him out with a mouthful of suds.

John Duval
    Small town attorneys: What they don't have to do!

This book is, of course, dedicated with love
to the real Alma Weinant, who was my mother

1

Wednesday, High Noon

in Alma's Converted Chicken Shed

To be perfectly honest, Alma Weinant was plumb disgusted. She'd seen dead bodies before and she wasn't impressed with this one. In addition to everything else, now this mess was in her way. She leaned on her cane, considering the situation. Which was more important, to deal with the dead guy right at this very minute, or to protect her reputation at community club? She sure did need to find that exchange gift for club before Duz caught her out here.

Well, yes, in fact, Duz should have been almost at Alma's by now, but when he saw the woman by the road, it didn't occur to him not to stop. He would never pass up a lady in distress, not even this "lady". It wasn't in his nature. Still, as he applied the brakes and methodically turned the truck in the center of the highway, he was also giving an amiable, dusty-shouldered, personal shrug, a private response to the comment he anticipated from his mother. "Douglas Ulysses Zane Weinant, you're late! Late, as usual." Well, she'd be right, right as usual. He sighed. Stopping now would definitely make him late.

Alma was out of the range of her Health Watch line, that was for sure, so Duz would have grounds to scold. On the other hand, at 91 years, hadn't she earned the right to move around her own place and not be tied like some naughty pup to a blasted 911 button around her neck? Think about it: heart attack? stroke? 'I've fallen and I can't get up'?... Well, all that stuff had happened already. She didn't like it, but shoot, she'd lived through 'em all, hadn't she?

She still felt pretty spry, too. Today, anyhow. It was a nice warm June day.

But then... Here was this corpse. And didn't bad things just always come in threes, though? Think about it. First there was the heart, then the stroke, and finally, the shingles in her left eye (Bingo! Strike Three!). Now here was this series of problems just today.

One of her girls – she didn't like to call 'em nurses – made her feel old – whichever girl it was who came on Wednesday mornings ... that one told her that she couldn't finish filling the pill boxes because there was no heart medicine. Lost, she supposed. Rolled under the furniture. The girl had shrugged. Mary ... was it Mary? Alma struggled to find the name in her glimmering memory. Mary, she guessed. She said it out loud to reassure herself. Mary. Mary had called Thomlin's Pharmacy and they told her it had just been refilled. Mary had called ... who was it? The other girls, whoever they were. Jeannie, one was. And Victoria. Pill bottle couldn't be found. That was Strike One. And ... Well, anyhow, thank goodness for local businesses. Thom, at the pharmacy, had finally agreed to send up more medicine.

The second thing was forgetting that it was her turn to bring the club gift.

Duz pulled up beside the woman, who stood near the road languidly waving her hand for him to stop. Oh, he knew who it was, all right, and he wasn't pleased. Alice Biederman, one ditzy lady. 'Pothead' would be a minimal description. 'Mushnoggin' or 'Shroombrain' might also apply. He always avoided going up to her and Mac's place. He did what neighborly business he had to do with Mac's dad, Reider, at the main ranch when necessary, but he knew how the mountains took off from the foothills up by Mac's, and how there were plenty of nooks and crannies among the brush and rocks where even the helicopters that patrolled these mountains would never nose the stuff out. Marijuana ... what was the point of it? But then again, Mac, the worthless little bastard, seemed to be doing a brisk business. Duz pushed his hat back off his work-sweated gray hair and smiled in spite of himself as he pulled to a stop beside Alice.

Oh, boy, she'd outdone herself today. Her freckled breasts

were squooshing out of a dirty, tight white tank top which also exposed a pale, bare midriff. She had on a short leather skirt, very short, from which extended long, pale, toothpick legs. The bareness of her legs was interrupted by Roman sandals which laced to the knee. Blood red polish on her toenails contrasted with the black of her hooked fingernails. Duz marveled at the number of bracelets she'd managed to pile on her skinny, bare, freckled arms, but he marveled even more at her rings. First there were the rings on her fingers, surely a dozen: death's-heads, ravens, wizard stones, unicorns, and serpents. But this was nothing. From her left ear sprouted four rings, five from her right. One from her nose, one from her navel, one from her lower lip, and god knows where else one might have found a hole on the woman into which jewelry had been injected. No, thought Duz, take that back. She was working her mouth, and as her tongue moved uncomfortably in and out, an occasional drop of saliva was released against her lips. As she slurped one back in with an impatient lick, he realized that the cause of all this oral action was a diamond-like stud that flashed in her tongue, about halfway up the length of the side, causing her to keep up a steady adjustment against her teeth and cheek.

After the array of bejeweled piercings, the short greasy purple hair topped by a backwards farmer's cap seemed anticlimactic.

* * *

In all of her years as a charter member of the Oozle-Onion Valley Community Club, she had never, ever forgotten to bring the exchange gift when it was her turn. And yet, there it was. Strike Two. She had completely forgotten to ask one of the girls to pick up something in town to give. This, she felt, could surely damage her reputation. People knew her for her dependability and wide knowledge of all the folks in the community. Now they would say she was getting old, was starting to lose her memory. Hmmm... Well? Maybe she was, but the less people knew about it, the better.

And now this third thing, Strike Three. Blasted body! She had so much stuff stored in her old shed. It used to be a chicken shed. She recalled the days when fat old hens bustled around the front of it, making the happy gurgling sounds that were chicken songs. The big old rooster, stripey-feathered and magnificent, rode shotgun, him arrogant and bossy... Her Doug. Fine man. She recalled when her and Doug decided to travel a little more, so they gave up on the chickens and hauled the shed up here to convert to a storage shed. Well did she remember the effort spent boiling water and carrying buckets of it to scrub the mess down, but after the old shed was fixed up, it had proved quite handy. You could get a lot of stuff in it if you used your head. She gazed with longing over the top of the body at the boxes beyond. Somewhere in those boxes would be a great gift for club. She just needed to pick a little old something and find the wrapping paper... but still...

Duz ducked his head to clear the door frame as he slid from the truck. When he was born, Alma had been impressed with the success of her great feat. She wanted the size of her accomplishment—all ten pounds, five ounces of him, and born at home, too!—reflected in his name. It would be Douglas, of course, after the baby's powerful and immediate progenitor. And Ulysses, after her own upstanding father, so like the Union general he had been named for. Then there was Zane Gray, her favorite author, describer of the sweeping vistas of the mighty West. "Zane" would give a nice expanse to the weight of the rest of the name. She conferred with her Doug, and he, preoccupied as men can be when planning how to provide for their nestlings, agreed.

As so often happens with plans, hers fell through. The sweet-tempered baby boy proved too mellow for the heavy name. Illustrating the old saw that it takes a village to raise a child, the community got to know him, then shortened the fine, long title to the less inspired monicker, 'Duz.' So it had been for sixty years now, and even for Alma the appellation at last stuck. In his more favored moments with her. After all, what's in a name?

Alma's eyes dropped back to the corpse. He'd been shot. Despite her old eyes and the bad light in the shed, she could see the bullet hole right in the middle of his back. She knew everyone around here, of the oldtimers and such. She peered closely at the body. Lots of newcomers comin' in. From what she could see of him, she didn't recognize this guy. But then, all she could see was his

4

back. He'd been sitting on a stack of boxes – her boxes, she noted with indignation – facing the piled boxes at the back of the shed. To his left was one of her good oak dressers that she had enameled all up in a bright and cheerful yellow, a little dulled now after thirty years. To his right, more boxes, a variety of cardboard cartons from various grocery stores, fruit packing plants, and other commercial establishments around the area, all filled with her treasures. In front of the corpse was a low table Doug had built for a coffee table in their first living room.

Drat the man! Inconsiderate! He'd got blood on it. Couldn't seem to muster much, though. Now when Grampa – her own grampa – cut his arm off at the sawmill that time! Now that was blood! She'd been just twelve then, and she recalled the family running and screaming and her and her brothers and sisters huddled near the porch, watching. What a mess. Couldn't save Grampa, either. Long ways to the doctor, those days.

There was a spot of blood beside the box he'd been poking in. Tentatively she touched it, wondering if it had stained the wood, then spit on her finger and wiped the spot up. She cleaned her finger on her skirt. Crowded among the boxes, he seemed to have been going through them. Her boxes! The one in front of him that his face had fallen into when he slumped forward was wide open. His hands were kind of just flopped on the table now, but they'd been in it, she could tell. Fingering her things! She felt violated.

Well, by gum, she had never failed so far to bring the gift to the club gift exchange when it was her turn. If she didn't take a gift today, some of the women would notice, might comment to each other on her age and suspect her memory loss. They'd talk. But it wasn't that she'd really forgotten the gift. She'd just forgotten to have one of the girls get something earlier in Peaseford, or even Riversmet. Victoria nursed in Riversmet. She could've done it, easy.

Now, what was it she'd been thinking about? She idly poked the corpse with the end of her cane, but he stayed in place. Oh, yes. She still had enough nice things out here. If she could get past this guy, there should be something that would make a very acceptable gift. With some pretty wrapping paper.

Duz was a small-time rancher who'd struggled to make a living with his little place ever since he inherited it from his grandparents. His parents used to carry him into the mountains on horseback before he could walk, and his early rambling atop ranch horses had left him with a slight bow to the legs from the long days of gripping the animals' sides. Perhaps the bow was increasing with the increase in his girth. His belly now drooped over his belt. The belly and his cheerful blue-green eyes enhanced his Santa persona at the Oozle community Christmas dinner. He resembled a very large, happy gnome from a sketch-book for the Brothers Grimm. He loved to laugh anyhow, sought out the best jokes from other ranchers, ribbed the neighborhood kids, and had a tendency to optimism even when others despaired. Anger was seldom an emotion for him; those who knew him knew that the only way to set him off was to show him a serious injustice. Only a few had seen the rare instances when that happened. Those few knew that in the face of such an injustice, he could demonstrate a white hot fury that pushed you away like a furnace.

Yes, Duz stood for fairness and an even hand even if it went against his own interests. He stood for freedom. He stood for secure property rights. A solid stand. He voted libertarian.

And no, he was not easily angered, but he had been angry last night. The goings on at the water board meeting had offended his deep sense of fair play. He had been mulling over the evening as he drove, mulling less from the perspective of his own preservation as a ranch owner than from the perspective of a man who feels that people should behave in an upright and decent manner. He had been mulling it over, worrying it like a newly discovered rotten tooth. Then he spotted Alice.

Squinting at one box just to the right of the corpse's head, Alma read the word 'paper' as the label. Ah, yes, right here: wrapping paper. With a grunt of satisfaction, she hooked her cane to the back of the box, pulled it forward, then, juggling the box under one arm, she clutched the cane in the other hand and limped into the house.

Setting the box on the table, she grabbed the scissors and slit the tape, then opened the lid. Her face fell in disappointment. She had anticipated a box full of saved paper from holiday occasions, the bright colors and pretty ribbons young people used nowadays. She still saved most of that paper, although in Doug's later years she and he had been able to afford store-bought wrapping paper, too. Instead of pretty papers, though, the box was full of old letters. Long and short envelopes shoved humbledy-jumbledy into the box until it was full. She did save old letters, especially if they were on pretty paper, but today! She glanced at her watch. Duz could well be here in ten minutes.

She closed the box, peering more closely at the label. Oh. Papers. 'S'. Letters and papers. Plural. Well. Maybe she should sort through these, but not today. After all, she probably still had time; Duz was always late, and today probably wouldn't be an exception. Gathering the box off the table, she shoved it into the corner behind the easy chair that she still thought of as Doug's. There.

She caught her breath for a minute, then hoisted her cane like a weapon and returned to the shed. Oh! There was that guy again! She reassured herself that she had known all along that he was there, but in a way he'd become irrelevant. She was running short of time. Club was at 1:30, and it was a quarter till 1:00 now...

It took two more tiring trips before she was able to come up with wrapping paper and a gift. She was very satisfied with the gift. You weren't supposed to spend more than three dollars, and back when she and Doug had gotten it, it hadn't cost more than that, she was sure. She was kind of sorry to have to give it away; it was a memory, like all souvenirs. She and Doug would never go to New York again, never get a chance to pick out such a pretty little bell together, shaped just like the Empire State Building. She had wanted to go outside the building and look down, and she could tell Doug was scared, but men didn't admit such things, especially not her Doug. He'd taken a deep breath, gone out, looked around with her... Ahhhh! The wind was blowing, making the building move. It was unthinkable, this, built so big and strong, yet going with the wind... She shivered, recalling, then shook herself and looked at her watch. Yes, indeed, it looked like Duz would be late again...

After the gift was wrapped, she made the obligatory trip to the bathroom. The bathroom at the clubhouse was not only hard to get to, but also it didn't have a riser. She washed her hands, then recalled that the shed door was still open. She headed back out, congratulating herself for remembering it. A closed door was the *key to the shed: Doug had fixed it good, and it and the wire mesh around the walls kept out mice and other varmints. She reached the door of the shed and gave a little start.*

Except, apparently, for this varmint! She'd forgotten this one. She stood staring at the body – an interloper with the temerity to invade her storage shed and get shot. Shot! In HER shed! He never should have been here in the first place. Far be it from her to call the sheriff in this fool's honor. She drew herself up to the full five foot one inch to which she had shrunk in the last few years and, holding her cloud of permed white hair high, she limped back to the house with dignity, thumping her cane as she went. She would just see about this. When he got here, she would tell her son about this intruder, and Duz would deal with him, you bet your sweet apples. But Duz was always late, and today was no exception.

2

Also Wednesday at Noon

At the Scenic Pullout on the
East Side of Highway 46

From Croysant, Highway 46 winds past what locals call "The Reservoir." Passing Alma's place and skirting Onion Valley, the road twists among the dobie hills that roll across the landscape, moving south, then east. Soon the elevation increases, and Highway 46 eventually works its precarious way along deep canyons, following old wagon train cuts against the challenging slopes, until it arrives at Stoney City. Stoney City nestles in the "real" Rocky Mountains. Real, because mountains are considered to be those things which rise steeply, cool and alluring, clothed first with quaking aspen and, higher, with blue spruce. Above timberline, the craggy visages of the mountains peer down, aloof and dignified. Real mountains are Colorado on a picture post card.

Around Croysant, though, it is different. Here, the dobie foothills present themselves as trashy, bare and barren, willing to sport only seasonal vegetation. What covering they wear is a melange of pinyon, juniper, and scrub cedar, with an occasional stand of cottonwood along their wrinkly creeks. They flaunt hardy grasses which quickly dry and yellow in the summer sun. They are bedecked with rabbit brush, smeared everywhere with sage. The effect of the whole is seedy and weedy, old mountains gone worn and shabby. For the lucky rancher with irrigation rights, though, the snow pack in the "real" mountains to the east grants water, and the dobie soils are willing to yield alfalfa, timothy, and other grasses to make hay for his or her cattle in winter.

Cattle. Yes, this is classic Colorado cow country, but no cattle were visible this June in the hot fields along the roadside. All the cattle were off to their annual summer vacation, munching native grasses in the distant mountains seen from the pull out.

Perched on the bar ditch, Alice's truck had stopped just short of one of the ubiquitous gulches that erosion grinds out of these aged dobie hills. It was a typical gulch, very deep, and dry at its depths. In her wispy, dream-possessed voice Alice murmured, "It has been an awful night."

Alice's pale blue eyes were rounded with thick black kohl. The eyes themselves were opaque, seeming, under the potentially pretty, thick lashes, to open inside into nothingness. They settled briefly on Duz then drifted past him, as if unable to track. She gestured listlessly at the old pickup truck which was sitting beyond them, it half leaning into the bar ditch north of the scenic pull out area.

"You haven't been here all night, have you, Alice?"

"Mac didn't come home on time, you know, Duz? So here I am with this freaking truck stuck in the freaking ditch."

Duz took it in. Yes, it was a freaking truck, all right—it had dings and bashes from one end to the other, its paint half gone, the body rusting out, the windshield boasting at least two sets of cracks spreading out from where gravel pebbles had shot up off the back road to strike the glass. And it did appear to be stuck.

"So," Duz ventured, "How did the truck get into the ditch?"

Alice didn't answer. She simply gazed vacantly toward her vehicle, but he noticed a deepening of color around her neck, the flush moving along the hairline and into her cheeks. He decided to try again.

"Would you like me to help you get the truck out?"

"I really hate this place," she said, her voice a monotone. She walked to the truck and opened the door on the driver's side. "And this freaking truck."

Duz watched her get in. A rock the size of a wash basin was wedged against the front of her left wheel. Maybe that was what was holding her up. She was starting the truck and he was jumpy about getting next to it to push the rock out by hand. He turned to his own truck and reached into the bed. Whoa! No shovel? He stared into his truck for a minute. He always had his shovel in his truck. Then he remembered. Last night. When he got home, he hadn't returned it to the truck. Now it was by the garage door. Shoot.

He walked over to Alice, who was pressing down on the accelerator but seemed to have forgotten to get the truck out of neutral. "Hey," he said, through her closed window, "Alice!" Loudly. "Do you have a shovel or crowbar or something, so we could move this rock?" He wasn't sure she could hear him. She looked up at him glassily, but she didn't respond, just looked back at the steering wheel and gear shift, a slight, puzzled frown on her face.

Duz looked again at the rock. He didn't want his hands, feet, or head in her way, that was for sure. He looked around hopefully, then walked to the back of her truck. Good. She had a shovel. He could get some leverage on the rock with that.

Gathering up the shovel, he moved to the front of the truck, avoiding the side mirror and noting that she had rolled down the window but was still staring at the driving apparatus. "I've done something wrong here," he heard her say as he passed. He decided it wouldn't matter whether he responded or not.

Just as he got a good grip on the shovel and set his feet, the truck gave a carnivorous roar and sprang backward. It had been sitting with its nose angled toward the adjacent pasture fence, its rear end slightly uphill, the whole truck just forward off the main flat of the tourist scenic pull out. The momentum of the lurching truck sent it spinning, kicking gravel, backwards into the pull out. Duz leaped away, wondering that he hadn't been hit by rocks, and Alice's head shot forward, then back, then bounced a little as she seemed to have gotten her foot off the accelerator, so that after a few feet the truck rocked to a stop, its engine sputtering and coughing.

After being frozen into the moment, both Alice and Duz moved. Duz started to walk toward her pickup, which had halted dangerously close to his own relatively shiny one. Alice stuck her head out the driver's window and, for the first time, looked directly at Duz and smiled. "Emergency brake," she shouted as he approached her. "I knew it was something real weird. The emergency brake was on."

With that, she gunned the pickup again, again spitting gravel, only this time her direction was forward. Again Duz jumped out of the way as she shot past him and trundled onto

Highway 46 toward Croysant. Only belatedly did he realize that she had left him still holding her shovel.

"Shoot," he mumbled to himself, then tossed the shovel in the back of his truck. He grinned. He'd drop the shovel off tomorrow or sometime. Old Alice probably wouldn't even miss it for a month.

3

Wednesday 1:45 (Late As Usual)

The Oozle-Onion Valley Community Clubhouse

"It's about time," Alma greeted Duz. She wasn't sure what time it was because, exhausted from her noontime adventures, she'd been asleep in her chair, but she knew it must be getting late, since Duz, who was always late, was now here.

Club was at 1:30, and granted, it was down the road less than a quarter mile, but he should know it took time for her to pull her old bones together, use the bathroom, wait for him to get her kitchen stool so she could crawl into his pickup, then crawl back out again when they reached the clubhouse. Some of the best gossip got gossiped early, before the meeting, and she darned well wanted to be there.

She struggled from her chair. "It's about time," she repeated. Now she had her eyes fully open, the left eye gently clouded over the brown iris, but the right still sharp, especially at a distance. The big number clock over the TV said 1:30. Well, there you go. Club would already be in full swing.

Duz had nothing to say. Sure enough, he was late again. He'd parked the pickup as near the door as possible to save his mother some steps, and he hurried to accommodate her rapid shuffle. When they reached the clubhouse he parked in the handicap spot. He walked Alma in and seated her in one of the two creaking desk chairs. They were chairs with arms and thus easier to get up from than the folders. Hallie Flute was already in the other. He acknowledged all the 'Hey, Duz' shouts of the women, and then, with great relief, headed for home. He'd more

than enough spring work to do, and he wanted to get at it. He
sighed. "Women!" he muttered, then chuckled to himself and
added, "God love 'em."

It would have been better had he been able to continue
thinking about the oddities of women, but despite his best
efforts, his mind drifted back to the previous evening and his
face sobered. He forgot Alice, Alma, and all the club women
completely as he again wrestled with the problem that had been
raised. He was going to have to do something about it, but what?

* * * * *

It was a difficult situation for everyone. What the women
most wanted to discuss was taboo, considering Victoria
Biedermann's presence. They'd hoped she'd stay home.

It wasn't that they didn't like Victoria. Although she and
Reider were newcomers, having only been here five years,
Victoria had proven to be a warm and sweet person, a
contributing member of the community. She faithfully attended
both the club and the local church. She was a certified practical
nurse who not only substituted when needed at the hospital in
Riversmet, but who had a faithful clientele of elderly in the
community for whom she cared. She was, in fact, one of Alma's
"girls." If they had to say what made them accept Victoria, the
women would have said it was her work as a nurse. Few would
have admitted that what they really admired was her stunning
good looks.

Victoria Biedermann, entering mid life, was as lovely as a
twenty-year-old. She had the long, tanned, slender legs of a
Barbie doll, a complexion as smooth as sweet cream, smoky eyes
that shone above chiseled cheekbones touched by sunshine. She
was a natural strawberry blond and her braids formed a tidy
Swedish halo over her delicate, heart-shaped face. Today she
looked smashing in a satiny, billowing-sleeved peach-tinted
blouse and trim, tan shorts. Her slender feet were tastefully
encased in brown sandals. The women smiled to her face, then,
in clusters of two or three, slipped back into the pantry to
"uh...help with the dessert." In fact, they spoke quickly and in
hushed voices about the Biedermanns.

Victoria may or may not have been taking part in Reider's scheme, and the women may or may not have personally liked her, but the bottom line was that it was simply good manners not to speak in front of Victoria, no matter what your final thoughts on her were. It did seem to be her husband who was causing the trouble. While they wished for a chance to just hash it all out freely among themselves, they were being careful to remain discrete.

When Agnes Michaelson, one of the hostesses for today, went to the pantry to check the coffee, Frieda Johnson crowded along behind her. Frieda had her hair freshly permed into tight corkscrew curls and wore a huge homemade polyester/cotton dress which looked good, considering that the shops did not carry her size. She wanted to talk about Reider and the water board, and had just said to Agnes, "I hear that Biedermann tried to attend the meeting last night himself. Can you imagine?" when Nancy Jane Barnswallowper, with her cropped hair and ranch roughened skin, stepped in the pantry door. She was dressed, as always, in well used jeans and a long sleeved Wrangler shirt, the cloth made soft by repeated washings, the last of which scrubbings had failed to defeat a large, greenish brown cow manure stain near the right elbow.

"Are you kidding?" Nancy Jane made a sour face. "I can imagine, all right. That son of a bitch will always be in the wrong place at the wrong time. Only this time they escorted him out as fast as his little banty legs could carry him. I was there."

Agnes, her face pink, made a shushing motion with her hand. "Hush, Nancy. Victoria's just around the corner."

"Well, it's true. You know, he was actually born in Riversmet. That's how that family of skunks got drawn back here—they smelled their own stink. I've got friends in Rivers' say that Reider gets it from his dad. His dad was one shifty land developer, all right, and his mother was a Las Vegas dancer that quit 'im when he was a kid. When the other guys were wearin' their Levis up to the ag building for FFA meetings, Reider was wearin' a suit, taggin' his dad around tryin' to gouge the local old folks for money to invest in shady land deals..."

Jilly Brown, in jeans and a tank top, had slipped into the pantry and was being smashed up against the cabinet by

Frieda's bulk. Jilly had brought the twins, as usual, and their shrieks could be heard from the other side of the building. They were playing skydiver off the community hospital bed, which was stored in the building's entryway. Although their behavior made Jilly nervous, more for the sake of the bed than for their health, she needed to hear this conversation. It could throw some light on her and Billy's position in the matter. "Wow!" She exclaimed, to keep Nancy Jane talking. "Is that true?"

"Damn right it's true. They run him and his dad out of these parts not long after he left high school. Talk about the wrong place at the wrong time...."

"Ladies," Doreen Van Doran, the other hostess for today and the current club president, interjected. She was a slight, refined appearing woman who didn't believe in saying things about someone behind their back that you couldn't say to their face. She could be a real spoiler on days like this.

"Ladies," she repeated. "The coffee and iced tea are ready, and I think we can start the meeting as soon as..."

Nancy was not to be put off. "...Talk about the wrong place at the wrong time. They say he ran for Canada after that, scared of the draft, but they didn't want the little weasel in Nam either. I bet he was insulted, never getting the call. He finally slunk back into America in the mid- seventies. Joined the Hippie crowd. War was nearly over. Nothing much left for the flower children to protest. Like I said, wrong place..."

Doreen was blushing. "Hush, Nancy," she admonished. "Victoria's just right THERE." She indicated the next room. "And Alma is here now. It's time for the meeting."

Reluctantly, the women edged from the room, looking longingly back at Nancy, hungry for the gossip. Jilly shot to the entryway to be sure the twins hadn't demolished the bed — and themselves. The other women settled in chairs that formed a rough circle near the front of the room.

If Victoria had caught any of the gossip in the pantry, she didn't let on. She was talking pleasantly with Maggie Merimeister. Maggie was also a former Californian, and they had been comparing news from their home state. Across the circle from them, Alma, her best friend Hallie Flute, and Donna Caswell, with Spit, formed a group. Spit was getting old now, much to everyone's relief. She was a hyperactive chihuahua and had, in her puppyhood, barked at everyone so hard that she shot out spit, hence her name. For years the women had braced themselves when they came to club, knowing that Spit would be all over them, clawing at their legs, tearing their slacks or pantyhose, and yapping to get on their laps. Donna would respond to Spit's enthusiastic socialization with sharp tugs on her leash, occasionally causing people in the vicinity to trip and fall as the unpredictable doggy line tautened and twined around their ankles. Only their innate courtesy and friendship with Donna and Bud Caswell allowed the club women to tolerate Spit. Then, one day—finally—people began to notice that Spit had begun to settle down. She'd aged. They forgot her earlier behavior. They came to expect her to act as she always did nowadays. She lay quietly, at peace on Donna's lap, occasionally twitching her gray haired skin as an itch rippled across her shoulder or hip, and letting her eyes drift sideways and then shut, only to raise her lids when dessert was in the offing.

Doreen opened her mouth to begin the meeting, but with the perversity and privilege of age, Hallie, Alma, and Donna kept talking.

Hallie was saying, shaking her head to emphasize her point, "... It's just real unusual. Big old beads. And the colors on 'em are real unusual, on the beads, I mean. Kind of a midnight blue and turquoise, real bright ... and silver and white and black ones, too, of course, beads, I mean, 'cause, like I said, it was a wizard, I think, taming a unicorn with a wand." She paused to consider, then finished, "At any rate, it was just beautiful, and real unusual."

Donna's resonant voice carried across the room. "So where'd you say you saw it?"

"Like I said, right there on Maggie's front seat."

Alma looked puzzled. "Didn't you come over on your four-wheeler, Hallie?"

Donna ignored Alma. "So, let's see it, Maggie. Where'd you get it?"

Bypassing Donna's question and answering Alma, Hallie said, "Oh, my bones was achin' today. Maggie offered and I figured I'd just ride on over with her for today."

Frieda, looking inquisitively beside Maggie's folding chair, said, "I don't see it. Didn't you bring it on in?"

Maggie had turned from Victoria and a look of agitation passed across her face, an unusual emotion for her. She was a collected woman, noted for her stylish, shoulder length brown hair, and for clothes so appropriate you failed to notice them. Today she wore a tailored off-white cotton pantsuit with a soft gray spaghetti strap top, the huaraches on her feet matching the woven straw purse next to her chair. "The purse in the car...," she hesitated, a little stammer. "It ... it isn't mine. A ... a friend of mine left it there." She finished with a rush. "I'm sorry if I misled you, Hallie. It does have lovely beads. I must get it back to ... my friend ... today."

"Oh, heck, no problem, Maggie. We were just gabbin'." Hallie grinned, exposing stunningly white teeth in her mottled brown face. She was always quick to tell anyone who admired those teeth that she had gotten them, mail-order, over fifty years ago and that they were "sure dandy," as good today as they had been when they first arrived. Truth told, Hallie was eighty-seven and she had sent for the teeth from 'Monkey Ward', as folks called Montgomery Ward back then, when Hallie was a newly married girl of sixteen. The catalog company had sent her a mold to bite to get the right fit.

Alma frowned. "I think I forgot to tell Duz something this morning."

"Duz's a big boy." Donna shrugged it off, jiggling Spit, who had to resettle herself. "He'll manage."

"But it was really a pretty purse," Hallie added. "I loved the beading. I never saw such big beads." She wanted to keep visiting and just forget the blasted club meeting. "It's too bad Duz got you here so late, Alma. You and me got some catchin' up to do."

In truth, the two hadn't seen each other for all of two days, and much of what they had to say would be the same thing they had discussed last week, since each had short term memory loss and tended to repeat herself, but the joy was in the telling. Hallie had been like a little sister to Alma ever since their one-room schoolhouse days up in Onion Valley. There were five kids in school there the first year Hallie went, and the other three were boys. Before old age, Alma had been a hefty woman. She used to carry Hallie on her back around the schoolyard at recess. She still had surprising power in her strong bones. As for Hallie, although she remained much smaller, she was sturdy. For years Alma referred to her as 'Little Old Hallie' and extolled her feats of agility to everyone she knew.

Until recently, Hallie had picked Alma up on her four-wheeler to take her to club, since she just lived across Dry Gulch from her friend. Dry Gulch was just that, another brushy ravine through which water ran only in springtime. You wouldn't consider going up and down the steep, crumbling dobie embankments, so Hallie had to cross the bridge and come up Highway 46 about a quarter mile to actually visit her friend, even though she was not much more than a stone's throw away.

Alma didn't like the ride with Hallie. In her opinion, "Little Old Hallie" drove like a maniac. One day, she finally got up her courage to shout her fear of the four-wheeler. She had to shout. She had said as much to Hallie before in a normal voice, but Hallie was just like Doug used to be. She was not just hard of hearing, she was selectively hard of hearing. She sometimes heard quite a lot, so you had to be careful. Then other times she didn't seem to hear squat. Well, to be honest, Alma had noticed lately that Hallie didn't seem to hear most things unless you were right in her face where she could see your mouth. At least that seemed to work.

Today Hallie wore homemade navy polyester slacks with a button front, and a flowered blouse sporting a tidy Peter Pan collar. The blouse had to be a little large to accommodate her widow's hump. (Both she and Alma favored flower prints. Alma's summery dress, which she was proud to be able to put on herself, was a chaos of pink, red, yellow, and blue roses entwined with bright green leaves, a veritable explosion of good cheer.) Hallie, as always, wore her lank gray hair short and straight, combed to the left and firmly in the command of a barrette placed at the temple to hold it back from her face. She needed the traffic cleared from her face because she had sharp, busy blue eyes which, like those of her forebears, had never yet missed a thing in the Oozle-Onion Valley area. This said a lot. The first Flutes, a roughshod bunch, had pushed into the valley as the Ute Indians were riding out.

Again, gentle Doreen opened her mouth to call the meeting to order, but temptation overcame the older woman. With a strange mixture of craftiness and naivete, Hallie said, "I heard that that was some water board meeting last night. It sounds like Victoria's Reider is causing quite a stir for us old ranchers."

A silent sigh passed among the gathered women, and they dragged their eyes self-consciously away from Victoria's face. Alma, not wanting to appear uninformed—(*Why hadn't Duz mentioned this? Maybe what she had forgotten was what it was he had told her?*)—Alma said noncommittally, "Is that right?"

"Oh, yes," Hallie said. She had a smooth, melodic intonation that made the 'oh' rise almost as if it were a question, while the 'yes' hung in the air, coaxing the listener to yearn for more. "There is a dispute over water, you know. It seems Reider Biedermann has discovered a defect, some sort of legal error, in all the deeds that go with the first ranches in this valley. Let me see—that would mean our place, of course. Mine and the kids and the part Ed Skinner holds now. And Duz and Carmen's, where Doug's dad settled. And Harris's, which would affect them and Michaelsons. Right, Agnes? And then, of course, Nancy's place, and Frieda and Pete's. And Billy and Jilly's. In all, seven old settler deeds, but because of the way land sales and inheritance issues have followed, it sounds as if it affects most of the people here in the Oozle area."

Alma hesitated, reluctant to reveal the depth of her lack of information on this issue, but curiosity got the better of her. "Sooo...what was it Reider discovered?"

"What?" Hallie scowled at her, projecting blame to Alma for not speaking up. Like deer frozen in headlights, the other women sat transfixed.

"I said," Alma shouted, enunciating clearly and emphasizing 'said', "I said, what ... did ... Reider ... discover? What ... caused ... the ... argument?"

"Oh," Hallie said. "Don't shout, Alma. I can hear you just fine. Reider discovered that the original deeds do not convey the water rights with the land. So he is going to file on them. For himself. Just like that! Now, isn't that a fine mess of fish!"

Victoria shifted in her chair, the sound loud in the tense room, but she remained silent. Doreen, however, cleared her throat and found her voice. "Um," she said. "Um, it's time ... it is time for the meeting to come to order."

"Oh," said Alma, her voice surprised and innocent.

Hallie didn't hear Doreen. Focused on Alma, she said, "Oh, what? Please speak up, Alma." Then, before Alma could say more, she added, "It would wipe us all out, you know. None of the ranches could function without their water rights."

Alma shouted. "I said, 'Oh,' Hallie. And also Doreen is trying to call the meeting to order." Now it was Hallie's turn to say 'oh', and then she subsided into her chair.

Doreen repeated, "It is time for the meeting to come to order. We will all stand and say the Lord's Prayer."

Now, let it be said that this was a community club and not a Christian organization, but be that as it may, the Lord's Prayer had been a part of every meeting since the club began. Whether in times gone by it had been a problem for anyone is difficult to say. Perhaps the community was completely homogenous then with respect to faith. Or perhaps it had been a problem, and the record just does not show it because people are usually silent on these matters. It can be said that the women of the club today were silent as to their personal feelings toward the prayer, although at each meeting the heart of each woman held its own emotion as the prayer was repeated.

At least two of the members would simply speak the words from the depths of their hearts, reaching for Jesus' touch as they always did when the prayer was spoken. Some spoke with a degree of automation that made the words meaningless and some felt the prayer brought them into a sweet unity with the other women. One of the current members was Jewish and one New Age, a woman who attributed the main act of creation to a female figure, a goddess. These last two let the words pass by, holding hands and secretly attributing a more general meaning to the ritual. Because it had always been a predominantly Christian community, few noted that their Jewish and Wiccan friends might, in fact, actually be different in preferred ritual or belief.

And back to the prayer: one lady sincerely believed that such prayers should only be said in the privacy of one's own home, but she longed for the closeness of the club, so she, too, tolerated the ritual. At least one woman had withdrawn from the club, not concurring with the prayer as the opening event. She did not at the time give her real reasons for withdrawing, feeling that it was unnecessary to "upset the apple cart." And so it went. Such is the nature of one small ritual: the speaking of this prayer in this public sphere had the power to silently sort out the women, eliminating some, uniting others, and causing a few to feel discomfort as they searched their own consciences at each instance of its repetition.

Today the union of their hands and speaking of the prayer sent the minds and hearts of the women present toward Victoria. Their primary emotion was sympathy. She was, they felt, a woman who went about her business and did her work well, a work that was important to the community. Not everyone was kind and patient and capable of nursing the sick or caring for the elderly. Most importantly, they felt that she was somehow separate from her husband, the scheming Reider. He was seen as the power figure in the marriage. Could she restrain him, they thought, she surely would. One or another of them may have felt a tiny itch of envy toward Victoria's relentless beauty, or a sliver of doubt as to her part when it came to Reider's doings, but for the most of it their sense was that she had made a real bad deal in choosing Reider, and was showing good Christian courage in sticking with him.

And so the Lord's Prayer was spoken, the women forming a standing circle and holding hands all around, and then, with a sigh of shared kindness toward their stricken member, they sat. Roll was called. It was never clear how many women belonged to the club, because all that was required to belong was to live in the Oozle-Onion Valley area, appear at the meeting, and give a contribution of one dollar when the bowl was passed. Perhaps there were eighteen, maybe twenty, members, of whom a dozen attended with reasonable regularity.

The main interests of the women appeared to be a good gossip and a plate of excellent pie or cake, completed by nuts and mints. This dessert was provided by a different member each time. Like a Muslim woman's veil, the gossip and dessert concealed the true face of the little club. This club was the glue which cemented the community. Held together by the clubhouse as a base and the dab of business done at each meeting, the community formed around the club. It saw itself as an entity and functioned as one, also. When political issues — issues of fire hazard, road repair, the right to drive cattle on public highways, the question of water and land development — when political issues arose, the club was there for the community to meet and define them. It was a town meeting, a Native American tribal council. Through the club the Oozle people had a forum from which to speak their thoughts, listen to their neighbors, and draw their own conclusions.

Frieda had just finished the treasurer's report and the reading of the minutes when Alma, not tracking on the business at hand, said, "I feel like I left something at home I should have done. It seems like I left the water on or something."

Hallie heard one word in all this. She nodded knowingly. "Yes, I agree. Water is always a darned big issue around here. Something like what Reider did could start a range war, I reckon."

The whole group, respect for the elderly cast aside, looked at Hallie in naked aggravation. They had just gotten everything settled down with respect to Victoria, had been ready to do orders of business, and now here was Hallie stirring it up again. Nancy Jane Barnswallowper, either out of sensitivity or, more likely, out of a genuine urge to comment, said, "Yeah, that's true. Water isn't even just economic. You know, a lot of the names of stuff out here is named after water, like Riversmet, because of where the Rowly River meets the Colorado."

A chorus of 'yes, that's true' greeted this comment, as the women felt themselves getting away from sensitive issues again. Jilly, holding a twin on each knee and feeding them cookies, said, "Yeah, there's Dry Gulch, over between Weinants' and Flutes'. That has to do with lack of water. And Peaseford. Named after that settler Pea, that forded the Rowly right there. Now, Pea. That's a funny name, too."

Frieda shrugged. "Well, people think Oozle and Onion Valley are funny, but Onion Valley, up there by the old Culpepper place ..." she nodded at Doreen, " ... Van Doran's place, now. And all the way down 46, past Caswells ... those wild onions, on a wet spring, they just used to make that whole piece of land plumb purple, a real purple blanket of wild onions. Real pretty, but it made the cows milk strong..."

"But see?" Jilly interrupted, not wanting to have her theme of water pre-empted. "You said on a wet spring day, and we ain't had a wet spring day now since Billy and I bought the Cooper place. It's real droughty out there—already big cracks in this darned clay soil."

Frieda resettled her bulk on the folding chair, which protested accordingly, and continued. "... And like I said, 'Oozle'..."

"Oozle!" Hallie was pleased to have picked up the word. "Shoulda been spelled 'O-U-Z-E-L'. Those settlers meant to name it after the water ouzel, that little dipper bird that lives by the mountain streams up above the Oozle Valley, dives right in and dips out whatever he can catch. Bobs up and down, up and down." Her melodic voice sang the words and the women paused, enjoying the phrasing. Then Maggie spoke up.

"Well, Croysant is a water thing, too, I guess." She pronounced it 'Croy-sin', just as the oldtimers in the area did. Pronouncing local names right could help you fit in. Maggie wanted to fit in. "They told me that it was supposed to be named 'Croissant'. A French explorer named it, they said. 'Croissant', for crescent, like the roll, because it sits right there in the crescent shaped bend in the river."

Donna took it up, contentedly scratching Spit's ears. "Yeah, that's right, Maggie. But just like with Oozle, when the people sent off to have it commissioned as a town, they spelled 'er wrong. Guess they didn't know their French. Heh heh."

For the first time since the meeting started, Victoria, who had been looking pale, sat forward. Color came to her cheeks, and she said, "Isn't it the truth? Lots of things have the wrong names. Or at least they are spelled wrong."

"Oh, yes," Doreen said kindly. "There is another one right here. Did you know that Rowly River was meant to be the Roily River, but it got spelled wrong, or else the commissioners couldn't read the founders' penmanship. The story was told to me that the first settlers came in the spring and the water ..." She hesitated, feeling by this time that 'water' might somehow be a dirty word, then forged ahead bravely, "...the water was really high, all full of rocks and limbs and mud being carried off from a good snow pack in the mountains, and everyone said that it was 'quite a roily river.'

24

But the true nature of the river got lost in the naming process."

"That is exactly right," said Nancy Jane Barnswallowper, folding her arms across her chest, leaning back and thrusting her feet forward. Her voice was authoritative. "Lots of water names. Lots of dumb oldtimer spelling. Hey, we can't all be educated."

Alma nodded. "But we can learn. I always thought of there being the three names misspelled in this area: Oozle, Croysant, and the Rowly. But they turned out to be good names. Always felt they were kind of pretty. And I always thought things came in threes, anyhow. I keep thinking something else came in threes lately ... something about what I was supposed to do before I left home ..."

"In a way there's more than three wrong names," Donna interrupted, persistent. Alma thought she was a little pushy. "How about the Cowpath Saloon? It used to be more formal, didn't it? They called it the Cattle Trail when they first started it. Because it's along the river there where they started the cattle out of the mountains and drove 'em down the trail to meet the train in Peaseford for shipping on out to Denver. Then the locals, kind of kidding around, kept calling it the Cowpath and they just finally changed it ..."

Doreen clasped her hands fretfully. Perhaps a tactful attempt would work. Speaking with exaggerated courtesy, she said, "Alma may need to get home to check her water. She may have left the hose running in the wrong place. Would that be it, Alma?" A worried shake of Alma's head, and Doreen pushed forward, "So no doubt the best thing to do would be to continue the meeting and get our business done, and have the refreshments Agnes and I have brought, then maybe we can all get home and tend to whatever it is we need to tend to. Isn't it something, how we all forget things before we leave the house?" She emphasized the 'all', trying to draw any blame or hint of excessive forgetfulness away from Alma herself.

Apparently the general discussion had satisfied them because Doreen was able to continue the meeting, making it through 'Old Business,' where they discussed fund raising and repairs, and then 'New Business,' where they discussed fund raising and repairs some more, with the addition of an item about a donation to be made by the club to the fire department, a long debate as to whether it should be fifty or seventy-five dollars, and concluding with a card signing for a neighbor on kidney dialysis and another for an elderly neighbor who had broken his hip.

Finishing up with the business aspect of the meeting, Doreen called for a motion to adjourn—moved and seconded—and then several of the women got up, some to help distribute the dessert, Frieda to collect the dollar donations, and Jilly to get the names into the cup for the gift drawing.

At every meeting, each woman put her name on a slip of paper and it was collected with the others into a cup, then one name was drawn out. The winner got the monthly club gift—a handmade item or something that cost $4.00 or less. The lucky winner was now obligated to provide a gift for next month's lottery. Last month Alma had won a "lovely set of handmade kitchen towels and a matching pot holder." Privately, she had commented, "Lot of good it does me, since I can hardly see the pattern and lord knows I'm not safe in the kitchen at my age," but to the women she had exclaimed over the gift, expressing her pleasure. Now, this week it was her turn to bring the gift, and Jilly was making the rounds of the group with a pencil and slips of paper, collecting the names. One of the twins would draw out the winning name.

Suddenly, almost inaudibly, Alma gasped. She flushed, not just from embarrassment, but from shame. "I remembered," she tried to whisper to Hallie. She needed to confide privately to someone who would be understanding. "There WERE three things this morning, the heart medicine and the club gift and ... I just remembered the third one. Oh dear, oh dear. It was important! I should not have forgotten!"

Hallie looked at her, befuddled. There was a good deal of noise and paper shuffling in the room. From the far side of the room, Jilly announced, "Victoria won," and a little gabble of pleasure at the justice of it all went around the room among the chattering women. Hallie leaned her ear toward Alma. "What? Speak up, darn it, Alma. What did you say?"

Flustered, Alma leaned closer. "Hallie, I forgot to tell Duz. I meant to have him deal with it... there is a body in my shed."

Hallie scowled. "There is a WHAT? A what in your shed?"

Her voice had gained decibels. Across the room, Victoria exclaimed, "Oh, how ... (*she paused*) ... how nice. How pretty! It's ... Oh. It's the Empire State Building."

Ordinarily, Alma would have been pleased, taking this chance to describe the circumstances under which the gift had been purchased, giving its recipient a good idea of its true value. As it was, she was leaning toward Hallie, near tears, trying to make her friend hear her voice over the shuffling and chatter.

"It's in my shed," she shouted. "A body!" Hallie was still looking baffled, and Alma screwed up the volume. "What I forgot to do is tell Duz that someone — some man — has got himself killed in my shed, and I wanted Duz to deal with it." She paused. Her voice tapered off. "But he was late, like he always is."

The clubroom fell silent, and every head was turned toward Alma. Even Spit's.

4

Wednesday, 3:00 P.M., Give or Take

Alma's Place

The door of the shed wasn't that big. Not everyone could see into the area at once. Jilly Brown, with the twins, and Nancy Jane Barnswallowper, the most agile club members, had arrived first and stepped inside, then Jilly snatched up the twins, who were all eyes, and beat a fast retreat.

By that time, the other cars were pulling into the yard and the women were climbing out and taking their places at the front of the shed, taking turns to see what was inside. Each viewing produced a funereal silence at the exit, but by the time the final parties arrived, clusters had formed and the women were gabbling like guinea hens.

Maggie, Victoria, Alma, and Hallie arrived last. Maggie and Victoria had taken time to ease Alma into the car's front seat and buckle her seatbelt with care. Hallie popped her younger eighty-seven years into the back seat, beside Victoria, on her own. When Alma was feeling anxious, her memory worsened dramatically, and she repeated her repetitions, unable to recall whatever it was she had just stated. In this case, she was having niggling doubts about her initial convictions concerning the man in the shed. The conversation on the short drive from the club house to Alma's home went something like this:

Alma: "He was a tramp, you know. Some kind of bum who shouldn't have been in my yard at all."

Maggie: "No, dear, you are absolutely right. No one should be in your yard..."

Hallie, from the back seat: "What? Could you please speak up?

28

Why would there be a trap in the shed?"

Victoria: "I just can't imagine..."

Alma: "Did I tell you? There is a tramp who is dead in my storage shed. Someone who shouldn't have been in my yard at all. I don't know what he thought he was doing there."

Hallie: "What kind of trap did you say it was?"

Maggie, turning to the back: "A tramp, Hallie. Somebody came into Alma's yard last night and died in her shed. A vagrant."

Hallie: "Vacant? The shed was vacant? Did he take Alma's things, then?"

Alma: "I'm not sure, but did I tell you about the body in my shed? I think it's a tramp. Somebody that didn't belong there at all."

Hallie: "So was it you that set the trap, Alma?"

At this point they arrived and took their places by the door of the shed, Alma increasingly agitated to think that she had let notice of this important event pass for so long, and yet somehow elated to think that at least something interesting had happened in her vicinity for a change. She leaned on her cane to the side of the others, evincing a certain sense of proprietorship of the scene.

Victoria was the first in this last carload to take her place among the women waiting to peek in, and she rose on tiptoe to peer over Donna Caswell's head. A blackbird sang out, and a whiff of fine perfume wafted across Donna from Victoria's person. Victoria leaned in, then she caught her breath, taking Donna's shoulder and gripping it so hard that she caused Spit, clutched in Donna's arms, to emit a protective growl. "Oh, my god!" she gasped. "It's Reider! But... but... he's been shot!" And with that, her grip on Donna's shoulder loosened and she slid to the ground in a good, old-fashioned, nineteenth century faint. Both Donna and Spit let out yelps, which alerted the clusters of women in the yard, causing several to spring toward Victoria.

"Oh, poor thing!"

"Quick, run into Alma's and get a cool cloth. I mean, get it wet, OK?" This from Nancy Barnswallowper, kneeling beside Victoria and holding up her head.

"I *thought* that was Reider, didn't you?"

"What a shock! Poor Victoria... we shouldn't have let her

see it. You really can see that bullet hole—and in his back!"

"Didn't anybody go for the damned cold cloth?"

"But we didn't really know it was Reider, from the way he has his head down. So how could we have known not to let her see..."

"It's right here, Nancy. And a glass of water..."

Victoria's eyelids fluttered. Jilly spoke, her voice worried. "We need to call 911."

"She'll be OK. She just fainted. Maybe we can get her in the house where she could lie down."

"I'll help. You get on one side, Nancy..."

"Maybe an ambulance would be a good idea... just..."

Victoria's eyes came open. Her voice was a murmur. "Please... take me home. I just want to go home."

"Oh, Victoria, you better not go home and be alone right now!"

"No, I don't mean call 911 for Victoria." Jilly had raised her voice over the cacophony of fussing around her. "I mean call 911 for the sheriff. That guy in there... I mean, Reider... he's been shot. He's been murdered. We need to call the cops."

This statement brought home the sudden realization of the truth. As abruptly as it had started, the chatter in the yard ceased. An uncomfortable hush settled over the group, and everyone kept her eyes to herself. Reider had been shot. They couldn't avoid that. And now that he *was* actually shot, dead in the shed, they weren't so sure after all that their sense that his being dead might be a good thing for everyone... at the least, maybe that sentiment might not be the best one to express just at this moment. And besides, how did he get there? How did he get shot, in the shed? Who... who among them... had done this? The silence among the women lasted uncomfortably long.

It was Doreen, always poised, who finally cleared her throat and said, "Well, yes, Jilly, of course. You are right. We need to call 911. Just... well, I guess I'm the president. I guess I'd best go do that right now."

Victoria was struggling to sit up. "Please... just please take me home." Her voice was pleading, her big gray eyes tearful.

"Not so fast, Girl." Nancy spoke heartily. "We need to get you into the house first, set ya down to be sure your head's on straight." With that, as if she were lifting an overweight calf, Nancy got both hands under Victoria's armpits and hefted her to her feet, Victoria wobbling and protesting. Then, putting an arm around her, Nancy steered her to the door and inside, where she parked her in Doug's old easy chair. Frieda followed, carrying the glass of water, her large face kindly.

The rest of the women had formed a fussing knot in the yard by the time Doreen emerged from the house. "Well," she said, not sure it was good news to everyone here, but sure she had done the right thing, "Well, they are sending people from the sheriff's department. A deputy should be here in a half hour. The main investigators are coming all the way from Riversmet, so it will be over an hour for them... and they are sending an ambulance anyhow, although I told them I thought it was not needed. So I guess we should just wait. They said not to touch the body."

Agnes looked at Alma, who was leaning heavily on her cane. "Alma, don't you and Hallie want to go inside and sit with Victoria? It looks like it could take a while out here."

Alma squared her shoulders and planted her feet firmly. She would not miss this for the world. "No, I do not want to go inside. I should stay here, where people are doing things. Get me my lawn chair out of that shed. Hallie can sit in Doug's. Get it, too."

The women's eyes shifted uncomfortably toward the shed. Finally, Agnes said, "Well, I suppose that would be OK." She stepped toward the shed.

Maggie chipped in, speaking with a certain sense of false cheer and good purpose. "In fact, Doreen, wasn't it just the body itself they said not to touch? It looks like a mess in there. A couple of us could tidy it up, get things cleared back, so it would be easy for the sheriff to get in to get at Reider's body... itself...."

Jilly, well up on her TV crime shows, looked troubled. "Look, you guys, you should just stay back. You're not supposed to mess around a crime scene."

"She's right..."

Hallie had caught the gist of the last exchange. "Alma, some of those boxes in there are real kittywampus. They could fall and something would get broken. You want we should go straighten 'em up for the sheriff?"

"The boxes..." Alma started, nodding her head and recalling that she had knocked down a couple searching for the club gift, but before she could continue she was interrupted by Maggie, speaking with authority.

"I really don't see that it could hurt, Jilly. So many of us have been in and out of there already. We'll just get the catawampus boxes and straighten them up. We can be careful not to touch anything whatsoever near the body."

"And some of us can straighten up out here," said Donna Caswell helpfully. She set Spit down, tying his leash to the gate. The women set to, Maggie and Hallie working in the shed while the others straightened up outside. Somehow getting carried away with the spirit of the task, Donna herself fetched a rake from the shed and went to the back lawn where she tackled a patch of dry grass that appeared to need tending, taking Spit with her while the twins watched from a nearby tree. The women were all hard at it when Victoria appeared again on the front step. She was standing erect and her color had returned.

"I really do need to go home, you know?" she called out. "I need to call Christa and Mac and tell them about their father, and to just have some time... could someone please drive me home? Maggie?"

Just then, the first official car pulled into the yard, and it was neither the ambulance nor the deputy. It was Hetty Beasly, the victim's advocate, who lived nearby in Croysant. Stepping from the car, she spoke in her smoke-deepened, commanding voice. "Hey there. It looks like there's been some trouble here. Hey, Alma. Hallie. Hey, Doreen and everybody. Hey, Victoria. You doin' OK?"

Victoria's knuckles showed white along the porch rail. "Hi, Hetty. I just want... I just would give anything to get away... to get on home. I didn't bring my car, but..."

"Umm-hmm. Just a minute, Honey. Let me talk to Alma, here." Hetty walked over to kneel by Alma, who was sitting upright and fascinated in her lawn chair. She put her hand on Alma's knee and smiled. "You doin' OK here, Hon? Ya got plenty of support? Somebody to call Duz or Carmen for you?"

Alma nodded, setting her chin. She knew how to deliver

what was expected of her when it was needed. "I am doing just fine. You're Hetty, aren't you? Hetty... um...."

"Hetty Beasly, Hon. And you *are* doin' fine. I can tell. I'll be back a little later, to check, OK? Meanwhile, maybe we should tend to Victoria." Hetty stood up and faced the women. She was fairly sure they had more than one concern about sending Victoria home, but she made her tone mellow, addressed them in general. "Look, I think it will be OK if I drive Victoria on home." She looked at Nancy Barnswallowper's skeptical face and said, "I will stay right there with her. It will help her to be able to reach her children, don't you think?"

Nancy burst out, her voice cynical. "She ain't gonna reach them anyhow. At least not Mac and Alice—they ain't got no phone in that damn tepee."

Her voice still soothing, Hetty smiled. The smile had a little edge to it. "I think we can arrange to get the word to them, Nancy. I will be sure all of this is taken care of." She knew it! Nancy was suspicious of Victoria herself. Ah, well. She'd do what she could and Sheriff Pat Garrett could sort out the rest.

Alma put her old, bony, blue-veined hand on Hetty's hand, which was still resting on her shoulder, and patted it firmly. "Hetty, you know, I am worried about one thing, and I want to apologize to Victoria. Victoria, I think I said that the man in the shed was a tramp. Now they are telling me he was your husband. I am real sorry. I didn't mean to be calling your husband a tramp."

5

Wednesday, 4:00 P.M. or Thereabouts

At Police Perimeters, Alma's Place

Deputy Leigh McCracken sent them scampering. The ambulance had arrived first, causing one final skirmish over the best place for Victoria. Nancy Jane Barnswallowper and her allies lost that one. A cursory check of Victoria's vital signs by the ambulance driver and she was loaded into Hetty's car to be trundled to her home. Lois, the other EMT, cautiously approached the shed, stuck in her head, then stepped in to check the vitals on the corpse and called out, "Nothin' to be done over here, neither, Ralph."

This made the club members feel somewhat guilty, as if they were wasting the ambulance people's time. These folks had to leave their cookstoves and fields in order to run these routes, and it would be rude to call them for nothing. When Ralph responded with, "Well, let's wait around 'til Garrett gets here," the whole group became subdued. Frieda, panting with exertion and dusting off her hands from her tidying endeavors, said, "You know, maybe I should just get on back home now. I don't see as there's much more to do here."

The ambulance driver, an easygoing man, but astute, said calmly, "Nah, Ms. Johnson. Ya' should hang out here a little bit yet. Those folks that are comin' will want to interview ya' all. You ladies just get yourselves some iced tea and find an easy spot to set. Better quit messin' around cleanin' up here, I 'spect." He grinned. "The big tough cops from Riversmet are like to accuse ya' of tamperin' with the evidence."

The club ladies did not grin back. Jilly caught Maggie's eye and made an "I told you so" face, while Donna set her rake by the backyard gate cautiously, as if it had become an explosive. At the mention of iced tea, Doreen and Agnes, the club hostesses for the month, shot their heads up like fire horses at the bell: they'd forgotten the refreshments! The murder had interrupted refreshment time! Back at the club house sat two large pans of Cherry Drizzle Goody just waiting for the whipped cream stashed in the tiny clubhouse fridge; there were also three dishes of nuts, mints, and special toffees, a large steamy container of coffee, and a pitcher of iced tea ready for the ice chips. Hesitantly, Agnes approached Lois, who was getting back into the ambulance. "I think Doreen and I should run up to the clubhouse and get some things... some food we left up there. It could help feed you and Ralph as well as Mr. Garrett and so-on..."

The EMT smiled and shook her head. All she said was, "I think you should not, Agnes."

It was at that point that Deputy McCracken pulled into the already bustling yard. She'd been patrolling Highway 25 between Riversmet and Peaseford when dispatch called. She was driving the least of the three patrol cars owned by Riversmet County. Except for the occasional disastrous incident involving some strange automotive disregard for the power of freight trains hundreds of cars long, each laden with tons of coal, not much ever happened on that stretch of highway. It made a patrol there a boring task. McCracken was thrilled to get the homicide call. She had hit the siren and moved at all permissible speed, but it still took nearly 40 minutes to respond to the 911.

Clipping off the siren and lights, McCracken stepped from the car at the top of the incline that began the driveway. She was silhouetted against the distant peaks, her back straight and her uniform bright in the lowering afternoon sun. She surveyed the scene, assessing the huddled women as if she expected one or another of them to step forward, shotgun at the hip, and blaze away at her. She would have been ready.

Unlike Victoria's delicate good looks and tasteful grooming, which sent secret shivers of envy among the club women, Leigh McCracken's appearance filled them with awe and a kind of dread. She had the unrestrained beauty of flourishing health and exuberant youth. Her deputy hat was pinned onto her hair, which flew fiery red and free around her face, and her mass of freckles showed proud and bronzed in the afternoon light. These women did not know McCracken. She was a Riversmet girl. But they could tell that she did things: she lifted weights, that would be for sure. Jogged, no doubt, and probably climbed mountains or played soccer. Perhaps she even stripped to her brassiere and twirled her shirt when her team won. If, that is, she wore a brassiere.

Like sparrows eyeing the mama cat, they watched her stride across the yard, taking in the layout as she went, and enter the shed. She stepped out and stated the obvious to everyone: "He's dead, all right."

Then she said, "Have you all restrained yourselves from touching anything here, at the scene of the crime?"

For a seeming eternity she was greeted by silence, then Doreen Van Doran, seeing her responsibility as club president, spoke up. "We were very careful not to touch Mr. Biedermann's body. We did help Alma so that you officers could get at things better."

McCracken scowled. "Which one of you is Alma? Why did you 'help' Alma? What is it you did?"

At this point, Nancy Barnswallowper, feeling testy, said, "We 'helped' Alma," using the same intonation on the word 'help' that McCracken had, "because this is her place. She is 91 years old and couldn't do it herself. And there, in that chair. That's Alma." She gestured at the fluffy-haired old lady in the lawn chair, a chair which had been set to best viewing advantage against the outside wall of the shed, not six feet from where McCracken now stood and closer than that to the body.

Having taken a short nap while the women bustled around her yard, Alma was again alert and ready, checking out the ambulance and police car on the other side of the yard, following the exchange with McCracken with interest.

"So... YOU are Alma?" McCracken focused in. "And this is YOUR place? Just what was it that you needed these women to do for you, Alma?"

Alma's eyes had narrowed and she returned McCracken's gaze with her good right eye. "I may be Alma to my friends here, but to you, young lady, I am Mrs. Weinant. I know your boss, Pat

Garrett. I used to baby sit your boss's mother. And I've known Abby Garrett, your boss's grandmother, since she lived in the old Bidwell house. You have no call to be snippy."

The club women were looking at Alma in amazement. How the heck did she do that, recall all that detail? They'd seen her when she couldn't recall what she'd done two minutes ago. Properly chastised, but still determined to do her job, McCracken said, "Mrs. Weinant. I didn't mean to be snippy, but a man has been murdered here on your property. We have to find out who did it, and why. Could you just tell me what it is these women have been helping you do?"

Alma frowned, her expression puzzled. "I don't know."

"You... don't know?"

"No, I don't know. Were they doing something? What were they doing, do you know?" This last asked sincerely, expecting that perhaps McCracken might give her a hint.

Stumped, McCracken said, "Well... I don't know. That's why I am asking. Mrs. Weinant, what do you mean, you don't know? You were right here. Didn't you tell them to do something?"

"No, I..." Alma started to say that she couldn't for the life of her recall; that, in fact, for the moment, she had no idea why all the club women and McCracken and the ambulance were even here, at her place, but before she could continue, Doreen came to the rescue.

"Officer, Mrs. Weinant has a wonderful long-term memory, but she has short-term memory loss. And she's been here in the sun for over an hour now. I'm not sure she can answer your questions."

McCracken scowled. "Well, then, Mrs. ..."

Doreen supplied the 'Van Doran.'

"Well, then, Mrs. Van Doran, what do YOU say it was that you were helping Alma with?"

"There were spilled boxes in the shed, and the yard had some things scattered that we thought we might help out by picking up. We agreed that if we tidied up that it might make your investigation of the crime easier." She paused, having come to realize at this point that maybe they had not taken the best route, then finished lamely, "We thought if we tidied up, you could get at things better."

Temporarily defeated by this dose of overwhelming niceness, McCracken rolled her eyes. "Look, all of you. You get. Stick around the place, so the sheriff can talk to you, but get out of this yard. Go into the house or something. Get away from this shed. I am going to secure this area with police barrier tape, and I don't want one single soul to go past it. I..." There was nothing more to say. McCracken stopped mid sentence, turned on her heel, and headed across the yard to talk to Ralph and Lois, who had gotten out of the ambulance again and were leaning against the side, watching everything with unspoken, but amused, interest.

The women "got." They scattered here and there, Jilly and Agnes helping Alma into the house while Alma commented, "I needed to use the restroom anyhow."

The rest of the sheriff's team was coming from Riversmet, so it was nearly a half hour after that before anything else happened. Restricted, the women were restive. They wandered in and out the back door, paced by the windows and looked out at McCracken putting up the police tape, stood around the back yard, walked by the flower bed (from which the storage shed and parking yard were visible) and assessed the status of the flowers. Shortly after they went in, McCracken stepped away from the ambulance and the two technicians crawled in and drove away, giving short waves and grins back toward the house.

After that, McCracken seemed to simply pace. Truth was, she felt rattled after her encounter with the women. She wondered if her comments had muddied the water for Garrett and Hobbs. Clearly the women's tidying had not been a good thing, but if she had foolishly set them up to resist the investigators' questions, that would not be a good thing, either. Oh, she sincerely hoped not!

She paced back and forth in the hot late afternoon sun, sweating in her uniform, and told herself to focus on looking for any evidence that might have been left by the busy women. She told herself that, but her mind wandered into the recurrent daydream she had about Sheriff Pat Garrett.

In the fantasy, he was pinned down by the gunfire of thugs. Smart as a whip, he outwitted them one by one, returning their shots with deadly accuracy. Then, just as he felt himself to be safe, one of the villains approached him unseen from behind.

Unseen by Pat Garrett or by anyone else but her, Deputy K. Leigh McCracken. The deadly thug was huge, much heavier than she or Garrett, but she was upon him without a thought. Now, let it be said that in the real world, McCracken was an expert in jujitsu. Perhaps that was why, at this point in the daydream, she always visualized in detail the many moves she would have to use to bring down the heavy, evil man and rescue her sheriff.

The object of the daydream was to get to the part where the sheriff recognized her feats and expressed his extreme admiration, not to mention his gratitude. The expressions of gratitude would probably be spontaneous, physical, and sweet. Unfortunately, McCracken most often did not get to the end of the fantasy; the jujitsu moves had become quite elaborate, the villain more detailed, and before she knew it, reality interrupted again... as it did today.

The women in and around the house saw her go down on one knee and squint at the ground a few feet in front of the shed door. She stayed in that position for several minutes, then stood back up and took a position by her police car, directing her attention anxiously down the road in the direction of Croysant.

It gave the women something to talk about. Like the repetition of the Lord's Prayer, homicide had asserted a certain power over them, silencing them, uniting them, and dividing them. They must think their private thoughts, most of which centered around the water board meeting, but they found they were suddenly unable to discuss their thoughts or the meeting, even though Victoria had gone from their midst. Some knew more than others; most had heard about Lew Harris's rantings, rantings which, until just this afternoon, had been written off as just Lew acting up again. Now they weren't so certain. Now they wondered what else had happened at that meeting that perhaps had been missed. Worse, now they wondered how much they should be talking about any of this to Sheriff Garrett when he arrived. Or to one another. They shot covert glances, wondering what the others were thinking.

While the time crawled by, they spoke of petty things: the dessert at the clubhouse, Alma's flower bed, a quilting exhibit, the pictures on Alma's walls. Watching McCracken was a diversion. When she knelt down, they were able to comment to each other at some length—what had she seen? What was she doing now? What next? Do you suppose she had word of the sheriff...? They hadn't expected to wish so strongly that any law officer would hurry up and make his presence felt in their community.

At long last, a second police car pulled up where the ambulance had been parked. McCracken stood talking to its occupants, then walked about the crime scene with them, obviously pointing out the place she had knelt by on the ground, gesturing toward the house—she was telling the investigators about the women's tidying up—and gesturing into the shed. The men looked at the sky; they seemed to be assessing the location of the sun, the nearness of the approaching evening. They returned to the police car, began pulling out a pile of equipment.

It took the women a few minutes of watching closely to realize that the one was videotaping the area, moving about carefully, trying not to disturb anything. The other had a still camera and he, too, began to take pictures, the camera flashing with each shot. He spent a lot of time in the shed; they could see the flashes and occasionally a portion of the photographer's anatomy—a foot emerging from the shed door, his head cocked sideways—as he worked to get all the necessary angles.

At this point Nancy Jane had had enough. She wanted to get a closer look. With her in the lead, the women trickled from the house one by one. Only Alma, who had gone into a sound sleep in her chair, remained behind. Hallie stood by the door a few minutes, then returned to maintain a protective watch over her friend. The others stood around close to the police tape, watching.

The photographers had put away their equipment and begun to take measurements and sketch the scene of the crime when the last police car in the county pulled into the yard. Detective Asa Hobbs stepped from the passenger side, and from the driver's side Sheriff Pat Garrett undraped his lanky, Gary Cooper body. Nothing else was Cooper. Sheriff Garrett, who had a good fifteen to twenty years on his thirty-some deputy, McCracken, felt most comfortable with what was left of his disappearing hair if he clipped it all off close to his scalp. This exposed a very round head and ears that protruded like Jughead's. Every morning he employed the old Mach 3 razor to drop any other hair in his cranial area except for a tiny, nondescript mustache that straggled across his upper lip and drooped noncommittally down each side of his chin. This produced an appearance that already had a tendency to startle, but the effect was enhanced by a scar that crossed his lower left cheek, pulled the mustached mouth slightly askew, then dropped down his neck toward his chest, to disappear at the front of his collar. A broad, flat, ugly, puckered, red scar.

Whenever he did think of his own appearance, which wasn't often, he would think, "Butt ugly." He would think, "Ugly as a sack full of assholes." Then he'd let it go. It wasn't a thing should bother a man much.

Today, he took in the scene before him: the peaceful looking little white house, the old, remodeled shed, the green lawn and blooming flowers, and the women waiting hopefully for him to resolve things, then turned to Hobbs and said, "Sure is a damn funny place to park a corpse."

6

Also Wednesday at 3:30 or so

At Duz and Carmen Weinant's Home

"Hey, Duz." Carmen tried shouting the greeting and waving her arms from two yards away because Duz was oblivious to her. He was perched over the front of the old John Deere tractor, totally focused on whatever he was doing with his screwdriver, and whatever it was he was doing was causing the tractor to belch smoke and pop so loudly that Carmen's voice stood no chance of breaching the din. Duz glanced up, grinned in a friendly manner, and simultaneously waved her away with a dismissive gesture of the screwdriver. Carmen raised her eyebrows and headed toward the tractor seat, making it clear that she intended to turn off the ignition.

If it is true that opposites attract, Carmen and Duz would be the poster child couple. While Duz was a one-time towhead gone through brown to dusty grey, in her youth Carmen had laid claim to raven black hair. It, too, was now grey, but a long, loose silvery grey that reminded one of a cloud-hazed sky on a moonlit summer night. Duz's sparkling, elfish green eyes could retreat quickly when they met Carmen's snap-back black ones. Duz was at base a nit-picky perfectionist who wanted every fence row straight and every irrigated patch to grow evenly green under the high, arid Western sunshine. Poking at the irrigation ditches with his shovel (it worn short and thin from long use), leaning on the old powdery grey quakie poles of a fence to ponder a new calf, he was a resident in the eternal Now.

Carmen, on the other hand, was a grounded and practical woman, ever mindful of past and future, ever sensible of the implications of things. A busy woman, she was active in community cultural events, and was an accomplished storyteller who volunteered weekly at the local schools. She and Duz were already grandparents many times over. With all that, however, if asked what she did, Carmen would say simply, "I paint fish."

That was how she saw herself: as a person who could take one subject, all of her life one subject, and see it over and over again, each time for the first time. Her paintings of trout, bass, salmon, goldfish, angels, and Piranhas—frequently wildly, colorfully abstract, often with startling naturalistic detail, always with surprising takes on perspective, scale, and pattern—hung in public buildings from Oozle to Riversmet and beyond, and always took a first at the county fair.

Carmen was a mosquito to her husband's bumblebee. Bumblebees seldom sting except in self-defense. Carmen, who barely topped off at five foot one and a hundred pounds, knew where to bite in, when necessary, in order to draw blood. Having just returned from a long day at an art exhibition in Riversmet, Carmen was intent on hearing the details of the Oozle Valley Water Board Meeting. On her way back through Croysant, picking up the mail, she'd heard gossip. She wanted to know what Duz would have to say about it, but he was intent on fine tuning the old tractor. When she made as if to march to the tractor seat to pull Duz's plug, so to speak, he shouted and gestured wildly for her to cease and desist, and she ground to a halt.

Wiping his hands on a stinky, oily rag, grinning devilishly, and pushing his hat back, he came for her, her still dressed in her town clothes, making her wave her own arms and step back swiftly. When he was close enough to be heard, he said, "What do you want, Woman?"

"I want to talk, Duz," she shouted. "P. D. says (she was referring to P. D. Quick, the Croysant postmaster) ... P. D. says that the board meeting last night was a disaster. He says Biedermann tried to attend it and was kicked out." They moved away from the tractor, which was left to sputter and cough on its own in the middle of the shed, and sat by the door on discarded lawn chairs which had missed the trip to the dump so often that they again had found a useful place in the family's lives.

Duz chuckled. "Too late. You should've woke up last night when I tried to snuggle up to you. I would have told you all about it. Every man has his price. But now ..."

Carmen punched him on the arm, a good-natured jab. "Cut it out, Duz! YOU should have come down to the exhibit today. It was beautimous, like the kids say. And our pictures were right pretty." She always called her paintings "our" pictures, a nod to the inspiration provided for her by Duz. "We did well, too. We sold three right off the bat."

"That's great, Carmy. And I just had a super day, too." His light tone bogged down in frustration, taking a sarcastic edge. "Tried to mark the wastefield. Broke the tractor. Took our Mrs. Alma to club and was pronounced late again. Oh ... and rendered roadside aid, for what it was worth, to the ever beautimous Alice Biedermann."

At this last, Carmen smiled. "Ever beautimous?"

Duz chuckled. "Even holy. What I mean is, filled with holes. She amazes the eyes."

"Was she high?"

"You be the judge. I was just trying to see what could be done to get her 'unstuck' from a big rock when she discovered that she had had the emergency brake on all along. She slammed her truck in gear, backed up, and took off ... no thanks to me."

"No thanks to you," Carmen echoed. "Sounds like it's been a day of double delights. Sucks for you, like the kids say. Mine was better."

"So what's your big complaint?" Duz started to put an arm lovingly across her shoulders, and Carmen, remembering her town clothes just in time, grabbed it away.

"I am complaining, Mr. Weinant, because P. D. told me the meeting was a mess, and I wanted to hear your take on it." Carmen's tone was serious, and Duz took the hint. His face sobered.

"You're right. It wasn't a pretty meeting. I can sum it up fairly fast. Like you say, for some reason Reider thought he could turn up there, and I guess he did have a right to be there, but it showed more gall than anybody there could handle. A couple of guys—I think it was Ed Skinner and Bill Brown—anyhow, they met him just inside the door when he was spotted coming in, and they sort of got on either side of him and half carried him back to the door. I was sitting a little way toward the back of the room, and I heard one of 'em say, 'Look, Biedermann, unless you came to undo what you started, you don't wanna be here.' "

"So did he say anything? Did he resist? Or did he say he'd give up filing on the water rights?"

"Nooo ... He didn't have anything to say. And it didn't look to me like he resisted at all. He looked funny, pale ... like he was real beat down ... they say that whole bunch up there is into the marijuana trade, and probably other drugs. I dunno. Maybe he was on drugs. Or maybe it was just a flu bug. But I remember thinking at the time that he probably couldn't have resisted even if he wanted to."

Just like Duz, Carmen thought. He'd try to give someone the benefit of the doubt in some weird way. She pursued her questioning, trying to visualize the evening. "So after they put him out, what happened? Did he hang around?"

"Oh, no. He took off. And you know Nancy Jane. She was there—the only woman. I guess she's the only woman ranch owner around here, and most of you wives were wasting your time at the library meeting ..." He half wanted to start teasing again, but Carmen scowled, so he resumed his narrative. "Anyhow, Barnswallowper interests were well represented. And after they threw him out, Nancy Jane sat by the door, where she could take in the meeting and look out, too, like some kind of guard dog to keep him away."

"Hmmm," said Carmen thoughtfully. "What then?"

"Well, Pete Johnson is the man with the paper ass this year, and he stood up and laid it all out. The bottom line is that there was some clerical error and the water rights to the seven original homesteads in the Oozle area were not conveyed on the deeds." Duz cleared his throat and frowned. "How Biedermann discovered that, I'll never know, but he did, and he filed on all of that water."

Carmen's face was skeptical. "He couldn't make that stick. That ... there must be some law ... those homesteads have been using that water for over a hundred years ..."

"Everybody last night said that. At times the noise got so thick in that room you could stir it with a spoon. But apparently

Johnson and Ed Skinner have followed it up clear to the state water commissioner, and old Reider might get away with it except ..."

"But if he actually took the water? These ranches would ... they'd dry up! Everything here depends on the water, and nothing is worth anything ... Oh. I suppose he would try to sell it back?"

"I don't know. I guess that would be one option. Or the way it is set up, he might be able to buy us all out and send us packing, then cut this land up into little housing tracts and develop it to make it all a suburb of Croysant."

Carmen gasped. "A suburb of Croysant—Duz! ... But you said, 'except' ...."

"Right. Two or three of the old timers said that there are papers somewhere that corrected that error on the first deeds. They are sure they recall that the error was discovered before this, and that they took care of it. But when us young guys," with this he winked at Carmen, "When us young guys tried to get them to tell us where the papers were, or even what they were, they couldn't say. Of course, everyone was worked up, so they couldn't think straight."

"But if there are such papers ... wouldn't they be part of the records, down at the court house?"

"You'd think so, wouldn't you?" Duz's face had clouded again, his voice sobered. "You'd think so." He sighed. "According to Pete Johnson, they aren't."

Carmen waited a beat, then said, "P. D. said something else about the meeting." She paused, taking in Duz's expression. She loved his perpetual optimism, and was most concerned whenever she saw it fade. The last time she had seen him this unable to keep his happy demeanor was last winter when they had rushed his mother to the hospital with her heart fibrillating wildly, ranging between speeds of 200 and 56. He looked equally serious now. "Something about Lew Harris," she added carefully.

"Well, I think it was ..." he hesitated. "I think it was just old Lew, spewing like he does sometimes. I guess ... well, I suppose he was expressing what we all felt, maybe, and hated to say."

"So. He did say what P. D. said he said."

"Yeah. I think his exact words were, 'We need to gather up

that son-of-a-bitch Reider Biedermann and subject him to a good, old-fashioned necktie party.' "

"Well." Carmen shrugged, patted her husband's hand. "Well, that's just talk. And talk from Lew Harris doesn't amount to too much, does it?"

Duz was suddenly quiet, and Carmen glanced up to meet his eyes. His expression was strange, troubled. "No," he said slowly. His voice was a murmur. "No. I don't suppose it does." Then he reaffirmed his statement, his voice stronger. "No, I don't suppose it does." He imitated her shrug, his voice again cheerful. "Hey, let me turn off the tractor and we'll go up to the house and get some iced tea and cookies. Okay?" Cookies were the only surefire way of luring Duz away from his work.

Carmen tried to search his face, but he was already getting up from the folding chair, so she said, "Well, let's do. I need to call Aggie anyhow and see how club went, see if she got Alma home all right."

Duz turned around. "I'll tell you what. Why don't we ... If you've got time, let's just run over. To mom's. It'd just take a few minutes and we could check and see if the old gal's OK. She seemed kind of addled when I picked her up. But then, I was late as usual, like she said, so that was probably the problem."

"Maybe." Carmen's eyes were at work on Duz's face, but by now it was noncommittal, so she decided to see if she could stir him up a little. "Speaking of late: where were you when I got home from the library meeting last night? P. D. told me that they said you just up and stomped out in the middle of Lew Harris's spiel, and that that was about nine or so. I got home at a quarter after ten. It must have taken you a hell of a long time to drive that ten minutes from Croysant to here."

The question was a challenge, and although he had been married to Carmen for over forty years, he was like Charlie Brown running to kick a Lucy-held football. He just couldn't stop himself from taking the challenge. On the defensive, he said, "I was upset, damn it. I came home and walked up to the divider box up on Clear Creek. I just sat there awhile, trying to get it out of my head what an utter, dry dust pocket this ranch would be without water rights. And trying to erase the image in my mind of the whole valley with houses all over it, fences and roads, and all the sage brush cleared and packs of domestic dogs after the deer ... later I dreamed about it. A nightmare. The houses in the dream were little, identical green squares, like on a monopoly board."

To hell with the town clothes. Carmen, her face soft and her eyes moist with sympathy, went to him and took him in her arms. "Oh, Duz."

A sufficient hug, then he held her at arm's length. "Besides, it's you that has to answer. A lot you really cared—you didn't even check whether my truck was in the garage or stay up to keep the lantern in the window, so to speak. You just crawled in the sack and conked out, limp as a sick jackrabbit. What if old Lew Harris had got it in his head it was me that needed strung up? What if he'd gone on a shooting spree?"

Now it was Carmen's turn to back pedal. "Oh, Duz—Lew Harris isn't ... and anyhow, I was so tired, and I felt you crawl in. I just didn't feel like talking and ..." She caught the renewed twinkle in his eye and finished, "And I've never been so pessimistic that I thought you couldn't take care of yourself. Just fine. Now, let's go see what Alma is up to."

7

Wednesday as the Afternoon Wanes

Alma's, Again

As Detective Asa Hobbs, amiable and chunky, ambled down Alma's driveway toward the shed, Sheriff Garrett stood by the police car, which he had parked at the upper edge of the sloping yard. He studied the assembled group of people, a group which at this point was beginning to grow by leaps and bounds as word got around. And he watched his deputy, Leigh McCracken, discharge from its center and boil up the driveway toward him. At 50, Garrett was intimidated by his vigorous and youthful deputy, as he had been by women in general for most of his adult life. Like other women he had known, McCracken seemed to have ideas about him. It was as if, flipping through a catalog, she'd found what she thought she wanted and filled out an order form, but he wasn't prepared to deliver on what she thought she saw.

As she approached him now, her face was a study in relief and eagerness to serve. He had a mouthful of nicotine-free wintergreen chew, and he twisted his lips around it over his teeth, adjusting the wad, jiggling his dangly, skinny mustache. Her first words, he knew, would be some kind of justification for whatever it was she had done before he arrived. Then, to his vast annoyance, she would ask for some direction as to what was to be done next, calling him "Chief" in the process. He squinted at her approaching form, adjusting his eyes to the late afternoon sun in the west. He had to rely on her; she was his top deputy. McCracken skidded to a halt in front of him. Although her hands stayed at her sides near her firearm, he had the distinct sensation that he'd been saluted.

"Sheriff. I need to talk to you about extensive disruption of the scene of crime by these club women. This disturbance happened prior to my arrival. After I arrived, I was able to secure the area. I have also located a possible blood stain on the ground directly to the left of and in front of the shed door. The photographers have been apprised of that stain. That would expand our theory of the crime."

Garrett noted the words "our theory of the crime," intrigued by what she thought 'our' theory might be, and braced himself for her next words. "So, Chief, what would you like me to do next? The women are getting unruly. Have you called for back-up? Should I order them to return to the house?"

Garrett grunted and worked his wad of chew with his lips. A man and woman walked past him, headed for the house. From having lived his full life in Riversmet, the nearest "urban" hub to Croysant—that is, it had a hospital, a theater, and a McDonald's—he had a nodding acquaintance with many of the people gathered in the yard. He had had occasion to see Duz Weinant and his wife at art shows. He was sure he recognized the passing couple as Duz and the artist. His guess was confirmed when he heard the woman say, "Good Lord, Duz! What in the world has Alma done now?"

Asa was already standing by the shed, looking in, where a flash of light indicated that the photographer was still at it. Garrett spit masterfully beside the driveway, dragged his hand across his mustache, beginning with the wrist and ending with a smoothing motion with the tips of his index and third fingers, then said, "Well, McCracken, let's go assess the damage."

They walked past Duz and Carmen, who had stopped just outside the perimeter tape between the house and the shed. The face of the normally jolly Duz was grim. He could be heard to say, "Oh, shit." Glancing over, Garrett nodded at them both, received no response. Duz looked pale and his eyes were fixed on the shed. Carmen, at his elbow, half whispered, "Oh, no, Duz. You don't think your mother...!" Of its own accord her hand sought his.

Across the highway, a minivan slowed to a crawl, a large family of bug-eyed kids and their mother gawping against the sealed windows. The van hesitated, halted, and pulled off the highway, discharging the lot to pour across the road in blatant defiance of the increasing traffic. From the same direction an old pickup appeared, slowed sharply, then pulled decisively in behind the van. Two men in straw cowboy hats stepped out and walked briskly across the blacktop to join the crowd. One could be heard to say to the first person he encountered, "Need some help here? What's goin' on?" Another small family group came walking up the highway, having accessed parking against a ditch bank a mile down the road. Behind them, a pickup jammed with teenagers in the truck bed slowed, the kids gabbling to each other and craning their necks as the truck edged into a defiant parking position, leaning, engine first, half over the sharp embankment that occurred just down the highway from Alma's home.

As he approached the shed, Garrett took in all this activity with annoyance. To his right, two old women had appeared on the porch of the house, one leaning heavily on a cane. She looked aggravated and she gave a shout which carried past him and penetrated the whole yard. "Duz! You're late. I thought I told you to take care of that body!"

This comment momentarily stayed the generalized bustle. Carmen and Duz, facing the shed door, twisted 180 degrees. Alma, scowling, continued accusingly, "It wasn't a tramp. It was Victoria's man. Why didn't you call the police? Doreen had to call for us."

At this point Doreen, club president, emitted a little yelp and headed toward Alma. She'd been standing with not only Agnes and Nancy Jane Barnswallowper, but also her own and Agnes's husbands, who had been on their way to the Culpepper place with a load of fence posts and mineral salt when they saw the activity. P. D.'s wife, Lucy, was there, too, having pulled into the old Cooper place, now owned by Jilly and Billy Brown, to avoid the difficulty in trying to park any closer. She'd simply hoofed it on up the road the quarter mile to Alma's, chalking the walk up to a good chance at a daily workout. It was never clear how community news traveled, speeding into Croysant, filtering around town, making its way to the post office and hence to Lucy Quick, as well as the rest of the world. It was only clear that it was very fast. Faster than e-mail.

Doreen was fast now. She made her way at a sharp clip across the silenced yard and took up her stand beside Alma, looking down into her indignant eyes. "Alma! Remember? You kept telling us at the clubhouse that you forgot something? And what you forgot was the body, to tell Duz that there was a body in the shed? Remember?"

Alma's face softened. "Oh, that's right. I remember now. Oh, yes..." She hesitated. "Duz didn't know ..." Then she looked Duz up and down, surprised to see him. "Why'd you come over here then, anyhow?"

Under her breath, Hallie said, "Which Bobby was that that was in the shed? Did they find the killer?" but no one heard her because Sheriff Garrett, rolling his eyes at Asa Hobbs, stepped away from the shed door and was now facing the gathering crowd. Before the general murmur could resume, and over Hallie's comment, he barked, "McCracken."

Deputy McCracken snapped to attention. "McCracken," Garrett repeated, "I want all of these people who were here when the body was first discovered to wait over there, in that side yard. They are not to leave. They are not to discuss this situation further. They may pull up chairs from inside the house, or sit on the yard swing, or stand until Asa and I can see the body. Then we will interview them."

"As for the rest of you folks," Garrett continued, directly addressing the crowd, "It wouldn't hurt if you moved along. You're hamperin' the wheels of justice." He paused, worked his chew. "But if you feel ya just gotta hang around where ya ain't got any business, then get yourselves back a little, up there past the gate, and let the rest of us get on with what we gotta do. Seems this poor man is dead and he deserves a fair shake to find out who killed 'im." Then he pointedly turned his back on the crowd, mumbling under his breath to Asa, "Not just which of 'em did it, but why the hell he ended up in this old lady's shed ..."

The photographer stepped out, nodded at Garrett, said, "I'm done," and went to join the videocam man in putting equipment away. The crowd had already begun to draw back; McCracken, taking her cue, was herding the club women into the side yard. Ducking his head to accommodate the low door, Garrett followed Asa into the shed.

Asa was looking down at the body, scratching the back of his head. "Well, this is gonna fuck up my daughter's wedding." Asa had planned to fly to Wisconsin the next day, to give his daughter away to a chap he considered to be a dope. He didn't like the idea, but he was braced for it. Now his tone was hurt, thinking of the complications that would arise from this homicide. His wife and daughter would accuse him of doing the murder himself, just so he could avoid the marriage that had become inevitable. He sighed, and Garrett sighed, too. Garrett knew what he had to do.

"Nah, go on," he said. "Me 'n McCracken can handle this. We'll call in the CBI if it gets too complicated for us."

Hobbs was not sure this was the outcome he wanted. He really didn't want to spend the weekend in Wisconsin watching Wise-Ass hitch up with his Coreen. On the other hand, no other available outcome was any good, either. He grunted, a grunt of assent, and both men directed their attention to the corpse, the stacked boxes around it, and the well-trampled floor under their feet.

It wasn't suicide. This guy had been shot in the back, so it wasn't likely that there would be any GSR, or gun shot residue, on the corpse's hands, but even so, the deputy who had done the videocam work had packaged the hands in brown paper bags. Just good police work. You never knew. For example, a couple of boxes looked pushed over. Garrett wondered if that was from the mob of women that had been in and out of here this afternoon. Or maybe something had gone before, and this guy had fought back against his attacker. That could mean there might be trace evidence — hair, skin, anything with DNA — under his fingernails. Garrett pulled his eyes away from the bagged hands and fingered the dark hole in the back of the shirt where the bullet had entered.

Without needing to comment to each other, he and Hobbs took hold of the shoulders and tipped the guy up for the first time, looking directly into the glassy-eyed face and down at the exit wound. Bigger than the one in the back, bloodier, the chest wall shredded. Again without comment, they grunted at each other. It was as they expected. Still holding the body aside, its longish, thick black hair flopping against Hobbs' wrist, they screwed up their eyes, looking at the angle the bullet had taken.

Hobbs said, "Right there," pointing with his chin to the surface of the thick-topped, homemade coffee table. The hole had been partially obscured by a small pool of blood, but now that he saw it, Garrett figured they wouldn't have any trouble digging out the bullet. They lowered the body back onto the table, and Garrett said, "Now. Let's us go talk to some ladies."

Back-up had finally begun to arrive from Stoney City, seat of the next county to the south. Those officers were moving about the yard, looking around, listening to McCracken. Garrett also noted the coroner's limousine jockeying its way past cars and people crowded along the highway. The Riversmet officers who had taken the pictures were waiting outside the shed, ready to begin the next phase of evidence collection. Detective Hobbs, his hand at the back of his neck again, scratching, spoke to them.

"Try for prints, but I doubt it," he said. "Get the I.D. off him and so-on, then Tom may as well take him for autopsy ... help him bag the body. You should find the bullet in the table he's down on. Anything else ... Let's see. Keep an eye on those boxes. Don't let those women mess around with 'em any more—we need to try to figure out what the hell brought him into this shed. Red, why don't you take out warrants to search this place and ... may as well get a warrant on the victim's place, too. Can't tell. Then get people ready to start goin' through boxes in the morning." He paused, thinking. "Oh, sure. And get some of those hotshots that are over here from Stoney City to start a perimeter search, start combing the area for the weapon."

Red grinned. "What we lookin' for, Cap?" Asa had a reputation in the department of being able to nail the type and size of a gun before any official ballistic feedback had hit the table. He shrugged now, pursed his lips.

"Pretty obvious, I think. You're lookin' for a .38. A Smith and Wesson .38 caliber." He looked at the shed, back at the crowd, lowered his lids. "May be a tough search. My money's on an old gun, been in somebody's gran'daddy's cabinet for quite a long while."

He'd just said this last part to grandstand; he really had no idea of age or make. Still, he could tell Red got a kick out of it. The kid chuckled, said, "We're on it, Cap."

Asa turned to follow Garrett, who'd gone into the house.

McCracken was watching the women in the yard like a good sheepdog, but Duz and Carmen had stated in no uncertain terms to her that they would be inside with Alma and Hallie, where the old women would have the benefit of toilet facilities and shade. When Asa arrived, Garrett was just settling into Doug's old easy chair and saying, "Why, yes, Mrs. Weinant, I do believe I do know you. I remember you coming up to have coffee and ice cream with my Nanna Abby, right?"

"That's right," Alma said approvingly. "Your grandmother used to grow the most beautiful roses there on the Bidwell place." She dragged out the word 'beautiful' and closed her eyes as she said it, imagining the flowers. "I used to walk through her gardens with her while Doug looked at your Grandpa's bulls. He raised fine bulls, you know, your Grandfather. Herefords. Most common breed in the valley back then. Doug usually bought from your Grandpa Carl whenever he got the chance." She smiled, warm with memory, and Garrett smiled back at her, recalling his own sweet memories of his grandparents.

Then Alma spoke again. "Does your Grandmother still grow roses, now they've retired to Riversmet?"

Garrett shook his head regretfully. "Oh, no, Mrs. Weinant. My grandparents both passed away some years back."

"Oh, my. I'm so sorry to hear that, Lyle. So sorry."

Garrett shifted uncomfortably in his chair. The old woman had mistakenly called him by his father's and oldest brother's name. He would have preferred not to be called Lyle, even under these circumstances. "Well," he said, "It happens to the best of us, I'm afraid." He was thinking, '*Enough chitchat. We need to get on the topic, here,*' but Alma interrupted his thoughts.

"Yes, you are right. About death. Happens to us all. A very young man, a new neighbor of ours, died right here in my shed just the other day. It has been on my mind all this time. I was the first one to find him, you know. It doesn't seem right to interrupt a pleasant visit, but I'm just thinking, since you are a sheriff, if perhaps you shouldn't investigate his death while you are here. He was shot, and you would think someone would want to know why he was shot."

Garrett, trying to follow this turn in logic, shot a glance at Hobbs, whose eyebrows had raised. Duz was sitting stoically and noncommittally in a straight-backed chair between the rabbit foot fern and the television, his palms open and resting flat on his knees, but Carmen was squeezing her knuckles and twisting her mouth, eyeing her mother-in-law, obviously trying to decide when to jump in. Alma turned to her friend, Hallie, who had been gazing rather stonily out the window at the club women assembled and restless on the lawn. "What do you think, Hallie? Don't you think Mr. Garrett should investigate that death in the shed while he's here? It could save him some time later."

Hallie ignored her, so Alma repeated her words, louder this time. "Hallie, I am asking you about that body in the shed. What do you think?"

Hallie fixed Alma with a pinch-lipped stare. Only her melodious voice cut the edge of her obvious aggravation. "Alma, you never will speak up. I have not been able to hear one word that was said here. You keep talking about trapping Bobby in the shed, but to save my soul — and I have wracked my brain — I can't think of anyone we know who goes by the name of Bobby. That man in the shed who is dead went by 'Reider'. Do you think the killer was named Bobby?"

This time Alma really blasted it out. "Not Bobby, Hallie, *body!* Body in the shed. And of course, we all know that the man was named Reider." In a quieter mode, she added, "I've just thought about that a lot. Reider Biedermann. Dead in my shed."

Hallie subsided, returning her gaze somewhat defiantly to the window, but, encouraged, Garrett said, "You've thought about it a lot, Mrs. Weinant? What was it you've been thinking about Biedermann being in your shed? Could you tell me?"

"Well, I was thinking about how things come in threes: first my heart attack, then my stroke, then the shingles in my eye. And then these problems lately—here was the heart medicine my girls forgot to order, and the body in the shed, and ... well, something else. I can't remember right now."

Garrett waited, thinking she was going to continue, but she simply cleared her throat and smiled at him, seemingly pleased with her contribution. The silence in the room lengthened until Carmen, tortured, burst out, "Duz's mother has short-term memory loss, Sheriff. I don't think she remembers what you asked her."

Alma glanced at Carmen, then back at Garrett, her face startled. "Oh! What did you ask, Lyle?"

Gritting his teeth, Garrett said, "I wondered what you thought about, when you said you thought about Mr. Biedermann being in your shed."

"Oh, that." Alma shrugged. "I just thought about how things always come in threes, and about spelling. And rhymes. Dead, shed. Reider, Bieder. How the vowels in the name Biedermann dance around in several tricky little ways — at least three. Our own name is spelled W-E-I- ... , and pronounced 'Wy-nant', with the 'I' as the long sound, but for Biedermann the vowels are switched, and Gritty told me once it is a German thing, because that name is pronounced 'Bee-derman', with the 'E' as the long sound. That wouldn't be so bad, but then Reider's parents shuffled the deck again and dealt him an 'e-i' like our Weinant name, only pronounced it 'Ree-der', like he was a book 'reader'. 'Ree-der Bee-derman'. Now, why do you suppose they did that? Maybe the kids teased him in school about it." She sighed. "Names. Kids tease about names, you know. I know it could be enough to make you want to change your name."

Both Garrett and Hobbs were torn between the sag their bodies were feeling at the length and irrelevance of her answer, and the fascination they were experiencing with her ability to be coherent in this odd logic. After a lengthy pause, Garrett accepted that she had finished and said, "But the name doesn't really explain why the man was in your shed, does it? Do you have any idea, Mrs. Weinant, why he was in your shed?"

Alma looked at him, a tiny puzzled frown creasing her forehead. "Who?" she asked.

* * * * *

There was no convenient place to interview the others, so in the end, deciding Alma and Hallie were harmless, they sent Duz and Carmen out and called the women into the living room, one at a time. They spoke with Doreen first. She responded to their questions with thoughtfulness, courtesy, and very little information. Garrett did note that no Onion Valley ranches, which included both the Van Doran's, known as the old

Culpepper place, and the Caswell's, would be affected by Biedermann's planned water takeover. Only the Oozle ranches were involved.

Doreen suggested that they interview Agnes next, then she and Agnes could invite people back to the clubhouse for refreshments. This, she said, might help the investigation by thinning out the press of people. As added incentive, she offered to bring coffee and dessert to the officers on the scene. When they yielded, she phoned her daughter, sending her scampering to round up more goodies.

With each woman interviewed, the investigators heard one or another version of the club meeting, the discovery of the body, and the water board meeting. Donna Caswell, carrying an over-stimulated and exhausted Spit, commented that probably no one felt comfortable to admit that Reider had gotten what he deserved, but that she, for one, was not afraid to say so.

Maggie Merimeister began her own interview with the old schtick about Garrett's name: "Sheriff Pat Garrett! Aren't you the man who brought down Billy the Kid?" and he gave her his usual answer, "No, Ma'am, I ain't that one." After a brief interval, she felt the need to continue. Shivering, she said, "I think it is creepy that that man has been sitting there in the shed, dead, all night, slumped over that table, and Alma never knew it. And he's still there!"

At this comment, Garrett raised his eyebrows. "All night, Mrs. ... He looked at his notes. Mrs. Merimeister? It is Merimeister — M-E-I, 'my-ster' — isn't it?"

This flustered Maggie. "Why yes, yes ... of course it is ... it ... Well, I just assumed ... I mean, I can't see it happening in broad daylight, can you? ... Well, I suppose it could, but less likely. But really!" She collected herself. "Really, I'm sure that blood on the table felt ... I mean, looked, dry ... dried ..."

Garrett came to her aid, his voice itself dry. "You're right, I think. Until we hear from the coroner, we're guessing that the man was dead since last night. Except for where the blood is thickest, under him, it has dried." He watched her as he spoke. He was sure that with his mention of the thicker blood under Biedermann she gave a somewhat delicious, additional dramatic shiver.

Most of the women discoursed on Victoria's good works as a nurse and her sad circumstances, first married to Reider, then widowed in this ugly manner. She had, they breathed, been so SHOCKED to see her husband dead in the shed. They described her stunned words, her drop to the ground in the "horrible faint." What did she say?

According to Frieda, she screamed and cried out, "They've shot Reider! They've shot my husband!"

According to Maggie, it was, "Oh, no, that man in there is Reider and (dramatic pause) they have SHOT him!"

According to Donna, who was closest to her at the time, she said, "Who is it? Who is the dead man? Oh, my god! It is my husband!"

According to Jilly, who found romance novels and the soaps to be her own perfect escape from the escapades of the twins, Victoria had moaned (softly) and burst into tears, then, just before she slid (almost lifeless) to the ground, she said (cried out), "How shall I live now that they have shot my Reider, the father to my children? We must find whoever did this awful deed!"

According to Nancy Jane Barnswallowper, she had gasped in surprise, then said, "Oh, my god! It's Reider! But ... but ... he's been shot."

"If you ask me," said Nancy Jane, her voice cynical, "That woman was a lot more surprised that he'd been shot than that he was dead."

"But," pursued Detective Hobbs, "She did then faint from the shock, did she not?" He looked at his notebook, as if trying to confirm.

Nancy shrugged. "Well, she did then slide to the ground, partially held up by a bunch of women, and her eyes went closed. Maybe she fainted."

Garrett frowned. "So you think there was something fishy about Mrs. Biedermann's reaction? Are you saying she *wasn't* surprised to find him dead, just that she was surprised to find him shot?"

Nancy pondered through narrowed eyes. "You know, I don't know what I think. Victoria's a nurse, but old Reider has always been the most drug out lookin' guy I've ever seen, ever since he moved here a few years back. And I use the term 'drug out' for a reason here—I don't know about Reider, but I'm no fool about what goes on up that road with his son Mac and that nut, Alice. Jesus, let me tell you! Those two never see a day without the benefit of rose-colored glasses. But Reider ... well, I do know he was plumb sickly lookin' last night at that water board meetin'."

"And you were there? You saw him?"

"Oh, yeah. I was there. He looked like shit."

Garrett scowled, looked down at his little pocket notebook, muttered, "hmmm." Then, "So. At that meeting, lots of folks were stirred up about the water, right? As I understand it, Reider was a real threat ..."

"Oh, yeah," Nancy said again. "He was more than a threat. He was a rattlesnake ... Lew Harris suggested a necktie party, but the way I figure it, someone just decided hangin' was too little, too late."

"Maybe," Garrett agreed thoughtfully. "But that doesn't explain why he was in the shed."

Nancy shook her head. "Nope, it sure doesn't, does it? Kind of a bummer for poor old Alma here, I guess."

And that was it for the club women. Needing some supper besides cherry dessert and coffee, some of the crowd had begun to trickle away. They took the women's compared stories of the interviews with them, coupled with first hand viewing of the body bag departing the shed and the investigators starting to comb the grounds for, clearly, (pause, lowered voice) "the gun." Carmen and Duz were now stranded alone in the side yard with McCracken. Much more than an hour had passed, but Garrett wanted to hear what they had to say.

Duz, whom Hobbs called in first, described his taking of Alma to club, his return home to work on the tractor, his uneasiness about Alma—some psychic thing, he guessed—and his and Carmen's return to all the fuss in the yard. Garrett asked again about the water board meeting and he gave a clear, tight description of the situation.

"Everyone," he concluded, "was very wound up. After all, no land in this area has any real agricultural value without irrigation rights. People have counted on the snowpack in the mountains for as long as I know. And they've counted on that snowpack thawing and coming out and being shared fairly, used to water our livestock and our hayfields. Just on principle, nobody should threaten that." His face had gradually flushed as he spoke.

Garrett and Hobbs, who knew the area well, could only nod their agreement. "Look, let us just have a few words with your wife, then maybe we can close this down here for tonight and your mother can get settled. Does she have someone to stay with her?"

"Oh, yeah," Duz said. "Mary told me she'd stay since Victoria couldn't be expected to. And the neighbors'll watch out for her."

Garrett eyed him thoughtfully as he went out the door. Was it odd that he seemed so unconcerned about his mother being in this house alone at the time of a murder? And wasn't he being overly relaxed about neighbors, one of whom must surely be a murderer? Or was it just the guy's nature, a normal reaction? After all, Alma hadn't been harmed.

Carmen's entrance interrupted these speculations. "Ms. Weinant, I just have a few questions for you, then maybe we can let things rest for the evening. I understand from your husband that you were at a library meeting last night, and that you were at an art exhibit today and missed the community club meeting?"

"That's right. Maggie dropped Frieda and me off at our houses last night. It was after ten. Then I had to leave early this morning, at six, to get down to Riversmet in time to set up for the exhibit."

Garrett smiled. "I'm sorry I missed it. I like your paintings. More fish, I presume?"

Carmen nodded, pleased. "More fish. We sold three—a good day. I've been working on the idea of silver in the scales, very close up. What it suggests or makes us feel."

Garrett stretched. He really was sorry he'd missed the exhibit. Plus he was wearing out now and couldn't, for the moment, bring himself to pursue the questioning any further. Hobbs spoke up.

"So you missed the club meeting this afternoon? Did you hear anything unusual about it, other than the main adventure?"

"No ..." Carmen hesitated, thoughtful. "I tried to call Patty Harris when I got home today, because she'll usually give me a blow-by-blow account if I miss club, but she didn't answer. I figured she just hadn't made it home yet, but when I got here, they said she never had shown up at the meeting."

Garrett was focused again. "Patty Harris. Is that ..." he thumbed his notes. "Is that Lew Harris's wife? The guy that spoke out at the water board meeting?"

"Oh, no," Carmen laughed at the mental image it gave her. "Lew's the old guy—he can be quite a curmudgeon. Patty's his grandson's wife—a lot younger than me. She ... well, she's just a sweetie. She teaches kindergarten down in Croysant. She looks kind of like a female Harry Potter in the face—the big glasses and all. I guess that's why Duz and I get such a kick out of it when Clint calls her 'my Hair Trigger Honey from Hartsville.' "

"Who calls her *what*??"

"Oh, her husband, Clint. He's a real sober, quiet kind of guy, with a dry sense of humor. He met Patty on the Eastern Slope when they were in college. She tutored him through freshman English at C.S.U. and I guess that was what did it for him. At any rate, she's from Hartsville over there and he just teases her. Here's little, sweet-tempered Patty, and here's Clint, when she walks in the room, saying, 'Well, if it isn't my little woman, the local firecracker. Who are you after tonight, if it won't get me into trouble to ask ...' "

Carmen caught herself. What was she saying? This was a murder interrogation, and her words might be put in a very wrong context. Now what should she do? She finished lamely, "... things like that. If you knew Patty, you'd know how funny that sounds. Which makes it worry me that she is probably sick or something today. Because she always goes to club ..." *Shut up,* Carmen told herself. *You are just making it worse.* She clammed her mouth shut.

Sheriff Pat Garrett finished making a note in his notebook, sat looking at it a minute, and said, "Hmmm." Then he looked up at Carmen and said, "Thank you for your time, Ms. Weinant. I'll be looking forward to your next art exhibit."

8

Wednesday After the Interviews

At the Cowpath Saloon

Jenny Threewinds, guitarist, receptionist, and occasional waitress at the Cowpath Saloon, exclaimed, "Why, I saw Reider just last night! He bought cigarettes here."

The chicken-fried, as gristly as usual tonight, caused both Hobbs and Garrett to twist their mouths around it like two toothless old hounds harassing their hunting season bones. McCracken had sensibly ordered burger. She glanced at her Chief, then took it upon herself to ask, "What time was that, Ms. Threewinds?"

They were seated near the wall under one of the many faded photographs of local mountains that adorned the place. Other decor consisted primarily of antlers and a set of large horns from a longhorn steer, which had been placed over the fireplace. A stuffed bobcat head hung near the door; and the glass-topped counter where the cash register sat featured a display of framed arrowheads and other Native American artifacts.

Jenny shrugged. "About nine. I'd been playing for forty-five minutes and I stopped to eat a salad. Reider just stepped into the front there, bought the cigarettes and left. He didn't eat or anything. About ten minutes later, I went back to play again, and from my chair I could see his pickup in that little parking circle out back." She gestured toward the back of the restaurant with a movement of her head. "It was dark, but I could see the outline of his head and the glow of a cigarette. He must have smoked awhile before he left. It wasn't too long after that that he took off."

McCracken had refrained from another bite of burger, concentrating on careful mental notes, but Hobbs and Garrett were each forking in new deposits and regarding Jenny with mild interest as they masticated. McCracken shifted in her seat, feeling the responsibility. "So," she said, "which way did he go?"

Jenny looked at her with some puzzlement. Since it should have been clear that nothing was visible from the window at the back of the Cowpath except the back of the Cowpath, she wasn't sure quite what McCracken was getting at. "Well..." she hesitated. "Just ... out, I guess. I mean, I just saw him back out of the parking place and go ... toward the front."

"So you couldn't say," McCracken was on a roll, "just whether Mr. Biedermann took a left, toward Mrs. Weinant's house, or a right, toward Croysant?"

"Well, I..." Jenny Threewinds was puzzled by the point of the question rather than the answer. The exit to Highway 46 from the Cowpath was obviously nowhere visible to a guitarist playing in the bar in the back. It was her turn to glance at Asa Hobbs and the sheriff.

Sheriff Pat Garrett had known Jenny Threewinds, nee Finkit, forever. They went through the Riversmet school system at the same time, just one year apart. Garrett saw her around then, thought of her as a 'cute kid.'

After graduation she left for the University of Colorado and took up pre-law. Before she'd completed a year, she slipped out of her classes and headed for San Francisco to protest the war in Vietnam. Garrett didn't think twice about her until she returned to Riversmet in 1992 to be with her parents. Her mother was dying of breast cancer. She hadn't been back a month before her father was diagnosed with pancreatic cancer. He was gone within the year. Jenny stayed.

After that, Pat Garrett saw her around. Saw her all the time, in fact—she seemed, somehow, always in his horizon. He'd dated her since she came back. Unlike his big brother Lyle's first two wives, whom Lyle had taken away from Garrett just as Garrett's interest grew, but before he could muster the courage to pop the question—any question!—and unlike other women he had spent time with ... unlike McCracken, unlike ... well, anyone ... Jenny Threewind's quiet, padded body, the long, loose brown braid down Jenny Threewinds' back ... those things comforted him like a peaceful fire on a cold winter night. Her thoughtful, grey-flecked blue eyes felt mystical to him. They sang of the cool, mist-ridden mountain spruce forests where he went to seek solitude and solace on long, hot summer days.

The bitter truth was, the reason it didn't occur to Sheriff Pat Garrett to propose ... anything ... to Jenny Threewinds was not because she made him uncomfortable, like other women did. It didn't occur to him because, in his eyes, Jenny Threewinds was a hippie. An Indian Wannabe hippie. The worst kind of hippie ... except maybe for the real druggie ones.

She didn't seem to be a druggie, although she'd lived on the fringes of the aging hippie culture in San Francisco for a goodly amount of time. She'd eventually returned to the University of Colorado to study anthropology. Working off campus, she met Native Americans at the Indian Center in Denver. She set out to learn Lakota. On the day of her graduation, she left for the Rosebud Reservation in South Dakota, where she married Mike Threewinds, and, working as a paralegal in his Native American law firm, immersed herself in Native American rights. She kept working at the firm after Mike was killed in the car accident in 1989.

She was an only child. When her parents died, she took her substantial inheritance, sent a third to the reservation, invested the rest in the burgeoning stock market, and wrote a will that considered the reservation's needs most of all. Then she drove east toward the mountains.

Locating a thirty-five-acre piece of dry pinion and cedar covered ground on the mesa southwest of Croysant, she bought it, set up her water tank, pulled a trailer house into the trees where she could see forever without being seen, and settled down with the old dogs, Spot and Roughhouse, that her parents had left behind. From here she would let the vistas heal her.

Sheriff Garrett, meanwhile, stuck in Riversmet, listened to Beverly Sills and Placido Domingo, tended his flower garden, contemplated the sunsets, mended his own clothes, and denied that he had a loss to mourn. He'd never been to her trailer in the cedars. He liked spruce trees, after all, and summer snow on the mountains. He didn't face the fact that somehow the best path for him, of the many that went to the mountains from Riversmet, always seemed to lead through Croysant and past the Cowpath Saloon. Yes, through Croysant, just south of which he always recognized a hunger or a thirst, a gnawing in his middle which could only be satisfied by an innocent digression into that restaurant that served such fine chicken-fried on a regular basis.

He chewed the last of a slab of it now, crunched at the grease-soaked flour coating, swallowed, then washed it down with a dose of duck-water thin Cowpath coffee. "So," he cut in on McCracken, his gaze meeting Jenny's, not without a degree of unacknowledged pain, "So, it sounds like Reider was still alive at nine or so last night. I guess we'll get the bottom line on that, too, when we get the coroner's report from Tom." He wiped a napkin across his already annoyingly stubbly chin, stuffed it next to his plate, and watched Hobbs continue to work over his piece of meat. McCracken took a tentative bite of burger, afraid to get too involved with the food, in case her boss needed her to step in again.

Jenny took advantage of this hiatus to say, "I saw someone else last night, but I'm embarrassed ... maybe even ashamed ... to tell you. I just ... at the time it didn't seem to be such a big deal." She'd brought her guitar to the table when she came over to sit with them, and now she plucked a couple of strings, nervously.

Garrett's eyebrows wiggled and Hobbs looked up from his plate. "That right? Who'd you see?"

"That's the problem. I don't know. I've studied on it all night, but now that I hear about this happening, I'm really worried."

McCracken's chin went up, her body edged forward in the chair. "Just what do you mean by that, Ms. Threewinds? That is a dubious statement, if I ever heard one!" She turned her eyes toward Garrett, expecting some good police work from him to get at the nub of what this Indian woman was hinting at.

Jenny rested her eyes briefly on McCracken, thinking incongruously just how pretty her red hair was, then let her gaze drift back past Hobbs to settle again on Garrett. "You see, Patrick," she began, "I thought I should have known the woman, but I didn't. Like someone you meet at a class reunion years later, somebody who's aged enough on the outside to be unrecognizable, but who still gives off enough of a whiff of that original person to make you think ..."

The lips on Garrett's poker face moved slightly. Nobody else ever called him Patrick. 'Garrett' acknowledged his lineage; 'Sheriff' gave him his due for his office; and 'Pat' ... well, 'Pat' was wishy-washy. 'Patrick' acknowledged his manhood. Garrett's eyes were soft upon Jenny.

McCracken waited for the Chief's next words. He would pin this witness down. She could see it coming. Garrett cleared his throat. "So you felt you knew her, but you couldn't place her," he said. Jenny nodded, frowning a little, thinking still.

It was Hobbs who pursued it. "About what time did this woman come in? I'm assuming she came *into* the Cowpath?"

"It was like Reider. She didn't really come in to eat or anything. She just came in the door at about ten o'clock ... the channel on the set above the bar over there was doing its break before the news ... anyhow, she came in and she ..." Jenny paused and flushed. "And she asked directions to Alma's."

McCracken was scandalized. "Asked directions to Alma's!" she burst out. "Asked directions to some poor old 90-year-old lady's house at ten at night? You didn't give them to her, did you?"

Looking increasingly guilty, Jenny nervously pulled at two strings on her guitar as she replied, "Well, yes. Yes, I did. You see ..."

McCracken gave a snort, but Garrett put his hand on her arm and said, "Let her finish." He pulled his hand back at once, but McCracken sat still, shut her mouth, and felt the tingle where it had touched.

"You see," Jenny continued, "I never think of this area as a dangerous place. We never lock our doors here. This lady claimed to be an old friend of Alma's who was just passing through on her way to Stoney City. She said ... she said she was unsure of her distances in the dark, but that she just wanted to say 'Hello' on her way through. Well, you know how sociable Alma is. It didn't seem ... at the time it didn't seem far-fetched to me. Of course, it all looks different now."

Having rallied, McCracken interjected, "Not very thoughtful, though," but Hobbs' deep voice overrode hers.

"So you gave her accurate directions..."

"Well, of course, it isn't difficult from here. Five miles up the highway, little white house on the right ... I did tell her that Alma would probably be in bed, and she said she wouldn't stop in if the light was out."

Everyone was quiet, mulling the implications. Garrett, who was pulling at his mustache, finally said, "Yuh. Interesting. Maybe nothin', maybe something. What did she look like, the woman?"

Jenny hesitated, then said, "Maybe about our ages—yours and mine, Patrick. Not your deputy's, of course." McCracken glared at her, but she was focused on trying to visualize the woman and didn't notice. "Our ages, but her hair was quite grey, a kind of grey that comes out of a box and looks all even and attractive. It was pulled up in a bun and held with a clasp that I remember was nice; it flashed in the light. She had on good clothes, too ... maybe not off the rack. They were beautifully tailored, maybe designer clothes. I ... she was fairly short, a little chubby, but the way the clothes hung, she still looked good. Except maybe ..."

Even McCracken recognized that Jenny was struggling to get the words right, so the trio of law officers remained silent while she thought. "Except maybe," she finished, "Her face. Her complexion and demeanor. Her bun was tight and it pulled her skin back. It made her eyes kind of ... kind of bulgy. Like those pictures in old biology textbooks of people with thyroid disease who have protruding eyes. Only not really that severe. Nothing important about that, except her skin was pale, kind of sallow, and she didn't smile asking about Alma, like an old friend anticipating catching up on old times. The way her face looked, well ... she seemed harried, maybe kind of grim."

"The grim reaper," McCracken mumbled under her breath. Hobbs grunted and Garrett sighed, rubbed at his scar. "Well," he said, recalling McCracken's words earlier, "Well. This may expand our theory of the crime."

"I'm sorry," Jenny said, and Garrett looked shocked.

"Don't be sorry! Someone asked directions, you gave 'em. What were you supposed to do?"

"Well, in hindsight ..." Jenny pulled at her guitar strings, cleared her throat, then said, "And you see, something else ... oh, geez. This just can't be important. I can't believe this." She rolled her eyes at her table companions, shaking her head. "I know you guys'll want to hear it."

The hamburger that had been cooling its heels on McCracken's plate became a prop to express her agitation. She stuffed her mouth, chewed busily, slugged at her lemonade, and ignored the grease that dripped on her plate as she leaned over it and focused on Jenny. Boy, this was going to take some sorting out. She was glad both Hobbs and Garrett were hearing this. As she chewed, Hobbs said, "Yeah, you bet we do. Shoot."

"Well, one reason I don't think I gave this woman as much thought as I should have at the time is that I was having a drink with Patty Harris. She came in ten minutes or so before this other person was here, and she was just ... well, just really angry and shaky."

Even Garrett had forgotten the shade of Jenny's eyes and was hanging on her every word. "Patty Harris? The kindergarten teacher?" He turned to Hobbs, in case he needed to refresh his memory. "That's the one Carmen Weinant said wasn't at club today. Clint Harris's wife."

"That's the one. She doesn't frequent this place often, especially the bar at night, but we all like her. I wanted to hear her out, because she said ... well, she just said she was really upset about that water board meeting. That Clint and Lew had come home, told her about it, and she just had to ... had to get out of the house for a while."

"So she was here when the stranger came for directions?"

"She was. She stayed a few more minutes, then she said she had to get on back home. She looked tired by then."

"So she left after the other woman had been gone awhile? Gone maybe ..."

"Gone maybe ten minutes. Or less. She left then. And ... well, I ... I don't want to repeat this but ..."

Hobbs echoed the word. "But ...?"

"But ... well, what she actually said was, 'I have to get on home and see that something gets done about it.' She said, 'Something needs to be done about that slimy, lower-than-a-snake-belly, poor excuse for a human, Reider Biedermann.' "

Everyone was quiet. Finally, Garrett said, "Wow. Well, what else, last night, do you think, Jenny?"

"Nothing that I can recall right now, Patrick. I'm too ... I'm beginning to wonder, myself. I'll try to think. I'll let you know ..." Her voice was worried.

"Maybe you better write it down, Jen. Write down the evening and get back to us."

9

Wednesday at Sunset

Back to Alma's

Blessedly, McCracken was staring out the car window. This gave Garrett space to ruminate as they drove to Alma's. He wanted to know if Alma could recall seeing Jenny's mystery woman, but he dreaded going back. Contrary to how others might assess him, Garrett was not a person who felt he dealt well with older people, and Alma's undependable memory made him especially uncomfortable. For one thing, she called him 'Lyle.'

His hand went to the ugly red scar that had puckered his lower cheek since he was a baby. Sure, he had issues with his older brother, but he didn't want to think his desire to avoid Alma was just because she kept calling him 'Lyle'.

He rubbed at the scar. He had to admit that he blamed it for the loss of several women. If he could just tell women that the damn thing had happened when he rescued a crime victim from a burning building in New York City, or that it was caused by a rollover while he chased drug dealers at high speed in L.A., or ... but no, truth told, he was just a local boy, a farmer's son, no closer to vice in Miami than a satellite dish would allow him. Nah, his beat was talking to spacey old women. He was never a tough cop hero. He rolled his tired shoulders.

The hero had always been his big brother. Lyle's ears were as sculpted as Garrett's were large; the hair on Lyle's head was thick and silky; Garrett's head was raw from the old Mach 3. Lyle's face? The mark of Adonis was upon it. Any goddess would go for him. And three had. It still hurt to think that Lyle had so easily plucked away ... and married ... the only two women whom he, Pat Garrett, had actively courted. And then had divorced them.

Bonnie and Peggy had seemed quite taken with Pat's lanky frame and sweet manner until they discovered they could snare the older brother, the handsome one. And it was Lyle who was the hero. At just seven years old, he'd pulled the two-year-old Pat away from a streaming horror of flaming grease. The toddler had clambered up against the stove to look, and had upset the pan into the burner, when he strove for a better handhold. His mom had been drinking. Not abusive, everyone agreed. The neighbors liked the family. Not abusive. Maybe negligent, though. Maybe negligent.

It had been Lyle who not only dialed the operator, but had the presence of mind to run for cold, wet towels. Maybe he'd learned this at school, Pat's brother. Whatever. At least he had known what to do. Garrett massaged the rubbery scar. Although Lyle was now on wife number three — this woman not second-hand from Pat — and had not yet settled on a steady job (even though by now he was AARP material), Pat still accepted him as the wiser, more worthwhile and experienced man. He respected him; he liked his company. He just didn't want to BE him. Or ... to be thought to be him, even by Alma.

On the other hand, it wouldn't have hurt to have had a little of Lyle's magnetism toward women. Any women. Even old women. Garrett and McCracken were approaching Alma's, as sure as doom. Only duty to office had gotten him this far. Garrett sighed, causing McCracken to pull her eyes from the passenger side window. She'd been busily scanning the landscape for potential clues. She was hoping to see something before the Chief saw it ... hoping to impress him. She assumed he'd been studying the area for clues, too, and was gratified that he'd seen no more than she. At least, not that he was telling her about.

"Well, looks like we're almost there," she ventured. Garrett grunted in assent. He could trust himself, he thought, to see through the guise of a witness who outright lied. Alma was something else. She could be telling a big whopper and telling the truth, from her perspective, both at the same time. If the woman who had inquired at the Cowpath had stopped by

Alma's last night, who knew if Alma would remember or not? She could say yes, or she could say no, and either response would be next to meaningless.

Damn. Alma's yard was still crawling with neighbors: good lord, didn't these people ever tire? People all over the place, bent, poking at ditchbanks, peering along the fences. "Helping." Searching for the gun.

"So, what do we do, Chief? You want me in on the interview, or ..."

Garrett looked appraisingly at his deputy. "See what you can do to make these people understand that they are not to touch evidence. Not the gun. Not the ... not anything else. Work with the Stoney City boys on that."

Alma was seated in her chair when he entered the house, her eyes bright but her cheeks a little flushed. She must be getting worn out. Did she consider everyone in this room full of people to be her friend? Protecting her? Or was she a little suspicious? Maybe worried?

Only Maggie Merimeister showed any inclination to depart. She got up as he entered, offered him her chair, and went to hug Alma, telling her to "take care." As she passed him he caught just a whiff of fine cologne, a subtle sniff of luxury and glamour.

Taking the proffered chair, the sheriff tried to decide how to get his question right for Alma with all these people still here. Whatever he said could confuse her. It could also start a back-wash of misinformation and gossip. As Maggie pulled the door shut behind her, Jilly Brown piped up. "It sure is a shame how something like this can make you feel distrustful of even your nicest neighbors."

Frieda, her bulk taking half the couch, laughed. "Which of us don't you trust, Jilly?"

"Oh, you know. The old timers are OK. But Maggie ... well, I always liked Maggie, but ..."

Agnes spoke up. "Why yes. She always has been most gracious to John and I. Lovely dinners. She had us over during the holidays, warmed the brandy, urged us to toast our toes by the fire ... and her beautiful house!"

Frieda interrupted. "Yeah, I like her house, too. Pete and I've been over there, got wined and dined royally—I think

Maggie enjoys her nip or two as well as her social hour. Yeah. And I'm sure Jilly and Billy have been up there, too, to eat ... but ... I guess that's part of the problem. Her house."

"You mean ...?"

"Well, sure. She comes in here, from who knows where ... well, we all know literally California, but I mean, why? She says she's a widow. Grass widow, more likely. And she buys the old Oozle post office, rips it apart one side down the other, no consideration for its history here in the valley, turns it into a mansion ... a castle. That takes money! And that big lawn! How does she keep the drasted lawn green? And four bathrooms, mind you! One woman and four bathrooms! Water being what it is, how did she get the taps for that? How much can one woman pee?"

Pete was sitting by his wife, pulled to lean against her by her weight. "Aw, come on, Frieder. You're just jealous. You'd get naked for weekly massages at Gail's, just like Maggie does, if you could afford 'em." He gave her thigh a meaningful squeeze just above the knee.

Garrett was trying not to imagine the portly ranch wife getting naked for a weekly massage when Jilly said, "You're right. Billy and I've been over to her place, too. She puts on a great barbecue. Hired Ed Skinner to provide the elbow grease on that one. Still, I can't help wondering where she came from. Really came from, I mean." Jilly was thinking of "The Young and the Restless," the beautiful but mysterious woman with amnesia who had been found by the road and who had turned out to be an escaped killer from the state prison. She added, "And I didn't see anything really personal at her place ... not family pictures or stuff. Even if she doesn't have kids, wouldn't she want a picture up of her so-called late husband ...?"

Agnes shook her head. "But she's been here two years, and she's never been anything but kind and generous ... how can we be so judgmental?" 'We,' of course, was Agnes's polite euphemism for 'you.' She didn't feel *herself* to be judgmental. Garrett, following the conversation, was trying to find an opening for himself. He glanced at Alma to note, to his dismay, that she'd nodded off.

John, Agnes's husband, was leaning against the doorjamb

nursing a cup of coffee, the kitchen growing dark behind him, his cadaverous Lincolnesque cheekbones and full beard somewhat ominous in the shadows, but his expression bemused. "So, Aggie, your point would be that excess wealth never looks so bad if it is shared. Right?"

"John ..." Agnes started to reply, but Frieda chortled, feeling understood. "Good point, John. Maggie's got it and she flaunts it. I say it disrespects limited resources. Limited environmental resources. Bottom line issue is the water she takes, you know?"

Frieda Johnson had one of those deeply carrying voices that Hallie could sort out of a blur of conversation. Hallie was parked protectively by the softly snoring and bubbling Alma, and this was her chance to chip in. Garrett wiggled his thin mustache in gratitude, hoping for an opening, as she interjected, "The water it is. The water here, that is surely the primary issue."

His relief was short lived. A quick rap on the door and the untimely entrance of McCracken silenced what might have been a promising discussion of the water dispute.

"We've found Mr. Biedermann's pickup," she announced to him and the group in general. "Over on a side road, just before a bridge that crosses the dry gulch behind this house." Two or three of those assembled murmured, "Oh, the road to Hallie's," but McCracken ignored them and continued, "It was pulled off the road, looked like somebody had tried to hide it."

Garrett nodded, dismissive. "Maybe Biedermann himself. I'll be out in a few minutes to look it over."

"And the blood stain. In front of the shed. I made sure they took it up to send in for analysis, Chief."

Garrett scowled. He'd forgotten the blood stain. He hated the idea that he would have to explain a blood stain outside the shed if it was Biedermann's blood and the guy had been shot in place, as it looked like he had been, considering the location of the bullet. He secretly hoped that McCracken was just stirred up and had located a grease spot from one of the cars or something. He was just beginning to reply when Alma gave a particularly loud snort and her eyes jerked open.

"Why, look who all's here!" she exclaimed, her face suffused with pleasure. "Doug and I ..." she hesitated, confused. "You are here for our anniversary, aren't you? Our seventieth?

Doug wanted ..." She searched their faces.

Hallie, hearing her clearly in the silence that had come over the room, said, as gruffly as a melodious voice like hers would allow, "Ah, Alma, doggone it. This ain't about your anniversary. You already did that when Doug was alive. These folks're worried about that guy gettin' shot in your shed last night. They're worried about your safety."

"Oh." Alma picked at the afghan someone had put across her knees. "Oh. Well, I just can't remember, you know. Can't remember like I used to." She eyed the people gathered in the room. "I used to have quite a memory, you know. Quite a good reputation for a memory."

Garrett shifted uncomfortably in his chair. He was reminded that he did need to know why it was the shed that had contained a corpse. Alma must have had something Biedermann wanted. Had he found it? Would someone kill again to get it? Where, after all, was Alma's son—wasn't he even a little worried about her safety, like these other people at least pretended to be? Then again, maybe the guy hadn't ended up in the shed of his own accord ...

Hallie patted Alma's hand. "Oh, didn't you, though? You knew everything about this community. A wonderful memory. You've been important here. Everybody knows that." She looked around the group rather fiercely, causing them to nod and mumble 'oh yeah's' and 'yups,' but the uncomfortable silence lingered. Garrett cleared his throat. He may as well plunge in.

"Mrs. Weinant, speaking of memory ... you wouldn't happen to recall if anyone stopped by to see you last night?"

Alma's gaze wobbled across the room to fix on Garrett's face. "Last night? I'm sorry ..." She hesitated. "I'm trying to see you clearly, here in the dark. Who you are. I've gone almost blind, they say. Shingles. I can't place who I'm talking to." The group shifted, looked uneasily around at the bright lamps, felt a pang of sadness and confusion.

"It's Pat Garrett, Ma'm. Sheriff Pat Garrett. Remember? This afternoon? You found a dead man in your shed outside, and we're trying to figure out who killed 'im."

"Oh. Oh, yes. I think I remember now. Who killed him. Yes.

What was your question?"

"Did anyone stop by this place last night, do you recall? Last night, late. About 10 p.m.?" Now that he'd started, Garrett felt more relaxed. Alma wasn't trying to lie to him; she was sincerely trying to work with him to defeat her memory problem. He could appreciate that. He could work with her.

"Last night at ten?" She screwed up her face. "No, no, no one ever comes by that late. That's when the news starts, you know. No one would come by here at that time."

"But last night. Usually, I understand, it doesn't happen. But what about last night? Did you see anybody? Man or woman?" He hesitated. "Maybe an old friend, someone you might have known from long ago?"

"Oh, no. Nobody ever stops by here at that time. I don't get that many visitors, you know. Absolutely not." The room, which had tensed forward, leaned back. An intake of breath, ready to commence discussion. Then Alma added, pleased with herself, looking sly, "But I heard shots."

"You what?" This time Hallie was peeved. "You said you didn't hear anything. Are you talking about what you dreamed just now? You dreamed you heard shots?"

"No, I didn't 'dream just now,' " Alma mimicked, fully awake, her dander up. "I'm talking about last night. Before the news. I heard shots. I just didn't say earlier that I heard shots because it didn't have much to do with the guy in the shed."

Garrett, all ears, was leaning forward. "Can you tell us what you mean? When did you hear shots?"

"Just what I said. People shoot around here all the time, at this thing or that, prairie dogs or whatever, and the shots I heard were a lot farther away than the shed. Down the road a good piece, I would say. I never thought nothing of it then and to be honest, I still don't."

10

Nine A.M. Thursday Morning

Sheriff's Office, Courthouse, Riversmet

"So. What you bettin' on the gun?" Detective Asa Hobbs looked a little like a toad, all sunken into the softly decrepit, earth-brown easy chair in Garrett's office. He was stalling. Coreen and Barbara Lee wanted him home to help pack; they had to be at the airport by two. He preferred here.

Garrett shuffled his feet under his desk, moved his chew, and gave Hobbs a knowing grin. "You're the expert. You've already made your prediction, so what is it? What we gonna find...?"

McCracken, passing by the door with an armload of paper-work, poked her head in. "We won't find it. They'll find it—all those people pokin' around that place. They'll find it and dump it down somebody's outhouse hole, and that'll be the end of that—ashes to ashes and shit to shit."

"Oh," said Garrett innocently, grinning. "Don't you think the Oozlites want us to find that gun?"

"No gun, no fun," McCracken retorted. She was loving this. Her red hair was staticky in the dry June office, wisps crackling out around her face. She would have liked to have stepped in, to playfully punch the sheriff's arm, but she sensed that such a move might be going too far.

Hobbs grinned back wickedly. "Macky's right. They'll never find the gun. Nobody. It's an old .38 out of somebody's gran'daddy's closet, not registered, not traceable ... and it's already down the outhouse hole by now. You're gonna have to make your case without the weapon."

"Well, you're lookin' at the man can do 'er." Garrett puffed his chest in mock pride. "I can do 'er, Manure. None of Hobbs' legendary facial recognition, but I've got the old folks for good and true reliable witnesses. Bottom line."

Asa looked at his watch. "Good thing, too," he said reluctantly. "Looks like I'm off to Wisconsin to see my daughter meet her doom with WiseAss, and I can't bail ya out, much as I might like." He grimaced. "You know what those two are planning for wedding music? Some rapper ... a female rapper, for Christ sake. Lida Meter. Ever heard of 'er?"

"Never did," said Garrett, while McCracken mumbled, "Maybe the name is familiar." Asa pushed heavily out of the spring-broken chair.

"Familiar. Sure thing. Familiar like Elvis. How about even a polka? 'F'ing WiseAss. The guy's got no class." Hobbs stretched, pushed up his untucked shirt to scratch at the round, fuzzy belly underneath with both hands. His expression turned serious. "Oh, well. You got a deputy keeping an eye out for the safety of the lady of the house. The Stoney City boys'll start organizing the contents of that shed of hers this morning ... see what we find there." Stretching. "There isn't a goat's chance in hell that any tire marks in the area'll have any meaning, now that the neighborhood mob has been and gone. I guess you'll be at the neighbors' next, checking up on this and that." Another thorough scratch, this one in the armpit. "Wish I could be here."

Garrett chuckled. "You'll be here in our hearts."

"Yeah, right." Hobbs shrugged, still procrastinating, still serious. "Anyhow, I'll be back Monday. I can pick it up with you then."

"Monday we'll all sit down over coffee and McCracken 'n me'll tell you how we solved it, INCLUDING where we found the gun."

Garrett's riposte really tickled Leigh McCracken, and she was just getting ready to throw in her last two-cents worth, something about digging around in outhouses, when a roar, a sound like the explosive burst of a cannon, whirled all their heads toward the front of the courthouse. For an instant they were still, frozen in that instant, during which they heard Edith, at the front counter, say, "What the hell was that?" Then everyone headed for the door.

The courthouse was entered from the street by a short set of concrete steps. The first floor housed the drivers license bureau, the county clerk's offices, and the sheriff's office. Two courtrooms and the D.A. took up the second floor, while the county commissioners, the treasurer, county attorney, road and bridge department, and various other officials of government held sway in the basement. People were beginning to inch out of the various rooms, peering cautiously up or down the stairs, as their location required, when another report sounded, echoing against the side of the building. Because of the location of their office and the nature of their occupations, the sheriff and his crew made it to the large, glass double doors first. A woman was standing on the second step of the courthouse entrance holding a double barreled shotgun. She was in the process of cranking two more shells into the chamber and they could hear her yelling. Garrett turned and held out his hand, palm open, to stay anyone who might have had ideas of stampeding out the front door.

McCracken, on her tiptoes to see past the sheriff and Hobbs, who had somehow gotten positioned in front of her, thought frantically of other exits. She was sure she could overpower that woman with jujitsu. How could she get around her without being seen? Then she heard the Chief say, "Keep these people inside, McCracken. I want to see what's going on here." McCracken followed the direction of his gaze and saw the gathering crowd. Shit. Was this all she ever got to do? Crowd control? "OK, Chief," she said, but her words came out sullen. She turned and began to make authoritative gestures toward the bank of curious faces, moving them back.

Another explosion ripped the air just as Garrett eased the door open behind the woman, who was facing the street. She was shooting into the air, but now he could distinguish what she was yelling. "Back off, you sons-a-bitches. The problem was solved, and you ain't openin' it up again. I heard you. I heard what you said in the restaurant and you just ain't gonna do it. Get your asses home and get 'em home now. Sit in your shitty little tepee and deal your way to lala land, but don't you cross the people in our valley again!"

On the street, past the courthouse lawn, two pickups sat

nose to nose, as if in a standoff. Neither truck was in the best of shape: the one had its paint half gone, its windshield crying for new glass, while the other was branch-scratched and covered with ranch dirt. On the sidewalk stood a young couple in their early twenties. The woman, her short hair an iridescent purple, was decked out in a skin tight, ankle length, rainbow-striped tube dress, split on both sides from the hem well up the thigh and topped with a shawl draped across her shoulders. She wore beach flip-flops and the rings in her nose and ears glinted in the sunlight. The man also had on beach flip flops, as well as stained, khaki, Banana Republic, multipocketed shorts. These he had topped off with a white T-shirt imprinted with a square sign that read, at the top, "Bush-league Seed Co." Below that the sign said, "Texas Homegrown Dope." It was illustrated with a picture of a potted plant, the American president's Alfred E. Neumann-like visage sprouting like a fruit from the middle of the foliage. Neither the man nor the woman appeared particularly daunted by the furious woman on the courthouse steps.

Their eyes flicked to the sheriff, who had stepped out the door behind the woman. "Get outta the way, Barnswallowper. We got as much right to that fucking water as our old man or as you or any of your fucking kind. He could file, we can file."

Ignoring the direction of their eyes, but suddenly playing to her audience, Nancy Jane Barnswallowper pulled the trigger again on the shotgun, causing Alice to cover her ears and cringe, while Garrett made a face in disgust. After the sound died down, she shouted, "No, you ain't gettin' past me, you bastards. You ain't gonna take good agricultural water and use it to line your filthy pockets and ruin a whole valley."

With that she turned and made a grand gesture, shoving the gun toward the sheriff. "Take it, by god," she said, grandiosely, "I probably broke the letter of the law. But if you are any kind of a lawman, you'll stiffen your spine and stand up for those of us in the right."

Unfortunately, the first part of her grand gesture was lost on Pat Garrett as, to his chagrin, he saw McCracken dashing hunched over toward the two pickups. She disappeared on the far side of them. He blinked, then scowled. Why the hell wasn't she inside dealing with people? Absently he took the gun and grunted. Alice and Mac Biedermann began, with some confidence, to edge forward.

Garrett moved his eyes back to Nancy Jane. "Look, Ms. Barnswallowper. And you two..." he included Alice and Mac with a dip of his chin, "... and you two, you all come on into my office and we'll get this squared away. Come along." Then he raised his voice. "And you, too, McCracken. Come along. The situation is under control."

McCracken's head shot up from behind the Barnswallowper vehicle. "Chief," she hissed, the half-whisper resounding incongruously across the lawn. "Chief, come here. I want to show you something."

Now everyone's head had swiveled back toward McCracken, and Garrett said patiently, "This might not be a good time, Deputy." McCracken shrugged, squelched, and emerged all the way from behind the pickup.

"Later then," she conceded. God, the man was aggravating. Maybe that was why she liked him, she thought.

Inside, Garrett gathered up Hobbs and sent the crowd back to their work, saying, "It's OK, folks. These people are just having a little friendly disagreement. We'll iron it out in my office."

In his office, however, his voice was furious. "What in the world do you people think you are doing? Ms. Barnswallowper, I am clearly going to have to come up with a major excuse not to arrest you on all sorts of grounds. And you two! You find out your father is dead ... has been shot dead ... and all you can think of is to get down here and carry on his dirty business? You don't even mourn him? I'd like to know what you have to say for yourselves!"

It was Alice's spacey, thready voice that took the floor. "You don't. Understand. Sheriff. He was a mean man, Reider was. I don't think any of us cared. About. Him. 'Cause ..." The words sounded like a litany, " 'Cause he didn't care about us." She glanced at Mac for backup, but he had clamped his lips shut and was simply staring at her and at Nancy Jane in the chair beyond her, a threatening stare. Alice was undaunted. "If he'd paid Mac what he was worth, we could've made it to San Francisco. That's where Reider and Victoria were from. San

Francisco. Wonderful Wonderful Wonderful. City." Her voice had faded away and she was gazing at the wall as if the city were spread out before her on its face.

Garrett started to speak but she started up again as if someone had pushed a button. "Wonderful. City. Reider, he wouldn't help us. Not a good man. Not good alive ... never helped. And no good dead. Mac says we probably aren't in his will, after all, so we have to get the water. Right, Mac?"

The younger Biedermann was looking daggers at her, but she had stopped speaking abruptly and resumed looking at the wall. The cessation of her voice left a vacuum in the room. Garrett let it hang, waiting. Nancy Jane sat silently and defiantly, her ranch-muscled arms crossed in front of her. Mac shifted on his chair, then finally spoke.

"I don't see as we did anything illegal, Sheriff. I don't see as you have a right to hold us here." He hesitated, eyed the sheriff and Hobbs. "Maybe ... maybe we need an attorney."

Garrett grunted, pulled at his chin. "It remains to be seen whether what you two are up to is illegal," he said finally. "You can go for now. We'll be keeping an eye on you. You may want to think carefully about what you do next."

Mac shuffled, eyed the sheriff, then stood, a faint look of triumph crossing his face. "C'mon, Alice," he said, and she stood to follow, trailing her shawl behind her and giving it listless little flips as she walked.

Hobbs stood at the door, watching them, then turned back. "They went on out. Apparently decided against trying to file on that water this time. Hard to say."

Garrett nodded. Hobbs was going to miss his plane or, at the least, piss off his wife and daughter. He decided just to send Nancy Jane away with a stern reprimand and a warning; he was sure she wasn't a dangerous woman. He would take the flack. Turning to her, he began, "As for you, Ms. ..." but McCracken, who had been fidgeting near Hobbs, burst in.

"Chief. Chief! Before you go any further, there's something you should know."

Sucking his words back in, resigned, Garrett turned to his deputy. "Right. That's what you said. So. What is it, McCracken?"

"There's a gun on the seat of the Dodge pickup down there, the one I take to be Ms. Barnswallowper's. It looks like a .38, at a quick glance. Don't you think we should have a look at it?"

Before he could answer, Nancy Jane Barnswallowper sat forward, uncrossing her arms. "It ain't illegal to carry firearms that ain't concealed. You don't need to make that gun part of your sheriff business. That shotgun, that's your business. You ain't touchin' that other gun without a search warrant."

Garrett stood up, rubbed his hand across his scar. All he said was, "Oh."

11

Thursday Morning, Near Noon

Victoria Biedermann's House, Oozle Loop

He never understood how they did it. It was particularly irritating this morning, when he wasn't sure whether he'd done the right thing in the first place. He'd released Barnswallowper on her own recognizance less than two hours ago, and already, here in Croysant, folk were abuzz about "Nancy Jane's run-in with the sheriff." Stepping into Coffin's Country Store, next to the post office, he could overhear the owner and Lucy Quick in the back discussing the incident.

"I heard she shot several times," Lucy was saying. "I'm surprised Garrett didn't throw 'er in the pokey. Seems he had plenty of grounds."

"Ehh," Coffin dismissed it, then mumbled something inaudible, followed by Lucy again. "Old Barnswallowper, she'd do whatever, wouldn't she?"

Garrett didn't want to hear it. "Hey," he hollered. "You guys got any non-nicotine chew?"

Coffin came out of the back, set a box of something on the counter, then, saying "ehh" again, chewing on a pencil, he rummaged around under the counter. Meanwhile, Garrett once more mulled whether letting Nancy go had been such a good idea.

It had been intuition. Sitting in the office and watching Nancy Jane while McCracken had gone out with an evidence bag to fetch the .38 — probable cause — all he could see was a settler type, rooted to the valley and unlikely to go anywhere else for any reason, a rough woman full of bluster but not full of meanness. He didn't figure she actually would have shot anyone with the shotgun, and he seriously doubted she'd shot anyone with the .38.

Besides, he was busy. It would be a waste of time to keep her without grounds—had she even had the opportunity to get at Reider, considering that all the neighbors placed her as one of the last to leave the water board meeting? And ... well, he liked her. She was a decent person, not as slimy as Mac Biedermann appeared to be.

Still.

Thinking back, he knew that maybe he should have had more doubts. Intuition. It could get you into a lot of trouble. He paid for the chew—three cans—then headed back to the car. He was glad that McCracken was in a talkative mood, anxious to rehash the adventure. It kept his mind off the possible error in his ways.

"So, what do you think of Biedermann's kid?" McCracken offered.

"Antisocial. One a' those kinds with a chip on the shoulder. May not mean anything, I suppose."

"I suppose not. Picked a dilly for a wife."

"Everybody's gotta have somebody, I guess." This comment temporarily sent McCracken's and Garrett's thoughts along different paths, and they were quiet.

Garrett turned left off the pavement onto Oozle Road, which dropped briefly as if for one last goodbye, then climbed vigorously eastward toward the mountains. Hayfields lay on either side of the road but they were punctuated with rocky outcrops and occasional larger hills. Flatlanders might call those hills mountains. Whatever land wasn't irrigated was dry, sporting its trademark patches of cedar, pinion, and sagebrush. Ranch houses and outbuildings along the way had a rough look, built from lumber dragged out of the mountains a century ago by the first settlers, cobbled together and still kept with limited resources.

At one point a nipple of land edged into the road, causing it to curve out widely before swinging back. A cluster of ranch buildings on the nipple looked resourceful, if not wealthy. The mailbox sign read "Weinant," and McCracken said, "That must be Alma's son's place. Wonder what he's been up to since yesterday?"

"Me, too," Garrett said.

McCracken sighed. "And speaking of sons, I wonder what Son Biedermann meant by that crack when he said that in one way he wasn't even Reider Biedermann's fucking kid?"

"He said that? I didn't hear it."

"Yeah, I quote exact. Come to think of it, it was after he left the office. I guess I picked it up when I went to get that gun—him and Alice were still hanging outside then."

The road grew steeper. Just before swinging right to run horizontally along the foot of the mountains proper, it revealed a large, ancient barn looming to their left. It was clearly no longer in use. Air showed between each of the weatherbeaten boards that would have been coveted by city people for use in paneling their modern rec rooms with 'barn wood.' Beyond the barn was a house built of logs, its demeanor as grey as that of the barn, squat and settled, the front stoop displaying a variety of chickens, cats, and a tired looking border collie. The mailbox, opposite the buildings, read simply 4486 Oozle, but Garrett hmphed. "This is the old Barnswallowper place. I don't see Nancy's truck up there, but then maybe it's parked in a shed or around back."

McCracken giggled. "Or maybe she had some shopping to do before heading home. A new .38 or ..."

Garrett felt his mood lighten. On a deal like this, McCracken wasn't such bad company. To their left, County Road K-4, a narrow, ungraveled track between crooked barbed wire fences, left Oozle and snaked sharply upward. Garrett gestured toward it. "We'll head up there next; it goes to the back of the Biedermann place, and that's where Mac and Alice are supposed to live."

To their right, an expansive flat opened out. It was green and well-watered, alfalfa already calf high and growing fast. A sign, hanging between posts set at either side of the lane that headed west toward the house, proclaimed it the Quarter Circle Lazy J ranch, and the sign at the mailbox read "Johnson."

"Where's the cows?" asked McCracken. It had just occurred to her that something was missing.

"They would already be up in the high country for the summer ... Bureau of Land Management, Forest Service ... over there." He gestured toward the big mountains and mesas to their south and east. Before McCracken could speak again, he added, "Anyhow, the next place is Biedermann's. McCracken, I've got a search warrant, but I won't use it unless there's a reason. I'm going to see if Mrs. Biedermann will just let you look around while I talk to her.

"Damn it!" he continued. "I wish we weren't always so short handed; I'd like you to be on hand for the interview, too." He paused, pushed his chew. "Well, just rove around a little. See if you notice anything out of the ordinary. Then drift back in and listen in on what she says. Don't say much yourself, OK?" He wasn't sure why he added the last. He just always had an uneasy feeling that McCracken was going to jump in and over-compensate if she perceived something wasn't going quite as it should.

"Yeah, Chief — will do," she said, and then they had turned left onto a well graveled lane, and were approaching a modern house built of huge, reddish spruce logs. It jutted out from the hillside on which it sat, looking incongruous and presumptive among the dry, brushy foliage around it, which it dwarfed. Leaving the car, the investigators walked beside a landscaped lawn to reach hewn log steps that led up to a large deck which faced the low mesas to the west.

Victoria Biedermann, expecting them, answered Garrett's knock on the door. Her long, slender legs were tastefully set off by a soft grey pantsuit. The silken hair glowed golden in the tidy braid, and her wistful, smoky eyes, looking up at Garrett as she opened the door, seemed to send a respectful question. The sweet cream complexion was pale, a modest button of color marking each high cheekbone.

"Come in," she said. "Can I get you anything to drink? A soda, or ...?"

Garrett felt the area around his scar getting warm; his disobedient left hand insisted on giving it a little rub as he said, "Oh, no. No, thank you, Ma'am. We will be fine."

He glanced around the large living room into which they were escorted. It had all the trappings of the Big Valley/Bonanza western culture — the wooden and leather furniture, the horseshoes made into lamp bases, the rock fireplace, logs of equal proportion stacked at the ready beside it, the Navajo rugs and prints from Russell and Remington gracing the walls.

On one couch sat a thick young woman with heavy, dark black hair, a swarthy complexion, and a pouty-lipped mouth that was set hard against what appeared to be either tension or anger. On the bear rug at her feet a child of about four was playing with a golden-haired Barbie. The little girl looked up and grinned at Garrett and McCracken as they entered.

"Mr. Garrett, this is my daughter, Christa. And her daughter, my granddaughter, Firene." Garrett nodded, said, "How do you do." He remarked to himself the resemblance of the daughter's hair to Reider's own thick mop. In fact, the whole daughter must resemble Reider, since she bore almost no resemblance to the willowy, elegant mother. "Ms. Biedermann, Ms ... hrmph ..." No one filled in the missing name, so he swallowed the sentence and continued.

"This is my deputy, Deputy Leigh McCracken. We both want to extend you our sympathy on the death of Mr. Biedermann." He paused, and Victoria lowered her long lashes in acknowledgment while the daughter simply scowled. Garrett plunged on.

"Our purpose here is to learn about your husband, Ms. Biedermann, with an eye to identifying his killer. With your indulgence, we would appreciate it if Deputy McCracken could take a short walk through this house while I talk with you and, um, Christa. Sometimes, the more we know about a victim, the faster we are able to do our job." Had he imagined it, or had Victoria involuntarily sucked in a breath when he'd asked if McCracken could go through the house? Perhaps not.

At any rate, she was saying, "Oh, no. Feel free to look around, Miss McCracken. If you have any questions, I will be happy to answer ... and won't you sit down, Mr. Garrett?" She indicated a large leather easy chair opposite Christa's couch. Garrett wondered if it had been Biedermann's.

Indicating a row of family portraits along the fireplace mantel, Garrett said, "The gentleman in those photos must have been Mr. Biedermann?"

"Oh, yes," Victoria said, sadness tinging her voice. She stood and selected a portrait showing a family group, man, woman, and two youngsters. "This was Reider and I, little

Mickey Mac and Christa, back when we lived in San Francisco."

Garrett took the portrait and examined it. Victoria had been beautiful, then, too, and, Reider, although short in stature, shorter by half a head than his wife, had been a handsome young man, his bad boy looks reminding one of the young Elvis. It was the same pouty mouth that was echoed in his daughter's face on the couch. Victoria picked up a second photo, obviously more recent. It showed a middle-aged, bifocaled, paunchy Reider seated by Victoria. About all that was retained from his youth was the thick, dark hair. "This is just Reider and I, last year on our anniversary. He wanted a photo to remember it. He was always so sentimental."

If possible, Christa's mouth seemed to turn down even further. "Give it up, Mother. Reider was about as sentimental as that asshole, Les."

With that comment, Eirene looked sharply at her mother, while Victoria simply said, "Oh, Christa," her voice sounding infinitely disappointed. She set the pictures back on the mantel, and Garrett, brows up, asked, "Les?"

"Les," said Victoria, turning from the mantel and seating herself on a straight-backed wooden chair with steer horns carved into the back. "Les is Christa's husband. Ex-husband, soon-to-be. He has behaved very badly toward Christa and Eirene, and Christa has had to leave him."

"Well, Mother dearest, very badly might be a euphemism. He was outright abusive. He abused me. He tried to abuse Eirene. And that — that will never happen. Will it, Eirene? That asshole."

Clearing his throat and rubbing his scar, Garrett said, "Abusive?"

"I think ... I think controlling would be a good word. He never hit you, did he, Dear? Just ..." She turned, somewhat imploringly, toward the sheriff. "You see, he wouldn't ever support the girls. Christa has been working two jobs. She works at the post office in Croysant as a substitute many days, then at least five days or evenings every week she works at the Harvest Apple in Peaseford. Waiting tables."

Garrett was looking assessively at Christa. "We believe your father was killed some time after nine o'clock on Tuesday night. Were you at the Harvest Apple then? Did you see anything that struck you as unusual?"

Christa looked disgusted. "You mean, do I have an alibi. You know, my shift ends at 8:30, and I still have this and that to do. Then I try to pick up Eirene at the sitter's there in Peaseford and get home and get her to bed. It's a long day for her. And me. I try to read to her, get her to bed, then I take a muscle-soothing bath – do you know how tired you can get standing, sorting mail from 7:30 till 4:00, then rushing down country to be on your feet some more, packing veggie tacos and Caesar salads to Peaseford's best? After I undo as much of the stress as I can, I go to bed."

She'd been talking in generalizations. Garrett said quietly, "And Tuesday?"

"I was alone after I got home – except for Eirene, of course. But maybe ..." Her expression changed, softened. "Maybe you could call Joh... uh, my attorney, John Duval. He's going to represent me in my custody fight with that asshole, Les. I phoned him after I got home from the restaurant that night..."

Garrett nodded. "Thank you, Christa. I will. And by the way, I really am interested in whether you saw anyone unusual that evening. Jenny Threewinds, at the Cowpath, saw a woman that night that was ... perhaps suspicious. Perhaps not." He let the significance of the event remain at the level of gossip.

It was Victoria who said, "Oh!" Then she said, "But just so you won't have to inquire, Sheriff. I left here at 5:30 Tuesday evening to do a substitute nursing shift at the Riversmet Community Hospital. It was one of those twelve-hour shifts. When I got off, I had breakfast with my friend, Susan Baker, picked up a few groceries, and came home.

"I really didn't expect Reider to be here. He always has ... had ... so much on his mind, you know." Her voice had gotten shaky, and she paused, composing herself. "So ... well, of course I had no idea. I just took a good nap when I got home, ate a sandwich, and went on over to the clubhouse." Again, she paused and swallowed. "I hate to miss club, you know. And I had no idea ..."

She was now crying, large tears slipping from the corners of her eyes, and a different daughter might have put her arms around her mother. Christa, however, looked at her with disgust. "You had no idea how lucky you'd just gotten. And it looks like you still don't."

McCracken had apparently finished her walk around the house, having slipped silently into an inconspicuous chair near the hallway door. Her voice swiveled all their heads. "So. Would you say that you and your brother had about the same feelings toward your father?" It wasn't a bad question, Garrett thought, with surprised approval.

Christa snorted. "Little 'Mickey Mac'?" Her voice was sour with sarcasm. "Do you know why he got expelled from the easiest community college from the easiest course to take in the Rocky Mountains? Our darling little 'Mickey Mac' was trying to get a certificate of photography from Buckhorn Community College — Buckhorn, mind you! — and they had to expel him because he kept wandering around, trying to get respectable local women to pose in the nude. The kind of women, mind you, who had to have the light off before they would take their clothes off in their own bedrooms. 'Mickey Mac' is a bum, like his father. Was."

Victoria had nothing to say. She sat with her eyes downcast, twisting her hands on her lap. After the silence had stretched like bad taffy, Christa resumed, her voice softer. "I'm sorry, Sheriff. I guess I'm a woman with issues. I don't feel much in common with my other family members. I'm the only one who doesn't hate it here, doesn't want to get back to San Francisco, despite what mother may say. Mac and his doxy Alice would kill to get out of here — oh, excuse me! No implications intended! I doubt those two would have inherited diddly from Reider. And all I will end up with is this short, fat body ..." She gave her chubby thighs a sharp smack and caught her breath.

"And Reider never made mother happy, no matter what she might tell you. But me ... me, I like it here. Except for that asshole, Les, I like it here fine. And I didn't need Mr. Deals-in-Graft to make it harder than ever for me and Eirene to fit in. As if the damn drug dealer reputation wasn't enough, he had to start stealing water."

Now Victoria looked up, her eyes moist but flashing. At each juncture in her speech she sucked in little gasping breaths.

"Christa, you know your father ... (gasp) has been under the weather now for ... (gasp) for weeks. I was trying so hard to ... (gasp) nurse him to health. He wasn't on drugs. He hated drugs."

Christa's jaw had gone taut again and she stared at her mother, shaking her head. "Oh, yes, Mother. I forgot. Pure as the driven snow, our dear parent Biedermann. Our Pappy." This last word dripping acid. "As for me, my money is on Alma Weinant's chicken shed being a drug drop. What do you say to that?"

12

Thursday Noon

Mac and Alice's Tepee

No one replied to Christa's outburst. Garrett had been leaning forward in his chair, his forearms on his thighs, his hands dangling loosely between his knees, watching and listening. When it became apparent that neither Victoria nor Christa intended to continue, he stood and thanked them for their time.

Garrett and McCracken turned right onto Oozle loop from the Biedermann gate, going back in the same direction from which they had come. Garrett said, "Well, Deputy. What do you think? See anything on your stroll?"

McCracken wasn't sure where to start. Her "stroll," as Garrett referred to it, had produced something that she didn't know how to process.

"Well, speaking of drugs ..." she started, hesitantly.

Garrett mumbled encouragement, so she continued, "According to Victoria, Reider was ... what did she say? 'Under the weather'? Anyhow, not in good health, right?"

"Right. Said she'd been trying to nurse him back to health for weeks."

"See, I remembered Barnswallowper saying how sickly the guy looked and ..." McCracken shook her head, groping for what was bothering her. "I can't see what the point of this is ... probably nothing. But ... somehow it doesn't fit. The thing is, the absence of something doesn't necessarily mean it's not there."

"Probably not." Garrett looked across at her curiously.

"But it ... it looked odd to me. I looked in the medicine cabinet in the family bathroom, and it was pretty normal — some Tylenol, some toothpaste, the usual stuff, whatever that is. Then I took a peek into the cabinet in the master bathroom. It was really empty. A tube of antibiotic ointment, some Advil, and a tube of toothpaste ... but no special drugs. No little brown bottles of prescription drugs. No special containers of 'I am nursing him back to health' drugs." McCracken made the quotation marks with her fingers in the air. "Just a drab, generic, medicine cabinet for Mr. or Mrs. Everyperson.

"That triggered a nagging doubt in me, so I started really focusing on looking. Just poking around, trying to see where they might have put them — bedside stands, kitchen cabinets, you know ..."

Garrett glanced over. "But you didn't find anything?"

"Nothing. Even all the wastebaskets were empty, except one. The one under the bathroom sink had a couple of feminine products, and something kind of odd, but hardly worth mentioning, either. I couldn't see how it tied in to anything ..."

Garrett primed her. "Odd? How?"

"Oh, it was a little statue of the Empire State Building. The metal it was made of looked kind of tarnished, like it was maybe an old souvenir or something. Maybe it was a toy or something that that little kid, what was her name ... Christa's kid? Maybe a toy she got tired of. I don't know."

Garrett's face had developed a contemplative frown, so McCracken forged ahead, trying to be clear about why what she had not found seemed odd to her. "Of course, it was a short time to look, so that medication could be somewhere and I just missed it. And ... well, the man was shot, not ... poisoned. I started to feel foolish, poking around for some sort of stuff that had to be legitimate medicine anyhow, so pretty soon I started just thinking about what else I might be seeing."

"Whoof," Garrett sympathized. "I've had that sort of nagging doubt before. Sometimes pans out to be something, sometimes not." He turned right, aiming the car up County Road K-4 toward where Mac and Alice's tepee sat on the back of the Biedermann land. Flipping off the air conditioner, he opened his window and rested his elbow on the frame. The Barnswallowper place rolled along to his left, some of it unirrigated and covered with sage. He drew in a heady, perfumed breath, a look of such pleasure crossing his face that McCracken, inspired, followed suit with her own window. "So. What else did you pick up?" he asked.

"Not much. Nothing, really. The house is relatively tidy; there's a well-stocked bar and it looks used — some unwashed drink glasses in the sink. Reider's desk is in a big old nifty office that I would love. Great view. The top of his desk was clean; nothing on his appointment book for the twelfth, and, since he was killed that night, that was the last day up. It was one of those religious, inspirational, daily calendars that you tear the sheets off, so nothing of his previous activities, and no notes for what he had expected to do in the next couple of days, had he lived. I didn't poke past this week, but I poked around in the drawers. He had a business card for John Duval, the attorney Christa mentioned. I suppose he had an interest in the custody hearing. Her kid being his grandkid and all."

"And that was it?"

"That was it." The road had tilted and was beginning a series of sharply upward spiraling switchbacks. McCracken's eyes widened. They had rounded a turn, and in front of them sat Nancy Jane's pickup, pulled against the gate beside a cattleguard that crossed the road. As their car crossed the cattleguard, both the sheriff and the deputy craned their necks. No one was in the pickup. Before their car rounded the next turn a series of shots rang out somewhere to their left. Bang. Bang bang bang. Bang.

Garrett slowed the police car to a crawl and they both listened. Nothing more. The car was groaning, struggling with the slow pace and the climb. After what seemed minutes of holding their breath, Garrett finally said, "Well, Alma is right, you know. Around here, people do shoot all the time. Prairie dogs or whatever. I guess ..." He let his voice trail off, still craning his neck, but kept easing the car upward.

McCracken, casting her eyes around, fought off the urge to mention that the shots might have been meant for them. He probably knew that. She trusted his courage.

In less than quarter mile more of steep, winding dirt road, Garrett squinted at a rough-hewn track that took off through the pinion and sage. "I think ... if I've got my directions right, I think this is it." He squeezed onto the track which immediately began to do a nasty number on the car. McCracken, jostled forward, bounced sideways, tipped to left and right, gritted her teeth, but Garrett grinned. "This had better be it."

Then the tepee came into view, nestled in a pocket behind a large rock outcrop, its front obscured by the scrubby trees. The old pickup sat beside it. Garrett grimaced, his own nerves giving him trouble. In the old days, it would have been revenuers or game wardens who had to approach places like this, not sure what to expect and unlikely to win the day. Now he and McCracken were in the hot seat. He glanced over at her young, freckled face, pale and worried under the deputy hat. She looked vulnerable. Gruffly, he said, "We need to be a little careful here, McCracken."

She nodded. Her eyes were busy, searching the brush and the outcrop behind the tepee. One hand was on the door latch, the other on the gun at her hip.

"This time," Garrett continued, "What we'll do is, if they don't cooperate, we'll pull the warrant."

McCracken nodded again, attempting to look purposeful, but it turned out that there was no question of anyone cooperating. No human was in evidence anywhere, neither in the tepee, which smelled like sour farts and burned grease, nor outside. They searched the area for several minutes with increasing confidence, then went back into the tepee itself.

After the comments made by Christa that morning, it was difficult not to see evidence of contraband everywhere. Jars of seeds and large beads sat on an overturned fruit crate by a propane camp stove. Also on the crate was a large plastic jar that had once held Tang. Picking it up and peering at it in the dim light, Garrett ascertained that it was full of empty pill capsules. Empty, he assumed, to be filled with whatever was cooking around here. Frisking a shirt wadded next to a pile of sleeping bags and blankets, Garrett pulled out two packages of cigarette papers. To roll marijuana smokes? He couldn't catch the smell over the general stench in the tepee. A mano and metate, looking as if it had just surfaced from an archeological dig, lay on its side beside a bag of plant fertilizer near the door. McCracken picked it up, sniffed inside the depression in the metate, wished she had some idea as to what peyote might smell like. As it was, she was just sorry that she had opened her nose in the atmosphere of the tepee.

A cupboard opposite the door yielded a stack of jerky, some apples and apricots which had apparently been dried at home, a bag of pretzels, and two boxes of baggies, often used, Garrett mumbled, to package drugs.

There was an ice chest beside what was probably the head of the sleeping bag pile. McCracken had gotten over her initial jumpiness about scratching sounds and shadows outside along the tepee wall, and she was now poking around in earnest. She set a plastic restaurant ashtray, full of cigarette butts, onto the tent floor and opened the lid of the ice chest. "Just beer and a quart of milk," she said with some disappointment. Garrett, looking over her shoulder, saw the beer cans and milk sitting in a layer of water, a few pieces of ice floating beside them.

"Yeah," he said, "But look here." A hewn log, big enough for sitting, had been placed beside the ice chest, and next to it was a stack of deer antlers. Behind the log was a neat stack of pipes chipped from the antlers. It was the tidiest thing in the tepee. Next to them, carefully placed, were the hand tools that had been used to do the chipping.

"To smoke it?" McCracken asked, knowing the question superfluous.

"To smoke it. There aren't any plants in here. Let's step outside ..."

McCracken laughed. "Yes, there are. Look over there, under the tarp."

"Oh, yeah." Garrett laughed with her. "The little mushroom garden. I saw that, too."

Outside, they poked around some more. There was a roll of tubing, probably used to carry water from their tank to the illegal plants, and some sacks, of the kind used to cover plants in early spring, plus a variety of other generic gardening supplies, but they weren't able to pick up the marijuana itself. They hated to give up; they felt like bloodhounds on the scent. Somewhere ... somewhere nearby, surely ... these two were heavily into growing the weed.

On the other hand, the country was rough. They could hunt here two weeks and, without a burst of luck, come up empty-handed. Finally, Garrett proposed they give it up and head back to Croysant for lunch. McCracken, her stomach growling now that they were free of the fetid air in the tepee, concurred.

As often happens, the trip back seemed to go much faster than the drive into the unknown. In no time flat, they'd reached the cattleguard. This time Nancy Jane was there by her pickup; she raised her hand in a cordial wave. Garrett stopped the car and leaned out the window. "Howdy, Ms. Barnswallowper. Nice day."

"Too dry, as always." Nancy Jane grinned, threw a mud encrusted shovel into the back of the pickup and walked around it, the better to converse with the sheriff and McCracken. McCracken felt herself staring at Nancy Jane's middle, where a .45 had been casually tucked into the top of her pants, the butt of the gun protruding. So, it had been her who had fired the shots. What had she been shooting at this time?

"I just thought," Garrett continued, seemingly oblivious to the gun, "That you might have seen the Biedermanns. Mac and Alice. We've just gotten back from their place up the road. Their truck is there, but there isn't any sign of life up there."

Nancy Jane snorted. "No police car is ever gonna find those two druggies at home. You wanta have a chat with 'em, you probably should park at my place and walk up, fairly sneaky. Quite a hike, though." She pulled the top off a weed which was brushing against her pickup fender, stuck it in her mouth, and masticated thoughtfully.

Garrett nodded, gave the conversation the appropriate mellow pause, then said, "Well, that's all right. We can talk to 'em later. I guess you're saying you didn't see any sign of 'em ... uh, wherever you were, either?" At this last he narrowed his eyes a little, regarding her closely.

"Nah, I don't see much of 'em. Nothin', if I can help it. I was just up ... dealing with some, uh ... trash, anyhow. As I figure it, this time ... well, it wouldn't surprise me that now that the heat is on, they've skipped the country."

"Maybe." Everyone was silent for a few more respectable moments, then the sheriff added, "Well, I guess we'd better let you get back to work. McCracken here is wantin' me to kick in for a little lunch."

Arriving back at Oozle road, Garrett turned left. "Let's have a look at the back part of this," he commented. "It's my understanding that it loops; we left Highway 46 ... what, about three miles out of Croysant? From there it goes up east here, the way we came, runs along the foothills, then just after the Biedermann main place it drops back to meet the highway again, right by the Oozle-Onion Valley Clubhouse. I think the loop itself runs about eleven miles, but that if you stayed on the main highway it's only about six miles from where it enters to where it exits."

This time it was McCracken's turn to grunt. She wasn't much interested in the length of the Oozle loop. She was trying to figure out how to get Garrett talking about Nancy Jane, the shots, the gun, the missing Mac and Alice, the tepee ... or if not that, then at least about Christa and her drug-drop comments.

Oblivious of her disinterest, Garrett continued. "It could be important because of the way Alma's house sits on the highway between the entrance and exit to the loop. Someone ... anyone ... could get to Alma's without being seen by others along that stretch of Highway 46. Or, if it was a question of passing someone along Oozle ... you see, if you went the one way, you would avoid ... see, there's the clubhouse and the highway entrance. Now, see? If you'd shot Biedermann and wanted to get back to your house, quickly, that is, not hide out for any length of time, and you lived on Oozle Loop, you could come this back way and not be seen by anyone along the highway or the main part of the loop. It's worth thinking about."

McCracken made an effort to make that what she thought about, failed, and was just at the point where she was ready to call time out on the topic when another of the Riversmet patrol cars appeared behind them. They'd passed Alma's already and were nearing the scenic pullout when a short, loud "waroo" from its siren caught their attention.

"Looks like Red," Garrett commented, pulling into the turnout. The deputy pulled out behind them and bailed out of his car, carrying an evidence bag.

"Hey, Cap! Look what we found right over there. Believe it or not! Right over next to that pond, there." He dangled the bag in front of Garrett's eyes. A .38 caliber Smith and Wesson revolver reposed inside.

"How about that. Over there by the pond? Not in it?"

"Nope, just beside it. Like somebody had maybe meant to heave it on in but had missed or something. Maybe they were in a hurry. Jim and me found it."

"Good police work," Garrett said, taking the bag and holding it up to peer at the contents.

"At first we figured it was a waste of time to hunt this far ... to try to hunt the whole country. Like Hobbs said, more likely in somebody's closet. But then we got to thinking about this pond and didn't figure it would hurt to nose around it ... Jim actually saw the glint of metal from the road and ..."

"You decided to take a look," McCracken finished for him. Red reminded her of an overenthusiastic puppy, jumping around all the time, trying to get approval. In fact, there had been one time when he'd had his paws all over HER. He never did that again

"We decided to take a look." Red nodded his satisfied confirmation.

"But not in the pond? Beside it?"

"Yeah. I can't figure that one. Why not go ahead and throw it on in? It was ten, maybe a dozen, feet this way."

"Well, this could be the little feller that did the trick," said Garrett, handing the bag back to Red. "So I guess you'd better get it on up to ballistics. And begin a trace."

Red grinned, taking the bag. "Already done, Amigo."

13

Thursday, a Late Lunch

At the Cowpath Saloon

They pulled into the graveled parking lot of the Cowpath while Garrett worked the mobile phone. He'd already talked to the office secretary, Edith. He'd asked her to get someone onto Victoria's hospital alibi. Now his ear was on hold, warming while he waited for John Duval's secretary to round the lawyer up from points unknown. He pulled into a parking space, stopped the car, turned to McCracken, raised an eyebrow, and shrugged, juggling the phone.

McCracken gave an answering shrug, pulled out her nearly empty water bottle, and finished drinking, secretly cursing herself for not bringing more. And a sack lunch might have been nice! She was famished.

Garrett checked his watch and looked with longing at the entrance to the restaurant. "Let's give her another two minutes to find 'em," he decided to McCracken, settling in. "I guess after we eat we'd better head back and walk the pond with those guys to get our own..." The phone in his hand burped, and Garrett interrupted himself.

"...Yeah. Duval? Yeah. Listen, you may be aware that we are in the middle of a murder investigation up here south of Croysant?" A pause as he took in Duval's answer, then, "Right. The chicken shed murder. Anyhow, we're just getting people close to the case placed with respect to where they were on Tuesday evening, at the time we think this thing may have happened."

Another pause. "Right. We're interested in a certain

Christa... in the former Christa Biedermann. She claims to have been alone at home with her daughter, Eirene, from about 9:00 p.m. on. She says she called you...?" A pause.

"I don't have her married name ... Yeah, I think you can assume we're talking about the same person if we refer to Christa Shipley. Right." Garrett fought the urge to ask the lawyer if 'Shipley' was a.k.a. "that Asshole, Les."

The attorney's voice droned in his ear. "That sounds close to what she said, then. About 9:30 or 10:00, as nearly as you recall? You didn't check the time, but could you give me any idea as to the substance of the call?" A longer pause.

"Right. Right. I hear you. Attorney/client privilege. Right. Thanks for the information."

Garrett dropped the phone into the holder on his belt, said to his deputy, "Right. The call seems to have taken place ... we could check phone records if necessary, but I doubt ..." He hesitated, looking thoughtful. "Duval states, and I quote, 'But I can tell you the call had nothing to do with homicide, and everything to do with Ms. Shipley's child custody case.' Whaddya think, Deputy—is the man qualified to make that judgment?" With that comment, Garrett abruptly bailed out of the car and headed for the restaurant, McCracken following.

As was traditional after the lunch rush, the "Please Wait to be Seated" sign had been swiveled to its other side, which read "Please Seat Yourself." Only two tables still had people. Passing them, Garrett and McCracken nodded, mumbled "Nice day," and "Sure is ... need rain." Garrett picked a table at the back, his eyes out for Jenny. He saw her emerging from the kitchen, her hips catching the swinging door, her hands full of coleslaw and cherry tomatoes to replenish the salad bar.

Rita, the waitress, came by to deliver water, pass them a menu, and assure herself that they wanted coffee. As soon as she had rid herself of the slaw and tomatoes, Jenny came over.

"I wrote it down, everything I could think of that happened here Tuesday night." She pulled a little notebook from her apron, sat between Garrett and McCracken, set the notebook on the table and, her finger on the first page, leaned toward Garrett in a way that McCracken felt was not entirely necessary.

"You see, I couldn't literally list everyone. Quite a lot of people were in and out. I'd figure that over the course of the evening we had maybe a dozen tables of tourists ... you know, you can tell 'em. People heading for the reservoir up here to go fishing—shorts, floppy hats, tourist tans ... and also drivers who've just seen the sign outside of Croysant and realized that they have ninety miles before they get to Stoney City and another chance at food. All of those folks looked normal—well, like normal tourists—so I didn't make anyone out as being different from anybody else."

Rita brought coffee and Garrett said, "Want a cup with us?"

"No ... oh, no. Not right now, thanks." Jenny waited while Rita took their orders for cheeseburger and fries, no mayo, and chimichanga, green sauce.

"Anyhow, a dozen or so tables of those. Then, maybe four or five tables with Peaseford people. I knew them, and I've listed them here, but I figured you were probably most interested in the Oozle Onion-Valley people, so I put them separate ..." She paused, thumbed the page over, "...on this page."

McCracken craned to see who she'd written as she kept talking. "First of all, Mac Biedermann was here early, about 7:30, I would guess. He was sitting at that booth over there, which is why I don't think he saw his father come in at about nine. See how that booth angles? He couldn't have seen the front from there."

McCracken cleared her throat. "So, was he here alone?"

"Oh, right. That's a good question." Jenny looked up at her appreciatively. "He had three friends, young men I didn't recognize. Maybe they were from on down in the valley, like Riversmet. They seemed to be just drinking and talking. Mostly drinking. Mostly beer."

Rita scooted plates, blistering hot, in front of Garrett and McCracken. The platter-sized chimichanga was buried in sliced tomato, fresh lettuce, and avocado, paper containers of green salsa and sour cream perched on the side of the plate. McCracken fought back a drool. Garrett said, "Thanks, Rita," as she filled their cups. Then he asked, "So, did the Mac Biedermann bunch stay all evening?"

"No, that's one thing I'm glad I noticed. The men Mac was with took off at a little after nine, kind of nodding, I'm not sure if shaking hands, but seemed to have agreed on something. Mac had another beer, then at about 9:30—you know, guys, I don't ... you can't quote me on most of these times. They're just my best guess. I did check with Rita to be as close as possible, though.

"Anyhow, at about 9:30, Alice Biedermann came in the front, stepped around to his table, and gave Mac a come along gesture. They left together."

Garrett, deep into his burger and looking at her list, managed to say, "This was after you had the drink with Patty Harris?"

Jenny shook her head. "No, that's not right. Patty came later. It was at least a quarter 'til 10:00. Then that woman came by, the one I still can't place," she paused, still bothered by her memory lapse, "and after that Patty left."

McCracken was still eating, but each forkful was smaller than the last. Feeling satisfied and chummy, she didn't mind including Jenny into Those-in-the-Know, provided she herself was on the inside information track with Garrett, so she said, "They found a gun. By Harris's pond."

"A gun? Do you think ... do you mean, *THE* gun? The murder gun?"

"Maybe. I guess you heard about the excitement at the courthouse this morning?" Silly question. That had been hours ago, so who could have failed to hear about it?

It turned out that Jenny had only gotten "one version," so they filled her in on the details.

Garrett finished the story with, "... and so it was McCracken, here, her good police work, that spotted the gun in the pickup."

"And now you have two suspicious guns?"

"Until ballistics gets done with 'em."

Garrett was ready to stand up when McCracken, relaxed and conversational, said, "So what can you tell us about the Harrises? As I understand it, Lew's the patriarch of the family and Clint's a grandson?"

"That's right. Lew and Lucky's only child, Michael, died in 'Nam in '71. Clint was just a baby then, maybe a year old. It must've been awfully sad. They say Lew dotes on Clint, as I suppose you would."

McCracken, interested, said, "That's so sad." Garrett squirmed. To put it politely, his whole digestive system was getting away with him. Now he had gas cramps. He wished the women would shut up. He needed to get up and move around.

"Oh, yeah," Jenny continued. "I guess Michael, the father, never got to see his son. It's too bad, too. They're such a nice family. He'd have been proud of Clint and Patty."

"I'll bet he would," said Garrett neutrally, thinking the stage was set to make their exit, but Jenny was happy to be without diners for a few minutes and had settled in for a good gossip.

"When cattle prices fell a few years back, Clint and Lew sold that piece of land across Dry Gulch, beyond the pond, to the Michaelsons. They sold a few acre-feet of the original irrigating water rights to them with the place, so they got a good price for it. That gave them capital to hold their own, I guess. Anyhow, they're flourishing now. It seems like every year when you come across the Harris cattle being driven up to summer pasture on Stoney Mesa, it takes longer to maneuver the car through them."

McCracken, honed in on Jenny, accepted a coffee refill from Rita with a nod, asked, "So their herd's getting up there in size?" Garrett gave up. Excusing himself, he told McCracken he'd meet her at the car.

The women gave him a dismissive nod. To McCracken, Jenny responded, "I'd say two hundred fifty, three hundred head. A lot for this area." She smiled and leaned in, confidential. "And between you and me, Leigh, they are going to need it. Now, don't spread this around, but Patty told me this. Her and Clint are in their early thirties, and Clint's been kind of funny about starting a family. See, not only did his dad die in 'Nam when Clint was a baby, but his mother died of breast cancer when he was twelve. His grandparents finished raising him."

"Oh, that's too bad. Were they hard on him?"

"Oh, no, I can't imagine that. It's just that he wished he had his parents, too. And he was afraid to start a family for fear that something would happen to him and Patty, orphaning their own kid. It worries him. Kind of a phobia."

"Ah, that's too bad," repeated McCracken. "What did Patty think about that?"

"She's a great person, understanding, understanding toward Clint, but you know ... Oh, god, Leigh. I shouldn't be spreading this around. I guess ...well, I guess I just felt comfortable that you would keep it to yourself. You seem like such a collected person and all."

McCracken was stunned. No one had ever thought of her as a "collected person" before. She wasn't sure how to respond, but Jenny continued before she could say more than "uhhhh..."

"But now I've opened my big mouth and the fat's in the fire. I won't keep you dangling. It's just that ... well, we all love Patty Harris. We know how she likes kids — the kindergarten kids just idolize her. And the whole community knew she hoped for a family.

"So anyhow, she told me Tuesday night that ... that a while back they'd finally agreed to try for a child. And it was Tuesday, the day of that water board meeting, that she learned she's pregnant for sure."

McCracken shook her head. "Hey! That's wonderful!" She allowed herself a vision of her own first child — hopefully it would be a gangly, large-eared kid. Redheaded, like her. Not bald. And without the mustache and scar. She shared a private giggle with herself, then, making sure to live up to her reputation of being "collected," she added, "I wish them well, and of course, Jenny (she felt this was the mature way to address the older woman, who was turning out to be not as bad as she had originally thought) ... of course, Jenny, I will respect your confidence."

Garrett was standing beside the police car talking on the phone when she finally arrived. Clicking it off, he said, "Well, we knew it would. Victoria's alibi checks out from square one. That last was Peggy at dispatch again. The Stoney City boys finally got back to us on the motel question. One motel in that 'big metropolis' and it takes 'em a day...! Bunch a' speed demons. Anyhow, they say nobody matching the description Jenny gave of that mystery woman stayed in the motel in Stoney City. Not just Tuesday night, but at any time within the last week. Whoever that woman was, it looks like she lied about her destination."

He grumped and shifted, staring up at the distant

mountains, which still had a small white snow cap. A promise of a trickle of water. "Now where do you suppose that woman went? Or *is*, now?"

14

Thursday Afternoon

Hallie Flute's Front Porch

Great minds. While Garrett leaned on the police car, contemplating the tiny snowcap on the mountains, Carmen Weinant was sitting on Hallie Flute's front porch, gazing glaze-eyed at the same mountains and thinking similar thoughts about water and the lack of it. She had to think about something, because Hallie and Alma had been at it for over an hour, rehashing all the details of the previous day, arguing over the small print.

She didn't know that Sheriff Garrett was sharing her thoughts, so Carmen didn't really think 'Great minds run in the same channels,' but listening to Alma and Hallie, she did think about minds. And water. And murder. She recalled watching the weather report this morning with Duz.

It seemed like there was always so much precipitation back in the New England states, and always a lot around the Great Lakes. The weather woman had frequent occasion to show her stylized clouds and raindrops over Florida, and even over Texas and California. But there was a big finger of space on the map that included New Mexico, Arizona, Colorado, and southern Wyoming, which that cheerful woman hadn't blessed for weeks. The deserts. The high, arid montane. A middle finger. When rainfall was denied like this, looking at that televised map gave Carmen a physical thirst.

This morning the woman had perkily shown a fairly nice storm front crossing to the north of them, right up there in southern Wyoming and northern Colorado. It might even splatter on Denver. It would miss everything else in Colorado, though, including the whole dry-as-a-prune Riversmet valley area. Carmen always had the eerie feeling that since North was UP on the map, the rain that the cheery weatherwoman showed falling to their north would somehow gather there, run down, and soak the areas here. To the south. It was like looking at a map of Egypt and not believing that the Nile River could really be flowing north. The map made it look like the water was going uphill. The reasoning part of your brain told you one thing, but the rest of you insisted on believing something else. Believing and feeling fogged your reasoning over.

Trying to get to the bottom of a murder was kind of like that. What looked downhill on the 'map' was probably not downhill in reality. The gut answer was one thing. The truth would probably be quite another.

And listen to Hallie and Alma take on about that body in the shed! They knew they were supposed to feel badly about Biedermann's death ... you don't just gloat over somebody getting shot. But the whole thing was just so EXCITING to them. Maybe the conflict between their real feelings and what they should feel was why they tried so hard to get every detail right. Maybe they were hoping to bring their feelings and the facts into alignment. They went on and on.

An odd thing ... after a while, she couldn't bear to listen to them prattle any more. And yet ... what made their minds, anyone's minds, work like that? How could it be that Alma remembered some things with such acuity that she left everyone else in her dust, yet in the next minute she'd completely forgotten the very topic of conversation? Carmen felt a kind of wonder toward the awesome mystery of what was happening here. What, after all, determined what Alma might recall and what she might forget? And, for that matter, what Hallie would hear, or fail to hear?

At this point, the two of them had discussed the shots Alma swore up and down that she'd heard Tuesday night, and they had agreed that shots were not unusual to hear, and repeatedly agreed with each other that Alma was right not to have mentioned the shots sooner to the sheriff. Besides, they reassured each other, the shots Alma heard were farther away and in the opposite direction from the shed, thus not relevant to the case.

Now they were on the topic of Reider Biedermann's character. They were establishing that he was not much of a man. Not a real man. Not a man of *good* character. Alma, her voice loud, making herself heard over Hallie's hearing deficit, was insisting that he had been a bigamist. Hallie, in turn, was questioning this assertion. Alma assured her that Victoria had told her so. Hallie asked her why Victoria would have put up with it, if that were the case and she had known it. She suggested that Alma may have forgotten what Victoria actually said. (A difference, apparently, between "said" and "actually said.") Alma, not one to back down, told her she wouldn't just make up such a thing. But Carmen could see that Alma wasn't as sure of herself as when she had first made the statement.

Carmen was glad she'd brought Alma over here to visit. They all needed to escape the general confusion around that place of hers for a while. Alma and Hallie had needed this privacy to hash things out.

Her eyes dropped from the distant mountains to Alma's place directly opposite Hallie's porch, where they now sat, and about seventy-five yards across the deep erosion in the soft dobie soil that comprised Dry Gulch at this point in its drop toward Croysant. She could see people, law officers, even now moving around the shed and in the yard. Mostly, they seemed to be working over the contents of the shed. Still rocking on the porch swing and looking across the gulch, she decided to put her two bits into the conversation.

"Hey, Hallie!" Carmen shouted, to get her attention and to help her hear. "I know you didn't hear anything Tuesday night, but I'm surprised you didn't see something going on over there. Your viewpoint from where you are here is excellent."

Both women followed Carmen's gaze, then Hallie, her liquid voice sweet in the warm afternoon, said "Oh, but Carmen, dear! Who said to you that I didn't see anything?"

Stunned speechless, it took Carmen a breath intake to rally. "You ... you saw something Tuesday night? I meant, specifically, Tuesday night. Something to do with the murder."

"Well, yes. I saw something Tuesday night, and at first I

thought it was to do with the murder, you know, dear." Hallie's voice was very composed. "Then later, when all the hubbub happened, I just decided that what I saw wasn't all that important."

"Well, probably not, then, Hallie," said Alma helpfully, willing to be supportive of any decision her friend might have made. Carmen cut in.

"But Hallie! What is it you saw?"

Hallie Flute fluffed herself in the old overstuffed chair, stuffing almost gone, that made up the lion's share of her patio furniture, and prepared to tell her story. Alma, in an armchair that had been dragged from inside, leaned forward. "You see," Hallie began, as if this were the crux of the matter, "I really don't enjoy television because of my hearing. The close captioning tires me." She took a long drink of tea. "And the programs, of course. They have become quite pointless."

"Yes, yes, I expect that's true," responded Carmen, fighting an urge to yell at the woman to get on with it.

"So," continued Hallie, "I went outside that night just to sit where you are now, dear. It was hot. I wanted to enjoy the stars and the cool evening breeze that was coming up." She looked at Alma and Carmen to see if they could appreciate the beauty of the scene with which nature had greeted her that night. Alma chimed in, ready to reminisce.

"Oh, Doug and I have done that so many times." She paused, orienting herself to the present. "When Doug was alive. We used to get out, enjoy the evening air and ..."

Carmen just had to cut in. "About what time was that, Hallie? What time were you out here ... enjoying the breeze?"

"Oh, about 9:30, I'd say. Boris spilled my teacup at about a quarter till ten." Boris was a majorly sized, butter-colored cat who was presently draped like an antimacassar across the arm of Hallie's chair. She patted him forgivingly. "I noticed the time on the clock when I went in to get a cloth to clean it up. So it must have been about 9:30 when I first settled in here."

"I think it must have been 9:30," said Alma helpfully.

"Alma," said Carmen, "How could you possibly know when she was out here? Didn't you say you were in your house watching television that night? And you can't see this far, especially at night."

"Well, yes, of course!" Alma gave Carmen a disgusted look. "I didn't say I knew it was 9:30. I was just pointing out that Hallie is probably right. She usually is right about such things."

Carmen rolled her eyes, controlled herself, and swallowed. This had better be worth it! "Sooo, what did you see at about 9:30, Hallie? Over in Alma's yard?"

"Well, like I said, I was enjoying the stars and sipping tea — it was hot tea. Even when the weather is hot, I still like hot tea at night. It's soothing in the evening. My folks always used to enjoy at good cup of hot tea ..."

Carmen must have made a strangled sound, because Hallie interrupted herself this time. "Well, anyhow, I happened to look down, right over there, and there was a heck of a commotion going on between Alma's house, there, and her outbuildings."

"A commotion?"

"Why, yes, dear. There were two people, men I think, pushing and struggling. One had a cap on. One of those duck-billed caps like ranchers wear so much nowadays. Now in my day, it would have been a real straw hat, but I believe the young men find this new kind of hat to be more comfortable. Or maybe they think they look better." Hallie smiled to herself and patted Boris, contemplating Alma's yard.

"Soooo ... two men struggled. And then did ...?"

"Well, the one with the cap finally left. Took his little car and just pulled on out of Alma's driveway. I'm not sure what happened to the other fellow in the end, because of Boris jumping up and knocking down the tea. But I do know it was quite a set to!" She settled back in her chair, seemingly finished. Carmen took in a deep breath.

"But Hallie! Why didn't you tell this to the sheriff? When he or Detective Hobbs were talking to you, why didn't you mention it?"

Carmen didn't ask why Hallie hadn't been more concerned about Alma at the time. It hinged on the true grit everyone expected of each other here in these mountains. Last year, Hallie and Alma had wanted to cross Stoney Mesa on one of the old dirt logging roads, and when they had encountered a fallen tree barring their way, they simply got out of the car, each took an end of the tree—granted, a small, dead tree, but nevertheless!—and they moved it. Two ladies, one ninety, one approaching, neither concerned that it might be too much for their hearts at that lonely high altitude. No, they moved the tree, did what they had to do, and proceeded with their scenic drive, no doubt commenting to each other on the beauty of the day and the many columbine, Indian paintbrush, and fireweed that bloomed that summer. Somehow, in Hallie's calculus, she had not perceived her friend to be in real danger Tuesday night. An intuition perhaps. A gut feeling. A trusting of Alma's can-do abilities ...

Hallie responded to the question Carmen did ask. "Why, Carmen!" Hallie said logically. "The man in the shed was shot. I didn't see any shots fired as those two fought, so I can't believe that what I saw was all that important to the sheriff. It wasn't, dear, do you think?"

15

Thursday Late Afternoon

At Duz and Carmen Weinant's Place

Dispatch was at it again. After lunch, Garrett and McCracken had walked the area around Harris Pond with a couple of the Stoney City officers, thinking something else might turn up. Nothing did. Then they'd gone back up the road to Alma's. The three deputies there were supposed to be working on the boxes. They looked dazed.

How it had all fit was anyone's guess. At this point, everything was in the yard, and the pile was humongous. The officers, beat after lugging the dust covered, cobweb encrusted boxes out of the depths of the shed, were arguing about what to do next. Jim, the Stoney City guy, wiping a dirty sleeve across his sweat-smeared forehead, was saying, "This is the kind of shit that gives people Hantavirus. This is dangerous shit—we shouldn't be breathing this shit."

The Riversmet deputy, Chad Harville, who was also the videocam man, laughed. "You wanna get extra money for drawing hazardous duty, Jimbo? This crap could jump out and bite ya." He picked up a stuffed rabbit that had been wedged in a basket between the boxes and wagged it toward Jim, making 'aurp aurp aurp' sounds.

Carla was the other Stoney City deputy there. She had only been on duty a month and was as green as the crabapples on the tree. She was taking in the exchange between Harville and Jim, considering how to get her oar in the water, when Garrett and McCracken pulled in. She decided to say, "Cheez it, the cops," and this comment was not negatively received, being for the most part ignored.

Harville stood up from where he had been squatting beside a box; Carla, dusting her hands, came to the front of the pile, and Jim set down a shoebox. He'd been trying to decipher the writing that labeled it. "Hey, none too soon," Harville said, as Garrett and McCracken approached. "We could use a little professional advice."

Garrett eyed the teetering stack of boxes and the empty shed. What the hell did these guys think they were doing?

"We don't really know what we're doing," said Carla. "I tried to tell these guys that we should put these in chronological order, look at the more recent first ..."

Garrett was pulling at his mustache. "I sorta figured they were in chronological order the way they were settin' in the shed," he said.

"Well, yeah," Harville scratched at his cheek, then his sweaty neck. "We kept that order, pretty much. Hard to tell here, I guess. We just thought if we pulled everything out, maybe somethin' big would jump out at us ... a rat or somethin'." He giggled, glanced around, but everyone remained serious, so he said, "Nah, just kiddin'. We thought we could save diggin' through every single box. I can't figure how we can go through all these boxes ..."

Jim interrupted, rounding on the sheriff. "Yeah. What's the point a' goin' through all these boxes, without we know what we're lookin' for? What the hell *are* we lookin' for, anyhow, Sheriff?"

Garrett wished he knew. "Like you say, I guess we're hopin' somethin'll jump out." He paused, thinking, and McCracken, by his ear, began to hiss to him. Garrett ignored her. He wanted to pick these people's brains while they were still untarnished with his own guesses. "Whatta you guys think this guy was diggin' around here for?"

McCracken kept hissing away behind him, and he resisted the urge to slap at her like you would a horsefly.

Raising his brows and pulling the corners of his mouth down, Jim said, "Well, for myself, I woulda figured it would be somethin' to do with water rights, considering what I've been hearin' about community sentiments. Your deputy there, though," he pronounced it 'dehpatee,' flipping his head toward

McCracken when he did, "Your dehpatee seems to think it was drugs. Ain't that what you're tryin' to say, Ma'am?"

McCracken reddened and Garrett shot her a brief, annoyed glance before facing down the grins of the other three. "Yeah, she's right. Could be drugs. Could be anything." Garrett let his eyes run over the pile again. The others quit grinning and Carla folded her arms across her chest.

"I suppose I sorta figured you guys'd look at the stuff nearest the corpse first. We maybe should assume he had some idea what he was after. You know," Garrett again took in the unwieldy pile, "The guy probably wouldn't have been diggin' in a box if it was a shovel or somethin' loose in the shed that he'd been after. Just for example."

Harville nodded sagely. "Yeah, we had a good look at that box he was into. I stuck it over there by the rosebush. Nothin' we could see in there."

Jim, grinning again, muttered, "Nice save, Harville."

"So, what was in it?"

"Whole gob of old letters to this lady lives here, goin' back a few years. Didn't seem to be any rhyme or reason why she kept 'em. They were from a variety of people, big variety of handwriting, some of it about as flowery as the stationery. I tried readin' a couple, and they were all about alike." His voice got sing song. "'Dear Alma, How are you? We are fine. The family's great except the half that's surely dyin'. We have the cutest grandkids in America so we wish you could see 'em ... blah blah blah yaddita yaddita.' You know, the kind of letters people write."

"So," said the sheriff, grinning wickedly, "Did you go on down through the box, check if any of the envelopes might contain ..." he paused dramatically, catching McCracken's eye, a co-conspirator, "drugs? Maybe several? Mary Jane? Cocaine? Ecstasy?"

All three deputies' eyes shot to the rosebush at the edge of the yard, where the one lone box was parked separate from the rest. "Uhh ...no, Sir. No sir, we didn't."

"Well," Garrett said, wooling at his chew, letting the thought sink in. "Wee...ll."

Finally Carla, courage up, said, "We'll definitely look, Sir, but I don't think, whatever we do, that we oughta ruin this lady's things, stuff she took care of for years. Not without cause. Probable cause. This stuff means a lot to ..."

"No, Carla, I don't think so either." Garrett looked at the stack of carefully packed items, ninety-one years, a living biography. "Tell you what. Why don't one a' you get on the horn, call a lady called Mrs. Doreen Van Doran. See if the Oozle Onion Valley Community Club will let us use that clubhouse, down the road that way, to keep these boxes in for a while, outta the weather. What there is of it. Once you get 'em down there, you keep a deputy watchin' 'em at all times. Don't want anybody takin' anything, or movin' stuff around.

"All right? And mark 'em, too, the order you found 'em in the shed, front to back. Then go through the front ones first, nice'n easy. Kind of keep your head open, what you might be seeing. Then maybe sort 'em out a little—this stack contains letters; this one contains ... well, clothes or whatever; this one, pictures ..."

"It just ain't that simple," Jim argued stubbornly. "Most of these boxes are a big mix. She's just like my own Granny. Come across a box in her closet, and she'd tell you that it was all stuff had to do with Uncle Del's mining expedition in Canada in nineteen-ought-six and how his in-laws reacted to it, or with when her and Granddad thought they might move to Montana and raise sheep, or with stuff she was collecting to show that Roosevelt was wrong, even though he brought the country around. Her sorting categories were all in her own head. This lady's sorting system probably meant somethin' to her, but I don't think we can decode her plan."

Garrett's head was beginning to ache. "Look, do the best you can. Just look through. Don't mix stuff up or damage it. Meanwhile, McCracken and me'll try to find out more about what this guy was after." Which, he thought to himself, was tail wags dog—if they knew what Biedermann was after, they wouldn't have to go through everything in the shed.

Glancing at the box by the rosebush, he said, "But that box... when you get done having another look, how about you make sure it stays somewhere separate from the others, where we can lay our hands on it easy. If you don't find nothin' in it. Of course, if you do, you call. Otherwise, mark it good. I still gotta funny feelin' about that box ..."

* * * * *

It was when they were back in the car, headed toward Riversmet, already halfway to Peaseford, that dispatch got them. When they had first called in, there was nothing, but now she asked them for a land line. Garrett wished she could just tell him what she had to say on the police radio, but everyone in the Riversmet valley area would have it on their police scanners and then any privacy for the investigation would be shot.

He handed the cell phone to McCracken. "Give the lady what she wants," he advised, resigned, and McCracken dialed in.

"Uh huh, uh huh," she said, then, "I'll be damned," then, "All right. I'll tell the Chief ...Yeah, I s'pose."

She shut off the phone, said, "Well, Chief, he really was sick, our Reider Biedermann."

"Oh, yeah?" Garrett's interest was back up. "Doc's report came through?"

"Yup. His doctor told our man that for the past six months Mr. Biedermann has been receiving medication for a very active case of AIDS."

"AIDS!" Garrett whistled. "Holy Toledo! Now, where the hell does this fit into our theory?"

"Plus, you may want to slow down and look for a place to turn around. Peggy says Carmen Weinant just called. She wants to see us before we leave the Croysant area."

"Hmh," Garrett grunted. "Carmen Weinant. So what does she want to talk about ... anything important?" But he was already slowing down, looking for a turn out.

"Doesn't sound like Biedermann's heirs would have to kill him, then," commented McCracken as the car worked its way back around the curves just outside Croysant. Garrett nodded, thoughtful.

"Good point. You sure don't have to kill a dying man to get at his money, do you?" Garrett worked his chew. "At least, right now I can't think of circumstances where that'd be necessary.

Unless there was a hurry." He eased the car around the-dog-that-sleeps-in-the-street. Then, "Damn bohunk town."

Duz Weinant was in his truck ahead of them as they rounded the turn that took them to Weinant's gate. He pulled the truck up to the tractor shed, got out, and grinned at them. "Howdy. Go on in the house there. I think Carmen's expectin' you."

Garrett and McCracken started up the front walk and the screen door on the porch squeaked open, held wide by Carmen. A sheep came trotting across the yard, baaing anxiously and honing in on the two law officers. Duz, sloshing up behind them in tall, mud-encrusted irrigation boots, laughed. "Ge' back, Fido," he commanded. "These guys don't wanna be part of your game."

Gesturing them into the house, Carmen said helpfully, "We don't have sheep."

McCracken caught Garrett's glance and raised her eyebrows, but Carmen smiled. "A friend gave us Fido when her mama died this spring, so we raised her for the grandkids. She's been kind of a cutey, but we don't have other sheep, so she thinks she's either people or a dog."

"Oh," said Garrett, following Carmen and McCracken into the living room area, but glancing briefly behind him, where Fido was nuzzling Duz so roughly that he kept losing his balance as he took off his irrigation boots.

"Please, just have a seat. Can I get you some lemonade or coffee?"

It took a minute for Garrett and McCracken to answer. Although the room they were in was the living/dining area of a standard old ranch house, complete with worn, comfortable overstuffed chairs and a couch, a desk piled with papers, letters, and agricultural journals, and a large wooden table covered with a colorful plastic tablecloth, their eyes and minds had been taken by the walls, across which swam dozens of bright-eyed speckled trout. The mural covered every wall in the room, as if the space in the room itself was a mountain river. One felt one was swimming underwater.

Trout—rainbow trout, brook trout, natives ... every manner of trout—peered from behind watery boulders, hid among roots and earthy overhangs, shouldered their way through the drooping limbs of downed spruce that bridged the falling mountain torrent. Fish everywhere, the walls shimmering with them, silvers, browns, and pinks ... but perhaps what most took the mind was that nothing about the mural was garish. How had the woman done that, brought forth a feeling of peace, an idea of immersion in a fantastic otherness, without jarring the senses by the bizarreness of it all?

McCracken, her eyes roaming the walls, found herself speechless. She thought she needed to either quit staring at them or say something, but she wasn't sure how to react. She was relieved to hear Garrett say, "Wow, Mrs. Weinant, that is some mural! Makes me feel cooled off, like I'm free and easy, right up there in Clear Creek on Stoney Mesa."

"Oh, that's good. And just call me Carmen." Duz had come in to sit down, carrying a glass of lemonade and a plateful of cookies, which he offered to the officers with a broad gesture. They both shook their heads, and Carmen continued. "I didn't mean to make a big thing of this anyhow, getting you all the way back up here and all, but I just thought you were nearby and it might be easiest to talk to you in person."

"And it's about the murder of Mr. Biedermann, right?" said Garrett, by way of encouraging her to continue.

"Right. I took Duz's mother over to Hallie's today. I figured it would be better if she got away awhile. It's such a hubbub down there, you know, bless her heart. So she and Hallie sat on Hallie's porch and hashed it all out. Now, I don't know how much you know about these two old ladies ...?" Carmen paused, looking inquiringly at them.

"As I understand it they are friends ..."

"Yes, that's true. Great friends. And they can sound silly at times, because Alma has the memory loss problem and Hallie can't hear. But you know, they have a lot of experience between them, and they are quite the sharp old gals if you can cut through their handicaps."

"I suspect they are." Garrett was wondering where this was going, hoping for something more concrete than advice.

"It might help to keep talking to them, getting as much as you can of what they know. You see, Hallie's place sits just across Dry Gulch from Alma's. Of course, it takes a while to get there, because the gulch deepens at that point, so you have to go around, toward the clubhouse, and cross by the bridge ... a little more than a quarter mile. But as the crow flies, the distance is short.

"Hallie has a pretty good view of Alma's yard from her porch. And she told me today that she saw a bunch of stuff going on over there on Tuesday night. I suppose, about the time Reider was shot."

Both Garrett and McCracken had perked up. "A bunch of stuff? Can you be more specific, Mrs. Weinant?"

"I'm hoping you'll talk to her yourselves, but basically, she described what she referred to as 'a heck of a commotion.' I gathered it was just outside the shed where Reider was shot. She talked about two men struggling—and here's where I felt inadequate. I came away not sure if she was describing a struggle over some thing, or like a fist fight, or what. She mentioned one being in a hat. I guess she said cap. And she said one drove away and that she didn't know what happened to the other one. I was so surprised that she had seen something and not told you all, that I just ... well, I just left it there. I thought you could follow up better than I."

Garrett nodded. "Thank you, Mrs. Weinant. We really appreciate your tipping us off. We'll most certainly arrange to talk to Mrs. Flute." He cleared his throat. "Neither one of you would have any guess as to who might have been fighting there? You didn't happen to drive by, see an unexpected car there, or anything like that?"

Both Weinants shook their heads. Carmen said, "Like I told you earlier, I was out that night. Several of us women were at the Friends of the Library meeting in Croysant. Frieda and I were with Maggie Merimeister. When the meeting was over she just came up the short way from Croysant, dropped me off first, then Frieda. We didn't go past Duz's mom's place at all."

"And it's hell for an alibi, I guess," Duz said, spreading his hands good-naturedly, "But I got upset at that water board meeting when Lew started cuttin' loose. I have to admit that the water loss threat from Biedermann had us all stirred up. Anyhow, I left ... I guess you could say walked out ... then. When Lew cut loose. That was about nine o'clock, I heard later. I didn't look at the time. I just came on home and walked up, all the way up to the upper divider box, where our water splits off from the shares that go down into the Rowly River. I wanted to just sit. Just be alone. If I'd gone by Mom's and seen anything, I'd've gone in. She usually never has anyone around that late at night."

'Usually never'? thought McCracken. Whatever. She had decided she should take notes, and she was scribbling like crazy to keep up. When he paused, she looked up. "Mr. Weinant, was Mr. Harris's outburst that bad, that you had to leave? Maybe one of the figures struggling in the yard might have been Mr. Harris?"

"You mean Lew? Nah ... it wasn't him. He's just a guy that the older he gets, the more he has to say, and the louder he says it. He's 86, I think. Little kid when my mother went to school. Little banty rooster of a man now, makes you wonder where Clint got so tall. His big speech was just kind of the last straw of this whole thing that sent me out the door."

McCracken pursued. "Sooo. You're saying that the older Mr. Harris would maybe be too small to get involved in ...?"

Duz laughed. "Ahh ... I guess not. Couldn't actually count him out just for size. Nor age. He's little, but he's wiry. He can spot a rabbit hunkered in the sagebrush fifty yards away. And he can pack a hundred-pound bale of hay without a grunt. It's just that I'm sayin' he's very much bark and damn little bite. I don't think he really wanted to take on old Biedermann. He just want-ed to get people stirred up." Duz brushed cookie crumbs off his jeans onto the floor and Carmen, watching, scowled. "He proba-bly thought he wanted to fight, if somebody woulda taken him up on it while his dander was up. I suppose."

* * * * *

Back in the car, McCracken stared at her notes. "The plot sickens," she mumbled, doing a reverse lisp. Garrett grunted. "Now I'm hungry again. Whyn't you call in, I'll head to the Stop n' Go in Peaseford and we'll vary our diet, get a little pizza."

"Yummy!" McCracken said, thinking, 'Oh, cool—not Mexican or burger and not the gentle Jenny, either. Things are looking up.' Her adoring glance at Garrett was cut short by dispatch. A land line again. She dialed in.

"Don't you guys ever tire of this cell phone," she kidded. Her mood was great. Then she said, "Mmm huh. Mmm. Wow. O.K., then. Thanks."

Garrett, already back to the delicate negotiation past the-dog-that-sleeps-in-the-street in Croysant, tipped his head, queried his eyebrows at her.

"Ballistics has checked in."

"And?"

"And it's the gun by the Harris's pond that matched the bullet from Biedermann. Not the Barnswallowper gun. And this one was loaded, just the one shot fired."

"Ah ... that narrows it again," said Garrett, rubbing at his chin.

"And ..." added McCracken, drawing it out.

"And what?" He cast her a sharp glance.

"And they already finished the trace. It was a new gun—wait'll Asa gets back and hears this!—it was a new gun, and you'll never guess who bought it."

"Who?" Garrett snapped. He'd had enough guessing games already. He didn't need another one.

"Our friend, Clint Harris. The grandson. Harris the Younger. How about that?"

Garrett took a deep breath and expelled it through rounded lips. "How about that," he said, shifting gears.

16

Thursday After Supper

At Clint and Patty Harris's Place

The thing that Garrett noticed the most about Clint and Patty Harris was how each kept glancing at the other. After the message about the gun, he and McCracken decided to go into Peaseford anyhow, get the pizza, then come back to see what they could learn here. As they pulled into the yard, Clint was doing what ranchers always seemed to be doing—coming from some sort of work somewhere, wiping dirt, maybe oil, off his hands with a rag. When they stopped the car in the circular driveway, they could hear western music pouring out of the house. It was old-fashioned, stand-by-your-man kind of western music, and Garrett thought he could hear Patty singing along with it.

He got out of the police car, nodded at Clint, and apologized first, saying he was sorry he hadn't had a chance to call ahead. Truth was, he could have called ahead, but he had an intuition that it might be best to catch them off balance. Clint nodded back, then turned, without speaking, to walk into the house. Garrett and McCracken glanced at each other, frowning, but then the music stopped and both Clint and Patty emerged from the door, Patty drying her hands on a kitchen towel. "Oh, hi!" she said. "I didn't see you pull up."

Garrett repeated his apology. Patty said, "Oh, that's all right." Then the two took positions on either side of the porch step, Clint leaning on the railing, Patty just standing, her arms folded over her stomach. Neither seemed inclined to invite the officers in. What McCracken noticed most was the stomach ... it surely couldn't be starting to bulge a little already? She made a point to move her eyes.

"We didn't get a chance to talk to you at Alma's on Wednesday, so we just thought maybe we oughta stop by," Garrett said. "As I understand, Mrs. Harris, you usually go to club, but you didn't go this past Wednesday?"

"No, no. I didn't go. I just didn't feel very well." Garrett tried to keep suspicion out of his eyes, but McCracken couldn't help but notice the slight, protective tightening of the arms. Aha, she thought. Morning sick!

"That's too bad. It would help to have another opinion as to what happened when Mr. Biedermann's body was found. Do you take time off from teaching to attend club?"

"Oh, I wouldn't do that! We just have eight kindergarten kids here in Croysant, and some of them ride the bus so far, we figure a half day is enough for the little guys. They go home and get a nap in the afternoon. And to be honest," her eyes sparkled, "many times, so do I!"

McCracken thought that Patty Harris was living up to her advanced billing. She had a pretty, lively face, a petite body with soft, curling, shoulder-length brown hair, and big brown eyes framed by Harry Potter eyeglasses. Her ready smile would invite any child to come learn from her.

Clint was another story. He was tall, gaunt, black-haired, black-browed. Unlike the thick, curly, Elvisy hair on the dead Biedermann, this guy's short hair hung straight, currycombed, stiff as a horse's tail. He looked like the classic settler type in a John Wayne movie, the staunch pioneer plodding beside the wagon train, prodding his slow oxen to move along. Eyes patient. Miles to go. So far he had said absolutely nothing.

Garrett had warmed to the vivacious Patty. "Well, I hate to do it," he said, genuinely reluctant, "But I have to ask where each of you were Tuesday evening, from about nine to ... oh, say eleven or so."

Again, the eyes caught each other. Patty said, "Clint brought Lew home a little after nine. Here. Lew lives in the old family house, right next to the road down there ... between here and the pond ... but they came here together. I guess Lew got real wound up at the meeting, and it embarrassed Clint, so he got him out of there as soon as he could pry him loose and brought him here. And they told me about Reider. About the meeting, how it went."

Garrett rubbed at his chin. "So then ... after that?"

"Well...," Patty hesitated, seeming to collect her thoughts. "Well, after that, I was about as upset as Lew. I had to get out of the house, move a little, so I got in the pickup and drove around awhile. Maybe Jenny Threewinds can tell you. I went there and talked to her. She's a real soothing lady."

"She mentioned it," Garrett said drily. "Said you were there about ten. Said you didn't stay long."

"Oh. Well ... good. I'm glad she mentioned that. And she's right. I was too worked up to visit long. I just came on home after that. And Clint ..." Again, her eyes met her husband's, briefly. "Clint was out back, in the barn. We have a lot of old run-down machinery, and Clint was stirred up, too. It relaxes him to work on stuff, to try to get it up and running. He didn't hear me come in. He was playing the radio back there. I just ... I just came on in the house and did up some chores and went to bed."

"And you? When did you come in, Mr. Harris?" Garrett made a point to direct the question at Clint, whose expression didn't change, although his eyes flicked toward Patty.

"He came in not long after that," Patty answered quickly. "I heard the radio go off in the barn, and sure enough, Clint wasn't ... wasn't far behind," she finished brightly.

"Is that all correct, Mr. Harris?"

For the first time they heard his voice. Briefly. "That would be right," he said.

"And where was your grandfather at this time?"

Patty said, "He always just goes on home. He takes the footpath. We call it the back pathway, because it doesn't run along the road. So after I left, he ... he just walked on home. On the back pathway," she repeated, nervous.

"It's good that you can account for each other," Garrett said. "You see, we've found the gun that shot Mr. Biedermann. It was found just down the road here, on your property. Right by the pond."

Again, Clint's eyes flicked to Patty, but he remained silent. Patty said, "Oh, my gosh!" Her hand went to her mouth.

"The problem is," Garrett continued, "We know where that gun came from. It has been traced to Bucky's Hardware. Mr. Harris, do you recall purchasing a .38 caliber revolver from Bucky's hardware this past December?"

Patty had blanched and again was holding onto her stomach, to the silent concern of McCracken. This time Clint actually shifted and opened his mouth as if to speak. Garrett, however, decided to pre-empt him. "It is that specific gun. I'm sure you wouldn't mind coming by the sheriff's office tomorrow to be fingerprinted. We don't know how your gun got there, by the pond. But it would be helpful to us to get you cleared from the picture as much as possible."

At this a surprising burst of red suffused Patty's face. Her voice was sharp and angry when she spoke. "Look, I don't know why you two are playing this game, but Clint will not at all find it a problem to come down to be fingerprinted. He's no murderer. And you had better fingerprint me, too. If either of our prints are found on that gun, they should be mine. Clint bought that gun in December and gave it to me for a Christmas gift." Her hands dropped to her sides, and they were trembling.

Clint was regarding his wife narrowly from beneath the heavy dark brows. "We'll be in." He spoke slowly. "There wouldn't be any reason not to find our prints on that gun. If it's ours." He looked as if he wanted to reach out to his wife, but she had averted her eyes from him, so he concluded, "But Patty's right. We're neither one a killer."

17

First Thing Friday Morning

The Office of Dr. Kenneth Thomson, Forensic Pathologist

Edith handed Garrett the pathologist's preliminary report when he walked into the office Friday morning. To say that it surprised him would be an understatement. He supposed he should have expected something like this Wednesday, when McCracken announced her find on the ground in front of the shed. It must have been blood after all. He berated himself for being so honed in on the bullet wound that he had more or less ignored her.

There were no photographs with the report. Dr. Thomson, who concerned himself with the feelings of families of victims of violent death, would not release autopsy pictures to anyone without a court order. Thomson saw no need for graphic portrayals of all that remained of someone's husband, son, or parent being spread across the front pages of the local papers. After rereading the verbal description, Garrett gathered up the keys to the police cruiser. Because he was the sheriff, he could look at the autopsy photos in Ken's office.

Pictures weren't really necessary. It was just that, in this case, he knew that seeing would be believing. There was something about the report, something ambiguous, that needled his subconscious. Maybe seeing the pictures and hearing Ken talk about the case, he could get a better feel for what was going on here.

Thomson left him sitting at a table with the photos, and he spread them out. The first was taken before the autopsy was started. It was Biedermann, all right. The next showed several angles of the head, shaved but before any cuts had been made. Underneath all that thick, black, curly Elvis hair, unseen by himself, by Detective Asa Hobbs, or by any of the deputies at the scene, was the bruise in question: "a blunt force injury of unknown origin."

The contusion was large, spreading over most of the crown of the head, the blood bubbling up in several places to form hematomas which were barely contained by the outer layer of skin.

Just below the crown, Garrett could see points where the force of the blow had caused the skin to tear, the small lacerations described by Dr. Thomson in the written report. It was from these tiny splits that the blood might have dropped which McCracken had found on the ground in front of the shed. Somebody had struck the guy hard with something on the back of the head and he had fallen, then rolled so that bleeding from those little openings left traces of blood on the ground that were somehow miraculously undisturbed by the club women.

Garrett looked up as Ken Thomson returned to the room. "So," he said, "not a pattern injury."

Thomson turned around one of the straight back chairs at the table, draped himself over it, and rested his arms along the back. Then, facing the sheriff, he said, "Nope. No pattern."

Garrett wrinkled his brow and ran his fingers over the area covered in the photo by the bruising. "No way to tell what could've done this, is there?"

The pathologist chuckled. "Something hard and deadly."

Allowing himself a grin in response, Garrett said, "You're a big help."

"That I am." Thomson was still smiling, but now his brows were raised, a question. They said that, despite his regard for Garrett, he had a lot to do. What else did the sheriff need to know?

"Mmmmph." Garrett was still thumbing the photographs. "I took it from your report that the blow was the cause of death?"

"Maybe. If the shooter was somebody else from the guy that hit him, a defense pathologist for the shooter could argue that." Thomson paused. "There was an awful lot of blood in the internal capsule of the brain. In the central portion."

Garrett had the impression that the doctor was hedging about something. He knew Ken. There would be no moving him until he felt sure of his conclusions. "So ... You'd suggest I wait to place my bets until you're ready with the final report?"

"I wanta see the blood scan for drugs. Shouldn't take too long. Early next week, with luck." He began to unwind himself from the chair, and Garrett got up, too, saying as he pushed the photographs back into their folder, "Any educated guesses on time of death?"

"When was he seen last?"

"As near as we can tell, about nine in the evening Tuesday. Lady at the Cowpath Saloon up there sold him cigarettes then."

"Makes sense. I was gonna say maybe eight or nine earliest, probably midnight latest. Based on what we got, that'd be my best S.W.A.G."

Garrett didn't need "S.W.A.G." translated. It meant 'scientific wild ass guess.' As far as Garrett was concerned, a scientific wild ass guess from Ken Thomson was as good as the next man's sworn statement of absolute fact.

18

Friday Morning 11:00 Sharp

Hallie Flute's Place

"They were pushing and shoving."

"But they weren't fighting over some *thing*? Not a box or something like that?" Garrett and McCracken had made a point of it, to be on time. They figured that Hallie would see punctuality as a virtue, and they were right. She was waiting for them with a pitcher of iced tea and a plate of boughten gingersnaps, ready to tell her story. They sat on the porch.

"Didn't look like it from here." Hallie squinted across the gulch as if seeing the squabble in Alma's yard for the first time. "It was dark, remember? What you can see there now, I couldn't see so good then. But it was moonlight, too. The yard was pretty bright."

"Sounds like you picked up on quite a little, Mrs. Flute," Garrett encouraged, his volume up full bore. McCracken was sitting in the chair Alma had occupied the previous day. She was hunkered down, scribbling notes.

"Oh, yes," said Hallie, still looking with narrowed eyes at the yard. She seemed to feel that the shouting from the sheriff was to be the social norm for the day, because she was shouting back. "The little guy, he had on a cap. The other one was bare headed. They pushed and shoved, and the bigger guy, he started trying to hit, but the little one ducked him."

"When you say bigger, are you saying he was tall?"

"Nah, not tall. I mean kind of heavy. Fat. Not much taller than the other guy."

McCracken looked up from her notes. "And that was it?

The little guy just drove away and ...?"

"What is that, dear? About the hay?"

McCracken repeated her question, shouting.

"Oh, no no no no no! I didn't say that. Before the little guy drove away, he whacked the big one with a hoe."

McCracken's eyes widened. Garrett hadn't told her yet about the bruise on Biedermann's head. As for Garrett, he gave a narrow-eyed nod. A hoe! That could explain some of this. "So," he ventured, "You actually saw one man hit the other with a hoe?"

"Well, what happened," Hallie said, enjoying the effect this new information had had, "What happened is, it looked like the big guy bent over. I'm pretty sure he bent over to tie his shoelace. That's what it looked like." Garrett made a mental note to have a look at the crime scene photos to see what kind of shoes Reider had been wearing. But why tie your shoelace in the middle of an altercation?

Hallie continued. "So anyhow, while he was bent over, the little guy sort of stepped sidewise toward that chicken shed and grabbed something. I think it was a hoe. He raised it up and hauled off and whacked the big guy real good." She nodded to herself, confirming the power of the whack.

Garrett was eyeing her. "You *think* it was a hoe?"

Hallie chuckled. "Guess I'd better be careful what I say, eh? That little lady secretary you got, she's takin' down every word. Maybe you oughta read me my Mirander rights."

Garrett snorted, stifling a guffaw, but McCracken flushed and opened her mouth to set Hallie straight. Secretary! Another snort, then Garrett, catching the twinkle in Hallie's eyes and the storm clouds in McCracken's, intervened smoothly. "Now, Mrs. Flute. You've seen McCracken in action, and you know she's my deputy, not my secretary." He grinned at her good-naturedly. "And where did you learn about Miranda rights, anyhow?"

Hallie took a satisfying sip of iced tea, then said, "Watch a lotta TV."

"Well, good place to learn, I guess. But I thought you said you were on the porch Tuesday evening because you don't like TV?"

Hallie shrugged. "Sometimes I do, sometimes I don't. I like

Regis Philbin." She pronounced it Phil-bine. Garrett decided to rein this in before it got too far afield.

"I do, too, Mrs. Flute. But you aren't under suspicion here for the murder, so you can tell us what you know. Deputy McCracken and I." He emphasized the 'deputy,' but McCracken, her flush gone, was still sitting grim-lipped, galled more by Garrett's amused snorts than by Hallie's initial comment. "Deputy McCracken and I need to know how sure you are that the weapon the smaller man wielded was a hoe."

"Well, I'm not real sure at all." Hallie was prepared to wax serious and helpful again. "He stepped over next to the shed ..." she squinted down at the yard, as if trying to see the action again. "He stepped over, grabbed something looked like a hoe, maybe a shovel. Then ... see how that patch of weeds there next to the yard ..." She paused, then continued.

"Now, those aren't Alma's weeds. She wouldn't have weeds like that in her yard. Those weeds go with the property that runs along the gulch."

McCracken, who had slowly activated her pen again, stopped. What the hell did weed elimination have to do with anything? But Garrett had been able to enter Hallie's perspective.

"Ah! I see. Those weeds are in just the wrong place. They blot out your view of some of the yard."

"Right," said Hallie, satisfied, then repeated, "They blot out my view of some of that yard. They grow up there every year. It's real aggravating."

"So what do you think you may have missed? Because of the weeds?"

"After the little 'un whacked him, the big man went down so low I couldn't see him anymore. It was after that," she looked significantly at McCracken, making her point about the sequence of events, "After that that the little guy got in the car and drove away."

"So the smaller man just left the other one lying in the yard?"

"No, I couldn't swear to that. Right after he whacked him, Boris jumped up here and made me spill my hot tea all over me and all over this good chair. So I had to get a rag and clean up."

"But it *looked like* the little man was alone when he drove away?" Garrett persisted.

Hallie looked thoughtful. "I think there was someone in that car. Not just when he drove away, but before. Someone was sitting there all during the fight, but they sat real, real still. Someone with kind of longish hair."

Garrett rubbed at his temple, and McCracken looked up, her brow wrinkled. "Someone else came with the little man?"

Hallie's voice was hesitant. "It ... well, maybe. Something about the person in the car ... something doesn't feel right. That person sat real, real still."

"Real, real still?"

"Real still. I'm thinkin'. Thinkin' and thinkin'. That's all I can really say about that."

They all sat silently, everyone thinking. What the heck had been going on in that yard? Finally, Garrett said, "Well, you have helped a lot. Lots of information. But ..." he rubbed at his jaw. "But weren't you worried the big guy would get up, maybe hurt Mrs. Weinant?"

"Well ... not really. See, I cleaned up the tea, and when I got back out here the car was gone and the yard looked empty and quiet. I guess it just felt like no one was there. Have you ever had that kind of feeling? I watched Alma's house, and I could see her movin' around, kind of her normal night time routine—first the kitchen light and her silhouette, then the bathroom, then the house going dark. Nothin' else happened."

"Nothing else ..."

"Nope. And there's my hearing—I don't communicate good on the phone. And Alma's heart—why worry her? She'da been up all night, stewin' around, if I'd called. I figured I'd go over and talk to her Wednesday morning, but everything looked normal over there then, too, and I had to take Boris to the vet. He musta ate too much spring grass, threw up all night."

Garrett and McCracken's skepticism must have shown on their faces, because she added, "Besides, by that time, wouldn't I look the fool if I made a big stir, told a big story about a fight in Alma's yard and then nothin' was there to show for it? People'd say I was losin' my marbles. They'd say old Hallie Flute was gettin' dotty. Folks'd be ready to put me away. Couldn't be on my own anymore. When I woke up Wednesday, it even felt funny to me that I'd seen that fight. Sure—hindsight is better than foresight! If I knew then what I know now, I'da called somebody that night." Hallie shrugged, but Garrett and McCracken looked at her with renewed understanding.

McCracken closed her notebook, ready to wind it up, but Garrett said to Hallie, "Just one more time. Are you sure the fighters weren't struggling over a *thing*? Some ... item?"

Hallie shook her head. "I didn't see anything."

Garrett worked his chew, stared down at the yard, which for the first time this week was empty of people. "What about you? You got any idea what Biedermann ... what anyone ... might have wanted in that shed?"

"No...," a pause, a release of air. "No, I've thought about it. I can't figure it. Alma hasn't got much that a thief'd want. Maybe you oughta talk to old Lew Harris. He's gettin' up there in years, and he's been around. Has about as much to say as the next guy in this community. And he ain't like me or Alma—he can recall stuff and he sees and hears like a hawk."

19

Early Afternoon Friday

The Old Harris Place

The noon hour was not a success. Previous efforts to drop in on her had taught Garrett that Friday was Jenny's day off, so he suggested to McCracken that they go on down the hill into Croysant and give the Lucky Lantern a try.

The thing about the Lucky Lantern was, whenever things weren't all that busy, the cook enjoyed coming out to visit with the diners. Now, things were *never* all that busy at the Lantern, because the cook was notable for his yellow, stringy hair, his inflamed zits and brown teeth, his red, chapped hands, and, especially, for his gift for gab. By serendipitous circularity of circumstance, this lack of customers gave him frequent opportunities to enjoy coming out to visit. He wasn't all that bad a cook. In fact, his chicken-fried far surpassed that which the Cowpath turned out. Still, people can be picky.

Garrett and McCracken were the only patrons this noon, so once the chicken enchilada and cowpoke barbecued bean special arrived, they found themselves the objects of a cheerful discussion of potential suspects in their present investigation, all topped off with advice as to how to proceed. The cook's conclusion was that it would be best to put the most pressure on the least likely suspect, because that person is usually the one who did it. This was a conclusion with which Garrett and McCracken were prone to agree in order to get an opportunity to deliver food, such as it was, to their mouths.

Once they'd made their escape, McCracken stood by the police car and shook herself like a dog, ridding herself of an invisible contamination, then crawled in and said, "What now, Chief?"

Garrett, whose intention of talking it over with her at lunch had been pre-empted by the cook's advice, grunted and took a healthy wad of peppermint chew to clear his tastebuds. Getting the wad settled against his gum, he said, "Well, I ain't sure. We got Mac and Alice Biedermann that haven't turned up yet, we got the Harrises and that gun, and then we got this business with Mrs. Flute. You know, McCracken, I didn't get a chance to tell you, but the pathologist's report showed a big bruise on Biedermann's head. Does look like somebody clobbered 'im. I don't know about you, but I'm gettin' a lot of information here, and not much crime theory goin' on to fit 'er into."

McCracken was trying to dislodge a stringy piece of chicken from between her upper left and center incisors without appearing trashy. "Well," she said, thinking it over, "I think the Harrises have motive. The water. But," she recalled the pregnant, and thus vulnerable, Patty, "But they don't seem to have had opportunity. I mean, their alibi ... but I guess it's just his and her word ..."

"Yeah," Garrett responded gloomily, starting the car. "And who was duking it out, back there in Alma's yard? If Mrs. Flute's right, that was close to the time of the murder. The one she described as the bigger man, the one that got hit, could have been Biedermann, pretty easy. But who was the little one? What was in that shed that had somebody fighting that hard, anyhow?"

"It does feel like we've got too much information ... I'm havin' trouble puttin' it together." McCracken took a deep swig of her bottled water and stared with resentment back at the restaurant.

"Yeah," said Garrett again, releasing the brake and easing the car onto the street. "And worse, I guess we better go after some more. My instincts tell me we need to have a visit with old Lew Harris. Just like Mrs. Flute suggests. Maybe he does have a guess about what Biedermann was after. In fact, maybe he had a personal interest. He's one we've heard described as a little, wiry guy."

It took less than ten minutes to turn around in the middle of the street, head south again on Highway 46 out of Croysant, and pull off in Lew Harris's yard.

Garrett caught on at once that this was one of those ranching family housing arrangements. Clint and Patty's place, nearby but not fully visible through a little orchard of gnarled apple and plum trees, was a modern modular home, approached by the graveled circular drive, surrounded with small patches of tidily groomed lawn and new trees spindling out of the ground, each protected by wire cages. Garrett guessed that it had gone into place when the grandson married.

Lew's place, on the other hand, was ancient, the upper and back parts frame, all cobbled against an even older log cabin in front that had probably been there since the late 1800s. The yard, partly graveled, seemed to have grown of its own organic accord, some of it making an effort to go toward the orchard, where the back pathway took off toward Clint and Patty's, some of it tippling and weeding its way down against an old barn, and another piece snuggling up to an open garage where a '76 Oldsmobile sat, looking well used.

The house itself was nearly smothered with huge lilac bushes that had finished their bloom for the year, leaving brown husks where the flowers had been, and with wild roses, both pink and yellow, which were going full tilt and which gave the yard a heady, intrusive fragrance.

Apparently Lew had seen them pull up, because he threw open the front door and crowed happily, "Come on in! Come on in!" He grinned at them with the same bright white teeth that Hallie Flute had flashed this morning, and Garrett figured that Hallie's explanation about the mail order catalog probably extended to these teeth, too. Lew's eyes were an excited blue, his stiff-bristled, thick hair a vanilla ice cream white.

"Me'n Lucky been expectin' you—heard you was goin' around talkin' to people in the community what knew somethin' about that Biedermann. Knew ya'd fur sure wanta talk ta us."

Us? Garrett shot McCracken an inquiring glance. Wasn't Lucky the wife's name? The deceased wife? They headed into the enclosed front porch behind the old man. He had on Levis aged as soft as flannel and held up with suspenders that covered red long-handled underwear. There was a slight bow to his legs.

His pale bare feet thumped busily across a wooden floor covered with linoleum, smooth and seamless, a style long since discontinued. Its mustard and brown flecked pattern ended a foot before the wall, where it had been firmly nailed into place.

Standing in the living area to which they had been led, Garrett realized why the old guy was in long underwear on this toasty June afternoon: the house, shaded on all sides and having sunk deeply into the ground over the years, was as cool as a block of winter pond ice held in sawdust. McCracken was rubbing her arms as they looked around.

The shelves and cupboard tops in the room were crowded with what appeared to be a collection of framed family photographs, with a generous surplus of unframed snapshots tacked to the log surfaces of the walls. Some showed a young man in army uniform standing between an older man and woman. Garrett figured it was the lost Michael, dead in Vietnam, between his parents, Lew and Lucky. This conviction was reinforced when he saw a picture of the uniformed guy with a young woman, surely the wife, and one next to it of the wife alone, holding a baby. Probably Clint. The woman looked sad.

In most of the pictures, it was easy to recognize the older Clint with his dark hair and deep-set, thoughtful eyes, but there were many pictures in which Clint was not the only child. Here, for example, a picture of what must have been Lew and Lucky, and with them three pleased-looking youngsters: first, a bright blond boy; then Clint; then a girl with long brown braids. And here: a photo of Lew, Lucky, Clint, and two entirely different teens, one of them an African-American, the other, perhaps, Japanese. McCracken pointed to one of the more clear-cut ensembles and said, "This looks like you, Mr. Harris, with your grandson, Clint, when he was younger."

Lew's eyes glowed. "Yup, me and Clint. I was younger, then, too, ya know." He cackled. "Tell ya what. Lucky here," and he gestured at an empty space just beyond where Garrett was standing, "Lucky can tell you all about these pictures better than me. Why don't you chat with 'er for a little bit, and I'll go get us some coffee."

McCracken looked wild-eyed around the room, seeing absolutely no one in the place indicated by the old man, nor anywhere else either. Garrett, on the other hand, was looking closely at Lew Harris himself. "You bet, Lew," he said. "We'd sure like a cup of hot coffee to wash down our dinner, and Mrs. Harris can tell us about these pictures."

When Lew had disappeared through the door, Garrett and McCracken's eyes met. McCracken made a circular motion near her temple with her index finger, her face a question mark, and Garrett shrugged, spread his hands, and nodded. Then he took her by the shoulder and faced her toward a thick bank of pictures along one wall. "So this one," he said loudly, his voice meant to carry, "This one shows you and your son Michael before he went off to Vietnam." He paused, letting the ghostly Lucky fill in, then said, "Yes, it was a terrible, terrible thing, that war. Too damn bad. What happened to them young men shouldn'ta happened to a dog."

McCracken, taking her cue and letting her voice project, said, "And who is this, Mrs. Harris?" She gave the significant pause, then said, "Wow! He really was a cute baby, little Clint."

Lew came in wearing heelless leather slippers and carrying a tray with four cups of coffee. He stopped dead one step into the room, stared, and said, "What the bejesus is the matter with you two damn fools? Didn't you hear Lucky say she had to go get a sweater? She'll be back in a minute."

He crossed the room, turned his back to them and bent to set the coffee cups on the end tables, mumbling under his breath about where law enforcement had managed to come up with a pair of fools like this. He finished his half audible monologue with, "Don' know how they can expect jackasses and women to do a man's work," plopped a bowl of sugar cubes down, and turned back toward them. He had Clint's beetle brows, turned white, and he raised them now in what looked like a layer of faked politeness intended to cover up what was an irrepressible layer of curiosity and real innate courtesy.

"So, I guess before she went upstairs she had a chance to tell you all about these pictures?"

"Well," Garrett ventured, feeling now more like an ass with every word, "She told us about family. But there are a lot of children ... young people ... in some of these photographs. She didn't have a chance to talk about them."

Lew scowled. "Well, I distinctly heard her mention the exchange students. Her greatest thing was to sow good for when fate dished you out ill. After Michael got killed, she brought so many young people here from all over the world ... Oh, that's right, she showed you the plaque. I heard that. She always shows the plaque."

The old man was getting agitated, and it was McCracken who managed to spot the plaque, sitting on a bookshelf among some sport trophies. It was a commendation from Youth For Understanding, praising the Harrises for their contributions to international student exchange. McCracken walked quickly over to it, said, "Yeah, Mrs. Harris was proud of this. She sure should be, too."

Garrett was looking more closely at the pictures. "All exchange students?" he asked.

"Nope. After Clint was out of high school, Lucky took in a lot of troubled kids from the cities, too. Helped a lot of 'em. They always loved Lucky. She mostly worked with a program called TRY, T-R-Y. Stands for 'To Rehabilitate Youth.'" Lew was on a roll now. "See this kid here? When he arrived here that spring, he was as sullen as a sick dogie calf. Hangdog, wouldn't talk to nobody, no manners. Lucky got through to 'im, big meals, little kindness, lotta work, taught him where he had to be responsible. Responsibility. That's what gives 'em a place in the world. That kid went back to school and straightened up. He started makin' good grades, graduated top a' the class. He was here three summers. I got to likin' him quite a lot."

He moved along the walls, peering closely at the display, picking out this young person, then that, some with sullen looks, some smiling. This one, he would say, was pregnant when she came ... full blown. Lucky had learned her how to care for the kid. And this one, he never came around. "Ended up in the hoosegow," said Lew, his voice half disgusted, half regretful.

At a bank of pictures by the kitchen door he stopped, his finger resting on a picture of a young girl with shining blond hair combed long across one shoulder. "This'n here is Lindy," he said. He peered at the date scrawled on the picture, making it out. "1995. But you know, this girl was the last one Lucky took in. I don't know why. She turned out to be a real nice girl after what she'd been through. Yup, she was a dandy after that. I don't know why Lucky won't take in nobody after her." He shook his head sadly, then looked toward the stairs.

"Yeah, I know, Honey. Coffee's gettin' cold. We was just talkin' about all the kids. All the kids you took in and loved. I miss ..." He hesitated, swallowed the last word, "... miss'm." He shuffled in his slippers over to one of the easy chairs and sat down. Garrett thought his back looked more bent, his step had less spring, than when he had first greeted them at the door.

The old man gestured toward the other chairs and the couch. "Well, damnit, si'down. You heard 'er ... Lucky wants to get you a plate of cookies, but she doesn't want you to wait. She knows you gotta find out what you gotta find out. So sit."

They sat. McCracken took a swig of the coffee. It was in an enamel cup, and even after sitting there ten minutes the lip of the cup burned her mouth. The coffee was as thick as tar. She covered up a gag as Garrett cleared his throat and said, "Well, we just wanted to talk about the night Mr. Biedermann was killed. We thought you could tell us about the water board meeting. Tell us anything unusual you might've noticed. During it, or after it. That's when we think Mr. Biedermann was shot, right after that meeting."

Lew nodded, looked solemn and wiggled his bushy eyebrows. "You know," he began confidentially, "I'm glad Lucky's in the kitchen. She doesn't need to hear this. I don't think she knows that I got a little out of hand at that meeting." He leaned back, satisfied with the thought, a bit pleased with himself. "I made threats."

"Threats?" Garrett repeated, his voice shocked, as if this were the first time he had heard this.

"Well, what he was doin' weren't right, and after they talked around on it, seemed like forever, I just pointed out that they oughta solve their problem once and for all by stringin' the dirty little weasel up.

"You know, Sheriff, nobody'd really mean to have a necktie party in this day and age, not even me, but the young 'uns took me about half serious. Kids are funny that way. What they need to take serious, they plumb fart off — pardon me, ma'm," he added, with a nod at McCracken, before continuing, "But when somebody's just lettin' off steam, they can get a real knot in their tails."

"Yeah, it can happen," Garrett said noncommittally, to let him continue, but Lew had placed his hand firmly over the top of his cup.

"No more right now, Honey." He indicated McCracken and Garrett. "You people want any more coffee? Or cookies?"

No cookies had ever appeared, since they would have had to arrive by telekinesis, but both officers burst out with a smattering of polite "Oh, no thanks, Mrs. Harris. Not now. Good cookies, though," responses. Garrett also covered his cup with his hand, looking up to shake his head and smile at the invisible Lucky Harris, while McCracken saw fit to rub her stomach with appreciation.

Lew was looking down with a hangdog look, and when the two had ceased their protests, he said, "Look, Honey, I'm sorry, I shoulda told you. I didn't mean for you to overhear this. But what's done is done—you need to go ahead and sit down, tell these people what you know, too."

There was a long silence, and just as Garrett was prepared to try to get the conversation going again, Lew nodded at the empty chair next to him, turned to the officers, and said, "Whaddya think?"

Taken aback, McCracken and Garrett looked at each other, groping for their next move, but Lew kept talking. "Ya see, I agree with her. Now that I think about it, I think Lucky's right about why that bastard was in Alma's shed. I just couldn't think so clear at first after Tuesday night, after gettin' so pissed off at that meetin' (pardon me, ladies), and then Clint and Patty were goin' at it. When Patty loses her temper, she can be somethin' else."

For lack of anything better, Garrett repeated, "Something else?"

"When she grabbed up her gun that night, I figgered poor little Clint had had 'er for sure, then she stomped outta the house. She was yellin' like a banshee. Sayin', 'Your dad's right, Clint—but you're too chicken shit to take on that S.O.B., so maybe a real woman's gotta do it.'

"And you know Clint. Right, Lucky? More upset he gets,

less he'll say. Yeah, he takes after you, Honey — the quiet kind are tough to fight with. But he followed 'er to the door and it's a good thing he didn't go no further, 'cause when she gunned that pickup outta the drive, she shot gravel back twenty feet. Coulda beaned him with one a' those rocks."

Garrett was twisting his left mustache so much it had formed a little roll by his upper lip. "So after that, you and Clint ...?"

"Ah, little Clint, he just walked on out. Never said a word. Went to the barn to dink around with the machinery, I guess. That's all that kid could ever see. Tractors and mechanics. Tractors and mechanics. Never a damn horse or cow ... Anyhow, heard the radio goin' out there after a few minutes. Me, I couldn't see no point in hangin' around after that. I took the back pathway home to tell Lucky about the meetin' and all. We watched the ten o'clock news together."

"But why ... why was Patty so angry?" McCracken ventured.

"I don' know. Do you, Lucky? Seems like she has just got an exceptionally short fuse for the last month or so ... always set to pick a fight with little Clint. Like everythin' he does gets her mad lately."

"Oh." A look of partial comprehension crossed McCracken's face, but Garrett's had gone completely befuddled.

"But you and Lucky ..." Garrett said carefully, "You know why Biedermann was in the shed ..."

"Well, sure. Like Lucky told you, Gritty was in that car accident that year. It scared Alma. She had to go over ta' Denver, spend time gettin' her on 'er feet." He sipped his coffee, relaxed, pleased that it had all been cleared up.

Garrett had never been so frustrated. He pawed at his scar, blew air from his pursed lips, shuffled his feet. How the hell could he find out what it was that the deceased Lucky had told them, having heard none of it? He figured if he alienated the old man, he would damn well never know what the ghost lady had said. He felt dizzy.

Looking directly at the empty chair, McCracken said in a conversational tone, "But Mrs. Harris, Patty is usually a nice girl, isn't she?"

There was a pregnant silence, then McCracken said, "That's

it. I can't imagine her planning real harm. I was just wondering if maybe she took out from home that night because she was thinking she was going to ... to beat Reider to the draw. To ... get the ... stuff ... in the shed."

"Ahhh," Lew said, nodding at McCracken with approval. "That's one idee." Then he shook his head. "But I can't see it. You know, like Lucky says, not too many of the young'uns recall when Alma was the secretary to the water board. I don't think Patty woulda thought about it."

He ran his thumbs up and down under his suspenders, giving them a little snap, thinking out loud. "I'm like Lucky. I'm just sure Alma woulda filed the deeds in the board files, ready to get copies. Just like Lucky says. Her and me figgered that'n out the day after the meetin', 'cause we knew there were papers somewhere that secured us old timers' legal rights. We remembered findin' out the problem on the deeds back then, then we remembered fixin' it. It's called *quit claim deeds*." He rolled the words in his mouth, pleased to have remembered the exact legal term to use. He repeated it. "*Quit claim*."

After letting the word sink in, he continued, "We all took out *quit claim deeds* right after we discovered the error about the water on the originals. But maybe, because of poor little Gritty, Alma didn't get the paperwork down to the courthouse."

Garrett and McCracken held their breath, afraid to interrupt his flow and have to refer again to the absent Lucky, but he continued this time without coaxing.

"It wouldn't a' been like Alma not to see that the deeds were properly filed, the originals returned to the owners and so-on. I recall us all sayin' we would hand 'em over to Alma so she could make copies for the board files, then she'd take care of 'em. But that was the year Gritty was hurt so bad."

The old man shook his head, looking worried, then he said to the chair, "Yeah, I know, Honey. Gritty's doin' pretty good now." He nodded vigorously. "Yeah, I know. It really can't be laid at Alma's doorstep. Us damn fools then ... We shoulda had enough sense to follow up on our own damn deeds, not just dump it all on Alma, poor old woman." He turned to Garrett and McCracken and shook his shaggy head again. "But you know how it is. Ya' get busy. Rely on the women folk. Can't expect us men to do it all alone." He rolled his eyes sideways at the chair. Garrett decided it was safe to interject.

"So you think Biedermann was after the unfiled quit claim deeds? Thinking to find and destroy them so he could make his water filing stick?" The left side of Garrett's mustache, released from its painful twist, had formed a corkscrew, which contrasted interestingly with the still drooping right side. McCracken, who felt she had entered some sort of alternative universe, couldn't take her eyes off it.

Lew didn't answer Garrett. He seemed to have commenced another discussion with his wife, and his tone was argumentative. "I know I shoulda thought of all a' this sooner. Maybe coulda saved the heat at the board meeting. Spared the sheriff some investigation. I just didn't, damn it, Lucky!"

A pause. Garrett's hand shot back to his mustache, his eyes fixed on Lew, who said, "No, I was not! Just 'cause I was lookin' out the winda' for the grass widder ... Yeah, yeah, yeah, so you always say. Yeah, sure, she's a good-lookin' woman, Maggie Merimeister, but she ain't my type. You're my type."

Another pause. "Yeah, you know I saw her get home over there ... after eleven ... Yeah, I do suppose you were gettin' tired a' waitin'. Look, Honey, I told you, I don't care fer her. I just wondered what she was ... Awww, Lucky. Awwwh. I shet the winda' and I came to bed, just like you wanted, right after she showed up. You didn't have to holler at me ..."

Another pause, then he lowered his head. "All right, then. We'll discuss it later."

Garrett and McCracken had begun to ease delicately out of their seats. Garrett tried, "Thank you, Mr. Harris ... ahmph ... and Mrs. Harris. I believe you've helped us a lot."

Lew shook his thick white hair as if to clear his head, shot the two a piercing blue glance, said, "Sure do hope so, Sheriff. And young lady. We're both plumb glad to help at any time, so you come back and see us when you can. We enjoy the company."

20

Friday, Late Afternoon

With Sheriff Pat Garrett

Garrett was not so insensitive as to let on that he was relieved about McCracken's Big Sister Soccer Tournament. She, of course, protested that duty told her to stay in Oozle. He could see from the look on her face that she would prefer death by anaconda to riding back to Riversmet with Red. Braving another foray into Mac and Alice's territory, in fact, would be cream pudding compared to the hour and a half drive with that big lummox, but Garrett encouraged her not to forego her commitment to the kids. "This isn't just a practice, McCracken. The girls are gonna need their coaches for the tournament," he said. "You don't wanna let 'em down."

With less sensitivity, Red added, "Get over it, McCracken. There are occasions when the sheriff can function pretty well without you. Come on. I need the company worse than he does — it's a long, lonesome drive back to the big city."

The truth was, Garrett wasn't that worried about danger from the occupants of the tepee, nor did he expect an earth-shaking discovery there. His primary hope was to get alone and clear his head.

The Oozle clubhouse had once been a one-room school-house. It was only slightly gussied up now for modern usage, and it had no telephone, so Garrett and McCracken drove up to let the deputies who were working there on the boxes know that they might be looking for quit claim deeds in some sort of file. And, Garrett felt compelled to add, "you might not." This sense of ambiguity about the truth of Lew Harris's proposal fueled his need to assimilate the information he had collected during the last couple of days.

Thus it was that McCracken and Garrett parted ways, McCracken lemon-lipped as she piled in the passenger seat next to Red. Garrett headed on up to the younger Biedermann's tepee. No Nancy Barnswallowper could be seen on the road this afternoon, but neither were there any Biedermanns around when he reached the tepee. The tepee looked as if it hadn't been visited since they checked it out yesterday. Garrett didn't poke through things much, but the truck sat in place, the stale smell still floated in the air inside the tepee, and he saw no tracks any fresher than his and McCracken's.

Back in the police car he left the door open and let his left foot rest on the ground while he mulled it over, eyeing the surrounding rocky outcrops and mauling his chew. Then he called dispatch. "Peggy, put out an APB on this pair for me. We're looking for a Mac Biedermann and his wife, Alice... Right ..." He continued to let his eyes search the surrounding cliffs while he gave the description, then he started to shut off the phone when Peggy said, "Hold on a minute, Sheriff. We have information on that gun that fired the fatal shot for Biedermann."

"Oh, yeah? What's news?"

"They've matched the prints. It looks like there was only one set on that gun, and they belonged to the lady who came by this morning. A Mrs. Patty Harris? That help you out any?"

"Maybe." Garrett grunted. He felt grim. Pulling his foot into the car, he added, "Maybe not. Thanks, Peggy."

He dropped the phone on the seat and pulled out of the drive, but instead of heading down, he turned right, taking the narrow county track on back into the mountains. It wasn't long before he reached a little mesa, pinion and oak brush giving way to stands of quaking aspen and the green bunch grass, sage, and wildflowers of the high mountain meadows. The dirt road had deteriorated to a path, a mine field of large rocks, and the police car was taking a beating. Garrett had just decided he needed to find a place to turn around when the path arched left and stopped dead in a stand of quakies that was flourishing beside a cold mountain stream. Garrett cut the motor and sighed with satisfaction.

He lay on his belly and drank, then for a while he just propped his back against a hard, fat aspen, stretched out his legs, closed his eyes, and let the water talk to him. It had plenty to say, yapping and gurgling as it hurried past, occasionally making grating and plopping noises as if annoyed to be drawn so rapidly toward its fate, to be spread-eagled and sun-scorched in the irrigation ditches of the valleys below.

Water. Garrett shifted his weight and sighed again, this time the sigh one makes when drawn back to duty. Taking a ballpoint pen and spiral notebook from his shirt pocket, he opened the book to the first blank page, where he wrote, "Weapons. Hard object. Revolver ... .38." After that he doodled, looking up at the shivering leaves and making treelike objects across the bottom of the page.

It seemed obvious to him that someone had gotten into a fight with Biedermann, somehow gotten the upper hand and hit him over the head. Maybe with a garden implement, if Hallie could be trusted. Then whoever it was must have drug him into the shed and arranged him to make it look as if he were going through Alma's boxes. Then they had delivered the *coup de grace*, shooting the unconscious man in the back. After which they had driven away. Not in a pickup, but in a car ... maybe with someone else in the seat beside them. Again, according to Hallie ...

He turned the page and went into a frenzy of doodling, producing not only a rushing stream but a pair of deer, a bird, and two trout swimming along the bank. That, he thought, is probably what happened. But who? Who whacked Biedermann? He turned another notebook page.

You usually were most suspicious of family members. Methodically he listed Victoria, Mac, Alice, and Christa. Victoria had an iron-clad alibi. She'd been working at the hospital, over ninety miles away, all evening and all night. But Reider's children all had had more than enough opportunity to get to Alma's during the critical hours between 9:00 and midnight. Christa, for example. Her alibi was slim, only the phone call that she made to the attorney, Duval. Which he had backed her on. But that could have been made from anywhere. And neither one was all that firm on the time of the call ... she could have gone before to Alma's, or gone after ... Garrett mumbled to himself.

He supposed he'd have to do a phone trace.

And Mac and Alice. They were right there. Jenny had seen them at 9:30 at the Cowpath, when Alice got Mac.

Family members. But it was the Harris's gun, and Patty Harris's prints on the gun. Clint was "working in the shop." Patty and Lew had "heard his radio in the shop." What kind of an alibi was that? No alibi, that's what kind it was! Garrett didn't write 'Clint,' but instead drew a stick figure with dark hair sticking up. He drew in a pistol at the hips and made the elbows bent, like the guy was going into an old West quick-draw.

And Patty. A drink with Jenny around 10:00, but it sounded like she hadn't gotten there until a quarter till ten, then had left shortly after. It was just minutes to Alma's — plenty of opportunity. Maybe.

He swallowed his urge to speculate, trying to be methodical. Methodical. Smiling to himself, he thought, "What about the people who were right there: Alma? Hallie? How about Lew? Lew fit Hallie's description, a small guy. Sure, they're old, but they had as much motive as the other ranchers. That business with Reider in Alma's shed going after rancher water must have felt to them like somebody spitting in church. A desecration. Together, they would have been a pretty strong force, especially if Reider was as sickly as he had been described.

Garrett gathered some skeletal last-year quakie leaves from the ground and mooshed them around between his fingers. Old people were not just useless dead leaves clinging pointlessly to the tree. There was usually a lot of piss and vinegar in the old dogs yet. Maybe they spotted Biedermann in the yard and argued with him to keep him from getting the deeds, then Lew hit him, then together they pulled him into the shed, then by the next day Alma forgot the whole thing and the other two were crafty enough to cover up ... Right, maybe. And maybe cows had wings.

Even so ... all that craziness, the stuff about the dead wife and all, and the handicaps, the hearing, the stalled memory — it could all be a coverup. Old people can be sly. Garrett poked at his notepaper, then began to make spirally circles. At least, even if the old folks weren't, someone was covering up. Someone wasn't on the up and up. Was it the ditzy Alice? Maybe she wasn't so spaced as she was letting on. And where were those two now, anyhow, Mac and Alice?

Maggie Merimeister. Now there was somebody whose alibi didn't hold water. Everyone agreed that Maggie had dropped Carmen and Frieda at their homes shortly after ten, but Lew claimed she didn't get to her own house, which from Carmen's was at best a ten-minute drive, until after eleven. Where the heck had she been for that ... well, at least half an hour? Probably longer ... What was she covering up?

And happy, jolly Duz — talk about somebody with no alibi! That guy might be all front: who was to say where he was, at the irrigation divider box or down killing somebody? All those light, cheerful spirits might be masking a hell of a dark secret.

Duz wasn't all that tall of a guy. Maybe he looked little to Hallie. Lew kept calling his big, tall clunker of a grandson "Little" Clint. Maybe Hallie thought of Alma's son as "Little Duz," so that she subconsciously believed the person who wielded the weapon was smaller than he really was. Or maybe Hallie had recognized Duz in the yard and was covering for him. Alma's son must feel like family to her.

And other people in the community ... Garrett closed his eyes and let the notebook sag. The alibis were intertwined, a seamless net which upheld everyone. Club president Doreen Van Doran and her co-hostess, Agnes Michaelson, who had a big stake in the water issue, claimed to have been preparing the club refreshments together, and they said their husbands came home directly after the water board meeting. Nancy Jane, who was godmother to the twins, had stopped by Jilly and Billy Brown's for a drink and to continue the water discussion; Pete Johnson had dropped supplies off at Ed Skinner's and visited awhile before heading on home ... and so it went. Everyone's alibi during the critical time period hinged on someone else in the community. Everyone in the community had a stake in the water. Garrett thought cynically that even the little dog, Spit, could claim to have been home snuggled next to his adoring owner, Donna, and she'd back him up. A dog needs a water bowl. It was a massive community coverup!

The community had gotten rid of Biedermann, and now they were sticking together to protect each other. It made total sense to Garrett, sitting by himself, cool in the dappling trees. If you looked at it that way, then it didn't matter who had done the whacking, dragging, and so-on, because all of the people involved were complicit in the crime. Garrett began to whistle to himself under his breath. This idea really had potential.

With Biedermann gone, the community had already started to settle down. Their water secure, all they had to do was ... well, play dumb. It was no accident, Wednesday, all those women moving those boxes around. And the absence of drag marks, where Biedermann had been dragged into the shed ... all blotted out by the busybody club ladies, "tidying up." The proliferation of stories — how Hallie saw this, and Lew saw that, and Maggie was maybe here, maybe there ... all this talk was explained by a shared coverup. If you saw it as a community planned crime, then really only Victoria herself, the wife, had a watertight alibi. It really opened things up.

Yes, alibis! If the community itself did it, that explained why everybody seemed to have an alibi ... Garrett drooped. The first hole in the lovely theory had reared its ugly head.

"Shit!" Garrett stood up and lobbed a rock into the stream. Of course it wasn't true. Several people had been left glaringly without alibis. If it were a community coverup, then Duz would not have said he was alone, at his divider box. And the Harrises would have had more backup than each other ... Lew wouldn't be relying on the ghostly Lucky, and Clint would have been seen, not just heard, in the barn ...

Which, of course, brought Garrett to the far worse problem. Why the gun? The community could easily have hidden a gun, hidden it well and forever. Why had that gun been found? Yes, worse: why had it been found with Patty Harris's prints on it — Patty Harris, the one person everyone in the community claimed to just love? And even worst of all, why hadn't it at least been sunk in the pond? To find it beside the pond, beside the pond and visible ... utterly pointless.

Garrett spun another rock at the creek, trying to get it to skip, then squatted back down on the ground. He'd been here over an hour and nothing was explained. He had to get serious.

OK ... Theories of the crime. Number one: Someone whom Reider had scared over the water rights issue had killed him.

How and why they met there in the shed wasn't clear, but maybe it was chance. Or word somehow got around that the deeds were at Alma's and ... but how did Reider know? Like Lew said, the younger people in the community wouldn't recall that there had been an issue about quit claim deeds and that Alma had them. Still, Reider seemed to have been resourceful. Maybe he'd just figured it out. Asked around ...

Or ... what if there were no quit claim deeds? What if there just should have been, but there weren't? Someone could have called Biedermann, told him there were deeds like that in the shed, then watched him and when he went to check it out, killed him. Maybe whoever did that was surprised in the act or panicked, just threw out the gun in their haste to get away ...

Either way, there was a good chance that now the deeds would not be found. At least, not until this all blew over. Not after those women had tidied and sorted—Garrett's money was on the Oozle women having found the deeds and hid them for some kind of "safekeeping" until it all blew over. If deeds there were.

Theories of the crime. Right. What about the drug motive? What if Reider had planned a meeting with the woman Jenny couldn't identify that same night at the Cowpath? What if? And something had gone wrong and the woman had killed him? Better yet—what if Mac and Alice had a meeting set up with the woman, then Reider, in search of quit claim deeds on the water, had surprised them? That would really explain quite a lot, wouldn't it? Not the gun, yet ... but something else could explain that. And if it was a setup like that, then there would be no drugs to find in the shed, either.

Garrett was just growing fond of this theory when he heard the unmistakable clop-clop of a horse coming purposefully up the path: Nancy Jane Barnswallowper, looking like Calamity Jane in her battered hat, western shirt, and chaps. "Hey, Sheriff! Come up to think it out in the clear mountain air, did ya?"

Garrett, jogged from what had become a reverie, stood and stretched. "Well, I suppose you got that right. You lookin' for a stray?"

Nancy leaned forward, resting her wrists on the saddle horn and letting the bridle reins go slack, which caused her horse, who had been clanking the bit in his mouth, to reach to one side and try to snatch a mouthful of lupine.

"Yeah," she said, her eyes moving through the trees even as she spoke. "I got a sick calf up here. Tried to treat 'er yesterday, she warn't sick enough yet. Took off with 'er mama and there wasn't any gettin' a loop on 'er. Thought I might be able to nose her out this evenin'. You ain't seen 'er?"

"Nah," Garrett said, paused, then said, "I been concentratin' on my own search efforts. You seen hide or hair of Mac and Alice?"

He thought he saw her eyes flick to the side, but she responded without hesitation. "Nah. Nah, never did see much a' them two, even on the worst of days." She grinned. "You figurin' a drug motive's involved in that shootin'?"

Garrett rubbed at his ear. "I ain't figurin' much of anything yet. Too much goin' on."

"Ain't it the truth." Nancy Jane gathered up her reins before her horse could tag another satisfying mouthful of flowers. "Well, I gotta get goin', maybe get home before dark. I'll let you know if your friends show up in their little Mary Huana patch."

"Thanks." Garrett watched her back, a graceful movement to the horse's rhythm, her rump adjusted to the saddle. What he did next would have crushed McCracken. He drove carefully down the car-jarring road, headed for Riversmet, and reached Peaseford at dusk, just in time to spot Jenny Threewinds hiking up the street with netted bags of groceries and produce dangling from each hand. With a feeling half melting and half hopeful, he pulled up beside her, rolled down the window, leaned over, and said, "Hey!"

"Hey yourself!" She smiled at him.

"Can I give you a lift?"

"Nope. Car's right over there." She gestured with her chin.

"Can I buy you supper?"

She shook her head. "Too much fuss, isn't it? I need to get back to my dogs pretty soon. Spot can take it, but Roughhouse misses me."

The 'isn't it' was encouraging. "How about," he said, thinking fast, "How about pizza?" He raised his eyebrows and nodded vigorously at her to get her to nod back.

It worked. She nodded back, her smile spreading. "Sounds good, Patrick. Let me put my stuff in my trunk."

Before he could answer, she jogged up the street, the net bags plopping against her legs. Patrick. He basked in the word as he took advantage of his official status, backing up three car lengths the wrong lane to save her the walk back.

The conversation over the pizza was quiet and easy. It drifted, threading around community gossip, the murder, Carmen Weinant's fish art, Duz's good nature. Garrett described his and McCracken's encounter with Lew Harris. "Is he always like that? Is he putting on, or does he really think his wife is still alive?"

Jenny was a hearty eater; she shook her head, disposing of a bite from her third piece of sausage and mushroom before answering. "Somebody should have warned you, you know? This community's like that—things go on so long that we get used to them, and even the strange stuff seems normal to us." A swallow from her second bottle of Dos Equis washed down the bite. Garrett, watching her eat, felt satisfied, as a parent might who is watching a child clean its plate. A piece of salad on the fork, then she said, "I take it for granted that I will set a plate for Lucky whenever Lew steps in the door of the Cowpath."

"I'll be damned," Garrett said. His was Coors. He was holding it to one, knowing that the car and the uniform put his literal off-duty status into an appearance of being on duty. He fingered the bottle. "Something has been bothering me since we left there this afternoon."

"What's that?"

"I knew that his wife was deceased, but I've been trying to think. I don't remember hearing how she died. After this afternoon, I started wondering if something else went on, something that shocked old Lew so that he can't accept her death. Am I just fumbling in the dark? Did she just die of old age?"

Jenny nodded and scowled, as if the question took some thought. "In a way, I guess you could say she did." She pushed her empty salad bowl aside and tapped at the table with her fingers. "She died from heart failure, like everyone does as a bottom line." She patted her mouth with her napkin and leaned forward, lowering her voice. "The rest is all gossip."

"The rest?"

"Yeah. See, Lucky Harris was kind of like a lot of the old settler types. The good part of her was that she was as honest, fair-minded, respectable, and good-hearted as one person can get."

Garrett nodded. "Don't we know 'em."

"And the bad part was that she was set in her ways. She could be very self-righteous and controlling. She was a bit of a nag."

"I see," said Garrett, who wasn't sure that he did.

"Anyhow, she and Lew took in kids from all over — international exchange students when Clint was young, then later on they took inner city kids, tried to get them some fresh air and stability. They did a good job, but as she got older I think Lucky kind of tired out."

"So she didn't do as good a job?"

"Oh, she cooked good meals for the kids, had them help, kept them safe. But she had a tough time standing the disruption, and some of the kids were like kids like that are — wild and sassy."

"Anyhow, the last girl that came to stay with them, her name was Lindy Zakely. I don't think the community ever learned too much about her background, but we all understood that the girl had had it rough. She was one of those kind of girls who had to run away from home. To get relief from her father, I think. She hit the streets and got on dope and got into prostitution, but I don't think at base that she was a bad kid. Just had some tough times."

Garrett figured that Jenny would never think anyone was a bad kid, but he kept that opinion to himself. Instead, he urged her to continue.

"Right. So, anyhow, this Lindy got into a program called TRY, which was one of the organizations the Harrises worked with, and she ended up here, with them. She spent a good year with them. I saw her around — she had real pretty long blond hair and warm brown eyes, and she was very sociable.

"But she was also just a teenager. She wanted to play. She wanted to get out, to meet other teens. She wanted to borrow Lew and Lucky's car. She wanted to get into Riversmet, see a movie or hang out. Coming from the city, it was real culture shock to her to end up in Croysant."

"I can see that it would be," Garrett said, beginning to get a sense of where this might be going.

"So anyhow, I guess more than once she and Lucky were overheard arguing. Lucky would be putting her foot down, demanding that chores be done or else, and Lindy would be yelling. In the end, it came to no good. Lucky was found dead at the bottom of the porch steps and Lindy was gone." Garrett's eyebrows raised and Jenny continued.

"Oh, just for a while. She actually returned after a few hours, admitted they had been arguing, and said that when she saw that Lucky had fallen and she couldn't help her, she got scared."

Garrett whistled. "How come I never got wind of this? Didn't they investigate, check if Mrs. Harris had been pushed or some such?"

"No, I don't think anyone felt like that was what happened. The girl said that she hadn't been near her, just yelling, and that it looked like Lucky had tripped. The coroner told Lew that Lucky had had a heart attack."

"And Lew accepted that?"

"There was no reason not to, actually. You know Tom Banks, the coroner. He's as reliable as they come. It was known that Lucky had high blood pressure; she was wound up like a top half the time. I think Lew thought the argument itself might have brought on the attack, but he knew kids pretty well. He didn't feel that arguing with Lucky was necessarily the girl's fault. In fact, he stuck up for Lindy. He said that was the way Lucky would have wanted it."

Garrett whistled again. "Maybe that was the way Lew wanted it, but maybe deep down he isn't so sure he did right by Lucky. Maybe that's why he's seeing ghosts."

"Maybe."

"Well, at any rate, it sounds like it was quite a shock. What happened to the girl?"

"This was about five years ago, I think. I remember it because the Biedermanns bought their place not too long after Lucky died. Anyhow, the TRY program was notified. Part of their rules are that parents aren't contacted until and unless a teenager wants them to be. I guess Lucky's death shook Lindy up pretty badly, because she agreed to have them reunite her with her mother. As nearly as I know, that's the last any of us around here ever heard of her."

"Hrrmph," Garrett said, shaking his head.

"So, you want to come on up to my trailer for dessert?"

Just like that. Garrett, his mind on the death of Lucky Harris, said, "Desser ...?" and then he blushed bright red, from neck to bald forehead, his scar the most crimson of all. Jenny smiled at him, and, Garrett, flustered, enveloped in an adolescent wave of shyness, made his biggest mistake of the day. Or maybe, of the year.

"Uh ... I ... It's nice of you to ask me, but I need to get on home." Maybe the words could somehow be sucked back. He wished. But they floated on, in the air, irretrievable. All he could do was add, his voice almost breaking with sincerity, "But I sure do appreciate your asking. I sure do appreciate that."

21

Saturday Morning

Oozle

Sometimes things turn up if your objective is not to have an objective. Like a hound trying to pick up a scent, Garrett roved here and there around the community, stopping to ask questions, digging for new information, and sniffing once more at the old. McCracken was with him. Her Big Sister Soccer team, the Wildcats, had won their first round and were scheduled for the next game at two, so she brought her own car and Garrett picked her up at the clubhouse.

They went to Mac and Alice's tepee first. There was still no sign of life. It was McCracken who noticed the marijuana plants. They'd been planted in plain view among the sparse foliage and ragged brush, scattered thinly, one here, one there, looking like weeds against the sage. They were drooping from lack of water.

A half dozen other stops, ending up at Alma's. Victoria was there. She'd just given Alma a bath, helped her dress, and was counting medications into the little pill boxes that were labeled for the days of the week, morning and evening, seven days. They knocked. Victoria spoke wanly to them at the door, telling them that she felt she might as well get on with her work since nothing had been resolved with respect to Reider.

"Nothing *has* been resolved, has it?" she queried, her grey eyes worried and earnest.

"No, ma'm. I'm sorry. We've been workin' on it pretty steady, but nothin's turned up." Garrett figured she had to be the only person in the community sorry to have Reider dead. Poor bastard. Maybe it served him right ...

"I was sure you would let me know if you had identified the person who shot him." She looked as if she might cry.

"Yes, ma'm, we would. I did have one question. We have a search warrant for your and Reider's home. You wouldn't mind if some of our people came up and looked around, would you? There may be somethin' there that Reider wrote down or left behind, somethin' that would give us an idea as to who was so angry that they wanted to shoot him."

She gave a little gasp when he said 'search warrant,' then she flushed, the color bright on her high cheekbones against her fair skin. "Well ... I was thinking the ranchers ... you do know about the water rights ... uh ... problem, don't you?"

"Oh, yes, we do," Garrett said, then added reasonably, "But if the motive were water rights, we think it would be one rancher, not the whole community. We still have a lot of detection to do to narrow it down."

"Oh," she said, sounding enlightened. "Oh, dear. I'm afraid I have been going through things ... sorting Reider's clothes and papers and so-on. I feel restless, you know? Maybe a little frightened ... until this is ... resolved." Tears had gathered at the corners of her eyes, and now they began to move unacknowledged down her cheeks.

"I'm sorry." Garrett and McCracken were still standing on the narrow steps, McCracken behind Garrett. He added, "Would you like us to increase our patrols in your area?"

"Oh, no, no," she said, finally wiping at the tears on one cheek with a slender finger. "No," shaking her head. "I am being silly, really. Whenever you would like to have someone come to the house, that will be fine. I hope I haven't disturbed things and ruined evidence." She ran her finger delicately over the other cheek. "And I'll bet you dropped by to visit with Alma. Come on in ... I'm sure she will like to chat. I can get you a cool drink if you'd like."

They accepted the drink to facilitate conversation with Alma, then Victoria went back to counting out the weekly pills. Alma clearly didn't recognize them, so the sheriff came close and reintroduced himself. "Do you remember me, Mrs. Weinant? I'm Pat Garrett. And this is Deputy Leigh McCracken."

"Oh, yes! Pat Garrett. Doug and I came to your home many

times to look at bulls. Your father sold Hereford bulls. And your mother used to grow the most *beautiful* flowers. I think it was either you or your brother Lyle who went on to become county sheriff." She had taken his hand and was beaming up at him.

"It was me, ma'm," he said, extracting his hand and taking a seat, assuming an invitation to do so. McCracken sat, too, her eyes examining the treasury of knickknacks on the shelves and the paintings and portraits thick upon the walls. "We just came by to see how you've been doin'."

"Well, I'm doing fine, thank you. Victoria's here today and she is getting a lot done this morning. I believe she has already hung out the laundry." Alma settled in for a good chat. Garrett noticed that she seemed oblivious to the recent death in her storage shed. Instead, they covered old times in the valley, discussing the habits and adventures of inhabitants long past.

Maggie Merimeister was just pulling into the yard when they finally bade their goodbyes and were stepping out the door. Victoria was outside, moving the sprinklers. Maggie bent over the trunk of her car. She emerged, carrying a box of bedding petunias and headed for the house. "Hi, there," she hailed cheerfully. "Don't you think Alma will love these? I just couldn't resist picking some up for her. The colors are terrific. She'll be able to see them."

"That they are," Garrett confirmed, and McCracken nodded, rolling her eyes. She hated this. She was stiff with boredom. She hated old times and she hated flowers. She wished there had been a shootout up at Mac and Alice's tepee.

"Would you like me to help you carry those in?" Garrett asked chivalrously. Maggie laughed.

"Oh, no. They aren't so heavy." She propped the box against the top fence rail, then added, "How're you coming on your investigation?" She tipped her head toward the shed, which still was set off by the yellow perimeter tape.

"Nothing new. We were just up today to talk to people, making sure we have the details straight as to what happened Wednesday ... not to mention the evening before." Garrett fished his spiral notebook out of his shirt pocket and thumbed the pages over, making a show, seemingly searching out Maggie's own statement.

"Here it says that you were at the Friends of the Library meeting on Tuesday night, and that you dropped Carmen Weinant and Frieda Johnson off at their houses before going home. I have that right, don't I, Ms. Merimeister?"

"Yes, you do," she said, leaning in, trying to see the notebook, but he closed it and returned it to his pocket.

"Now, you didn't see anything unusual while you were out that evening? Since I spoke with you Wednesday, you haven't recalled anything we should know that you may have forgotten then?"

Maggie frowned, an expression of thoughtful concentration. "I haven't thought of anything at all, Sheriff. You mean, like strangers in town or something, right?"

"Right," he said, giving her time, then added, "As I understand it, you went straight home after you dropped off Mrs. Weinant? You must have arrived home at about ... well, by 10:30? Would 10:30 p.m. be correct?"

Quickly, Maggie said, "Yes, yes, that would be ... right. From Carmen's it's about ... yes, about fifteen minutes. Yes, so I must have been home at about 10:30 because ..." Her eyes shifted from his face to McCracken's, "The library meeting got out before ten and ... yes, that *has* to be right." She nodded strongly, affirming her words, then added, "And I suppose that it's important, isn't it? I mean, he must have been shot ..." She gestured with her head again toward the shed, "Sometime in that vicinity. So you need to know our alibis and all? I was alone after I got home, you know. I live alone. There's no one to say I really got there." Her expression had become anxious.

Soothingly, Garrett said, "Yes, Mr. Biedermann was probably shot at right about that time. We need alibis, of course. But it also helps to hear from people that were out and about, whether they happened to see anything unusual." He smiled at her. "And it just doesn't sound as if you did."

"No! No, I just didn't. I'm sorry." She wiggled, shifting the petunias to her other arm.

"Well, thanks anyhow. We'll be on our way. I hope Mrs. Weinant enjoys the petunias."

In the car, Garrett said fiercely, "Someone is lying."

"Yeah." McCracken was chewing gum vigorously. "Lew

Harris said it was after eleven — maybe a lot after eleven — when Merimeister rolled in." She hesitated, then added, "He was watching for her while Lucky waited in bed." She managed to keep a straight face, saying this last, but her voice thickened with mirth. Garrett let it pass.

"Right. And Carmen Weinant claims to have been in bed by 10:30. She claims she was asleep when Duz returned from the divider box ... So, who do you believe, Deputy?"

"I dunno. Merimeister's got the shiftiest eyes."

"I can agree with that." They had arrived at the clubhouse. It was time for McCracken to take her own car back to the Big Sister Soccer game in Riversmet, and Garrett wanted to visit with the deputies who were laboriously sorting Alma's boxes. He parked.

"I can agree with that," he repeated, "So those shifty eyes would rule her out, according to the cook at the Lantern, right?" He chuckled at his own joke, and McCracken laughed out loud. She was still smiling as she headed for Riversmet. She sure loved to share a joke with the sheriff.

Garrett ended up babysitting the boxes at the clubhouse while the two deputies doing the sorting went to Croysant to get lunch. It looked like they were at least eighty percent done. No drugs. No file of deeds. He poked around idly, awed by the mountain of memorabilia Mrs. Weinant had collected.

There was stuff ranging from plastic flowers, labeled "For Memorial Day," to books by B.M. Bower, Gene Stratton Porter, Harold Bell Wright, Will Rogers, and others, all taped and worn with the reading, some with the covers actually sewn on as one would sew a torn sock. He wandered back to the box that had been set aside, the one Biedermann's hands had been in when he was shot. It seemed irrelevant now, since it looked like he'd been clubbed outside the shed, then had his hands placed in a box at random. Nevertheless, Garrett couldn't resist ruffling down through it again.

On top was a pile of letters, most of them on flowery scented stationery which still carried the heavy odors of lilac and rose perfumes despite the passage of years. They had been banded together, but the rubber had rotted and broken, so that now the pile was loose in the box. A plain envelope sliding among the flowery ones caught his eye. Idly, he picked it up and took out the sheet of paper it contained.

It said simply, "Tell your mother I didn't hurt you, Darling. I never wanted to hurt you. I just wanted to love you. Your precious Pappy." Feeling slightly guilty, Garrett slipped the paper into his pocket.

He knew the deputies had checked all these envelopes for drugs. Two photo albums lay at the bottom of the box. The picture corners had been fitted into little black pyramids which were then glued to the album page. Most of them had come loose and merely reposed on the same general page where they had started. He checked behind the others for ... what? Drugs? Minute traces of anything.

Nothing there. He spent the rest of the time looking at the album pictures, which featured old timers in the valley at various social gatherings. He knew many of the people, all of them looking young then, most of them dead and gone now. His grandparents figured in a half dozen of the photos.

By the time the deputies returned, he felt tired, burnt out. He decided to head down the valley toward Riversmet, but he only made it as far as the Browns'. Glancing over, he saw the Weinant pickup parked in the yard; now there was somebody it might pay to kick back with for a few minutes. He pulled in.

Billy Brown supported his ranch with his mechanical skills. He had never met a broken piece of farm equipment which he couldn't cobble back together, and because everyone liked his work, he tended to know who had the spare parts for every failed rake, mower, baler, manure spreader, marker, and what-have-you in the valley. He wasn't too shabby at constructing something new to meet the occasion, either. Clearly Duz Weinant was a customer. Billy had on a welder's helmet and was going hammer and tongs after something that was protruding from the back of Duz's pickup, while Duz stood by, ready to assist. Getting closer, Garrett saw they were working on a hay spear, used to carry twelve hundred pound bales from the stackyard to the field to feed the cattle in winter.

As befit the occasion, Garrett walked over next to Duz's pickup and leaned up against it silently, staring along the truck bed, averting his eyes from the superheated sparks of the welder. Duz acknowledged him with a nod and a grin, not attempting to talk over the bursts of sizzling sound. When Billy finished and raised his goggles, he said, "Howdy, Sheriff. How ya' doin'?"

"Not bad, considerin'. Looks like ya' had a pretty good breakdown there."

Duz shook his head. "I was gonna quit feedin' the mother cows and them calves in the north forty on May fifteen, and this sucker lasted through the fourteenth and called 'er quits. I just said the hell with it and opened the gate on the flat and let 'em at the green grass. Plenty a' time now till fall, but I figgered poor ol' Billy could use the business sooner than later."

Billy wiped the sweat that was pouring into his eyes and grinned good-naturedly. "Anytime. Wouldn' want ya' to go huntin' up a piece of new equipment, anyhow. You'd be payin' the bank all them big bucks a' yours and my kids'd be goin' hungry."

"Wouldn' wanna do that. You got somethin' special on your mind, Sheriff?"

"Nothin' in particular. We haven't had any big breaks in the shootin' over there at your mother's. Thought maybe you guys might have an idea."

Billy Brown, still wearing his gloves, got a grip on the hay spear, which was obviously heavy. He made an effort to turn it over, then Duz and the sheriff got hold and they lifted, trying to allow Billy to get a better look at the other side. Grunting with the weight as he spoke, Billy said, "Maybe I oughtta take the fifth amendment here ... oof ... but I'm kind of an innocent little fucker ... unh ... so I guess I can safely say ... urrrNF," this last with a heave to get the part a little farther past the tailgate, "I guess I can safely say that I been too busy rejoicin' to do much sleuthin'."

Duz sniffled and wiped at his nose with the back of his hand, then said, "Aw, now Billy ..."

"No, I got an American right to say that I hated that son of a bitch," Billy responded.

Garrett didn't hear him. His eyes had been sorting through the pile of tools and other miscellany that had been shoved aside in the back of the pickup to make room for the hay spear: barbed wire, crowbars, salt blocks, shovels, baling twine, a fence stretcher, a plastic bucket ... a fully representative, if disorganized, profusion of ranching equipment. As the hay spear moved, his gaze caught on the flat back of one of the shovels. It had been shoved helter skelter under the other tools.

Something ... He leaned over, squinting into the truck at it. As he put out a tentative finger, Billy said, "What ya' got there, Sheriff?" He and Duz came around and stood on either side of Garrett, peering down to try to see what he was looking at.

"I'm not sure," Garrett said. "There's not much of it, if it is. Where have you been using this shovel here, Duz?" He pointed to the shovel in question.

Duz reached over to get the shovel, but Garrett said, "No, don't touch it. You see the one I mean, right?"

"Yeah, I do. I see the one you mean, down under that stuff there. But that ain't my shovel. I never noticed it in there, but you can see that it ain't my shovel. See there? Both my shovels got the blades sharpened, and they're kinda heavy duty for irrigatin'. That'n is old, worn down to half its original size. Looks like it gets used, now and again, but look at the nicks there in the blade. I couldn't get no good outta that."

The sheriff shot him a curious glance. "That's all fine, but where'd you get it? How'd it get in your truck?"

Duz looked baffled. "My golly, Sheriff! Beats me! I don't have any idea whatsoever." He was scratching his head.

Billy's eyes were running from the sheriff's face to Duz's. "Jesus Christ, Duz. How the hell can you be packin' around somebody else's shovel and not know where it come from?" There was a pause, then he added, "And what are you seein' about it, anyhow, Sheriff?"

Garrett pointed. "See this here? And this? And this? If I'm not mistaken, those are splatters of blood. They're little. And dried. So they ain't real clear ..."

Billy and Duz leaned closer. Billy said, "I'll be damned. It does look like ... yeah, it could be blood. How'd it get bloody, Duz?"

Duz was still shaking his head and frowning. "Like I said, it ain't my shovel. I absolutely have no idea what it is even doing back there. I've always got so much shit ... well, I just never paid any attention ... it's the last thing I would think to do, sort out the junk back here." He looked sheepish. "Unless I lost somethin'. I guess I'm pretty trashy. Carmen gets onta me ..."

Wonderingly, Billy continued to shake his own head. "Jesus Christ," he repeated, then said, "I suppose it ain't necessarily ... well, I mean, you think this shovel was in the shed, got splattered when Biedermann got shot? Or I suppose it could be animal blood? Maybe a dog or ...?"

Garrett felt grim, but he forced himself to speak calmly, as if it were all no big deal. "Look. We can clear it up pretty easy. Why don't I just gather this particular shovel up and bag it. I can drop it off at the crime lab. I'm headed that way anyhow ... they can tell us what kinda blood we got here and maybe even have a clue about whose shovel it is." He held his breath, not wanting to have to push his authority, while Duz Weinant continued to look with genuine perplexity at the offending shovel.

Finally, Duz, pulling at his chin, said, "Well, it don't make me no nevermind. That ain't my goddamn shovel, and I can't for the life of me figger what it's doin' in my truck."

22

Monday Morning Nine o'clock

Sheriff's Office, Riversmet

Garrett had not even had a chance to set foot in his office Monday morning before things started to pop. Clint and Patty Harris, holding hands, were waiting by the door to the back offices. Edith had let them in that far. Garrett looked over at her and scowled. Edith emigrated from Mexico thirty years ago, and she'd been working as receptionist for the sheriff's offices for the last twenty of them. She loved her job. A single mother, she'd raised her three kids by holding this job. Her name was Spanish, not pronounced 'Eeedith,' but instead, 'A-deet.' Her fiercely inventive approach to her work usually charmed Garrett, but today he wasn't charmed. He had wanted time in his office to get paperwork done before the problems of the day hit. Edith, apparently, was not sympathetic. She gazed back at him, raised her eyebrows, and shrugged.

Giving up, Garrett growled at the couple, "Come on back to my office." He snagged a cup of coffee from the counter top by Edith, snarling at her as he did so, "Way to go, *A-deet*." She just smiled innocently, keeping her eyes on her typing.

He got the Harrises seated in his office. They took straight back chairs and pulled them up to his desk, ignoring the easy chair by the bookcase. When he got himself seated, Patty began.

"We finally had some pillow talk Saturday night and realized we had to come see you."

Both of their faces were glowing. For Patty's face to glow would not have surprised him, but Clint's face was all aglow, too. To Garrett, Clint didn't look like the kind of guy who would ever glow at anything. Must have been *some* pillow talk, Garrett thought. What he said was, "Well, if you have something to tell me, I'm anxious to hear it."

Garrett was surprised that it was Clint's rusty, seldom-used voice that he heard next. Clint said, "You see, Sheriff, we were protectin' each other. I didn't stay at that water board meeting to the end. My dad, he gets to blowin' and goin', and it kinda embarrassed me. I just told him to come on, that we were goin' home, which we did. When we got there, Dad and I told Patty about the meeting and she got real upset." Patty gave his hand a squeeze, and he said, "We were both mad, I guess. We fought."

Patty threw in, "I've been on a short fuse lately."

For the first time, Clint grinned. "See, that's the problem, Sheriff. Patty don't get mad much, but when she does, you better get outta her way. But the last couple months she's been mad at me ever' time I turned around. I never knew when I was gonna step into a box of rattlers."

"I'm sorry," Patty said, eyeing him softly.

Clint returned the look before continuing. "So anyhow, I felt like she'd been about crazy enough lately to do anything. After we fought a few minutes, she just grabbed her gun and ran outta the house. She yelled something about how if I didn't have the guts to deal with Biedermann, she would, then she gunned the pickup outta the drive and left. She was gone quite awhile, at least forty-five minutes. I didn't know what she'd done, and she wouldn't tell me because she was still mad when she got back."

"And Clint," Patty interjected. "Clint told me he was in the barn working on the tractor from the time I left until he came into the house. He came in after the news had been over awhile, and, to be perfectly honest, I didn't actually see him. I just heard the radio in the barn. He's a guy where still waters run deep, you know?"

Garrett nodded. He was sure she was right about that much. She continued, "So after I heard about Biedermann being dead, I was afraid ... I was afraid maybe Clint hadn't really been in the barn. I ...." At this point, Patty Harris swallowed a sob of contrition, then continued. "I thought maybe I'd goaded him to do something we would regret all our lives."

Clint picked up the narrative. "So when you came around,

askin' questions, we were each protectin' the other one. I didn't wanna tell you nothin' because I was afraid it would get Patty in trouble. And I guess she was doin' the same, standin' by me. We just couldn't even talk to each other after that. We weren't mad anymore, just scared."

"Then Saturday night," Patty continued, "I broke down. See, I had two secrets I was keepin' from Clint, and I just couldn't hold out on him anymore."

"Two secrets?" Garrett said, and thought: Well, A-deet was right again. This may be worth the early morning hassle.

"Yeah, two. See, I kinda went ahead and secretly threw away our birth control pills a few months ago. I'd decided we just had to start our family, but Clint and I had been at logger-heads on it for years. He was so cautious. He wasn't sure we could do right by a kid.

"So I found out I was pregnant, but I couldn't get up the courage to tell him. I was afraid he'd blow up at me. I had this whole fear thing built up out of thin air — every time he came in the room I was ready to fight him, because I thought he was going to be angry about the baby."

"But of course I wasn't." Another soft look headed both ways. "I want this baby."

Patty nodded. "Both of us scared, I guess. See, it always pays to confront your fears. Once I told Clint about the baby, we just started talkin' and it all came out. The other part, too. About the gun."

Was it possible that Garrett's big ears moved forward? Or did he just lean in? "Gun?" he prompted.

"See, Sheriff. I have a secret vice. I couldn't bring myself to tell you about this. It is ... well, it is a crime. A petty crime, I hope. Just fines, maybe. Which I am willing to pay. But it is so embarrassing to think it is going to get out. Now all the neighbors ... I wouldn't tell *you* if I ... if I didn't see how serious this is."

Maybe he felt his own ears move. Garrett tried to pull back and give her space, afraid he might break the flow, but she went on.

"Tuesday evening, when we fought, Clint clammed up like he always does. It's a mean way to fight, because you don't know how to get the air cleared, so it leaves you stressed. Here was Clint looking like a tornado all over his face, and here was Lew, hopping around like a little fighter cock, so I just did what I always do. I yelled awhile, then left.

"I took the gun, got in the pickup, and went down the road shooting up every single sign that I could find. I ..." At this point Patty blushed, needing to swallow to continue. "I ... just love, absolutely *love*, to shoot up road signs." This was followed by a bubble of silence.

It was likely that Patty didn't realize that both Garrett and Clint were stifling grins. Garrett was fighting to look stern, and of law enforcement countenance, while Clint was keeping his eyes straight ahead, muzzling both amusement and pride.

"All day long I am so goody goody around the kids and parents and other teachers, and Clint is a wonderful man whom I hate to nag, but he does irritate me. And old Lew patters in and out. And you never know when he's brought Lucky along. So it just ... it just *helps*, sometimes, to be bad. To go do something that ... that flaunts authority and flies in the face of the rules. So ... Well, it's like a hobby. I shoot up signs." She looked up. "I'm sorry, Sheriff."

After a minute, Garrett found his voice. He had to restrain the urge to say, "Aw, it's all right."

Instead, he said, "Well, Mrs. Harris. For now, what we need to know is where you went, Tuesday night, and what you did with the gun. Was it you who threw it by the pond?"

She looked anxious. "Oh, no! No, not at all. I drove up Highway 46, toward Alma's, stopping and shooting away and reloading and shooting again, but I was so stirred up it wasn't helping. Before long I gave it up. I was gonna go home, but I just ... couldn't face Clint for a while yet. So I went on down to the Cowpath. I don't do that very often. I had a Sprite and poured out my troubles about the baby to Jenny Threewinds, and that helped a little. She's a soothing person. After that I went home. The ten o'clock news wasn't even half over when I left the Cowpath."

"And the gun?"

"Oh, I am so ashamed. I didn't put it away or anything. I left it right on the seat of the pickup when I went into the

Cowpath to see Jenny. Right in plain sight of anyone. And you know, nobody up our way ever locks a car. I left the Cowpath, but I didn't think twice about that gun until Wednesday evening.

"I stayed home from club; I'm one of those who gets morning sick all day, so it wasn't till Wednesday evening that I heard about Biedermann being shot in the shed. I went out to look in the pickup for my gun. It was gone."

"But you didn't try to report it or tell anyone?"

"I was afraid it was Clint. I was afraid he took the gun after I pulled into the yard. He would've had time after that to take it. I had this whole worry scenario in my head, him seeing Biedermann drive by and taking the gun and jumping in Lew's car and following and seeing Biedermann go into Alma's and him following him in and shooting him. Stupid. A stupid idea."

Patty Harris shook her head at the stupidity of her idea, while Garrett, not so sure, tried to sort through the information he was carrying in his head.

Clint cleared his throat. "What do we do about those signs, Sheriff? I never paid much attention to 'em before, never need 'em when you live in a place, but I drove on down there and she's pretty much got 'em riddled. Can we pay you for 'em?"

Garrett had to draw his attention back to consider this subsidiary problem. He'd been pinching his mustache and leaning forward on his desk, his head resting against his hand while he concentrated on the story. The best he could come up with was, "I'm not sure about the signs. Let me check into it, and we'll have to get back to you."

All of them shifted and shuffled, a feeling of completion having entered the room. The Harrises made a tentative move to stand, but Garrett cleared his throat. "I have a delicate question to ask you. A question on another subject that has been bothering me. Have you got another minute?"

They nodded and resettled, and he continued. "If this makes you uncomfortable, Mr. Harris, let it go, but Jenny told me that your grandmother died while she was in the middle of an argument with a young girl. A young girl who, I understand, was part of a youth rehabilitation program. I believe her name was Lindy Zakely. What I have been wondering about is, do you have any idea what it was that your grandmother and Lindy Zakely were arguing about?"

It took them a minute to shift gears. Clint blinked, then said, "Well, it was Patty who heard snatches of the argument. She was hanging wash, and ... well, Gramma didn't talk much, like me, but when she did, she had a real carrying voice, and Lindy was a yeller."

Patty nodded. "I didn't hear a lot of it, and I didn't realize until later that Gramma Lucky had fallen and that Lindy left. At first it worried me, because I thought maybe I could have helped her. She had clearly hit her head on a box that was sitting there, and I thought ... but the doctor told us in no uncertain terms that the failure of her heart was what caused her to go down. She was dead before she ever hit the ground." Both Clint and Patty's faces had sobered. Clint looked tired, Patty pale.

"But anyhow, I just heard snatches. I kind of put it together. Lucky always stuck up for the kids; she wanted them to make it. She wanted Lindy to stay and finish school here and to be sure she came out clean—I mean by that drug free—and strong enough to have a life, but it sounded like Lindy had decided to leave. She was ... from what I could hear, I think she had seen her father in the area, or heard that he might come back to the area, or something like that. She was really afraid of her father. She hated him. He abused her, you know. It was because of him that she ran away in the first place."

Garrett cleared his throat. "I see. Well, thanks for setting me straight on that." He looked at his watch, then stood, saying, "Thank you for coming in. You've been very helpful."

Although they didn't touch, they seemed to lean against each other going back down the hall to the exit door. Garrett, thoughtful, watched them until they left, and had just gone back into his office to try to get at his paperwork when his office door opened again. Asa Hobbs stood there, grinning in at him.

"Gotta minute?"

"Got as many as you do. Welcome back, Cowboy! How was the wedding?"

"Don't talk about it. How's the investigation?"

"Short a good detective. We're movin' on it, but most of the movement's in circles. I've got deputies from here to Stoney City tied up guardin' houses and boxes. Got McCracken down at the crime lab, tryin' to get a little hurry-up. Got no officers available if somethin' else breaks loose, and I got lots of information with no special theory."

Hobbs chuckled. "So I got a little a what you ain't got. Time. Fill me in. Then I also got a little somethin' to add to your fun."

"*You* got somethin'...?"

"I couldn't just go out gallavantin' around and leave you all the work, now could I, Mr. Garrett? But tell me what ya' know so far." Clearly Hobbs was happy to be back.

Garrett told. He gave him the rundown, laughing when he got to the part about the .38. "McCracken'll be madder than hell that she isn't here to listen to you gloat about your prescient powers when it comes to guns. And she'd like to rub it in about it gettin' found after you sayin' it wouldn't."

Hobbs chortled. "I'll just bet she would."

"And," finished Garrett, "Besides this deal this morning with the Harrises, I guess the other most recent thing I learned was that they got done goin' through those boxes yesterday evenin'. No quit claim deeds. No drugs. No motive."

"Does that surprise you?"

"Not as much as some of this other stuff has."

Hobbs was sitting in the easy chair, looking toadlike again. "You say that Mrs. Weinant, the older one ... she says she heard shots on Tuesday night?"

"The Patty Harris deal probably explains that. It also tells me that the old gal isn't as dotty as you might think. Sounds like Harris really went wild, shot up signs all the way up the road."

"I s'pose. Could be. Well ..." Detective Hobbs, ready for his part, rummaged in his breast pocket. "You ever hear of Kid Lida Meter?"

"Who?"

"Kid Lida Meter." Hobbs had extracted some folded papers from his pocket. He thumbed the top one off and handed it to Garrett. It was a photocopy of a glossy promotional picture, a picture of a person of questionable gender with spikey hair, a ring in the nose, heavy army boots, and bulky shirt and pants. "That's her. Kid Lida Meter. She was the rapper at my little Coreen's wedding."

Garrett stared at the picture. "Shit!" he said. You could see why Hobbs had been unnerved by his daughter's choice of wedding musician.

"Yeah, she's a ugly one, ain't she?" Hobbs chuckled again. "Music wasn't too pretty either. Whatever. Water under the bridge. But anyhow, I brought that picture. Look real close at it. Anything about it look familiar?"

Garrett squinted at the picture. The woman did look familiar. Mac and Alice were still gone. Was it Alice Biedermann? No, that was just the nose ring. No, she looked like ... but who?

"So, did you figure it out?"

Garrett shook his head. "Looks familiar, but ..."

"How about this one?" Hobbs handed him the other piece of paper he was holding. It, too, was a photocopy of a glossy picture. The woman in it was older, and the picture looked as if it had been taken when styles were different, maybe ten or twenty years ago. "Well?"

"I've seen this woman. She was ... well, I think I saw her in a movie called ... called *Ramses the King*, kind of an epic film ... she would have been supporting actress..."

"Marla Mary Meter?"

"That's her. That's the name. She was a big name in movies a few years back ... Ahhh! Kid Lida Meter ... Marla Mary Meter. Related?"

Hobbs grinned. "Like mother and daughter. I saw that rapper and it ate on me and ate on me. Finally, I got it out of Coreen and Wiseass just before they left for the honeymoon. Who she was. She's Marla Mary Meter's daughter."

"Well, how about that. I think Marla Mary used to do rhythm and blues before she turned out to be too glamorous for that and ended up in films. Too bad she couldn't have done some R and B at the wedding." Garrett gathered up the photos and handed them toward Hobbs.

"Oh, I ain't just tryin' to hype up celebrities here," Hobbs said, making a pushing gesture toward the papers. "Take another look at the photo of your friend, Ms. Marla Meter. You sure she doesn't look familiar, if you think of her in another context?"

Garrett stared at the picture again and shook his head. Hobbs, he knew, had a great skill with respect to recognizing faces, but he himself had trouble placing anyone if they weren't where he saw them in the first place. It helped if they wore the same clothes, too. "Nope. I don't recognize this lady at all."

"Marla Mary Meter dropped out, you know. Disappeared a couple of years back with the fan magazines screaming like crazy, rumors of husband number five deserted at the altar, rumors of death by drug overdose, rumors of kidnapping ... and none of the rumors confirmed. Seems that at least to some people, she's a missing person."

"A missing person," Garrett echoed, still trying to get a read on the picture.

"Missing to some. But I'd bet a real pretty penny that you have run into her several times in the past week. Marla Mary Meter. How does that name sound as a stage name or a variation on Maggie Merimeister?"

"Well, I'll be damned," Garrett said. Like an optical illusion, the alternate personality in the picture clicked into place.

23

Later Monday Morning

Riversmet County Courthouse

It was past ten and Hobbs had gone back to his office to play catch up, but after the early morning rush, Sheriff Garrett couldn't concentrate on his paper work. He found himself doubting everything and everybody about the case. He stacked and restacked a pile of forms, put his feet up on his desk, and fiddled with a pen while staring out the vertical sliver of window that sidled down beside his bookcase. Nothing made sense. Finally, he wondered if quit claim deeds were the solution that Lew Harris had trumpeted them to be. He decided to head for the county clerk's office across the hall and find out.

Once he had unfolded himself from his chair and stepped into the big hall that was central to the building, however, he had to give in to the restlessness that was possessing him. He ignored the county clerk's door across the way and climbed up the heavy stairs, where he stood at the top, again gazing out a window and wondering if he should just forget the paperwork here and head back up to Oozle. To do what? His legs carried him on down the hall.

Without assimilating them, he read bulletins that were fixed to a board that hung beside the D.A.'s office. Victim advocacy. Right to counsel. Finally he swung around the corner and idled beside the courtroom door, reading the docket. Smith vs. Harcourt. Attorneys Loren Sweeney and Harvey Katzenbinder. Gaston vs. Jamison. Attorneys Jim Barstow and John Duval. Ah, sure. John Duval. He could ... should try to follow up with John Duval. After all, Biedermann had had a

Duval card on his desk; what was that all about? Next case: Beekerman-Shipley vs. Shipley. Attorneys John Duval and Loren Sweeney.

Huh? Beekermann? Was that Christa? Christa *Biedermann*? Hadn't Duval said that her married name was Shipley? He peered closely at the entry, as if somehow the letters would rearrange themselves if he looked hard enough. Beekermann. Biedermann. Hadn't Christa ... or was it Mac? ... hadn't one of them said that Reider wasn't even their father? Or maybe the clerk had just typed it in wrong.

He scratched his chin, then turned on his heel to return to his office. This one he needed to get straight. He would have Edith set up an appointment for him with Duval as soon as possible. The Beekermann-Shipley vs. Shipley (was it 'that asshole, Les'?) hearing was set for 1:00 p.m. He decided he would be there.

So, he thought, Alma and her three's, eh? First Maggie Merimeister had proved to be someone else with a different name, and now it looked as if at least one of the Biedermanns was perhaps not Biedermann at all, but Beekermann, for whatever that was worth. If Alma was right, and everything came in three's, who else in this illogical world would prove to be an impostor with another name?

He made it back to the door of the hallway leading to the sheriff department offices, where the Harrises had accosted him that morning, only to look up and see McCracken standing by, waiting. His face must have fallen because as she stepped forward she said, "Sorry, Chief."

"So, you didn't get the report yet?"

"No, I got the report. I'm just not sure you'll be real pleased with how it went."

"Oh, boy." His voice was tense; he was beginning to get a headache. "How'd it go?"

"Well, first of all, they finally managed to get a DNA cross-match on that blood I found in front of the shed."

"Well, good. Was it Biedermann's?"

"No, it wasn't." McCracken shuffled through the papers she was carrying and produced a report. She turned to lay it on the reception counter, the one on which Edith was leaning with both elbows and a fascinated expression on her face. Garrett followed her pointing finger to the relevant lines of the report. Sample A did not match that of the victim, but originated from a person unknown. Sample B did not match that of the victim, but originated from a person unknown. Sample C ...

Garrett was reading the report out loud, and Edith said, "Wowsy. That can be a clue or a disaster, huh?"

Appreciatively, Garrett nodded. "You said it, A-deet. 'Person unknown' plops it back into the misty realm of fable. Maybe the attacker ... What else you got, Mac?"

"They really went over the shovel, Chief. The only prints on that sucker were Duz Weinant's."

Garrett gave a low whistle. "I'll be damned. And the spots that looked like blood splatters?"

"They were blood splatters." McCracken was sorting papers again, laid the report on the counter and read from the filled-in blanks. "Sample A—matches that of all samples from victim. Sample B—matches ..."

Garrett interrupted. "I get the picture. Sounds like the shovel that whacked Biedermann. And it sounds like it was wielded by Duz Weinant. Shit." He pushed the papers around on the counter, then said, "Or maybe it wasn't. Look, A-deet. Give the D.A. a call, and I'll run down to my office and get the path report. McCracken and I need to go and have a chat with her if she's in."

* * * * * * * * * *

Their "chat" with the D.A. lasted nearly an hour, escalating to heated argument and then back several times, Garrett doing the talking and McCracken merely squirming in the hard-backed chair. It didn't take the course that Garrett would have liked it to take. They looked at the report and discussed opportunity: Who was completely without an alibi? Duz Weinant. They discussed motive: Who was so deeply upset by the water issue that he had left the board meeting before any of the other members? Duz Weinant. They discussed personality: Who seemed always jolly, so jolly that it felt unnatural ... a man who must have a dark side? Duz Weinant. Finally, to whom, of all the people Garrett had interviewed, did the evidence point?

Well, the D.A.'s theory of the crime was that it was originally a crime of passion, the victim struck in anger with the back of the shovel, perhaps killed, then dragged into the shed as a cover-up.

After that, something more sinister happened, something truly cold-blooded. According to the D.A., the murderer must have gone to the Cowpath, perhaps to get a drink to ease his nerves. He went edgy and worried, afraid the victim might revive to tell what had happened or, maybe worse, to return to his scheme of water theft. Maybe he would come around and threaten Alma ... in fact, that may have been the issue that got him cold-cocked in the first place. Whatever it was, the murderer ... Weinant ... was not happy. Then he spotted the gun in Patty's pickup and recognized a perfect opportunity. Instead of entering the saloon, he put on gloves and took the gun, leaving Patty's prints but not his own, and returned to the shed to deliver the *coup de grâce*. Weinant would feel secure to do this because no one would suspect him of trying to incriminate his friends, the Harrises. Such was the D.A.'s theory.

But why, argued Garrett, who felt increasingly uneasy with the fit between crime and criminal the more the D.A. felt secure that the crime had been solved, why the gun beside the pond?

Easy one, said the D.A., who didn't know any of the people she was preparing to indict. "Duz Weinant wanted the gun to be found. It didn't point to Weinant. It pointed to someone else; for all he knew, it pointed to the old guy, Lew Harris, right?"

The D.A. was a logical and convincing woman. She was also opinionated. The less Garrett felt comfortable with Duz as prime suspect, the more convinced she became that he was just too timid to act on a sure thing. By the time the three had chewed the evidence to death, it was noon, and the D.A. stood up and said flatly, "Arrest him."

"*Arrest* him?"

"You have probable cause. It all lines up. This guy, the Weinant guy, he did the job. That guy in the shed, Garrett, what you're thinking is that he was a bad piece of work. You think it over. There isn't one person up there that you would like to see convicted of killing him, because it sounds like if anyone deserved to get it, he did. And it sounds like all the rest of the community is made up of the good guys. But that has nothing to do with justice. Somebody up there is a murderer, and the evidence tells me that justice will be served if you get up there and pick up Duz Weinant before he just 'kind of disappears,' like Mac and Alice Biedermann did. Thank god none of the real evidence pointed to *them*."

After this diatribe, all Garrett could say was, "Arrest him?"

"Yes, Sheriff. Think about the evidence. Think about who most likely knew about those deeds in his mother's shed. Nice guy or not, you do have a duty."

Garrett said, "We'll see," but when they left her office he had begun to believe the D.A. was right. All the evidence pointed directly at Duz Weinant. If he were thinking objectively, wouldn't he think Weinant was the guy? Arresting Duz would keep him where they wanted him, he rationalized. It didn't mean Garrett would have to stop the investigation.

He walked heavily down the stairs, McCracken tagging behind, and turned to face her at the landing.

"What do you think, McCracken?"

"It ain't him, Chief."

"Because ...?"

Her face reflected his total misery. "It just ain't. I don't know why."

"You don't know why." There was a long pause. "Well, Mac. I guess you better go up and arrest him, then."

"Me!"

Garrett looked at his watch. "I gotta go sit in on a court hearing at 1:00. You never know how long they will take." He was dumping on her, and he knew it, but he just couldn't bring himself to do it.

"So I gotta..."

"Yeah, Leigh. You gotta go bring him in."

24

Seven o'clock Monday Night

At the County Jail

Even in her wheelchair, Greta Amelia (after Greta Garbo and Amelia Earhart) Anderson (her married name) was one brisk, no-nonsense woman. She and her husband, Mel, were both electrical engineers. They had sent their three children to good colleges and they gave their grandchildren problems in mathematics before they ever hit age three. Children, they said, should learn clear thinking early on.

Alma pleaded relentlessly for Greta and Mel to visit, but when they visited they nearly drove her crazy with their efficiency. Greta, wasteful, would throw out left-overs before their time. Alma griped and grumbled. Greta, disruptive, would clean and rearrange Alma's cupboards and closets while Mel did repairs around the place, confusing Alma's sense of space. "You have disorientated me," said Alma. Then the time would come and they would go, leaving emptiness behind. Alma, alone, wept.

Greta Amelia was storming up the jailhouse ramp now. No one in the world could get under her skin as effectively as her big brother, Duz, and she was ready to confront him.

Early on, in the life of the community, her beautiful name had been condensed to a nickname; because of her willingness to tackle everything from dirt to donuts, her family and schoolmates had termed her 'Gritty.' 'Gritty,' however, was just not enough for Duz. At every opportunity, he taunted her with "Shitty Gritty." The worst part was that behind her back at school, kids began to join him in expanding upon the moniker. When she caught a couple of them giggling about "Shitty Gritty," she kicked them good and ended up in the principal's office.

Word, of course, got home to Alma, and Duz got his mouth washed out with soap. It seemed, for the most part, to end there, although at a class reunion a few years back she had overheard someone say, "Can that be Shitty Gritty? The one over there in the wheelchair?" She could no longer kick them, but she barely controlled her urge to get close enough to ram them with the wheelchair.

Well, now that damn Duz was at it again. How could he have gotten himself jailed, for Christ's sake! For homicide, for Christ's sake? She leaned forward in the chair, urging it to speed up. Didn't he know she had things to do? He just was not effective. His happy-jolly-joker-this-and-that put him in danger of being misunderstood. She just hated the big klutz. That was probably why she had dropped everything she was doing, when Carmen called, and caught the first plane headed this way out of Denver.

Once her wheelchair had popped off the top of the ramp and she and Carmen had been processed and were being conducted to the cells, she felt a little calmer. On the way over from the airport, Carmen had told her all that she knew, but now that she could talk to Duz in person, she expected to get to the bottom of things.

Even in a jail cell, Duz was Duz. When the warden let them in, he greeted them with the same hospitable solicitude and happy smile that he would have exhibited had he been welcoming them into his living room. "Glad to see you two," he said, and one sensed that he would have offered cookies and cakes had it been within his power.

Gritty opened with, "So Duz. What's going on here?"

"Well, Saturday morning Billy Brown and I were working on the hay spear. I suspect Carmen told you about that. The damn thing broke just before we were done feeding in May, and I wanted to get it fixed as soon as possible, because you know how stuff comes up. Speaking of which, when I get out of here, I need to fix that fence at the lower corner next to Nancy's place. I was just getting ready to get to it yesterday and ..."

Gritty interrupted drily. "And your point would be, you

needed the hay spear to kill your next victim?"

Duz looked up at her and laughed. "Ah, come on, Grit. You and I never get to talk ..." He paused, unable to resist joking, "Except when I'm in jail. I just wanted to visit a little bit."

Carmen, whose brow wore an uncustomary worry line, said, "Cut it out, Duz. This is serious. You need to get to the point. They only gave us a half hour here."

Duz made his face sober. "Well, okay. Bottom line is, get me a good lawyer and send him over. They got a sample of my blood. I'm not sure I should've let 'em do that. And one thing I do want to get at, before we get on other subjects, is that Sheriff Garrett is real interested in some water deeds he thinks I may have."

"Water deeds?"

"Yeah, Gritty. Carmen told you what was going on with this Biedermann trying to file on old rancher water, right?"

"She told me."

"Well, Lew Harris remembered that Mom was secretary of the water board at the time that the ranchers realized their original deeds did not have water rights settled. I guess they took out quit claim deeds, but it was the year you got hurt and those deeds got as far as Mom and no farther."

Duz got up from the edge of his bunk and began to pace. "It sounds like they think that Biedermann found out that Mom might have the deeds, and he went up to destroy them. Then they think that I went up and caught him there.

"They think I either remembered about the deeds, too, and tried to stop him, or that I perceived him as threatening my mother. Either way, they figure I clobbered him with the shovel, then drug 'im in the shed and shot 'im."

Carmen said, "Wow," but Gritty said, "So did you?"

"No, of course not. I don't go around hitting people with shovels." He hesitated. "*And* if I did, I wouldn't go get somebody else's gun and shoot 'em afterwards. Especially not an unconscious guy. Not in the back. *And* if I did, I wouldn't get my friend's gun so that my friend would be incriminated for my own crime."

"I would think not," said Gritty drily, "But why do *they* think you did?"

"Like I started to say, Saturday while we were fixin' the hay spear — oh, but anyhow, I wanted to tell you, Carmy, that they are sure that somehow I have those quit claim deeds. You should probably expect some guys with a search warrant to be up to go through our stuff. They think I'm bein' shifty and just won't tell 'em where they are."

"And are you?" asked Gritty.

"Jesus Christ, Gritty, get over it! I have no idea where the damn things are ... I wish I'd known before all this happened and old Biedermann would still be alive to concoct some other harebrained scheme."

"Okay, so we believe you," Gritty said, speaking for both herself and her sister-in-law, who, however, was looking with narrowed, assessing eyes at Duz as she might at a fish she was about to place into a new perspective in one of her paintings. "But," continued Gritty, "The best I seem to get out of you is that you were making plans to spear ..."

"Come on, Sis. I'm just tryin' to tell the story straight, because this part is important. See, the sheriff came up while we were fixin' the spear. It was in the back of my truck, and we were all leanin' over the side, workin' and talkin', when he looked in and thought he saw blood on a shovel in there."

Gritty started to say, "And did he," but she could see that finally Duz was on point, so she figured she'd better shut up. Duz continued.

"Anyhow, he asked if he could take the shovel for testing. I didn't think twice about that. I knew I never killed nobody. But I was real baffled about the shovel."

"Because ...?"

"Because I never seen that shovel before. I still can't figure out how it got in my pickup. And when Garrett came down to see me, he told me the blood was, for sure, Biedermann's. DNA tests. I really don't know what's goin' on, but I think all I need is a good lawyer. After all, I didn't kill the guy."

"Duz," Carmen said, "When I called the sheriff, he said that your fingerprints, and only *your* fingerprints, were on that shovel. How could that happen and you not have seen the shovel before?"

"I dunno. I suppose I moved it over to get at somethin' back there. Somebody must have killed Biedermann and put the shovel in my pickup, then I just didn't pay attention." He spread his hands, a bid for understanding. "Carmy, you know how the back of my pickup looks."

It was true. Alma had always described Gritty as "the neat one." She didn't mention the potato chips, pop cans, and tinker toys that crunched under everybody's feet in Duz's room, nor did she elaborate on the little trucks that tripped everybody on the porch step, the ropes left out in the snowstorm by the yard fence, nor the bolts, rocks, and weeds found in pockets in the laundry. She left that part unsaid, which made it said enough.

Gritty rocked her wheelchair back and forth. It was her equivalent of tapping her toe. What Duz said made sense, as far as it went, but she wasn't as trusting of the court system as he was. A jury could well not believe Duz. He had always come off as a little too mellow to be true. And how many murderers claimed in court that they *did* kill the victim? The D.A. could convince a jury that, heck, why figure some other guy planted the shovel when Duz's prints were all over it and it was Duz who had every reason to want to see the end of Reider Biedermann?

She didn't voice her doubts. Instead, she said, "We have the question of where the quit claim deeds are now, right? Have they looked in the shed?"

"Have they ever!" Carmen exploded. "They took every single box down to the clubhouse and moshed through them. They were *their* version of careful, I suppose, but I felt bad for Alma."

"Right. So ... okay. I'll work on that. Then we also have the question of who the heck would kill for the sake of water and throw that shovel in the back of you guys' truck. Any ideas, people?"

"Look, Gritty. You know 'em," Duz said. "Try to visualize 'em, our neighbors, any one of 'em, takin' a murderous swipe at Biedermann. I've been thinkin' about it. Yeah, I can see 'em mad. I can visualize Lew Harris hoppin' around with his nose all bent out of joint. Or I can see big John Michaelson figurin' he'd have a talk with Reider, then maybe losin' his temper. Stuff like that." He paused for emphasis. "But I can't imagine any of them mean enough and mad enough that they would carry out that kind of a murder — whack the guy, then have time to think about it, then go get a gun, and *then* shoot 'im in the back. With a stolen gun."

An expression of distaste. "It was Patty Harris's gun. Garrett told me that. I got the impression Garrett felt he shouldn't be telling me stuff, but that he was gonna give me the best chance to defend myself that he could."

And that, thought both of the women, would be the way that Duz would think. It would never have occurred to him that the sheriff might have been trying to get him talking so that he would incriminate himself. Duz always thought the other guy was somehow well intentioned and on the right side, until .... Gritty fidgeted. She wanted to get on the road and start working on this problem.

Carmen said, "Maybe it was a different motive. It just about had to be a different motive, and someone besides the people we know around here."

Duz started to comment that he supposed that was true, but Gritty interrupted. "Has anyone talked to Mom? What does she think about all this?"

"Ah, Grit, you know Mom. She found the body, then she forgot to tell anybody for two or three hours."

"Well, yeah, Duz, but she did tell somebody, didn't she? Eventually? She remembered under the right circumstances. Maybe ..."

"You think you might be able to jog her memory? That maybe she knows something we don't? Something about why somebody would do it, maybe, or maybe she saw something that she forgot ..."

"It won't hurt to try. It looks like I'll be staying for a few days," she started to turn her wheelchair, "and Carmen and I can talk strategy on the way up. Maybe you'll think of something down here, too. Looks like you might have time enough on your hands." At this last statement Duz got such a pained expression that she was sorry she said it. Naturally, he would be stewing about the spring ranch work not getting done because he was sitting in this cell.

"Look, Duz," Gritty said, "You know we'll do everything we can to get you out of here as soon as possible. You know that."

"I know that, Grit." He looked as if he would have liked to give her a hug, but she and her brother had not been raised as huggers, so she squeezed his hand, then headed down the hall. Carmen, who did take time for a hug, had to run to catch up. When she did, they both turned for one last look at their embattled male. He was standing by the bars looking after them, a smile on his face that was sweet with the longing of a pup dog left chained to the garage while the children ran to play. He extended a hand through the bars and waved. They waved back; it would be hard to say which of them, at that instant, was the more resolved to get him out ... guilty or not.

The minute she had the car on the main road, Carmen said, "Look, Gritty, I didn't want to talk about this in the jail. I know better, but I've got television ideas about all jail cells being bugged and I can't shake 'em. But anyhow, tell me again about how Duz used to lose his temper when you were growing up with him."

Gritty's face was grim. "Right. I kept thinking of that, too, but I figured it would offend him to bring it up. He was kind of small when he was a kid growing up. Littler than the other guys his age. When I saw him lose it, it was always in circumstances where he thought some big wrong was being done, and where he thought he had to fight like hell because he was up against somebody bigger or he was taking on more than one person."

"So he was a little guy who was mad and scared?" Carmen said, "Maybe kind of like one of those Vikings ... I think they were called berserkers? The reason it reminds me of that is that I think you have told me that ... well, you know what's worrying me. You've told me that he would kind of black out when he got like that. That's what the berserkers did in battle, I think."

"Yeah, he did. It was scary. Sometimes it took him a day or two to fully re-enter reality. The worst time that I remember him doing it, and the last time, was when he was a teenager. Two big guys had me cornered in the barn at a big family whoopty-do. You know, I was always sassing, and these were second cousins once removed, boys, and they had me backed up in a stall. I was about twelve and they were about Duz's age, about sixteen. Old enough to know better. But they were getting carried away, and I was so dumb and innocent, I was just being a smart ass, still.

189

"Duz came in just as one lifted my dress. When he saw what was going on, Carmen, you know, he did pick up a board and he knocked the biggest guy over the head. The big old ugly lummox, he didn't even drop, and the board broke. But both guys turned and came at Duz, and he fought so hard, and I got into the fray. I swung a milk bucket and hit one guy on the arm. It left a major bruise."

"Did you and Duz get hurt?"

"No, that was the thing. Duz got this crazy look on his face, and I'll tell you, not too many people would have wanted to tackle him at that point. As soon as they could, those two broke and ran. Then Duz grabbed me and shook me so hard, it hurt, and told me to get up to the house and stay there and mind my manners. It was one time I did what he said."

"The circumstances seem a little different than this deal. I can't imagine old Gentle Ben Duz getting that mad at Biedermann."

"Not unless he came across Biedermann doing something he shouldn't be doing to somebody else, and that somebody else isn't talking. The thing I remember about that time he lost it in the barn—the thing that worries me—is that it took him two days to get his head on straight again. When I tried to talk about it, he didn't seem to recall the incident. I'll bet he still doesn't. Like he'd had an epileptic seizure or something.

"And he was still in a daze all the next day. Dad would send him to do something and he would just 'duh' around about it, get it half done. He wasn't himself. Maybe it was ... just worry. I don't know." They both lapsed into thoughtful silence.

Carmen stared at the road in front of her, trying to recall that night, last Tuesday after she'd gotten home from the meeting. She hadn't thought twice about Duz. She'd been tired. She figured he was at the water board meeting and would be home soon, so she'd just crawled into bed and gone into a light sleep.

It didn't seem long after that that Duz had slipped in beside her, and knowing he was safe, she'd nestled down for the night. But hadn't she heard his ...? Duz had told her, told the sheriff, told everyone ... that he had come home about nine and walked up to the water divider box. He had spent a long time up there, alone, thinking. Then he had come home to her.

She'd been expecting to hear his pickup pull into the yard from the board meeting, but he said he had come walking home to her. Then he had slipped peacefully into bed beside her. But hadn't her expectation been fulfilled?

She tried to remember. Hadn't she heard his pickup pull in—even in a light sleep, she knew the engine of that pickup— hadn't she heard it pull in, not long before Duz came up the stairs?

25

Eight o'clock Tuesday Morning

Alma's House

Gritty resisted her natural instincts. Her natural instincts were to say, "Hey, Mom. We've got big problems here. Your son and my brother, Duz, is in jail because of that body you found out in the chicken shed. We gotta sit down and come up with what it is that really happened to that guy, or Duz's gonna be walkin' the old Green Mile. For example, where did you store the quit claim deeds that year?"

No, Gritty couldn't do that. In the first place, Alma hadn't been told about Duz being in jail. Gritty had spent the night with Carmen, where they rehashed their strategies and brain-stormed ways to jog Alma's memory. Taking her to Biedermann's funeral today would be one. People would be there. Who knew what Alma would come up with? Friendly morning chats would be another. Shocking her, by telling her that her best, favorite, and only son was in jail on suspicion of homicide would definitely not be the memory jogger of choice.

The problem of her unannounced appearance on Alma's doorstep was resolved rather easily. When Alma, her voice melting with joy, said, "Why Gritty! I didn't know you were coming!" Gritty replied, "Oh, Mom. Didn't you remember that I told you I had a couple of days off? I thought we might ..." she cleared her throat. This was pushing it. "I thought we might get some spring cleaning done, maybe go through some of the boxes in the shed or ..." She gave her mother a hug and plopped down in a chair.

Alma looked worried. "Honey, I think some other people

have been going through those boxes. I believe the shed is empty right now. I don't know if they ... I just don't understand what they think they are doing with my things, but everyone seems to think it's the right thing to do."

"Really!" Gritty said. "Well, now that I'm here, we'll have to see what those people are up to. Has somebody been up already to get you your breakfast and meds?"

"I don't know." Alma looked around sharply, as if someone might have sneaked in and medicated her when she wasn't looking.

"Which one would have come, Mom?"

"Well, now, there's Mary. And Victoria. And sometimes," she finished roundly, proud to have remembered every name, "Sometimes there is Jeannie."

"And who would be coming this morning?"

Alma smiled. She knew irrelevant questions when she heard them. "I really don't know, Sweetie. Are you hungry?"

Gritty almost said she had had a bite before she left Carmen's, but she caught herself. Instead, she got on task. "Oh, no. I just thought I'd call and tell whoever would be coming that I would feed you breakfast, if that would work for them." She rolled across and rummaged in the papers by the phone. The list of health care nurses turned up about fifth down and she had a stroke of luck because Mary was just heading out the door when she rang to volunteer her services. Alma's "girl" was glad of the break.

It wouldn't be fruit and cereal. Alma loved a hearty meal, so they sat down at last to bacon, eggs, toast, juice, and coffee. Alma was thrilled with the coffee. "I don't drink coffee every day," she exulted. "Dad and I used to love coffee, you know, but I don't suppose it is good for my health now I'm getting older, is it?"

Over breakfast Gritty continued to wrestle her old urge to confide in her mother. She had to tell herself that it just wouldn't work any more. Instead they discussed the health of Uncle Frank and the beauty of the petunias donated by Maggie Merimeister. An opening finally came when Alma said, "You know, it seems so many people have been around here these days. I don't know when we have had so much company." Gritty seized the moment.

"Really, Mom? Why has there been so much company lately?"

"It has something to do with the shed, those boxes in the shed. Maybe people wanted to see what I've been storing out there all these years. There are some very good things there, you know."

Gritty felt awkward. She didn't want to disillusion her mother about the value of the boxes in the shed, but ... "Mom, P.D. told me you had a body in the shed. I don't think he knows what he's talking about, does he?"

It had been the right comment to make. Alma looked relieved. "Oh, yes. That's what it was. I just could not for the life of me remember. I forget so much these days."

"I know, Mom." Gritty patted her hand. "Whose body was it? Did P.D. find it?"

"Why no! Of course not! *I* found that body. Are people saying somebody else found it?" That's good, thought Gritty. Getting the dander up might keep the focus.

"Oh, no. I was just wondering. When did you find it?"

"Yesterday, I think it was. Lots of people came over and they took out boxes and so-on. The sheriff was even here. The man was killed, you know. Shot."

"Shot! Oh, Mom, that must have been a shock! What did you do when you found the body?"

Alma chuckled. "Now *that* I remember. I was just so embarrassed. You see, I was trying to get my club gift, so I was thinking about that, and I forgot to tell anyone about the body. Did I tell you that I keep forgetting everything these days?"

It was clear that this conversation could go in more than one direction. Gritty hoped she was choosing the right one. "So did you find your club gift? It must have been hard to look for anything in the shed with a body right there."

Alma nodded, vindicated. Only her daughter Gritty would be perceptive enough to realize the frustration she had felt that day. She could almost feel it again now.

"Honey, you just don't know. I wanted something nice, something I could be proud to give. I should have remembered to have one of my girls pick up something in town, but I forgot, so I didn't want to embarrass myself with trash. But when that man turned up in there, well ... I thought I shouldn't touch him or move him."

"That would be right," Gritty affirmed. "You are not supposed to disturb the scene of a crime."

"Well, I didn't disturb it ... much. I brought that box over there in, and it didn't have anything, so I just left it there." Alma gestured vaguely across the room. "Never had a chance to get it back out. Then I looked through and finally found that little Empire State Building bell, the one Dad and I got in New York. Do you remember that?

What box? Gritty's eyes sought the box. She saw nothing. The conversation about the bell was an uphill climb, but she restrained herself, letting her mother tell about the trip to New York which had taken place years ago. Alma's face flushed with pleasure as she relived Radio City Music Hall and the visits to fancy restaurants after riding the California Zephyr to New York all the way from Colorado. Alma had reached a lengthy description of the speed of the train, the scenery, and service in the dining car when Gritty decided it was safe to interject.

"Mom, you said you brought a box in from the shed ..."

"I what?"

"You said, earlier, that you brought a box in from the shed when you were trying to get a club gift. Where did you put the box?"

"Did I say that? I just don't remember things like I used to, Gritty."

"Did you bring a box into the house? When you got the club gift?"

"Well, I don't know. Let me see. Seems I ... seems I may have. Now why did you bring that up?"

"Where did you put it? The box?"

"Why, I put it right over there. Behind Dad's chair. I told you that!"

"Oh," Gritty said, looking. Sure enough, the corner of a box was barely protruding from behind the chair. Then Gritty, to be kind said, "Oh, that's right. You did tell me. I'm sorry ... I forgot."

Alma felt tired. Sometimes today's youth could wear one down, she thought, the way they never listened to anything. Gritty smiled at her.

"Let's get your meds and settle you down," she ventured.

"Then I'll clean up around here, pick up the breakfast dishes and so on. Maybe, while I'm at it, I can take that box back out to the shed for you?"

This all sounded fine to Alma, who sat in her chair and nodded off. Gritty wheeled around the table, gathering dishes, and as Alma at last dozed, she made a run for her father's chair and the box behind it.

It took her quick hands less than fifteen minutes. She called Carmen on the kitchen phone, speaking quietly. "Mom's asleep, but why don't you come on over. It probably won't mean much for Duz—they'll only have our word that he himself hadn't hidden them in here or something. But for what it is worth, the quit claim deeds were here. They were in one of those accordion files, marked 'Oozle Water Board,' and smashed down under clippings and letters in a box behind Dad's old chair."

26

Tuesday Morning, Nine o'clock

Peaseford: The Office of John Duval

"Yes, he changed the will." John Duval was clearly not happy to have to talk about it. He had averted his eyes, a behavior that affected Garrett the way that Duval always affected Garrett. Whatever attorneys were supposed to look like, somehow Duval just didn't fill the bill. The sheriff never saw him as an officer of the court. Every time Garrett encountered him, he saw a member of a lineup.

Garrett pondered why. Duval consistently showed up in court in Levis, running shoes, and a large-plaid (maroon and blue today), crumpled cotton shirt, the buttons on the button-down collar loose, leaving the collar to curl and flop. He always had an incongruously expensive-looking fountain pen jammed into the shirt pocket. He was a young man—early forties, at most, would be Garrett's guess—but he suffered a high, bald forehead, which he attempted to cover by combing long strands of his few remaining greasy-looking brown locks upwards and sideways across the shine.

That was the way he dressed, but it wasn't that. No, it wasn't the way he dressed or combed his hair. Those were just personal eccentricities. And the shirt was clean. Garrett considered Duval's demeanor as the man spoke. He decided that his subconscious urge to arrest him came from the attorney's hooded eyes, lids half down as if to cover sneaky, sly, criminal thoughts. There was also the mouth. It was slack, as if dropped neutrally into the face, but just at the tips of the lips it curved up slightly, soliciting permission or understanding from some unnamed authority. Garrett tried to be objective whenever he had to deal with him, but face it, the little runt looked shifty.

It had been tough going with him today, too. Garrett had followed him into his office, folded himself into a chair, and opened with the question as to whether Biedermann had a will. The thing was, he hadn't been sure that Duval was even Biedermann's attorney, but because he and McCracken had come away knowing Duval's card was on Reider's desk when they visited Victoria, he decided to bluff. When he asked the question, a dull flush crossed the attorney's face and his eyes shifted, then he invoked attorney-client privilege. He didn't want to talk.

Garrett shrugged. "Look, John. We have the CBI on this case. And we have people working with N.C.I.C., getting background on the Biedermann family. At one point or another, you're going to have to cough up what you know or somebody else will tell us anyhow. It may as well be from you to me, and it may as well be now rather than later." So finally, Garrett, running his bluff as far as he could, got the man talking.

Yes, Reider Biedermann had a will. Yes, he had changed it. "He changed it three times, in fact," Duval continued. "The last time was Friday before last."

Garrett nodded knowingly, as if this were what he had suspected all along, although, in fact, he had been dismissing this line of inquiry as irrelevant to the case. Now he said, "Tell me about that."

"I didn't draw up his original will. In that document, he willed everything he had to his wife at the time."

"His wife at the *time*?"

"Right. He was married to the mother of his third child up until about five or six years ago, and the will was a simple paper leaving everything to her. But it was a bitter divorce. When he and Victoria moved here to Croysant, he came in and changed that first will. I wrote the new document for him, as well as the next two."

Garrett wasn't sure just which part of this juicy slab of new information to pounce on first. He played it cautious. "So Reider was restless about who should get his money?"

"I guess you could call it that." The glance Duval shot at

Garrett seemed to hold some unspecified resentment. "The first will that I made for him directed his money toward Christa and Mac, his oldest children, the ones by Victoria. Which made sense, I thought."

"But what about his ... what about Victoria? His ... would she be his ... second ... wife?"

"Biedermann only had the one wife, and she was very well off to start with. She was a single child of wealthy parents. I think the only reason he ever had a will directed toward her is that she held her own money over him. It was a marriage with a contract."

"You're telling me that he and Victoria weren't married? But aren't Mac and Christa ... didn't you just say that the wife was the mother to the *youngest* child?" Garrett was trying to get the picture; it didn't make sense.

"Right. Reider and Victoria lived together before he met the woman he married. Victoria had Mac and Christa then. Then he met the other woman and married her. As I say, it was no doubt for the money. They were divorced five or six years ago. That was when he went back to Victoria."

"Whom he had never married?"

"Whom he never married."

Garrett sat a minute staring at the carpet, rubbing his chin, taking all of this in. "So now I don't understand the business with the will changes. Who did he decide to name as beneficiary, if not his children? Or was the change ...?"

"No, he changed the beneficiary twice. To be honest, Sheriff, and you must know this by now, Biedermann was a sociopath. He had no sense of moral responsibility, no conscience. He was lascivious and greedy. He liked his women either rich or very young. Until the family got wise and dumped him, he lived like a hog on his father-in-law's wealth, all the while cheating on his wife in every way you can imagine, both sexually and financially. His version of the Aquarian revolution was to find out who needed the drugs and then deal them ..." Duval was finally talking, on a roll. He stopped to take a drink of water, then continued.

"And he didn't bother to leave the kids out of his sins. All three of those kids got pretty heavily into drugs. Then the son-of-a-bitch got AIDS.

"They say there are no atheists in the trenches. About a year ago, Biedermann got religious, so to speak. He apparently quit drugs, and with his new-found purity he got self-righteous. The second time he changed his will, he dropped Mac and Christa like hot potatoes and made it in favor of Victoria. He had me write into the document that Victoria was his 'fragile, nurturing angel.' "

"His fragile, nurturing angel," mumbled Garrett, visualizing the delicate, Dresden-doll-like nurse. It fit.

"Right. And he stipulated that Victoria was to remain drug free and keep any and all of the inheritance away from Christa and Mac ... He had me put, 'no wealth should adhere to Christa and Mac, of whom I am ashamed.' " Duval's face had grown very dark. "The bastard ... as if he were a saint ..."

Garrett was shaking his head. "Wow. Quite a shift ... was there a lot of money?"

"I never knew for sure ... probably a lot. Probably drug money that he had ..." Duval's shoulders shifted, a shrug. "Laundered. I talk like I'm a shrewd big city lawyer, but I really don't know about that kind of thing. I'm just blowin' it out my ass ... relieves pressure." Garrett could tell that once Duval decided to tell the story, he had relaxed. He'd been divorced for years; maybe he was like Garrett, missed having somebody to confide in. Even his eyes had quit shifting away from Garrett's, and he managed to give him a sincere glance. Garrett pursued.

"So there were three will changes, right? From the wife to Mac and Christa, that's one, then from the kids to Victoria. That's two. What happened then ... you said the last change was recent?"

"Yeah, he came in just the Friday before he got killed and had me write up a new will while he waited. He wanted to sign it right then. He left all of his estate to his other daughter," Duval paused, then added with what sounded like a sneer in his voice, "The *legitimate* one."

"I'll be damned," Garrett said. "I'll be damned," he repeated, and paused, thinking. "So that's why Christa was listed on the docket for yesterday as 'Beekermann-Shipley.' She was never Biedermann's legitimate kid. Her nor Mac."

"Right. Victoria's name is Beekermann, and that's the legal name for her children. At least, that will be Christa's legal name once she is free of that asshole, Les."

Garrett's head shot up, expecting to see Duval grinning, but the attorney looked to be dead serious. Apparently Les Shipley's reputation had become a fixture that went with his name. Garrett decided to continue.

"OK, so we have Christa Beekermann and Mac Beekermann, both out with respect to inheritance, and the other child in ... and I take it now that Biedermann is dead, it will be her that stays in. Who is she? Or where is she?"

"I don't know where she is yet, but I've got people working on turning her up. We need her for the reading of the will tomorrow ... her name's Lindy Zakely."

This brought Garrett forward in his chair. "Lindy Zakely?! Isn't that the girl that was out here with the TRY program a few years back? The one that was staying with the Harrises when Lucky Harris died ... *that* Lindy Zakely? The one that was afraid of the father ... who wouldn't stay when she heard he was coming here?"

"That's the one."

"Holy shit. *That* Lindy Zakely." Garrett whistled. He was thinking of Alma's three's ... three children, not two. Three changes in the will. Three people with different names: Marla Mary Meter was Maggie Merimeister; Christa and Mac Biedermann were Christa and Mac Beekermann; and now, Lindy Zakely, who by rights should have been Lindy Biedermann. What next? What Garrett said was, "Shouldn't she have been called Lindy Biedermann?"

"My understanding is that after her parents divorced, both she and her mother took her mother's maiden name." Duval looked tired. "So, Sheriff, is that all you needed to know? I have court again before noon ..."

Court. Garrett rubbed his hand across his forehead, thinking. He'd originally come to talk about the court case yesterday, the one he had attended. He pictured the dark, short, sullen Christa Bieder ... uh, Beekermann, and cleared his throat. "Well, right. I appreciate that you have been forthcoming ... there were just one or two more things. Maybe we can make them brief ..."

"About ...?"

"About Christa. As I understand what you are saying, she wouldn't necessarily have known that the will had been changed and was no longer in her favor, would she?"

An unexpected storm crossed Duval's face. His hooded eyes opened and the slack mouth tightened, losing the upturn of the lips. "Look, Sheriff, in case you didn't pick up on it when I said it earlier, Reider Biedermann had a full blown case of AIDS. He didn't need killing by Christa or anybody else for purposes of that will. He was a goner anyhow."

"Right." Garrett was still scratching his forehead, a gesture of puzzlement. "I was just ... clarifying my thoughts. See, yesterday when I sat in on that custody hearing, I kept noticing that when Shipley's attorney was making his case, the magistrate was suppressing a number of statements that Biedermann might have made, HAD HE BEEN ALIVE. Shipley's attorney kept trying to get various information admitted that would have come from Biedermann, and you objected. Hearsay. Apparently ... well, if Christa were the one to have killed her father, her motive wouldn't have been the will, anyhow, would it, John?" Garrett was encountering a dark scowl backed by surly silence, but he persisted.

"I gathered that had Reider Biedermann been alive, he planned to come to the hearing and testify, but not on behalf of his daughter. Isn't that right?"

Duval had half risen from his chair. "Look, do you want to charge somebody with homicide here? It was my understanding that you arrested Weinant. You already have your man ..."

Garrett ignored his statement. Speaking calmly, he seemed to be continuing his line of thought. "Biedermann was about as amoral as a man can get. He somehow had gotten self-righteous about drugs, and he was going to testify against his own daughter. He was going to tell about Christa's use of drugs, which might have cost her custody of her child, Eirene. Right? And loss of Eirene would be one thing that Christa wouldn't ... couldn't ... tolerate. Isn't that right, John?"

Duval didn't respond. He was glaring furiously at the sheriff. Garrett said, "Well, I think I've taken enough of your time. And I thank you for it."

He got up and started across the room. Duval began to speak, as if talking to himself. Garrett paused. Duval said, "You know, Christa never touched so much as a joint after she became pregnant with little Eirene. She loves that little girl. She named her Eirene because it means 'peace,' and that is all that Christa asks for, is for Eirene to have peace and the normal life that Christa was never able to get. That asshole Les wanted to take it from the little girl, too. Christa doesn't miss drugs. She's motivated. And she's clean. And ..." His voice seemed to break. "And she's a good woman."

Garrett started to turn back, maybe to say something, but the attorney's head was bent over his desk, his muscles rigid, his hands fisted. Garrett turned back to the door, thoughtful, and made his exit. This was the man who was Christa Biedermann, A.K.A. Beekermann's, only alibi.

27

Tuesday Before Noon

Sheriff's Offices, Riversmet

Sheriff Pat Garrett planned to get back to his office in Riversmet and think. He wanted familiar ground to sort things out. He intended to go in, bar the door, and tell A-deet to hold the calls ... even if it were Hobbs, who should be around shortly. Peace and quiet—that's what he wanted.

It was not to be. The long drive between Peaseford and Riversmet gave him some time to review facts, but no sooner had he stepped into the courthouse, ready to organize them, than he was cornered. This time it was Carmen Weinant and Greta Anderson.

He wasn't sure how Edith did it. She raised her head and looked him directly in the eye over the top of her glasses, all the while continuing to type at a furious, unforgiving rate. Could she really be getting the right sequence of letters on the paper even as she met his glare? Pausing ever so briefly, she said, "They called, and I suggested that they come on in. Dispatch told me you were on your way quite some time ago." Her voice grimmed down on the "some." It was his fault again.

Silently Garrett cursed dispatch and Edith, not to mention the french fries and chili dog he'd cozied down for breakfast from the Prairie Dog, Riversmet's version of the Wienerschnitzel restaurant chain. The breakfast stop had allowed time for Weinant and Anderson to beat him to the courthouse, thus allowing Edith to imply that he was late. It was also, he assumed, the source of the warning rumbles in his belly.

Out loud he said, "Thank you, A-deet. Mrs. Weinant. Mrs.

Anderson. Would you like to come on down to my office?" With a chivalrous gesture he escorted them through the door and down the hall, shooting one final glare over his shoulder at the receptionist. Gritty, clutching a large box on her lap, wheeled ahead, and Garrett thought, "Duh. Let me just try to guess what that is." His stomach growled and he felt irritated with the world. Surprising how quickly things could turn up with these people once Weinant was incarcerated.

Once everyone was ensconced in his office, Gritty spoke first, abruptly. "Sheriff, this box contains the quit claim deeds you have been searching for."

Garrett nodded. "I see. You have found the deeds." The words were noncommittal, but the tinge of irony in his tone was enough to send a quick flush of anger across Gritty's face. She addressed the issue directly.

"Of course you have no reason to believe Carmen or me, any more than you believe my brother, but we will tell you the truth anyhow. Duz had no idea this box even existed. I found it by talking to my mother. I got her to think about the day she found the body and she was able to recall that she brought a box into the house by mistake." Gritty leaned over and set the box on the floor.

"As you can see, it is heavy. She didn't want to carry it back to the shed, so she stuffed it behind my father's old chair. It has been there since that day."

Garrett rubbed at his scar. "Well, I thank you for bringing it down."

Carmen sighed. "You are quite welcome, Sheriff. After we found the deeds, we put everything back in the box in roughly the same order in which we found it. The deeds are in an accordion file on the bottom."

"All right."

"And, Mr. Garrett," she continued, her tone now as edgy as Gritty's, "You know as well as we do that Duz did not kill that man. Given the evidence so far, I suppose you have to hold him ... department politics, perhaps ... but you *must* still be trying to find the person who actually did it. Right?"

Garrett spoke carefully. "We always welcome new evidence relevant to a case."

"Are you going to Biedermann's funeral this afternoon?"

"Do you think the funeral will be relevant to this case?"

A question for a question. Gritty frowned, but Carmen kept her face neutral and forged on. "We're working on triggering Alma's memories. Maybe she knows something she hasn't been able to tell you. We plan to take her to the funeral, and we'll take Hallie and Lew also, just to get them all reminiscing. After the funeral, we'll take all of them to the Harvest Apple and buy them a dessert; they love to get out, and maybe the atmosphere will be conducive to turning up information that hasn't surfaced so far."

Garrett knew he shouldn't say it; he was annoyed with himself, but he just could not resist. "And do you plan to bring Lucky Harris, too?"

Both women's mouths opened, then closed. They blinked, then caught the upward tremble of the Sheriff's lips. It was Gritty who rallied. "We'll invite her," she said, her voice solemn, "But she doesn't enjoy crowds as much as Lew."

Garrett allowed his smile to complete itself. The atmosphere in the room had lightened. He said, "It can't hurt to see what they might say. I'll join you. Maybe Detective Hobbs, too." He paused, then added, "And I may bring Deputy McCracken, too. She's quite a perceptive listener."

Carmen and Gritty seemed satisfied. Leaving the box behind, Garrett saw the women out, following them down the hall in order to pick up a cup of coffee from the acidic brew Edith kept available in the coffeemaker on her countertop. Sipping it should jar him awake while he sorted all this out.

Edith glanced up, as if accidentally noticing him. "Ah, the Sheriff. The very fellow I need to see." She rummaged on her desktop. "A messenger just brought this over from Dr. Thomson's office." She handed him a letter-sized brown envelope. "You better get busy, *Jefe*. I wanna see this case get movin' here." A devilish grin slipped across her face, but before he could respond her fingers were back at her keyboard and she was frowning at it, looking innocent.

Bringing coffee and envelope, Garrett stopped at Hobbs' office to ask if he wanted to go up to the funeral with him, then he went on back to his own office. Scooting aside paperwork which was accumulating on his desk, he pulled out the letter from the pathologist.

It concerned the blood scan that had been done on Biedermann's body. Garrett mumbled his way through it; a lot of it was technical, but he got the picture. When he'd finished reading, he stood up and headed for the door, talking to himself. "Right. Alma and her damnable three's."

A young couple holding a baby were sitting on the cracked vinyl of the couch in the reception area. They glanced up, then went back to dandling the baby. Apparently they weren't waiting for him. That was a switch.

He leaned over the counter, narrowing his eyes at Edith. "So, Ms. A-deet. You wanna get this case movin', right?"

"Only if you do, *Señor*," she said, her hands resting on the keyboard. "Need some help from a *profesional*?" Her eyes danced at him.

"Know where I could find one?" He grinned.

"At your service, *Compadre*. Just ¡*anda*! ... *Tengo mucho trabajo*." She made typing movements with her fingers.

"*Mucho trabajo*, eh," he repeated, shaking his head. "I shouldn't even bother you with actual sheriff's office business, *mucho importante* lady like yourself, but I will presume upon you, even so." The mother had begun to watch and listen to their conversation, joggling the baby on her knee as the father thumbed a magazine from the end table.

Garrett reached over the counter and snagged a memo pad and pencil from Edith's desk and began to write, speaking as he wrote. "I'm going into my office for a moment of quiet time. *Uno momento* ... silenso." He figured the last word was good enough, since he had no idea what it might really be in Spanish. "I ... need ... to ... think. No company down there, okay? Peaco and quieto?"

Edith stretched, her hands clasped together over her head. "I gotcha, boss. Everyone el shuto-upo." She giggled.

Garrett smiled back. "And while I am down there, all alone, *thinking*, I would like you to do these things." He turned the paper and Edith stood up in order to see it better. The mom cocked her head, too, sorry she couldn't see it from the distance of the couch.

"I understand McCracken's on patrol. Call her in; I need her this afternoon."

"She'll *mucho gusta* that," said Edith, with neither grammar nor subtlety, but the sheriff ignored her.

"Next, I'd like you to get hold of our friend, Mr. John Duval. Now, A-deet, this could be tricky. I want you to suggest to him that it will be in Christa Shipley's best interest to come up to the crime lab and volunteer a blood sample."

Edith frowned. "Tricky?"

"He's not gonna want to do it, but you need to point out that if he doesn't, we can get the court order and so-on, and that it will look the best for Ms. Shipley if she cooperates up front."

Edith was still frowning, but she said, "*Bien*. Go on ... what else?"

"Right. Call the crime lab, let them know she may be in. Here is what I want them to look for." He indicated the writing on the paper, and Edith read it through, her lips moving, then said again, seriously, "*Bien*."

"Finally, A-deet, I need you to call the hospital for me. I've developed a certain interest in some of the activities of a Ms. Victoria Biedermann." He pushed the paper on across to her. "Here's what I would like to know."

Edith held it, reading, her frown deepening, then her face cleared. "Oh. I see." The father had put his magazine down and both he and his wife were leaning forward with undisguised interest. They were clearly disappointed when Edith looked up to give a brisk nod and say only, "I'll do it, Sheriff."

Garrett smiled sweetly at her. "Thanks."

Edith looked back down at the paper. "Do you think Mrs. Weinant is in danger, then?"

Garrett took a deep breath and blew it vigorously out between pursed lips. "I'm not sure. We'll watch."

28

Tuesday Afternoon

From Peaseford Funeral Home to the Harvest Apple

Half an hour before time for the funeral, the folding chairs were filled, and by a quarter till two the standing room was gone. Garrett could tell that it was a crowd formed of curiosity rather than respect. Extras who came out of respect to a large funeral usually waited outside the door, spilled down the entrance steps, and lingered on the sidewalk. Latecomers here craned their necks, gawked around, then finally drifted away, leaving behind a room-sized funeral crowd.

While signing the guest book, Garrett overheard a kid of about ten say, "I dare you to go up and look."

The kid's buddy elbowed him smartly. "Shut up. Don't be a doofus."

"You chicken? Just look in 'n see, can you see the bullet hole. Double dare you."

Of course, any such aspirations toward corpse observation were thwarted because Biedermann, in accordance with Victoria's wishes, had been cremated. All that was left of him would presumably be found in the specially purchased brass urn resting on the cloth covered dais at the front.

Beside the remains in the urn was a collection of memorabilia that Victoria or someone had arranged. This was common local custom. Available for viewing by the mourners today were a pair of Reider's fancy new cowboy boots, some Native American curios, the expensive Stetson that Reider had worn around the community, and a large portrait of Reider in his young, handsome,

Elvisy-looking days ... all items meant to be definitive of the man that had been.

There were also flowers, Garrett noted, and old-fashioned western music emanated softly from a CD player concealed somewhere among them.

A larger crowd like this had its advantages and disadvantages. He didn't feel conspicuous. He was standing next to Hobbs and McCracken, all of them propped up by the east wall of the room, and there were clusters of people in front of him as well as to his left and right. When they had first entered, they had drawn attention, since it looked to the curious as if law officers might be the most interesting thing to come out of the day. Once they failed to do anything noteworthy, however, the interest faded and people's eyes again went to the front, to their programs, or to their neighbors. The crowd now conveyed them a decent anonymity.

On the other hand, although not seen, he couldn't see very well himself. He had to crane his neck to attempt to see who might be in attendance. Chairs had been held empty in the front row for the appropriate late entrance of immediate family and close friends, and he was at least able to watch this entrance.

No close friends presented themselves, but because of age, Alma, Lew, and Hallie, with Carmen and Gritty in attendance, were taken to the front row. Promptly at two o'clock, the funeral director escorted in a pale and teary Victoria, beautifully coifed, her slender, long-legged body stylishly draped in a black silk pantsuit. Christa stumped along behind her, her jaw set, her eyes directed straight forward, her heavy black hair pulled severely back and held with an incongruously flowery clasp, and her hand gripping little Eirene's hand so hard that Garrett felt he could see the whiteness of her knuckles even from where he stood.

Eirene, who had her grandmother Victoria's fair and delicate complexion, was gazing about uneasily, her big, china blue eyes restless in her solemn face. When they passed John Duval, sitting on the aisle about halfway to the front, she smiled at him. Duval's eyebrows raised above the hooded eyes and he smiled back, coming perilously close to conveying a look of tenderness.

And that was all. The funeral director helped the women

and little girl into seats, then proceeded to the front to begin the service. "Mr. Reider Biedermann, cattle rancher and esteemed friend and neighbor, was born in Riversmet, Colorado, on July 24, 1951 ..." he intoned.

McCracken leaned in and up to Garrett's ear. "No Mac and Alice," she whispered, the air from her lips setting the hairs in his right ear to tingling, which threatened to trigger an all-systems alert in the rest of his body. Under cover of the shifting and sighing in the room, he gave the ear a good rub before he responded, then he met her eye, nodded, made the appropriate face and a quick, hand-spread gesture to acknowledge her observation. It was, the gesture said, a mystery.

His eyes returned to the front of the room and his mind began again to circulate on the case. The quiet time in his office hadn't been that productive. No matter what, there had been that box on the office floor left by the Weinants. It intruded on his logic. In the end, the primary benefit of his office time had been to allow him to deal with his rumbling stomach, gaseous as Vesuvius. Finally, he took Gas-X, opened his office window, and left.

He took Gritty and Carmen at their word that the box contained the deeds. He didn't take time to open it. What bothered him was that having the deeds turn up so promptly at Alma's house had no logical redemptive value for Douglas Ulysses Zane Weinant. It only indicated that the deeds had been there—somewhere—all along, and strengthened the argument that Weinant and Biedermann were struggling to get at the deeds in the shed when Biedermann was struck by Weinant's shovel. Briefly, he wondered how difficult it would be to trace the ownership of the shovel. That could help.

One thing was clear: rationally, everything they had turned up so far pointed directly at Weinant ... opportunity, motive, access to weapons, all of it. Rationally. But intuitively, Carmen Weinant was dead-on when she said that Garrett knew perfectly well that Duz didn't do it.

He had a funny feeling in his gut about Weinant; something was not right about the role he claimed in the whole scenario. But he could not accept him as a murderer. If nothing else, the *modus operandi* belied that role. Weinant was not a back shooter.

Still ... why the shovel? Why the gun, lying by the Harris pond as if planted?

And now there was this new evidence: what the Biedermann blood scan had told him. Sure, Weinant could be fitted into that framework, too, but to do so required the man to become a contortionist. A whole new time frame, layer of opportunity, and so-on, needed accounting for.

The pianist had taken her seat, and a buxom local woman was crooning a dirgelike version of "Home on the Range" in a very frail, nasal voice. The words scarcely reached the second row, but the vigorous accompaniment conveyed the idea of the music. Garrett's eyelids drooped to half-mast, giving his eyes the hooded appearance of Duval's, and he let the rest of the service wash over him.

His body quiet, his mind got as busy as a pack rat in a cellar, scurrying here and there to gather facts, sort them, and deposit them in the appropriate mental heaps. Only when the crowd began to stir and shuffle, readying themselves for departure, did his lids raise again. He had an inkling. Yes, indeed, at last he had a coherent inkling.

As tradition demanded, Victoria, Christa, and Eirene stood to one side beside the exit and accepted hugs and condolences. Most of these came from the club women, their men hanging behind them. Many of those who had assembled simply made a run for the border, no doubt sorry they had wasted their time on a boring afternoon.

McCracken, Hobbs, and Garrett courteously stood in the line to take Victoria's hand, then Christa's, and tell them they were sorry for the loss of their husband and father. Victoria expressed her tearful gratitude to them. Christa, sounding sullen, said, "Thoughtful of you to come." Garrett assumed the statement was ironic.

The investigators had started for their cars when Jenny came up behind Garrett and gripped his elbow. "Patrick," she said, a little out of breath, "Patrick, it's her."

Garrett stopped. "Who?"

"Her, Patrick! The woman who stopped in at the Cowpath that night. Right over there—see? Getting into the red car. And now it's as clear as a bell to me ... I know who she is!"

Hobbs and McCracken had both stopped and their eyes all turned in the direction Jenny indicated. Two women were getting into a rented red sports car; one appeared to be middle-aged; the other one, very thin and with long hair, was young. Both were blond. "One of those?" Garrett asked.

"Yes. The older one ... but I know who they both are. I was watching them from where I was standing, just to the front of you. They were sitting in the middle of the room, very unobtrusive. Don't stare," she commanded.

Garrett would have averted his eyes, but the women were oblivious to the crowd. They were already in the car, the older one in the driver's seat, and starting up.

Before Jenny could speak any more, Garrett said sharply, "Oh! Oh, that's who they are." He wheeled on Hobbs, who was chewing a fat wad of gum and watching the women. "Hobbs, follow those two. We have to make sure where they're staying. I don't wanna lose 'em again."

Hobbs nodded. "Who you got, Sheriff?"

"The girl'd be Lindy Zakely." He looked at Jenny for confirmation, got it, and continued, "And the woman'd be her mother. Biedermann's ex-wife. Right, Jenny?"

"That's right. There they go."

As gracefully as a wolverine after caribou, Hobbs began a deceptively slow amble toward his own car. Before the little red car turned the corner, his ambiguous brown Ford had slipped quietly in behind it.

Garrett turned back to Jenny. "Thanks, Jenny. I got a pretty good look at 'em." McCracken, at his elbow, said, "Yeah, thanks."

Jenny said, "You were sure right on it, you guys. Do you want to hear about how I happened to know her?"

Garrett glanced around. Several people had slowed to listen. At the curb, by handicapped parking, he could see Carmen and Gritty loading Alma, Lew, and Hallie into a van. Alma and Hallie were in, but the middle door of the van was being held open and Lew was making odd gestures toward it. Garrett realized that they had also brought Lucky and that Lew was chivalrously helping her to get in. "How good could things get?" he thought ironically. He cleared his throat.

"I'll tell you what. McCracken and I've agreed to meet the Weinant contingent over at the Harvest Apple for a little while. Can you join us there?"

Jenny shook her head. "Nah. Rita just agreed to cover for me for the funeral. I can't leave her alone with the evening crowd."

"How about we join you at the Cowpath after we meet with these people? We can talk better up there anyhow."

"Sounds good," Jenny said, and, taking Garrett's hand, she leaned in to give him what McCracken chose to view as a friendly peck on the cheek before she left.

Garrett and McCracken worked their way back up the street toward the police cruiser, stopping to exchange pleasantries and not-so-pleasantries with a number of the old-timers who had come down to the funeral. The pleasantries had to do with it being nice to see one another and the possibility of rain. The not-so-pleasantries had to do with what in the hell Garrett was thinking of to have arrested Duz Weinant. Any fool could see that he had the wrong man.

Since Garrett tended to agree with them, it was difficult to mumble his way politely out of the situation, but mumble he did, and with McCracken taking a warrior's stance behind him, red hair shining and arms akimbo, her hand resting loosely near her gun, he managed to make it to the car. Before he could get safely in the door, Nancy Jane Barnswallowper encountered them to assert that even if Duz *had* clubbed and then shot Biedermann, he deserved a medal rather than jail time. " 'Esteemed friend and neighbor,' my ass," she snorted.

Garrett looked her in the eye and said, "You know, Ms. Barnswallowper, you may be right. We'll see what we can do." With that he made a smooth dodge, slipped into the car behind the wheel, made the assumption that McCracken was in place, and pulled out. Nancy Jane, her legs solid to the ground and her hands on her hips, stood watching them go, shaking her head.

In the five blocks to the Harvest Apple, Peaseford Valley's upscale restaurant, McCracken managed to ask, "Where do you think Mac and Alice Biedermann are?"

"I can't figure it. Maybe they took off for California."

"But you'd think they'd want to be here for the funeral, at

least. And didn't you say they'll read the will tomorrow?"

They had arrived at the Harvest Apple. "You'd think so," Garrett said noncommittally. He noted that the van was parked in the handicapped space and was empty. He was glad the oldsters were already in the restaurant; he hated to have to accommodate Lucky. For one thing, he wasn't sure what her handicap was. Besides being dead.

The Weinants, Lew, and Hallie were seated at a large round table in a fully windowed corner of the restaurant. All of the seating was secluded by heavy doses of ferns hanging thickly at uneven lengths from the low ceiling, and the round table itself was boxed in with wooden planters of live pansies and geraniums. A table cloth done in a bright red, green, and brown design, which featured large baskets tipped over to spill out copious varieties of harvested apples, covered the table, and was itself covered with a washable layer of clear plastic.

Seating at several of the tables was rough benches done up to look like apple boxes, but this table was surrounded by seven sturdy wooden farm chairs and Gritty's wheelchair. Garrett and McCracken took two of the last three empty chairs which were indicated to them, being careful not to sit in the other chair, which obviously was occupied by Lucky, because Lew was leaning toward it in intense muttered dialogue. The others were involved in ordering pie and coffee.

Hallie and Alma were aglow; after a lifetime of cooking on a shoestring, and from scratch, for large families plus dozens of relatives at the holidays, not to mention haying crews and every stray cowboy that happened along, nothing could be more fun than eating out and having someone else at the stove. Hallie ordered with a flourish, proclaiming that she wanted cherry pie, and stressing the lovely foreign sounding *a la mode*, then Alma trumped her by asking for pecan pie, and "don't spare the ice cream."

Garrett couldn't buck this enthusiasm. It had been long enough since his chili dog breakfast. Feeling self-righteous, he ordered the house specialty, French Apple-Walnut pie, and requested a double scoop of French vanilla to top it off.

Looking a little cowed, McCracken settled for a slice of rhubarb pie and added meekly, "Please. No ice cream. Just a glass of tea."

When the waitress left, Lew opened the conversation with, "Well, Sheriff, what'd ya think of the funeral? Right smart bunch of people turned out to bury the little bastard, wasn't there? 'Scusin' my French, Ladies."

"It was a pretty big funeral."

"Most of us just there wishin' we could peek in that vase, make sure old Biedermann was for sure in there, so we could rest easy." Lew cackled heartily. "Guess we couldn't tell now, the state he's in."

McCracken looked at the empty chair. "Lucky, did you get a chance to talk to Lindy Zakely? We noticed after the funeral that she had been there." Garrett was impressed. McCracken was getting good at this.

There was a brief period of quiet, everyone directing their gaze toward the empty chair, except Hallie, who had not heard the question and was using old fingers to fiddle open some sugar packets. Garrett wondered what each of them thought Lucky was saying. He hoped Lew would translate, as he seemed to be wont to do. At least that would get them on even ground again.

Lew said nothing, however, although he looked aggravated, so Carmen ventured, "Well, that's too bad, Lucky. Maybe she'll drop by to see you later." Then she nodded, as if Lucky had agreed with her.

Alma and Hallie were now ignoring the pretenses of the young ones. Their eyes were fastened on what was important, the waitress. She was dressed in the Harvest Apple costume of attractive, form-fitting coveralls, cut short to reveal plenty of leg, and a duckbilled rancher's cap, the bill turned fetchingly to the back, and she was over by the waitresses' work station, collecting onto a round tray the drinks they had ordered. "I'm hungry," Hallie grumbled. "Wish she'd hurry up."

"She seems slow. She must be new." Alma's voice, geared for Hallie's ears, roared across the room. The waitress gave a visible flinch. Alma could see pretty well from this distance, but she didn't note the flinch. She noted that the girl's back was to her, making her precise identity impossible. This was just one more eyesight annoyance.

"I dunno. I think I've seen her in here before. She looks just like that little guy I saw fighting in your yard that night." Hallie chuckled, but Garrett looked up sharply, glancing over at the woman filling coffee at the beverage center. Hallie continued, "Same kinda cap. Wouldn't it be funny if some waitress killed old Biedermann? Maybe he was having an affair and two-timed somebody." Garrett blinked. This was the restaurant where Christa worked. The decibels in Hallie's voice matched Alma's, and the waitress could be seen to stiffen before she turned with the loaded tray.

Gritty, feeling businesslike, cut in. "Well, anyhow, Mom, they were talking about Lindy Zakely. You remember her?"

Reluctantly, Alma pulled her attention from the approaching tray of beverages. "Well, of course I remember Lindy, honey." Her tone was irritated and condescending. "She used to stay with Lew and Lucky. Poor girl."

Poor girl? Garrett decided it was a general comment, not a comment on the Harris's hospitality. Alma continued, "Why would you bring her up? Have you heard from her?"

"Didn't you see her? She was at the funeral. We were just talking about her. She was with another woman, probably her mother ..."

"Maybe I forgot to mention, but I sometimes forget what people say. And I don't see as well as I used to, Gritty. You know, I can see fairly well at a short distance, but I can't see to read ..."

Gritty wobbled at her wheelchair impatiently. "I just wondered if you recalled her."

Alma was not to be put off. "... And you had me in a bad place there at the funeral, Gritty, right up at the front." Her tone was accusing. "Hallie and I could hardly see anything—everyone was sitting behind us." The waitress had begun to set drinks around the table.

Lew, his voice raised and cranky, said, "Alma, did you hear Lucky? She wants to know if you still hear from Lindy."

Alma fixed Lew with a withering glance. "Lewis Harris, if I've told you once I've told you a hundred times. Lucky is dead."

Garrett's mouth dropped. He expected a wave of shocked silence to greet this tactless pronouncement, but instead Carmen said, "Now, Alma ..." while Lew drew himself up to full fighting cock size. "Alma, you're blind as a bat and you got deafness in both ears. Don't go tryin' to make me out for a crazy just because you can't even hear Lucky talkin' and can't see her when she's right across from you."

"Lew, I may be blind but I ain't deaf and ..." Alma began, but Hallie had spotted a second waitress coming in with the tray of pie. In an annoyed tone she said, "Put up them knives, you two old fools. You gonna drag your arguments to the grave?"

This did produce a brief, stunned silence. Neither Alma nor Lew was fond of hearing about graves. At that point, however, the second waitress began to try to get the pie orders straight again so she could distribute the plates. Before the last piece had hit the table, everyone was digging in. Garrett had to admit that it tasted damn good, the taste enhanced by the prevailing elderly food frenzy.

Lew finished half his pie, wiped his chin, and said stubbornly, "So, Alma, since you couldn't hear Lucky, I'll say it a little louder fer ya. What she said was, 'Do ... ya ... still ... hear ... from ... Lindy ... these ... days?'"

Alma, chewing and satisfied, took it for what it was worth this time. "I don't remember. I don't think so; not for a few months."

Gritty pounced. "Is that right, Mom? Did Lindy write you after she left Harris's?" Alma continued to chew, more interested in the pie than in the conversation.

"Of course she did." This was Hallie, feeling like it was necessary to be sure that these young people were getting what was obvious to everyone else. "She wrote Alma for years. Alma showed me the letters. She was an abused child, you know. She was scared of her father. That was why she left here."

"And her father was Reider Biedermann?" This was Carmen, holding up her end.

"Yes, of course. She left when she found out that Biedermanns were coming here. It was a funny deal. Those other two, Mac and Christa, were the first children, but they were illegitimate, I say. Alma says Reider was a bigamist, but I figure he was just an adulterer." She thought a minute, chewing. "I guess that doesn't apply if he was divorced, though. But then how does that Victoria fit? To me, she seems like the real wife."

"I don't know ..." Gritty started, but Garrett cut in.

"Alma, did you keep the letters?"

Alma looked at him as if he were a school child who had had a serious lapse of attention. "Of course I kept the letters. They were on the most beautiful stationery. That was why Reider was digging around in my shed. His hands were right in that box of letters when he got killed. Don't you remember? We talked about that."

Garrett wanted to say, "We did?" but instead he said, "Oh. I guess ... I had forgotten. So ..." he blinked, a quick mental sorting, "So ... he wanted the letters from Lindy. But why?"

Alma shrugged. "I don't know." She had one more bite of pie left, which she disposed of, chewing thoughtfully. Garrett watched her, thinking irrelevantly, 'her teeth are browner than the other two's. They must be her own. I wonder what Lucky's teeth ...' but at this point she added, "Those letters had a lot to say about what Reider did to Lindy. He was cruel. I think she needed somebody to confide in. Sometimes people like to confide in *me*." This last was said with an edge of pride, and followed dismissively with, "I suppose she decided to turn him in for incest and told him she'd use the letters as evidence. He wrote her back a couple of times and she sent me those to keep ... it was an admission on *his* part." She wiped her hands thoroughly on her napkin, peering down with her cloudy eyes to see if she were missing anything, then said, "Thank you, Gritty. That was very good."

Hallie and Lew and Lucky all joined in a chorus of thanks to their hostess. The waitress appeared, carting an ice tea pitcher and a coffee pot, and everyone accepted refills. Hallie took a long, satisfying swig of tea, then leaned back and said, "Isn't it odd that Alice Biedermann and Maggie Merimeister both purchased such an unusual handbag? They almost looked like the same purse to me."

Garrett glanced around. Everyone at the table looked as perplexed by this statement as he was. It wasn't just that their minds were still on Alma's comments. It was that they had no clue about what purses Hallie was talking about.

Hallie also read their faces. Turning to Alma, she said, "Alma, don't you remember? Last week at club, I was telling everyone about Maggie's handbag. She brought me up to club, and I was quite taken with the handbag, but she left it in her car."

Alma said, "You know, I just don't remember things like I used to. Sometimes I can't remember the simplest ..."

Hallie looked thoughtful. "On the other hand, come to think of it, while I was telling about it, Maggie seemed embarrassed. She said that it wasn't her bag, anyhow. So maybe it was Alice's, after all. But how did it get in Maggie's car?"

Carmen, trying to track, said, "But why would you think that it was Alice's? I mean, and not somebody else's?"

"Oh, I saw Alice carrying it today. Or one just like it."

McCracken sat bolt upright. "You what? You saw Alice at the funeral?"

"Well, not actually at the funeral. She was outside before it started, hanging back from the rest of the family. I thought she and Mac would come in with them, but I guess Mac didn't make it." Hallie snorted. "He was probably layin' up in that tepee takin' drugs, left his poor little rabbity wife to cope with it all alone. They say he's that kind."

McCracken couldn't get over it. "You saw Alice *alone*, outside the *funeral* home?"

"Right. She never came in, though. But she was carrying that purse that I thought was so pretty. The one that I thought belonged to Maggie."

McCracken shook her head, amazed that Alice had turned up and that she hadn't spotted her, but Garrett said, "You thought it was Maggie's purse because you saw it in her car last Wednesday. Is that right, Hallie?"

"That's what I said. I guess you didn't hear me." She looked disgusted at the sheriff's hearing problem, then added, "Why? Is the purse important, somehow?"

Garrett closed his eyes. Facts. Facts. Shuffling facts. Aloud, he said, "It may be."

A face appeared in the hanging ferns that screened the table. "I thought I heard familiar voices over here. Hi, Gang! Hey, Alma!" A sturdy young woman in a nurse's uniform emerged.

Carmen and Gritty said, "Hi, Mary." Gritty continued, "Sheriff, Ms. McCracken, this is Mary Planter, one of Mom's regulars. I bet you just got off down at the clinic, Mary?"

"Yeah. Busy day. Some kind of summer flu going around ... lots of little barf bag kids. Thought I'd pick up a pie to take home so that my hubby wouldn't be too crestfallen not to get a seven-course meal tonight."

"They have excellent pie here," Alma judged, while the two younger women said, "Good idea," and Lew said, "Lucky and I like to take pie home from here now and then."

A general and pointless pie discussion followed, with Mary finally saying, "Well, Guys, I've gotta go. Nice to meet you, Sheriff, Ms. McCracken."

"Nice to meet you."

She turned to go, then turned back. "Oh, and Gritty? One reason I stopped ... I just wanted to remind you to pick up a refill for Alma's medication. Remember, I mentioned it this morning. It looks like we came up short again."

The fern rustled at her back as she left, and Alma shook her head, disgusted. "See, I told you. Things always come in three's. This is the third time that those girls have misplaced my medicine. Let's hope it is the last time now for a while."

Garrett's hand had gone to his mustache. He began to twist it slowly, thoroughly, his eyes distant. He didn't notice that the waitress brought the check and that Gritty picked up the whole tab, which made McCracken nervous, lest their good manners be questioned. As they exited the building, he intercepted Gritty on the sidewalk.

"Ms. Anderson, may I speak to you in private for a moment?"

She wheeled to the side, out of earshot of the people busily loading into the van. McCracken had her hand under Alma's elbow, helping to hoist her, and Carmen was politely waiting for the ghostly Lucky. Hallie was saying loudly, "It is so aggravating. I could hear perfectly well in that restaurant, but now I can't understand a word you're saying, Lew. Did you say it is windy? I don't think it's all that windy ..." to which he responded, "No, damnit, Hallie, I am trying to talk to you about Lindy. Lindy! LINDY! LINDY ZAKELY!"

"Oh," said Hallie, the rest of her sentence disappearing with her into the van.

Gritty leaned forward, said, "What is it, Sheriff? Didn't any of that help you?"

Garrett nodded, but his face was grim. "A lot of it was helpful. And I appreciate your efforts. But Ms. Anderson, I just want to ask you to do something tonight and tomorrow morning, if you will. It is very important, and you need to do it without fuss and without telling anyone."

Gritty's face became worried. "Of course! Anything I can do to help ..."

"You must administer your mother's medication yourself. Check the prescription bottles. Be sure it is the right medication; if you aren't sure, don't give it. Just call me. And then you, personally, take the dose to her and watch that she takes it. Don't let anyone else give it. And I mean not anyone," he repeated, looking over at the van. "And be sure that someone doesn't give her a second dose."

"She will be confused. She forgets whether she has had her medicine or not."

"You must watch, Ms. Anderson. It should be just for tonight and the morning. But it is you who must watch."

29

Tuesday Late Afternoon

Croysant

Garrett was back in the cruiser with the phone propped against his ear by the time McCracken had helped install the old folks in the van. He was making notes. "So you followed up on both leads from the hospital? Right. Thanks."

He started to click off, then said, "Oh, and A-deet? Any word on Christa Shipley? Did she come into the lab?"

After a minute, shaking his head, he pressed 'off' and said, half to himself and half to McCracken, who had just bailed into the passenger side, "Well, no word there. Didn't figger Duval'd make it easy for us."

McCracken cocked an eyebrow at him, but he ignored it, setting the vehicle in motion. "Well, Deputy," he said as they cleared the stop sign leaving Peaseford, "Do you need to make any arrangements with the home folk? It looks like this could be a long evening."

"Nah, it's okay, Chief! No problem." McCracken felt an electric surge of excitement pulse through her muscles and belly. She shifted on the seat, watching the prairie dogs ahead of them scuttle off the pavement and careen down the embankment, then dash for cover as Garrett, clearly impatient, cranked the cruiser up to sixty-five, leaning it into the sharp curves. "Do you think ..." she paused, trying to decide how to phrase it, "Do you think somethin's comin' down tonight, Chief?"

"Nah," he said, driving with one hand and scratching his nose. "Nah, not yet tonight." He looked thoughtful. "But I do think I got some a' this figured. Wanna hear how I see it?"

Trying to keep an admiring, do-I-ever tone out of her voice, McCracken leaned back. "Sure, Chief. I'd like to know what you got."

He only had time to sketch in the basics before they pulled into the parking lot of the Cowpath. Giving up all pretense, McCracken said, "Wow! It fits, doesn't it? And you got a plan?"

"Yeah, maybe I got a plan." Garrett popped open his door, swung his boots out onto the gravel. "Let's hear what Jenny has to say about the ex, make sure our details are right, then ..." She didn't hear the rest of his sentence. He was already halfway up the walk, and she had to scamper to catch up. She thought she heard him say, "Then I'm going to need you to go undercover."

The Cowpath felt soothingly dark and cool after the relentless afternoon glare outside. Both McCracken and Garrett were wearing dark glasses, and as they slipped them off, McCracken thought incongruously of the movie, *Men in Black*. Well, at least their problem wasn't aliens. She straightened her shoulders and took in the room, then shared a grin with herself. Just Croysantians.

Jenny was strumming a sweet-stringed folk song in the back by the bar. Her voice was rich and clear, carrying past the early drinkers and locals to the tables of tourists and their kids stopped for dinner in front before stretching daylight savings time to tackle the long, curling mountain drive into Stoney City.

They picked a booth near Jenny in the back, catching her eye as they sat, and when she finished the song, which ended mournfully with the death of lovers in each others' arms, she joined them, scooting in by McCracken. She had fresh flowers in her hair.

"I think I was psychologically blocking it," she began. "See, where I knew Betsy Biedermann was from my hippie days back over thirty years ago. I know how you hate hippies, Patrick, and I must not have wanted to get into that era with you. Like I say, I think I blocked it subconsciously. I wish I'd remembered her sooner."

Her thoughtful, grey-flecked blue eyes looked worriedly across the table into Garrett's, causing him to say, "Nah, it's okay. Only guy I know can put faces and names together from that long ago is Hobbs."

"Well, anyhow, maybe a little background will help," Jenny continued, her eyes holding Garrett's. "For good or ill, I dropped out of the University of Colorado in '70. I guess the hippie movement peaked that year, but of course when you're in the middle of something you don't know that. You don't see it that way.

"Nixon was Prez and he spoke against protesters, making us out to be traitors. May Fourth of that year was Kent State. To me, our own people shooting our own students on that campus was bringing the war straight home to this soil. To me, the war protest was in full force. I was pre-law, you know. Really politically minded and very idealistic. I thought the war was wrong and I was scared for the Vietnamese and the boys our government was sending over there.

"So, to make a long story short, I followed the protests around the country for a while, trying to do what I could, then ended up just at the rim of Haight-Ashbury, in San Francisco. By that time the war effort was tapering down, both from the point of the army and from the point of the protests. Still, I was a true flower child. I liked the hair and the clothes. And the music ...

"But I didn't do drugs much. Lots of people I knew, they were into anything ... quaaludes, LSD, you know .... You could get amyl nitrate across the counter for a quarter in those days. It was supposed to be used as heart medicine, but the druggies used it for sex. It was grampa to Viagra.

"I didn't like that stuff ... you could see it wasn't the way to go. But early on, even while I was still in Boulder, I'd go to the campus hangouts ... I'd go up on the Hill, go into the Sink to smoke pot and be cool ... I used pot for quite a while, then I gave it up in '83, when I came back to Colorado. So I did know about drugs."

McCracken was fascinated. No wonder Jenny came off as a little ditzy; maybe she'd fried some of her brain. Rita came by their table and they asked for coffee and a double order of mozzarella sticks.

Jenny continued. "But I'm dragging this out. The time you need to know about is 1977. The war was over in April of '75, and by that time most of the hippie stuff had died down. By then I was doing kind of the same thing I do here. There was a little organic foods bakery there, with natural grain breads and rolls and so-on, and fresh vegetarian soups, and people came in and sat around, reading and drinking tea and eating. I worked there, waited tables and played my guitar and sang. I wasn't all that far out. My folks would come by to visit from Colorado; they didn't think of me as a kook.

"Still, I'd been part of the movement, and I knew lots of people. Some of our bread and tea in that cafe was very special, drew people in, if you get my meaning. One of the people that hung out there was a guy named Pappy. That was the only name he gave. He would say it was short for papyrus, that he was really Egyptian and needed a harem, then he'd laugh.

"And he could have been Egyptian in one way – he had dark hair and dark eyes, a good beard. He was short, but he was really handsome. He'd come on to me and to any other woman that crossed his path, and a lot of women fell for it. In fact, he did have a regular little harem going, and each of them seemed oblivious to the existence of the others.

"He had one little thin blond gal that must have been ten years younger than he was. She had a frail beauty, but she was a real Twiggy, and she was obsessed with him. She'd follow him around, turn up even when he seemed to be trying to shake her. She had two kids by him. At least she said they were by him. One came after he married the other woman ... As for him, he treated her like dirt. Used her, sent her on errands and worse ..."

Rita came by and refilled coffee. McCracken knew this was going somewhere. She asked for a dinner salad and leaned into the space against the wall. Garrett also asked for salad. French dressing. Jenny, into her story, smiled Rita away.

"So, anyhow, another one of the people who came by was a little cheerleader type. Except for being blond, she was the opposite of the thin girl. She was cute as a button, almost chubby, and bouncy. The perky type. The first girl looked drug out, older than her years, but this other girl was well cared for. She really was older, my age, but her folks were wealthy importers of Asian art. She'd been doted on since the day she was born, and maybe kept a little naive.

"At any rate, she'd done college and the sorority and some travel in Europe, and because she was intelligent she began to hanker for a bigger world than the one her parents handed her. She wanted adventure, and she came down to Haight to try to find it." Jenny took the first sip from her cup and drew back in surprise. "Oh, oops! This is already cold! I didn't remember I'd ordered coffee. I usually drink tea."

She scooted the cup aside and continued. "Well, anyhow, that's okay. This is where my story ends. That girl and I hung out together for a while, until we realized that our tastes were quite different and we went our separate ways. Unfortunately, before we did, I introduced her to the guy I just described. The one called Pappy. The lady killer."

Garrett spoke for the first time. "And Pappy was Reider Biedermann?"

"Pappy was Reider Biedermann. I'm so stupid, Patrick. I never did make the connection until just today at the funeral. He looked so much different then as compared to here in Croysant. And I'm not sure he made the connection with me, either. He sort of just saw women as things, and I don't think he ever individualized me as being different from any other woman."

"And the two women ...?"

"Well, of course, the little pale girl that had the babies in the commune? Now that I've put two and two together, that was Victoria. The babies were Mac and Christa ... of course, they were tiny, then. I didn't see them much. And Victoria changed. She ... I guess you could say, she bloomed. At least she got stylish."

"And the one who was your friend, she married him ...?"

"She fell like a ton of bricks when I introduced her. Those pouty bad boy looks of his drew her like a magnet, and I know, Patrick, as I am sitting telling you this, that what drew Pappy was the money. I don't know what happened after that. Like I said, I returned to Colorado in '83 and changed my lifestyle ... but I doubt that Reider gave up either his women or his drugs after he took up with Betsy."

"Betsy ...?"

"Betsy Zakely ... the woman at the funeral today. And the woman who came in here that night. The woman he married." Jenny fell silent, absently drawing a circle on the tablecloth with her finger. Then she said, "You know, now that I realize who she is, I feel so sorry for Betsy. Terrible things must have happened between her and Reider. She looked old that night; her hair is probably grey under that bleach, and she looked so grim and angry. I think ... I think if she hadn't been all made up, maybe a face lift ... I think she truly would have appeared a broken woman."

Everyone at the table fell silent. McCracken felt a warmth emanating from herself toward Jenny. Jenny, after all, was trying hard to cooperate with the law, and it was understandable that she had not recognized those people after all those years.

Garrett broke the silence. "Let's go over the time sequence one more time, Jen, for the people who came in here that night." She nodded, and he got out his notebook. "Mac was here first, right? And he left with Alice at 9:30."

"That's right."

"Reider came while Mac was here, but you don't think they saw each other. Neither one was still here when Patty Harris came, right?"

"They had both gone. Patty came about ten till the hour, I think."

"Did we tell you she had been out shooting up road signs?"

"No, you're kidding me!"

"No kidding," McCracken chipped in, while Garrett chuckled. "She uses it to relieve stress. Keep that one under your hat, okay?"

Jenny laughed and, making a zipper motion across her lips, said, "I'd never have guessed it of her!"

"So, anyhow, at about ten, Betsy Zakely came by and asked directions to Alma's. And she was angry. Right?"

"Right." Suddenly Jenny was afraid she saw where this was going. "Oh, but wait! I'm not sure she was *that* angry ... I mean ..."

"It's okay. I'm not sure she was that angry, either." But Garrett was frowning.

Jenny screwed up her face, trying to be sure. "Mac Biedermann, then Reider, then Mac left with Alice, then Patty. While Patty was here, Betsy dropped by, then Patty left.

"Any sign that evening of Maggie Merimeister? She comes from California, too, you know." Garrett waited, interested, but she looked baffled and shook her head. "All right, then. Thanks,

Jenny." He turned to McCracken.

"Deputy, I think it's time to go ahead with our plan. I need a minute more here with Jenny while you get on the horn—we gotta start with some calls."

Looking interested, Jenny stood and let McCracken slide out of the bench. Quietly, Garrett addressed his deputy. "First, call Maggie Merimeister. Tell her we would like to see her, and that we will be by her place at about seven tonight."

McCracken nodded crisply, and he continued. "Then call Greta Anderson. Make sure she's at Alma's. Tell her we would like to talk to her and Carmen. Tell her we will be up in just a few minutes. Ask her how Alma's feeling."

"Yes, Sir." McCracken wheeled on her heels. Her adrenaline was pumping. This was going to be a good night.

Jenny sat back down across from Garrett, her eyes questioning. To her surprise, he reached across the table and took her hand. "Thanks for the information, Jen. Thanks for all the information. About the drugs, too, and about your past."

"You're ... you're welcome, Patrick." She shifted her hand slightly, trying to return the warm squeeze it was receiving, and she examined his face. How could such an ugly duck be so beautiful? A tender smile washed across her face, then she saddened.

"Oh, Patrick," she said, "I know how it bothers you. But we do have to accept one thing."

Soaking up the warmth from her hand, he barely heard her, but he emitted an appropriate "Ummhh?"

"Patrick, in spite of everything, you know, you may think they're gone, but we're still here. There will always be hippies. I will always be a hippie." She moved her hand, a weak attempt to extricate it.

Rita, coming up behind them to do refills, shook her head and slipped away, walking slowly, her ears tipped back. Garrett repeated his "Ummh," squeezed the hand to prevent its escape, and said, "I know."

30

Tuesday Evening at 6:00 P.M.

At Alma's House

"So you're planning to use my mother as ... as a decoy!" Gritty had been stirred up ever since the Harvest Apple discussion with Garrett, and this just frosted the cake. She'd called to waylay Alma's regular caretakers, telling them that she herself would tend to her mother's nursing needs and administer her medications tonight and in the morning, just as the sheriff had suggested, but it wasn't enough. She felt pinned down in this claustrophobic little place. She felt short of breath.

She'd paced, wheeling from window to window, while Alma dozed in her chair. She looked out at the once benign highway and the trees that now menaced on every side. She stared at the shed. For the first time, it hit home that a real murder had been committed there. Duz ... well, she knew her brother wouldn't have done that. Not that way. Not trying to frame friends. Which meant ... which meant there was a murderer loose. Didn't they say that once you had murdered, it wasn't such a big deal to murder again? Until they found him, any of them could be a target.

Such were her thoughts, and now she rocked her wheelchair back and forth with little jerks and looked grimly at the sheriff. "Honestly," she added, "A decoy. That is not such a good idea."

"I think it is," he drawled, his hands relaxed on his knees. Then, as if reading her mind, he added, "Ms. Anderson, you believe that when we arrested your brother we arrested the wrong man. If that's true, there must be a murderer loose. Don't you think that the best way to keep everyone safe, and especially your mother, is to find out who committed this homicide?"

"What about entrapment?" Gritty snapped. "You use these tactics, you'll get the right man and be unable to prosecute him because you entrapped him, then how safe will we all be?" She gave the impression that she thought Garrett and his brand of country-boy sheriffs were slow in the mental department.

"Yeah, I know." Garrett spoke mildly, running a hand over his head, the shaved pate already bristly from neglect. There was never time when he was in the heat of an investigation. "Gotta have a little faith in the law, I guess. There's been a time or two when we knew what we were doin'." He grinned at her, a placating smile that wasn't returned.

McCracken, still not fully briefed, wasn't sure, herself, as to exactly what was coming down, but she had plenty of faith in the law. "We'll take every conceivable precaution, Ms. Anderson," she said. "There'll be plenty of manpower around, including you and Ms. Weinant."

Carmen, who had been listening to the exchange between Garrett and Gritty, ignored McCracken; she didn't think of herself as manpower in a situation like this. Her tiny mosquito body vibrating with tension and her black eyes studying the sheriff intently, she interrupted. "Look, Sheriff. Don't you think that if you place an elderly woman in the position of peril that you propose, you should have her son present as well as her daughter? As for me, I can't conceive of consenting to your proposal without having Duz present."

The expression that crossed Garrett's face seemed close to amusement. "You're one step ahead of me, Ms. Weinant. Yeah, I've been thinking it might be wise to have your husband here. We can probably arrange for a deputy to bring him up. Will that help?"

Gritty turned to her mother. "What do you think, Mom? Do you understand what they are asking you to do?"

"Why, sure," Alma said, her voice calm. "They just want me to write a note that might help catch the murderer. I could sure do that. But I can't write, because I can't see, so I don't see any point in talking about it."

"Alma, you know you can write if someone guides your

finger," Carmen said. Garrett was relieved. Sure enough, the Duz agreement had made her an ally; more than assurance of Alma's safety, she wanted her husband out of jail. She continued, "We can get some of your pretty stationery, the ones you haven't used for a while. And we'll tell you what to say, help you keep on the lines and make it neat ..."

Gritty persevered. "But my point is, Mom! They aren't just talking about sending pretty little notes. They won't tell you who's going to receive the notes. And they want you to be here, tomorrow night, after Duval reads the will to Reider's family. It will look like you are here alone ... if the real killer comes ..." Gritty was trying to be very clear. Could Alma understand this? "Mom, listen to me! If the real killer comes, I'm worried about your safety."

Alma fixed Gritty with a cloudy brown eye. "But I won't be alone, will I?" She put the emphasis on 'alone,' causing Gritty to wonder if she got the point at all, but before she could say anything, Alma continued, "I heard this nice boy say that he would be here, and his young secretary." She paused to squint at McCracken.

"Young Lady, you know you have the most beautiful red hair. It just glows. You'll have to hide good or the killer will spot it."

So maybe she did get it, Gritty decided. Alma's mind was unnerving, what it did and didn't do. Now her gaze had returned to Gritty. "And I heard just now that you and Duz and Carmen will be here. At any rate, I've known Lyle all his life, and I think he would be sure that I'm safe."

Carmen frowned. "Who's Lyle?"

Garrett's hand was back at his scar, and his voice was resigned. "Me. I'm ..." he cleared his throat, and the words came out choked, "I'm ... Lyle. It's ... it's Mrs. Weinant's other name for me." What the hell had his brother done, he wondered, that had made such a big impression that his name was the only one Alma could recall? He sighed.

"Good then. It's settled." Alma reached for the phone. "Help me dial Hallie."

McCracken was across the room in a single bound. "No!" she said, staying Alma's hand. "You can't call anyone. No one else must know about this, just us here in the room."

Alma's face fell. "But this! This is important, isn't it? Hallie would want to know. She would want to be here to see who the killer is!"

Garrett cleared his throat. "Mrs. Weinant, we can't have anyone else know just yet or the killer may get frightened and not come."

Alma nodded, but she was still looking with suppressed longing at the phone. McCracken and Carmen were kneeling next to the bureau, trying to get at the phone jack, which was well boxed in behind it. Finally, resigned, Alma said, "Gritty, where's my girl tonight? Nobody came. Who should have come? It's already past six thirty ..."

Patiently Gritty said, "Mom, I told you. Tonight and tomorrow morning, I can manage. It will give everyone a little break, then ..." She paused, looked askance at the sheriff. "One of the women is supposed to come by tomorrow evening at six-thirty. I really do need the help for bathing and so-on. Will everything have gotten settled down by then?"

Garrett nodded. "Oh, yes. I expect everything will be resolved, or close to it, by then. Her caretaker should be able to — safely — resume all of her regular work with your mother." He emphasized 'safely', but Gritty did not relax.

There was a knock at the door and Red stuck his head in. "Here's that box you wanted from the clubhouse. The one the victim had his hands in."

"Thanks, Deputy."

"You going through it now?" Red made as if to come in, his eye on McCracken across the room, but Garrett shook his head.

"Ms. Anderson and Ms. Weinant will look for the letters and let us know what they find. When you finish your shift at the clubhouse, you'll want to get some sleep. We'll be needing you tomorrow evening for a little something different." Garrett smiled at him, and he left, reluctantly.

Garrett glanced at his watch. "Deputy McCracken and I have an appointment we have to keep. Ms. Weinant or Ms. Anderson, if we can dictate the contents of the note to you, then you can help Mrs. Weinant write it out in her own hand. We'll need two copies."

Gritty was looking curiously at McCracken. She was a distinctive looking girl. It was hard for Gritty to imagine the deputy being undercover. All that she said, however, was, "I guess we're ready. I seem to be outvoted here. Deputy McCracken will need time to prepare herself to deliver the notes."

"Right." Garrett felt in his shirt pocket and pulled out his notebook. He waited while Gritty took up one of her mother's writing tablets and a pencil, then read:

> *'At last, I am able to remember what I saw, and I've written it down so I won't forget this time. I think it would be best for you if you come alone to my house at _____. We must talk privately.*
> *Sincerely, Mrs. Alma Weinant'*

Gritty looked up. "And about the time?"

"Four o'clock, afternoon, will do for the one note. Five for the other."

McCracken had stood, Garrett assumed in preparation of leaving, but to his surprise she went to kneel by Alma, her face concerned. She patted Alma's arm. "Mrs. Weinant, there'll be a lot of people coming by tomorrow evening. Even your son. So you mustn't worry. The people who come will almost all be your friends."

Alma accepted the patting with a sweet smile. "Oh, that sounds wonderful. I love to have my friends drop by."

31

Tuesday Evening, 7:30

The Biedermann Tepee

Garrett, satisfied with himself as he pulled out of Alma's driveway, said, "Well, that'll bait the hook. Let's see what we get when it hits the water."

McCracken, who still wasn't sure how the plan all fit together, chose to nod wisely. She assumed that when it was necessary, the chief would tell her what she needed to know. They pulled into Maggie Merimeister's parking area.

Garrett had to concede that the grounds were a cut above anything else in the area. They'd been xeriscaped by a professional. Having once been cleared of boulders and trees with great labor by early settlers, the area again boasted cedar and pinion in careful groupings along the road, then rock gardens clumped like bonbons around the house. Scrub oak, wild rose, and sage were being encouraged among the rock gardens, in which cactus, yucca, Indian paint brush, and a variety of other native plants were cultivated. In one, a small water flow made its appearance near the top of the built-up rocky hill, then ran artfully among the stones to disappear somewhere near the bottom and presumably drop to the real creek bed, which was one of the natural accessories of the estate and which was already nearly dry for the summer.

The house itself would have been unrecognizable to those who had once used it as the first post office in the area. An architect had curved the newer adobe structure into the arms of the land, allowing it to embrace the tiny old log building and amplify it into tasteful square footage in the back. A southwestern touch saw pueblo pots decorating the shaded entryway, and kokopele windchimes sang gently along the eaves. The whole of the place gave off an air of wealth and pleasant tranquility. Neither of these qualities suffused Maggie's flushed face as she opened the door to their knock.

"Yes, hello, Sheriff Garrett ... Officer McCracken. I ... uh ...," she glanced across her shoulder at the interior of the house, "I ... understand you wanted to speak with me about ... something? Would you care ... to come in?"

Garrett's voice was cool. "I'm not sure. This is about a certain purse."

Maggie's face became genuinely befuddled. "A purse?!"

"Last week you drove Ms. Flute to the regular meeting of the Oozle Onion-Valley Community Club. That was on Wednesday, the day Mrs. Weinant discovered Reider Biedermann's body in her storage shed. When Ms. Flute rode to the meeting with you, she was quite taken with a certain purse that was lying on the front seat of your car. Do you recall that purse?"

The flush had left Maggie's face. In fact, she had paled, and she was clearly not sure what she should answer. After a pause which was long enough to cause McCracken, who realized she had no idea where Garrett was going with this part, to shift on her feet in anticipation, Maggie finally said, "I see. I thought you were here about ... about the murder. Yes, I recall that Hallie ... Ms. Flute ... very much liked ... the pattern on ... on that purse."

"We would also like to see the purse, Ms. Merimeister. Could you get it for us? Is it here?"

"It's ... no, I'm sorry, Officers." Maggie squared her shoulders, seeming to pull herself together. "The purse ended up in my car by mistake. I have returned it to its owner."

"By mistake." Garrett could see Maggie's features shift. The actress. He knew she was preparing a story about how the purse got in the car, but he sidestepped her. "Is the owner of the purse here now? In your house?"

The air seemed to leave Maggie, and her head turned uncontrollably to glance over her shoulder again. "Why ... why no! Of course not. Why would the owner of the purse be here ... now?"

"I can see your point," Garrett said calmly, then again distorted her intended meaning. "This is not a good time for her to be here. I'll tell you what; since she has your car, maybe you would like to ride along with us. We're interested in speaking with her, and it will help if you're there, too."

Maggie took a deep breath. Her shoulders became even more straight and her hand tightened on the door handle. Squarely facing the sheriff, she said, "Yes, then. All right. I feel chilly; just let me get a light sweater."

McCracken shot a glance at the sheriff. Was the woman going to try escape? And from what? What had they caught her doing? Garrett simply put his hand on McCracken's shoulder, guiding her into the house as they stepped casually in behind Maggie.

Maggie disappeared down the hallway that departed from the foyer to the left and they could hear her rustling around in the back. Then McCracken caught the odor. She darted her eyes toward the large living area that opened off the foyer to the right. Several windows were open and the room was aflutter with a soft evening breeze from the east, but McCracken was now absolutely sure what she smelled. Marijuana. Someone had been smoking pot in here. She turned to consult with Garrett, but Maggie had returned. McCracken was surprised to note that she really was wearing a sweater. Garrett, oblivious to his deputy, took the lady's arm and, guiding her toward the police cruiser, said, "Good. Let's head on up."

Within seconds, McCracken understood that they were headed toward the tepee. The foothills were still bathed in light from the west. McCracken watched them roll by; she felt as if she knew this part of the world by now. The three people in the police cruiser didn't talk, making the only sound the occasional crackle and comment of the radio, but McCracken had begun to get an inkling as to what Garrett was up to. She breathed deeply, readying herself for any action that might come from any of the hard core drug dealers that awaited their arrival.

When they pulled up next to the tepee behind the little black Mazda that Garrett had noticed missing from Maggie's yard, McCracken's eyes had already taken in all of the surrounding hillside. There was no movement. Unwary of any potential danger, Garrett slid out of the car, opened the door for Maggie, and said, "Let's go, Ms. Merimeister. It shouldn't take us too long to get this cleared up."

No one began shooting at them. McCracken rounded the car and then spotted Alice sitting tight up against the door of the tepee. She was hugging her knees, which were covered by a richly patterned, full cotton skirt from which her slender brown bare feet protruded. The skirt was topped with surprising taste by a deep-plum colored blouse and then by hair which, by some miracle, didn't match. Instead, it had already begun to grow out from its spiky purple arrangement of the previous week. It formed a pixyish brown and lavender cap that approached her ears. Her large blue eyes were on Maggie and her face was disconsolate. "They *did* find me," she said to her.

"Honey, I think they knew where you were all along."

Now McCracken knew. It wasn't the clothes and hair that made Alice look so different. She still had to mouth around the tongue ring, occasionally sucking spit, and the other rings were in place in her nose and ears. But what was different was that she wasn't high tonight. It surprised McCracken. Somehow it made Alice seem young and vulnerable, like one of McCracken's Little Sister Soccer girls.

Garrett said, "Alice, we have just come to talk to you about one of your purses. We heard about it because Ms. Flute thought it was unique and pretty. She said it's beaded, large beads, with a pattern of a wizard taming a unicorn. Would you know the purse I'm talking about?"

"Yeah, that purse." Alice's intonation was flat.

"Would you happen to have that purse here? At your tepee? We'd like to have a look at it."

Alice lowered her head to her knees. Through the cloth, they heard, "It's in Maggie's car." Aha, thought McCracken.

Garrett turned to Maggie. "With your permission, Ms. Meter ... uh, I mean, Merimeister?"

Maggie reddened. "I don't think it would help to deny you permission at this point."

Giving McCracken a slight nod indicating the car, Garrett turned back to the hunkered Alice. His tone was gentle. "Alice, before we talk about the purse, let's clear something up that's puzzling me. I think I've guessed where you've been for the last few days. It's my guess that you've been hiding out at Ms. Merimeister's. Is that correct?"

Alice looked up at him from her knees, scowling. "No crime in that, is there?"

Garrett squatted down facing her, his butt brushing the heels of his boots. "Well, so far I haven't seen any crime in anything anyone has done around here." He glanced up significantly at Maggie, who had taken a protective, arms folded position beside Alice. "Deputy McCracken and I are just trying to get some facts straight in order to investigate the murder."

The car door behind him closed with a small clunk. The hills seemed possessed of a preternatural quiet, as if holding their breath, against which the sound of McCracken's footsteps stood out like a slash of red in fresh snow. Without looking at her, Garrett took the purse, which McCracken handed over his shoulder. He glanced at it almost idly, squinted more closely, then moved it about in his hands as he looked back at Alice. "One question we had, for example, concerns the whereabouts of your husband. We've been searching high and low for him for nearly a week and haven't heard boo. Can you tell us where he is?"

Alice's eyes reddened. "Not really." She sniffled and wiped at her nose. Apparently it didn't make the ring hurt her nostril, Garrett thought, remaining quiet. After a minute, she added, "He took off. I don't know where he is."

"Did he say anything before he left ... say why he was going, or where? Anything like that?" Garrett's hands were feeling along the purse, detailing the wizard, poking at the clasp. "It could be helpful."

"He said he was going because he was scared. Barnswallowper keeps shooting at him. I think *that's* who you *should* arrest." Alice sniffled again, but her jaw had tightened and Maggie's hand was on her shoulder.

"*Shooting* at him? Ms. Barnswallowper has been shooting at Mr. Biedermann?" Garrett's fingers began to twist at one of the large beads on the purse, but his eyes didn't leave Alice's face.

"Yeah, you know. She hates us, you know? Says we're California hippie scum. She shoots right toward us whenever she gets a chance and when we scream and try to get away she'll holler that ... that uh, oh, oops, she thought she saw a prairie dog. Then she'll laugh and put her gun away. Then she'll say something like maybe the real dogs oughtta go back to their drug masters or some such."

Garrett's fingers had stopped for the moment. "She shot at you even on your own land?"

"Wherever she could catch us."

"And that's why Mac left? Because he was afraid he would be shot?"

"Yeah, I guess." Alice's lip trembled and her head went back down to her knees.

"Where did he go?" Garrett's fingers were working on the beads again, twisting away at the one he had started on before.

"I dunno. He said California." She was speaking through her skirt again. "He said to me, and I quote, 'Fuck it. The old man won't be any help anymore. I may as well get the fuck out of here and get somewhere I can get a life.' Thus spake Methuselah." Alice glanced up, pleased with her quotation and unaware of any inaccuracy. No one met her look, so her head dropped again.

The bead came loose in Garrett's fingers. He set the purse on the ground beside him, retaining the bead. He said, "But Alice. You were the one who most wanted to go to California. Why didn't you go with him?"

Alice's face came up again. It was scarlet. "You know perfectly well why. He wouldn't let me. Mac Biedermann was just like his old man. He didn't give a shit for anybody besides himself and now he's fucking gone and I am fucking glad. You know? Now do you get it? He dumped me like I was a piece of shit."

The fingers smoothed the large, gaudy bead, turning it over and over. Maggie's eyes had long since dropped, taking in the movement of Garrett's hands as if it were the swaying of a cobra. McCracken, too, was mesmerized by the moving fingers. Only Alice and Garrett himself seemed oblivious to the actions of his hands.

"Well, that clears that up," he said. "You're probably right. You are no doubt well rid of him." Garrett spoke reassuringly. He shifted in his squat, reaching in his pocket to pull out his pocket knife.

"There are some other things Deputy McCracken and I would like to know. For example, I'm curious as to how this purse keeps ending up in Maggie's car. Last Wednesday it was in Maggie's car, too, when she went to community club. That was before all the excitement, before you took up hiding with Maggie. Can you tell me how it got there then?" As if idly whittling, Garrett slid the blade of the pocket knife around the center of the bead, cutting it open along a fine seam concealed by the pattern.

Maggie started to open her mouth, but Alice fixed the sheriff with a defiant stare. "I love Maggie. She worries about me. Nobody in my own fucking family ever worried about me. They have no clue whether I'm alive or dead, even at this minute. Not right now, not ever! They don't give a shit. But Maggie always knows where I am. She's scared for me."

Garrett tipped the bead and a sugary white powder flowed onto the ground. For the first time Alice glanced at the activity going on with Garrett's hands. She shrugged and gestured casually toward the powder. "So that's why Mac beat the crap out of me last Tuesday night."

Still as if his fingers were an entity of which he was totally oblivious, the sheriff said, "Mac beat you?"

Alice sniffled again. "Sometimes. Tuesday night he did, you know? Tuesday night he sent me out with this purse, told me to drive the truck down to the Cowpath and get him some cigarettes and that somebody would meet me outside and offer to trade me purses, like always. I was to just trade and come on back home. I wasn't supposed to look in the other purse until he got it, then I could have it. Same deal as always. Big fucking deal. A different purse, maybe twenty bucks in it for me ... I hate purses. I wouldn't carry a purse across the fucking floor if that bastard didn't ..."

McCracken frowned. "But you carried one today!"

"I took that purse there to the funeral. I thought Mac might be there and I could hand it to him, tell him where to put it ..."

Garrett leveled his eyes at her. "So, back to a week ago, Tuesday. I take it you didn't make the trade then?"

"There was that same guy that always met me, like he said,

but I couldn't find the freaking purse. It was gone. The asshole got so freaking pissed. He shook me. Called me a pig whore bitch and he wouldn't give me the purse for Mac, even though I told him Mac had sent him the purse, that purse there you've got, and would make it right or whatever. I said I just misplaced it, it would turn up, but he hurt me. It was Maggie got him stopped."

"Maggie!"

"She's real brave. She saw him doing that and she jumped out of the car and said, 'Stop, you son of a bitch, we are on to you and I just called the cops on my car phone,' and he turned me loose and I ran back to her car."

"You were with Maggie? I thought you were in your truck ..."

Maggie took a deep breath. "I was coming home from the library meeting, Sheriff, just like I told you, when I saw Alice's truck in the pullout. Like she says, I do love her. This is rough country here. It isn't always the friendliest place to people they think of as outsiders. I'm so tired of being labeled a newcomer. I get lonely, and Alice has been a true friend to me, another daughter."

Garrett nodded. He picked up the purse and stood up, using his heel to grind the cocaine from the bead into the ground. "Another daughter," he repeated, his voice skeptical.

"From how you said my name, a minute ago ... you know, 'Meter'? I suppose you know a lot about me already. I guess you know that I have an older daughter, the rapper, Lida Meter." Even as tense as she was, her motherly pride showed through.

"I've heard of Lida Meter."

"She's good, isn't she? And Alice looks enough like her to be her little sister."

For the first time, Alice's face became animated. Wiggling to adjust the bulky skirt, she stood, too. Her voice was excited. "Maggie says maybe now that I've got Mac out of my system, maybe I can go with her to meet Lida. That would be so maximal!"

The sun was moving low in the western sky. The sheriff's face remained stern. Turning the still unopened purse over in his hands, poking at the other beads, he said, "So. Let me hear again, this time in detail—accurate detail—what you did Tuesday night, Maggie. Explain this purse, that night."

Maggie sighed. "It isn't such a big deal, Sheriff. I dropped off Carmen and Frieda after the Friends of the Library meeting, just like I told you. I really did. I didn't lie to you. Then I came on around Oozle the back way, and when I was passing the scenic pullout I saw Alice standing beside her truck. I pulled over and asked her what was wrong."

Alice cut in. "I was so relieved it was Maggie. I pulled out to pee, then that freaking truck freaking would not go, and I was already scared about Mac being pissed."

Maggie smiled indulgently. "When I pulled over, Alice just told me her truck wouldn't go and that she was supposed to be getting cigarettes for Mac. She didn't say anything about the purse." Her face darkened. "I hate that damn Mac. I tried every time I saw her to get her to get away. He had to control her every move, and I was as worried as she was that night that he would rough her up if she didn't do what he said."

Alice's eyes widened. "Maggie was right, too. When I didn't get the purses switched, he grabbed me by the arm when I got home and told me I was too stupid to trust with my own head." Alice looked at Maggie. "Then he twisted my arm and hit me on it. He always tried to hurt me in a way that people wouldn't see it, so I told him to quit because I couldn't wear long sleeves in this hot weather. He just laughed, kind of mean, and told me people would just figure the bruise was another dingbat tattoo." Her lip trembled. "Dingbat. That's what he said." She turned so that they could see the bruise on her upper arm. It had turned a sickly purple and green. McCracken silently agreed that when Alice had been done up like she was last week, most people wouldn't have thought twice about the bruise.

Maggie picked up the thread. "So the rest was pretty much like Alice said, although I didn't know about the purse switch and I am not so brave as she says. I just didn't know what else to do to get the guy stopped."

Garrett grunted. "So where did the purse turn up?"

"It had fallen under the seat. When we drove away, Alice told me what happened, so when we thought nobody was following us, we pulled over and pawed around. It was right there."

Alice had fully perked up; she was interested in the recap of this story. Now she cut in again. "And that's when I decided, screw it, let's see what's in that purse, so we opened it up. Boy, was I surprised! All there was was some pot! I had thought he was dealing big drugs that he got from his father, but shit! It was just some of the stuff we grow up here on our place. See?" Before Maggie could stop her, she reached over and took the purse from Garrett's hands, undid the clasp, and pulled out a plastic bag. Holding it up, she continued.

"There was more in here that night, of course. So when I pulled it out, Maggie said, 'Wow! I haven't seen any of that stuff since I left California,' and I said, 'well, shit, let's smoke some,' and she laughed and said, 'well, shit, why not?' and so we did ..."

Maggie's face had turned furnace red. She spread her hands in a placating gesture toward the sheriff. "I don't know what made me do it. I was so upset that night ..."

Alice nodded. "Yeah, Maggie and me was nerved up about that guy and all. First we kept lookin' back, worried he'd pop up like a Stephen King spook or somethin' leerin' in our window, you know? And we locked our doors. Then we each had a joint and after that we were way relaxed. I think we had more than one." She giggled.

"No wonder Mac thought I was a noodle head—I guess I was by the time I got there. We smoked awhile and Maggie told me about how shitty her husbands have been. She only liked the second one, and he died of a brain tumor. Boy, that was a shitty deal. And this last one is the worst. He's got an alimony settlement from her from their divorce! Can you believe that? *She* is supposed to pay *him*! At least when I divorce Mac, I won't have to pay him anything. He might find me and kill me, but he can't get money out of me." Her voice tapered off at the thought of Mac hunting her down, then she sucked in air and saliva and continued.

"Maggie's ex, he sure does want to get at her money so bad. That's why she's hiding out here in Croysant. She told me if he finds her, she won't have hardly a cent left. I hate husbands." Alice had run down; she simply stood, shaking her head at the grim reality of it all.

Maggie was still beet red. Gently, she said, "You're saying too much, Alice honey." To the sheriff and McCracken, she said,

"I should have told you. But neither Alice nor I was near Reider that night, so I didn't think it was important. We relaxed, like she says, then I drove her home. Which I would not have done had I known what was in store for her from Mac! I'd have taken her with me then. But I went on home alone and thought that was the end of it. I didn't know ... didn't know someone had just been murdered, just up the road from me." She gave the delicious little shiver that Garrett had seen her do on the first day he interviewed her. Watching her now, he attributed it to her life as an actress. She continued.

"And don't you see, Sheriff? And Ms. McCracken? It was important to me not to get a bad name here in this community ... I like this place. The people. I thought maybe ... I had hoped I could make a life here ..." Her hands dropped to her sides and an expression of true sorrowing crossed her face.

Garrett reached across and took the purse back from Alice. He removed a make-up kit and two twenty-dollar bills, handing them back to her, then he handed the purse to McCracken. "Alice, it looks to me like something illegal was going on involving your husband and his father," he understated. "With your permission we will retain this purse and look into the matter."

Alice nodded numbly. Neither woman was sure how to take what Garrett had just done. He said, "As for now, Alice, you need to get back into Maggie's car and go on home with her. It'll be more comfortable there to plan your future. You need a future, but you need one *without drugs*." His eyes met Maggie's, a stern look, and his brows raised in a question. "Most people around here aren't very tolerant of drugs, newcomers or not ... And we will be restricting this area around the tepee for when the investigators come. They'll be interested in the activities of your husband and father-in-law." He stressed the words 'husband' and 'father-in-law.' "You understand?"

Now Maggie caught on. "Thank you, Sheriff," at first unbelieving. Then, "Oh, thank you, Mr. Garrett. Yes. It must be. A future. And without drugs." She was near tears. Taking Alice's elbow, she started to steer her toward the Mazda.

McCracken was frowning. "Wait a minute."

Maggie sagged, and Garrett looked at his deputy, his brows raised. What now?

McCracken, holding the purse with one hand, with the other was scratching through her thick red hair in frustration. "Alice, I just need to know, before you go ...," she looked over at the old truck which had been parked for days now beside the tepee. "How did you get the truck home? Is it still broken? I guess Mac went down the next day ...?"

Alice shook her head. "Oh, no. Not Mac. He was too damn lazy ... he made me walk back down that night. I'd left that damn purse in Maggie's car again, like you know. I was hungry, so I grabbed some pot and stopped a couple of times with it and walked all the way back to that turnout. It took me hours. Then I slept in the truck and smoked some more. Well, I guess it must have been about noon when Duz Weinant came along. While I was trying to get it going. The truck."

Garrett, who had turned toward the police cruiser, stopped in his tracks and turned back. "Duz Weinant?"

"Yeah. He's a nice guy. I heard you arrested him for killing Mac's old man, but I think you're wrong. I don't think he did it. It was probably Victoria, the ice queen, shot him." Alice chuckled. "The ice queen. Iced the old man." Then she sobered. "Duz, like, that day. He was going to dig me out, but he didn't have a shovel."

McCracken said, "Were you stuck?" and Garrett said, "He didn't have a shovel?"

To Garrett, Alice said, "Well, he did, I think, but ..." then to McCracken she said, "I was kind of stuck ... there was a rock, but ..." She closed her eyes and gave her head a shake. "I don't remember, you know? I was tired and kind of high and my arm hurt ..."

The sun had gone down and the last light was going fast. Garrett peered through the gathering twilight at the girl. For some reason Alma crossed his mind. "Look, Alice. Please try to remember."

"About being stuck, you mean? Or about the shovel?" She bit her lip. She felt as if she were just one memory away from the safety and security of Maggie's car. Her eyes reddened again, and she said, "I can't ... I can't really remember. There was something about a shovel. Like, he didn't have one so he said he would use mine."

She stared over at the old truck, a look of genuine perplexity crossing her face. "He said something about how he could use our shovel, and he got it out of the back of our truck, but ... but Sheriff!" She shivered with the evening breeze. "That can't be right. That can't be right at all. I must be losing it ... losing my mind! A pothead, just like Mac said."

For the first time, tears began to streak her cheeks. "I know ... I'm so sure ... I think Mac and me didn't carry a shovel in our truck. Not that day. Not ... No. We *never* did."

32

Wednesday Afternoon at 4:00

By Alma's Converted Chicken Shed

"The thing is," Alma thought, "There just really isn't any reason for Gritty to be so blasted jumpy and tense." The hot afternoon wind, which Alma hated, had died down. You could see how Gritty might be jumpy with that wind, but that was no excuse for all of her wiggling around now. Alma considered the situation. Sitting here in her lawn chair, in the shade, on the east side of the shed, you could hear the blackbirds starting up again, ready for evening, and you could get a good look at the mountains.

Most of the snow was gone except on the high peaks. What was it Hallie always said? On June fifteenth, if there was still snow in the seven deep gulches coming off Pioneer Mountain, then the irrigating water should hold pretty good for the summer. Alma squinted and counted. Looked like just five gulches had snow. She wished Gritty would get on back out here and sit with her. She wasn't sure she was seeing it right. She glanced at a car coming up the road. Nobody she recognized off hand. Gritty was taking her sweet time.

And why was it Gritty'd gone in the house? Seemed like she said she was going to get her and Alma some lemonade for while they sat out here. Alma snorted in disgust. She didn't need lemonade; she just wanted to sit here in the shade in the companionship of her daughter and have her daughter sit still for five minutes. Or was it that Gritty thought she heard the phone ringing? Alma couldn't recall. Whatever, it seemed like Gritty'd been unusually skittish all day, even for her.

Alma got a grip on her cane. Maybe, she thought, I should

go on in and see what's holding that girl up. Clutching the wobbly arm of the aluminum lawn chair, she began unsteadily to hoist herself when she realized that the car had pulled in and was parking a little ways up in the yard. She sat back and watched with interest.

An attractive young girl had gotten out and was approaching Alma. She was thin, but she had a nice tan. She wore tailored khaki shorts, sneakers, and, Alma noted with approval, her white knit shirt, tucked in, had sleeves and a collar. Her long blond hair was parted on the left, pulled to the right and tied with a ribbon, causing it to cascade forward over her right shoulder in a loose, comfortable veil. "Hi, Alma," she called cheerfully.

This was Alma's good visual range. She recognized the girl at once and burst into a welcoming smile. "Why, hello, Lindy! I sure didn't expect you to drop by today. What brings you back to this part of the country?"

A brief expression of puzzlement crossed Lindy Zakely's face, but her deep brown eyes retained their warmth as she stopped near Alma's chair and squatted to her level. "You didn't expect me, huh?" She raised her head and looked carefully around the empty yard. There was no evidence of other cars or people. "You just sittin' out here by yourself, takin' in the sun?"

Alma looked disgusted. "Gritty was here, but she took off. You remember Gritty, my daughter? She lives in Denver."

"So. She headed back to Denver," Lindy affirmed, smiling, "And here you are by yourself. But you sure did recognize me, didn't you?"

"Oh, sure. I can't say you've grown since you were here with Lucky and Lew, but you've matured. You've become quite a young lady! But even so, I'd know you anywhere. You're a beautiful young woman."

Lindy took Alma's hand and squeezed it. "Thank you, Alma," she laughed. "You always were perceptive. Now tell me, what have you been up to lately? I haven't had a letter from you in quite a while."

Grimacing, Alma said, "Up to no good, I guess. I don't write much any more, not letters. I can't see, you know. I'm losing my eyesight."

"That's too bad," Lindy said, searching her face. "I always loved your long newsy letters, and I miss them. I suppose you just write notes now?"

"And I don't remember things very well," Alma said, continuing her train of thought. "So ..." she tried to think how her part of the conversation and Lindy's fit together. "So, I guess that's why I have to write notes."

"That would be a good enough reason, I suppose." Lindy was frowning.

"But as I recall," Alma added, "You haven't written too much lately, either. I think someone was looking for your letters just the other day. I can't remember ... but it seems like they were looking for your letters for some reason, and somebody said you hadn't written a lot lately." Alma smiled. "So, tell me what you've been doing now?" She didn't notice that Lindy's expression had become watchful. Carefully, Lindy began to speak.

"Do you remember that I was studying environmental biology at the University of Colorado? I was getting close to graduation, Alma ... just next year, I should have graduated."

Alma missed the nuance. "Oh, that's nice, dear," she said. "I wish I could be there."

Lindy's smile was gone, and she sat back on her heels. "Well, I don't think you can, Alma. Be there, I mean. You know this summer, in just two weeks, I was preparing to go into the field. I was going to document the behavior of conies up on Cottonwood Pass for my senior thesis. I was going to go with a good friend of mine, Zack, and I was really looking forward to it."

"Well, that sounds wonderful, Lindy!" Alma felt uncomfortable with the negative tone of Lindy's statement, but she chose to focus on the good part. "You know, Doug and I used to just love to go and watch conies. That's those little pika things, like rabbits," she added, as if Lindy might need an explanation. "We'd take a picnic, and sometimes, if we were real quiet, we could get them to come out from the rocks where they were hiding ..."

"Yes, that works, doesn't it?" Lindy interrupted darkly, but Alma kept talking, "... and lots of times they would gather up the grass and flowers and build little haystacks for the winter ..."

This time Lindy cut in sharply. "Alma, do you know what AIDS is?"

Alma stopped talking abruptly. "AIDS?"

"Right. Do you know what AIDS is? The sickness that is spreading all over the world, killing people by the thousands ... millions? Do you know what it is?"

Looking baffled, Alma said, "Why, yes. Yes, of course I know what AIDS is. It ... but I must be confused! I thought we were talking about your school and looking at the little conies. Were we talking about AIDS?"

"I guess now we are." Lindy had averted her eyes. Looking at the ground, she said, "Do you remember all those letters I wrote you? Do you remember how I told you that my father ... my father raped ... me?" She choked on the word 'rape,' caught her breath and continued. "Do you remember that he forced me and hurt me and that is why I ran away, why I ended up in the TRY program? At Harris's?"

Alma's voice was no longer happy. Gently she said, "Why, yes, Lindy. You told me all that. You and I wrote ... but you got away from him. And now he's dead. He died right here, you know, in this shed." Alma's glance at the shed resembled that of a tour guide pointing out the main attraction.

"Yeah," Lindy said bitterly, her eyes back on Alma. "Yeah, I needed to confide in someone, and you were always so kind. I thought I could trust you. Telling you about what Reider Biedermann did to me — getting it into the open — that helped me more than anything ever had helped before. It helped me get my life back on track."

"But that's good!" Alma said, fully alert now. "I'm glad you got things back on track. I heard you even got all of his money. That should help, shouldn't it? And didn't you just say you were going to go watch conies? Isn't that what we ..."

"I was, Alma, but I'm not, I don't think, not any more. Not with Zack. Not with anyone. Reider had AIDS, Alma! When he raped me, almost ten years ago now, when I was just a little girl, he was already HIV positive. And he gave it to me."

"Oh, Lindy." Alma's old chin began to quiver, her cloudy eyes tearing. "Not you. Not with AIDS!"

"And you know the worst part?" Lindy shifted positions,

her voice not sad, but angry. "You know the worst part? That son-of-a-bitch knew at the time that he was HIV positive. When my mother divorced him in 1994, he told her he had it. She didn't know about me, then. About the incest. She assumed he told her just to mock her ... to get even over the divorce."

"Oh, Lindy," Alma said again, but before she could continue, the door on the passenger side of the car opened and a woman in a tailored business suit emerged and walked briskly toward them, holding her hand out toward Alma.

"Hello," she said in a cultivated voice. "You must be the Alma Weinant I have heard so much about. I'm Betsy, Lindy's mother. You always did so much for my daughter."

Lindy's face had taken on a pained expression. "Mother, just once could you ever wait and tend to your own business? This conversation is between Alma and me. You said you would wait in the car."

"I'm sorry, honey." The woman's hair was worn in a tight and tidy bun which seemed to emphasize her slightly protruding thyroidal eyes and her sallow complexion. She had a soft, curving body that looked as if it might be prone to yielding to the forces of life, but her back was rigid and her tone steely, despite the apology of the words. "I'm sorry. It seemed as if you had taken quite a long time, and I thought I would see if I should come ... help."

"No, you shouldn't come *help*," Lindy said grimly. "As I tried to tell you, this ... it's me who needs to talk to Alma."

"But that's all right, Lindy. I'm glad to get to meet your mother, and ..." Alma was smiling again, and she was studying Betsy.

Lindy interrupted. "No, I'm sorry, Alma. I just ... I wanted to see you again. You were always a good friend to me, and I wanted to tell you about the AIDS in person. And then, I wanted to clear this up." She pulled Alma's note from her pocket.

"This note ... it says you recall what you saw ... that I should come at 4:00 today to talk." She hesitated. "I'm not even sure you wrote this, Alma. It doesn't sound like you. It sounds like some kind of blackmail note. Did you write this?"

Alma took the note and examined it, her eyes narrowed. "Yes, yes, I did. I particularly picked this pretty stationery."

Again Lindy interrupted. "But the note doesn't make sense. It says you recall what you saw — but I haven't been around you. What do you mean, what you saw? You didn't see me, not last Tuesday night, nor any time lately. Alma, what is it you thought you saw? What did you want to talk about?"

Betsy had stepped back, her eyes watchful. Alma handled the note, her face puzzled. "No ... no, I haven't seen you until just today." She shook her head. "That note doesn't have anything to do with you, Lindy. It has to do with the murder. It must have gone to the wrong person." She looked up, her good eye finding Betsy. "I think the note was meant to go to your mother. It was her I saw."

Inside the old converted shed, an audible gasp was stifled, going unheard as Betsy stepped forward and her daughter said, "What!?"

Alma nodded. "Why, yes. Like I told the sheriff, last Tuesday night I heard shots. I went to the window, just over there, see? From about there to here is the distance where my eyesight is good, and it was moonlight that night." Alma interrupted herself, mumbling, "You know, I'm not sure the sheriff got all this. The boy always seems a bit distracted ... I don't think he likes his name. But I'm pretty sure I told him."

Lindy had been stricken dumb, her mouth partially open, but Betsy had taken several strides forward. "Told him what?"

"Why, told him that after I heard the shot, I saw a woman standing outside the shed door, right over there. I didn't know who it was at the time, but now that I see you, Mrs. Zakely, I know it was you. I couldn't figure what you were doing here, and I would have called somebody, but then you got in the car and drove off, so I thought that whoever you were you were all right. Everything quieted down after that, and I could see Hallie's lights, so I just made sure the door was locked and went on to bed. I was going to tell Duz the next morning, but I guess it slipped my mind."

"Slipped your ..."

"And now that I know everything, I can see that was a mistake, because it was clearly you who shot Reider. You shot your ex-husband." Alma looked satisfied. "And that was certainly a good idea, Mrs. Zakely, considering what he did to Lindy."

At last, Lindy regained her voice. "Mother! You? You were *here*? You shot ..."

Betsy flinched. Her eyes were not on Alma, but on Lindy. "Well, yes, honey, I ..."

"But you said ... after I told you about the HIV ... after I told you that I had it and couldn't for the life of me figure out who ... Mother, I begged you! I didn't ever, ever, ever want to see Pappy again or have him know where I had gone ..."

Betsy's large eyes had grown bloodshot, her face splotchy. "I'm sorry, honey. I was so ... I was so angry!"

"But you came here! Here, after you promised me that ... we decided it had to be Pappy, and you promised me! You promised me you would go back to California and let it go."

"I meant to. I meant to let it go, but the car ... the car just seemed to head over the mountains ..."

"Didn't you even get it? He repulsed me! Remember how he even wrote me after I changed my name back to Zakely ... that yukky letter about 'just wanting to love me' ... I never got over being afraid of him, afraid he would find me again ... Oh, Mother, how could you?"

"Closure! Lindy, I needed closure! I hated him, too ..."

"But how did you find him?"

"Your grandfather kept tabs on him—a matter of self-interest—then after father died, I just followed up."

"I don't mean that! What in the world were you two doing in Alma's shed? How did you ... you find him in this shed?"

"I didn't, honey! Like I said, I just came for closure. He was at his house. The little strumpet Victoria wasn't there ... out doing her goody goody nursey thing, I guess. So I confronted him. He looked terrible, pale and gaunt. He said his head was pounding." Betsy chuckled grimly. "He was stunned to find ME at his door."

"What do you mean, you confronted him?"

"Just what I say. I told him he gave you AIDS. I told him what a shit he was. I'm afraid I worked myself into a frenzy."

"And with no consideration for me, for what he might do to me. Oh, mother ..."

"No, Lindy ... No, honey. I did. I did try to do right about what you wanted. I told him ... I told him the AIDS had killed you. I thought if he thought you were dead, he wouldn't ever try to find you again. You see?"

"You told him I was *dead*?!"

"I told him I was going to turn him in. I told him he was guilty of rape and incest and murder from the knowing transmission of AIDS ... and you know what he did?"

"Oh, Jesus Christ, Mother. What? What did he do?"

"No remorse. He never said he was sorry ... nothing. He just said I could tell everyone I wanted to, that I had no proof of incest, that you couldn't testify because you were dead ..."

"Mother, you knew Pappy. Why the hell do you even think it is a news item that he didn't care? He never cared."

Betsy paused, knotted her fist and held it to her belly. "I just ... I guess I never quite gave up ... even after all these years ... on getting him to ... to really feel something. Anything." She lowered her head. "He didn't, though. So I still wanted to get him, so I thought fast and I told him that the letters you wrote Alma would," she swallowed, "would function as testimony in lieu of your living statements. In the back of my mind I'd started to build a case, planning how you would go up against him as a witness in court and take him down, but I didn't want to tip him off that you were really alive, so I embroidered quite a story. I talked about your stay with Harrises, that you had friends all over, and how you wrote to Alma, all the details ..." Betsy sighed, then continued.

"He just said that Alma would have burned those letters years ago, so I told him that Alma promised you she would keep them because they were on such beautiful stationery. I never met Alma, but I remembered you mentioning her, and how you liked to write her on your good paper."

"That's right, too. I do love beautiful stationery," Alma interjected, causing both women to jump. Her face was animated, having watched the exchange with great interest. "I thought that Reider was after those letters. I saw that he was pawing through them when he died."

Now it was Lindy's turn to look perplexed. "I guess ... I guess it explains why he was here. But Mother ... I don't understand. I thought you confronted him at his house."

"I did. But I got a little afraid of him myself. He looked pale, frowzed up, wild-eyed, like a madman, so I put on a brave front, flounced down the walk and left. I started toward Stoney City. It was so quiet, the mountains and canyon, and no one passing, and I drove and thought, getting more and more frantic. I was afraid he didn't believe me. He was always so crafty. I was afraid he would realize that you were alive and try to track you down and threaten you. Just as you were afraid he would."

"Fine time for you to decide that," Lindy muttered.

"I'm sorry, honey," Betsy said once again, wringing her hands. "I did what I could. I got my courage up and went back to his house. I don't know what I was going to do ... tell him I wouldn't call the cops, I guess."

"So ... did you?"

"He wasn't there. I went in, even, looked around, called out. Nobody. I was getting irrational. I guess you could say I panicked. At first, I thought he was already on his way to hunt you down. I started back toward Croysant, thinking to catch him.

"Then when I hit the highway, it occurred to me. He would try to go for the letters. Alma, this one thing, I did right. I got worried about you. I was afraid he would hurt you."

Alma looked worried and said somewhat irrelevantly, "Oh, my! I wouldn't want that!"

"So I stopped at that restaurant down there, the one just outside of Croysant? And I thought, well, it is a small town. Somebody here might know Alma."

"Of course," Alma said indignantly. "*Everybody* knows me."

"That's what it seemed. The first person I asked knew you. I told her I was on my way to Stoney City and running late, but just wanted to say 'hello' to you and was turned around because it was night. I told her I was one of your old city friends, which was a little true. I was nervous as a cat, though. I was getting more and more scared of what Reider might do."

"You could have called the cops," Lindy said drily.

Betsy looked aggravated. "I told you, I was trying to respect your wish about not having Reider know about you. That's why I didn't call the cops, as you put it. Besides, at that point I didn't know if he was here or what."

"So you just forged bravely through the night ..." Lindy's tone was sarcastic, but Betsy ignored her.

"When I walked out of the restaurant, it was very moonlight. I happened to glance down into the front seat of a pickup that was parked by the walkway, and there was a gun lying right there. I'm not good with guns, but I was scared. Somehow, I got the idea that if I had a gun, Alma and I would be safer.

"The pickup was open, but it wasn't my gun. I used a kleenex to pick up the gun. I had to carry it like this." Betsy demonstrated clumsily, holding an object at arm's length with the thumb and first finger. "I don't like guns; I carried it barrel down. At the time, I was thinking I would just borrow it for self defense, then I would bring it back. No one would even know.

"So once I had driven a little ways, I put on my driving gloves and looked the gun over. I figured out it was loaded, but I didn't think I'd have to use it. That's what is so awful. I will never forget what happened after that."

"You shot him. In the back." Lindy's voice held both amazement and disgust.

"When I got here, I saw Alma's lights on, but there was a faint glow in the shed, so I parked and brought the gun with me. I was crazy with fear and anger. I was so sure that he had heard the car, because the night was quiet, and I expected him to just pop out the shed door. I thought he would try to hit me.

"But nothing happened and I kind of sneaked up on the shed. When I looked in, he had his back to me. He was leaning against a chest of drawers next to him, and one of his hands was resting in the box on the table in front of him. I guess he was thinking what to do next. I started to call his name, then I just lost it.

"I thought of what he'd done to you, how it would probably kill you, what a worm he was ..." Betsy was acting out now, her hand twitching as she once more experienced the heft of the gun. "I raised the gun. I held it steady on his back for several seconds. I wondered if he would turn around, but he didn't, and it started to be a challenge. You bastard, I thought! You dirty, bloody, slimy, shitty bastard. And I thought, I can do this. I can do the world a favor ... no one needs that dirty, slimy ..." Betsy's hand was raised, shaking, holding the imagined weapon. "I thought, again, I can do this. I can do this one good thing. And I did. I pulled the trigger." Betsy flinched, then smiled. "God, it was loud. Oh, god, it was great!"

Betsy's blotchy face had streaked with tears and she was trembling, still holding her arms in front of her as if holding the gun. Lindy went to her. "Yes, you did do the world a favor." Her voice had softened. She put her arm around her mother and gently pushed down her extended arms. Betsy leaned against her and kept talking.

"It was dreadful. He fell forward, right into Alma's box! I wasn't sure ... it sounds stupid now, but I wasn't sure he was dead. The flashlight came loose and rolled onto the floor, and when it hit it felt like ... felt like he had done something. I was so horrified." She passed a hand over her face.

"I just went numb. Instead of going in to see if Alma was okay, or instead of returning the gun, or calling the police, or anything, I bolted. I drove so fast for a couple of minutes, then I thought, 'I can't keep this gun,' so I pulled over. I saw some water shining in the moonlight on the other side of the road and I ran across. I threw that gun ... that damn gun! I threw it as hard as I could."

"In the pond?"

"I don't think it went in. I didn't hear a splash. I tried to look for it, but the moonlight made the bushes shadowy, and I couldn't see anything. I was shaking so hard. I thought I would throw up, but I didn't. In the distance I saw car lights coming and I thought, 'Oh, no! Oh, no!' and I ran and got back in my car and started driving again before the other car passed me."

"Where did you go, Mother?"

"I kept driving. The more I drove, the less I wanted to face up to what I had done. I played music, distracted myself, listened to commentators. I finally got tired and pulled out to sleep before I got to the Eisenhower Tunnel, but I couldn't sleep. Then I recalled a trick my parents had taught me about doing business. I told myself to act like what I wanted to have happened, had happened. The actions would help make it true. I decided to act like nothing had happened. I took the car back to the rental and caught the first plane back to San Francisco."

Alma looked very satisfied. "This does explain a lot. You didn't tell a soul. No wonder the sheriff was having such a hard time figuring out who killed him."

Betsy was leaning against Lindy and didn't answer. It was Lindy who said, "Alma, it's just you and I, even now, who know. Maybe they won't ... maybe I could just get in the car now and take her away. Even if you said anything," she said, looking at Alma assessingly, "It would just be your word against ... ours. I could say ... I could say mother was with me ..."

Betsy looked up. "I'm sorry, Honey. That's not a good idea. I can't get over it. I'll keep thinking about it. I'll have to face it anyhow. There's no life for me now."

A voice said, "And Lindy, your mother does have other problems." Sheriff Garrett stepped from behind the shed and put his hand protectively on Alma's shoulder. "Others have heard what she had to say. We now know what happened, and we will have to deal with it."

"Why, hello, Lyle," Alma said, pleased. "Where did you come from?"

Red came up from the lilac bushes near the house. Garrett said, "We've been keeping an eye out for you since the murder, Mrs. Weinant." He patted her. "Red, you'll need to take Mrs. Zakely in to Riversmet. I'll stay with these folks while you use the phone in the house to have dispatch send our car over from the clubhouse."

"So you have to arrest my mother for murder?" Lindy's voice was tight, her arm protectively around her mother.

"Oh, no, Ms. Zakely. We'll have to take her in for questioning. She didn't kill Reider Biedermann. The D.A. may have some lesser charges. We'll see. But it's not possible to murder a man who is already dead."

33

Wednesday Evening at 5:00

Alma Stays By the Shed

All of them kept staring at McCracken, but Red was the worst of the lot. He and Carla brought the car down to gather up Betsy Zakely, and Garrett was glad to get Red out of there. When McCracken asked if she should stay undercover for today, Garrett hadn't known what he was bargaining for. Now he figured Red's departure was all that would get his deputy's mind back on the job. As for Garrett, he had to admit that he was having trouble keeping his own eyes off her. She wasn't the same person.

Her long red hair was gone. What was left was a fuzzy little bald knob. Almost, he thought with dismay, like his own ugly pate. The hair had been dyed before it was removed, giving the illusion that it would grow back brown. The freckles were still there, discordantly red and oddly feminine, but she was in a homeboy outfit. Her bulky pants slouched over Nikes, and a ring dangled from one ear. One of the tattoos had been especially artfully placed on her well-developed, bare, left biceps. He'd been horrified to see the tattoos, especially that one, the enchained, half-naked woman, until she laughed, telling him they were just decals. She was nuts! Why did she think that impersonating Alma's great-grandson meant looking like a gang member? He sighed. Apparently it had worked. At least the Zakelys bit when she delivered their note. We'd see about the next one.

In her own car, Lindy followed the police car bearing her mother away for questioning. After they'd gone, Gritty rolled in her chair out of hiding behind the house, and Carmen and Duz exited the shed. Everyone wanted to talk. They were stirred up about the fact that Alma really had heard the shot with which Betsy plugged her ex-husband. They couldn't get over it. Sure she'd *told* them, but her way of explaining the shots hadn't made sense to them, so, as if she were a child, they hadn't listened.

And they couldn't get over Biedermann's being already dead when he was shot. Garrett didn't comment. "We have very little time," he said. "Does anyone need to use the bathroom? How about you, Mrs. Weinant?" His eye caught again on the oddly bald homeboy. With an effort he moved it along. Alma, obviously so excited she wouldn't miss a minute of this for anything, declined.

"All right then. Now, Mrs. Weinant," he said kindly, "As you can see, we're not quite done here. We still don't know who really killed Mr. Biedermann. Another person may be coming by, and this time I want Gritty to be with you. All right?"

"All right," she said eagerly. This was better than anything she'd ever read or watched on the television when she was able to see. Perry Mason, she thought, pleased at remembering the name. Just like Perry Mason. On the other hand, she wished she could remember who it was who'd just been here. Oh well, it didn't sound so important now. Everyone seemed more interested in the next arrival.

Garrett interrupted her thoughts. "Good," he said. "Now this time, the rules are different. You just sit back and relax. *Don't say a word.*" He gently shook a finger at her. "Can you do that for me, Mrs. Weinant? Let Gritty do the talking and you take it all in, all right? Just listen, in case we need you as a witness in court." He glanced at his watch. At best they had ten minutes.

"All right," Alma said, but Gritty said, "Me?"

Garrett heard a car coming up the road from down country. "Time to take cover. Everyone!" As quickly as a rabbit he himself disappeared into the rosebushes by the shed, but Gritty could hear his voice as the car came into view. "Gritty, that's Reider's other daughter pulling up. You're going to try to find out the path that shovel took to end up in the back of Duz's pickup. I'm pretty sure she knows the answer, if anyone does." Carmen and Duz could be heard shuffling on the apple boxes in the shed, but the homeboy had disappeared like a ghost.

The car turned into the gate and Gritty muttered, loud enough for Garrett to hear, "Thanks a lot for the lead time, Gomer. I just love being able to plan my moves ahead." Fortunately, she couldn't see Garrett behind the shed. He was grinning.

Christa's short legs dropped from the driver's seat of the car. In the back was a child's car seat. Garrett couldn't tell if Eirene was in it, but Christa made no move to take her out if she was. She came hesitantly across the yard, her eyes fixed on the two women sitting beside the shed. It was Christa who spoke first.

"I know Alma, but who are ... oh, I know you. You're Alma's daughter. The Denver woman." She pulled the note from her pocket. "Was it you who wrote this?"

Gritty wheeled forward, her hand extended. "Yes, I am Alma's daughter, Greta Anderson. And you are?"

Christa ignored the proffered handshake. "I'm Christa. No last name necessary. I think you know who I am, because I think you wrote this note. Then you hired somebody to deliver it— some weird-looking little gang monster. That wasn't any relative of Alma's that brought it. And your mom couldn't write something like this, anyhow. She has a hard time with her eyes, don't you, Alma? I came alone, like it says, but I think this note is a trick. I think you or somebody else wrote this note." Christa's face was grim.

Gritty cleared her throat. How could she do this? It was wrong. It was entrapment. "Well," she started, thinking of Alma at the window that night, hearing shots, looking out at Betsy Zakely. "Well, I did help her. But ..." No, she decided, saying that much wouldn't be lying. She continued. "I did help her, but she ... picked the stationery and wrote the note."

"Hmmph." Christa eyed Alma. "Is that true, Mrs. Weinant? You saw something? You wrote that note?"

Alma, concentrating on remembering that she *wasn't* supposed to talk, smiled and nodded. Gritty was silent, trying to think. The shovel ... focus on the shovel.

"So what is it you think you saw? And why do you two want me out here by myself? Are you going to try to blackmail me? Is that what you want, Greta Anderson?"

It came together. Gritty burst out, "No, no! Of course not. Don't you understand? Alma's only son, my brother—he's in jail. And we know he didn't kill your father. Surely you can understand that we're worried about him. We think ... Christa, do you know ... could you tell us how it is that the shovel that killed your father ended up in my brother's ... in Duz's pickup? That's all we want to know! Just that. Just about the shovel." Gritty hadn't realized how much she really did want to know about the damned shovel until she actually said it. To her annoyance, her tone became pleading as she spoke.

"Yeah, right." Christa was looking from one face to the other. "Yeah, right, that's all you want to know. What makes you think your precious little brother didn't put the shovel there himself, fingerprints and all? I suspect he got riled over the water deal, got pissed at my father dearest, otherwise known as the master skunk, and with poetic justice, he let him have it with an irrigating shovel."

"It wasn't Duz's shovel."

"It wasn't mine, either," Christa said, then caught herself. "Look, I don't know what you saw, Alma, but Reider Biedermann, the original asshole, was shot to death in that shed, and I didn't put him ..." There was a long pause, then, "I didn't shoot him."

Gritty cleared her throat and said quietly, "I don't know, Christa. But you need to understand ... the autopsy showed that Reider was already dead when he was shot."

Only Alma's eyes had tracked to the road. Both younger women, focused on their verbal duel, had failed to hear the approaching car. Now it made itself known with squealing brakes, splattered gravel, a sharp turn into Alma's driveway. Screeching the car to a halt, Duval yanked open the door and ran toward the clustered women. Garrett peered back toward where McCracken was hidden. "Don't come out, McCracken," he prayed under his breath, "Not for just a minute," but the bushes remained quiet, no homeboy in evidence.

Duval was worked up to the point of tears. "Christa!" he shouted. "Damn it, Christa! I begged you not to come out here. Don't answer. Don't say one word more than you already have.

Can't you see this is a god damned trap?!"

He began to dervish around the yard, peering behind the trees and in the shrubbery. "Garrett, I know you're here ... AHA!" He was peering into the shed, where Carmen and Duz cringed on the apple boxes. "AHA!" he repeated. "Snitches! Stooges! Stoolies! Sly little skulking puppet-mice ... where is your puppet *master?*" He ran past them into the empty shed and kicked at the back, then whirled and was out the door before their astonished mouths could speak.

Running back to Christa, he took her by the shoulders and said, "No more talking. No more, girl! I know the sheriff is ..."

Garrett, emerging from the rosebushes, finished the sentence. "Right here, Mr. Duval. I take it you represent Christa Beekermann-Shipley?"

Duval, his button-down collar flapping loose, his bald head glistening in the hot afternoon sun, and his hooded eyes and neutral slack mouth as animated as Garrett had ever seen them, whirled to face his adversary. "And *I* take it, Mr. Garrett, that you have chosen to specialize in entrapment?"

"Well, maybe a little," Garrett conceded calmly. "We're mighty interested in the travels of a particular shovel that was used for no-good here about a week ago Tuesday night. Maybe it's a good thing you're here. Maybe you can help us track that shovel."

Christa was looking up at Duval with an expression that was as astonished as everyone else's. "What ... what do you want me to do, John? I really don't think Alma saw anything and ..."

"What I want you to do," Duval said, looking at Garrett, "is to get in your car and drive away. Drive home, while I keep these wolves at bay. I'll follow. Where's Eirene?"

"At the sitter's," Christa responded, taking a tentative step backward, but Garrett interjected.

"Christa, before you run, you must understand that there really was an eyewitness to the altercation that took place in this yard last Tuesday night. The battle has been described to us in detail. Despite what Mr. Duval says, you would be better off not to play cat and mouse with the law at this point."

"Alma did see it?"

Duval made a shooing motion toward her. "He didn't say

that. He just said there was an eyewitness. Not who. Not what they saw. You know, if there was a good eyewitness, they would have made an arrest long before now."

McCracken had slipped from hiding and was slouching nonchalantly against the picket fence. She looked like she should be decorating it with gang graffiti. Duz and Carmen, out of the shed, had protectively flanked Gritty and Alma, but Carmen's head was cocked toward Christa, her attention focused on her. Her eyes were deeply thoughtful.

Garrett stepped forward and took Christa's right hand. "That's quite a cut you have there, Christa. It looks sore. How did you get that cut?"

Christa snatched her hand away and Duval stepped between them. "Leave her alone, damn it! Let's go, Christa."

"Yeah, leave her alone, Sheriff." Carmen's voice flowed silvery, trout in deep water. "I know Christa. She always just wanted a normal life. She told me herself. She wanted to live here, bring Eirene into the community like a normal kid." Carmen's hair caught the evening breeze and tangled outward, unexplained.

Garrett turned toward Carmen and said patiently, "I understand, Ms. Weinant. I understand what she wanted. But sometimes life doesn't deal us the cards we wish we had. There was blood there, by that shed. An eyewitness saw the blow with the shovel which drew that blood. I need to find out about that blood. And about that shovel."

Christa was biting her lip. Carmen said, "So Biedermann was human enough to shed blood. We can believe that. Somebody hit him ... not Duz or Christa, but someone ... and ..."

His voice very quiet, Garrett said, "DNA tests can identify even the tiniest of blood splatters. The blood by the shed was not Reider Biedermann's. Nor was it your husband's, Carmen. Look at Christa's hand." Almost reluctantly, everyone's eyes shifted to Christa's hand, which she opened even as they looked, as if the hand itself were a surprise to her.

"I come from a ranch," Garrett continued, "And I have had such a cut as you see there on the palm of Christa's hand. My cut was from a large splinter on an old shovel handle. I don't know what Christa's cut is from. She won't tell us. I do know that once we get a writ to get a sample of Christa's blood, the DNA will tell if it is the same as the blood spilled here on the ground by the shed last Tuesday night."

Carmen took a step forward, her voice distressed. "But what about Eirene? You don't want to arrest a young mother with a child. Alma didn't see ..."

Garrett looked at Carmen sharply, his eyes assessing. Good cop, bad cop? He said, "No, Ms. Weinant. Alma didn't see the blow with the shovel. You seem to have forgotten ... we have another witness." He gestured toward the house perched on the hill on the other side of the gulch. "Hallie Flute was awake and on her back porch last Tuesday night. Watching. Don't you recall?"

Duval's eyes, angry, followed the direction of Garrett's gesture, but Christa's had dropped, staring at the incriminating hand. Duval said, "Christa, these people are trying to frame you, and ..." but Christa interrupted him, her voice barely audible.

"You talked, Carmen, about Eirene." Christa looked up, her eyes meeting Carmen's. "Well, that is what is important here. My little girl, Eirene. My whole life has been a lie, you know. That asshole, Reider Biedermann, he pretended to be a loving father to me, but he was scum. He never married Victoria. He toyed with her, with my mother, like a cat with a mouse. She wanted marriage more than anything, but he would just hold out the promise, then snatch it back.

"Less than a month ago he mocked her, told her that he planned to leave her. He told her he had another woman and planned to change his will. He implied he was going to marry somebody else, but I guess from the way his will read that the other woman he had in mind was his darling little legitimate daughter." The word 'legitimate' came out in a lump.

Duval looked sick. His hand hovered near Christa's shoulder, then dropped. "Please, Christa ..." he pled. She ignored him.

"I was never an innocent little girl with a sweet, protecting daddy. I was never cute little Christa Biedermann with Barbie dolls and pretty clothes, or even toy horses and ranch clothes. I was an ugly little bastard whose father used her whenever he couldn't find a grown-up woman to get it off with. He mocked

266

me, just like he mocked Victoria. He'd come in my room and say, 'Come here, Biedermann. Come to Pappy. Or should I say Beekermann ... you probably don't even know what your name is, you stupid little drugged out goon.' He mocked me for taking drugs, but he was the one who started me on them, even before I was born ... he'd kept Victoria drugged out long before she had me. And Mac! Mac even tried to use me, until I bashed him one day." Her eyes went up briefly to meet Garrett's and a satisfied smile slipped across her face. "I didn't use a shovel. I used a baseball bat. And I got him good."

Christa's eyes dropped again. "I didn't want that life for Eirene. I thought nobody would love me, and when Les Shipley paid attention to me here in high school, I was in heaven. As soon as I could, I married him and we moved into the trailer next to his folks. It took getting pregnant with Eirene to get him to commit, but I thought it was worth it. It was such a relief! Such a relief to get away from the hell where I was raised ...

"Then Eirene hadn't been here even two years when one night I caught that bastard fondling her. Oh, god ... that dirty, fucking asshole, Les! I never dreamed he'd turn out to be a replay of Reider Biedermann. Oh, god, I am so tired ...."

Alma spoke crankily. "Lyle, you know better than this. This child has had enough. You need to let her alone."

"I'm as sorry as you about this, Mrs. Weinant," Garrett replied grimly, "but a murder was committed here last week. For the sake of justice, and for your son's sake, we must find out what happened."

Taking Alma's hand, Gritty leaned into her line of vision and nodded. Alma turned to catch the eye of her son, but he'd gone into the house. He emerged with a chair, which he set beside Christa. Then, looking awkward, he beat a hasty retreat. Christa watched him return to where he'd been standing by Alma, then sat with resignation in the chair.

"It's no big fucking deal, Sheriff. I whacked Reider with the shovel. You know it; I don't even know why I have to go through it all, telling it all, but I will, if it makes you happy."

"If you'd rather wait, you could make a statement ..."

Duval closed his eyes, his face filled with pain. Tentatively, his hand found Christa's shoulder and rested there. "Do you have to arrest her?"

As if she had heard neither of them, Christa said, "I didn't plan it, if that helps. I was so worried about ... about that custody hearing. Reider was paranoid ... a paranoid, schizophrenic, sociopath. After he told Victoria he was changing his will for another woman, he decided she was plotting against him. He stewed around about that and of course couldn't figure out what she was doing because she wasn't doing anything. But he was fixated on the idea.

"Finally, he got hold of me and told me that if I didn't find out what my mother had up her sleeve, he was going to go to that custody hearing and tell the judge all about my heavy drug use.

"He wouldn't have stopped with the truth, Sheriff! He wouldn't have told how I never took anything once I learned little Eirene was coming. He was a born liar. He planned to smear me so bad that I would never see Eirene again. Les would have her." Christa's knuckles tightened on the arms of the chair. "Think about it. His own granddaughter! Reider was going to be sure that a child molester would have custody of his own granddaughter."

Christa's jaw set and she looked into the distance. "Last Tuesday night, I got off work at the Harvest Apple. I picked up Eirene from the sitter's and headed home, worried about that hearing and dog tired. Just out of Peaseford I overtook a damn truck that was weaving all over the road. I couldn't get past, then all of a sudden I realized it was Reider's. I followed for a while, just worrying and thinking, then I got a bright idea.

"I would follow him wherever he was going. I thought he was going to his house, but I really didn't care where. What I thought was, was that I would make up a story about Victoria, something that would get me off the hook, something that would keep Eirene safe.

"I thought all the way up the road, trying to come up with something. Then he started doing funny stuff. He stopped at the Cowpath, and he sat in the car there maybe ten minutes and smoked. I kept tailing him, but he didn't go home. He went up here past Alma's and went down in the dry wash toward Hallie Flute's. I stopped on the highway and waited, turned off my lights. I was getting more curious than anything. After a little bit, he came walking up the road, walking as unsteady as he drove. I couldn't think what to do. He walked right past me and came up here to Alma's." She closed her eyes, the image clear. "I could see him weaving along up the road in the moonlight.

"When I saw him go into Alma's, I started my engine and drove by, like I was just an innocent passerby on the road, but I craned my neck and looked down there. Reider was just standing in the yard, looking around like he was lost. I didn't know what to do.

"Eirene was asleep in the back in the car seat, and I started wondering if he would hurt Alma or something. I decided I should see what he was up to, so I turned around down at the next wide place and drove back. I got out of the car, but I locked the doors and put the keys in my pocket. I was worried he might try to snatch my baby." Christa shivered and folded her arms across her ribs, huddling into them. "I guess it was fate. He succeeded in taking her, no matter what I tried to do."

No one knew what to say. Both Gritty and McCracken could be heard to swallow in the loud silence, and Christa continued. "Just my presence pissed him off. I asked him what he thought he was doing in Alma's yard, and he called me a nosy little snot. He told me that whatever he was doing, it was none of my business. I have to admit, the madder he got, the madder I got. I am his biological child, after all. Spawn of the devil.

"I accused him of planting drugs here, making this place one of his drug drops. He laughed at me. He said that he wouldn't dare tell me where his drug drops were because all the drugs he could supply would end up in my nose. But he looked funny — he was wobbly, kind of pale and weavey.

"Finally, he told me that I could kiss off my baby forever, that he would see to it at the hearing that I never saw her, ever again. I've never hated anybody so much in my life as I hated him, you know? He was a great liar, and I fully believed he could pull it off. I ran at him, and I started hitting him with my fists.

"Reider was always a lot stronger than me. He grabbed my hands and started pushing me around, and all the while he was saying awful stuff, like, 'What's the matter, little girl? Don't you love your old Pappy, little girl? Maybe at least Eirene can learn to love her Grandpappy—I have a few things I can teach her, don't I? Don't I? Once Les and I get the ugly old mother cow out of the way, we'll know how to take care of that little girl, take care of her right ...' That's the kind of stuff he said, pushing at me, forcing me around this yard ..." Christa shuddered, but she did not cry, and her lack of tears intensified the horror of everyone in the group. Perhaps they should have told her then to be quiet, to let it go, that no more need be said, but they had to know. Their compassion was overcome by their terrible need to hear the ending of the story.

Christa took a shuddered breath and continued. "Then a funny thing happened. I don't know why, but he suddenly seemed weak, out of breath. He dropped my wrists and the next thing I knew he had bent over and grabbed his knees. He was gagging, sucking at the air like a fish out of water. I was just frantic. I had to get out of there; I had to get out of there with Eirene, but I thought he would catch me before I could unlock the car." Christa looked up and directly fixed Garrett's eye.

"And now, Sheriff. Now comes the part you wanted to hear. I was scared, and frantic, and I looked around, and right there," she gestured, "Right there, in front of that shed. There was a splintery-handled old irrigating shovel. I grabbed it. I grabbed it so fast, and when Reider seemed to catch his breath and started to raise up, I lifted it up and brought it down with all the force I could muster. I didn't think or feel anything. I didn't feel the handle of that shovel splinter and cut into my hand. I didn't even notice it was bleeding until I got home, then I spent nearly an hour working the splinter out." She looked down again at her hand with the same surprised expression she had shown before.

"He fell forward and I just thought I had knocked him out. I ran to the car. It was weird, like I was on slow motion or something. I got out my keys, got the car open, and I kept looking back, thinking he would be up in a minute, crazy mad and ready to kill Eirene and me both. I didn't think about the shovel until I was out of the yard, but I had jammed it right in the front seat with me. The handle was poking up near my head. I drove a little ways, then I pulled off at the scenic turnout, and guess whose truck was there? Our darling little Mickey Mac's." A strange, ghostly smile crossed the woman's pale face.

"You have to give me credit. I really wasn't thinking. What I did next was just a gut reaction. I got out and got one of Eirene's clean nighttime pull-ups from the back of the car, and I wiped and wiped and wiped on that shovel handle, where I'd touched it. I was just like old Lady Macbeth. I was 'out damned spot' all the way. Then I stuck the thing in darling little Mickey Mac's truck. On the way home, I thought, 'Let him explain it. Let that son-of-a-bitch explain it.' As for Duz Weinant, I never expected him to have to explain anything."

Duval was still standing rigidly at her side, holding her shoulder. His eyes had gone closed during the last part of her narration, and Garrett suddenly realized that there were tears on his cheeks. Christa looked up at him now and said, "There is one thing. I didn't hit him with the sharp edge of the shovel. I used the back, just to knock him out. Will that count for anything, John?"

34

6:30 Wednesday Evening

In Alma's Living Room

Chad Harville and Jim, the Stoney City guy, had been propped against the back of Alma's house awaiting orders, and Garrett sent them to Riversmet with Christa (under arrest for assault until more information became available, Garrett said) and Duval, who insisted on riding in the cruiser with her. Duval knew that the other information Garrett wanted was a blood sample from Christa, and he was determined to bring a halt to that endeavor. After the cruiser pulled from the yard, Garrett spoke to Gritty.

"It's too late, isn't it, to get Alma's caretaker stopped? I wondered if it was a good idea to have more people around here tonight. She looks exhausted, and I still have some things I'm going to have to settle up here before McCracken and I can leave ..."

Gritty looked at her watch. "It's Victoria's night, and I'm afraid she might have left to come over by now. She's very prompt ... an aspect of nursing, do you think?" Gritty's face looked tired and wrinkled. "Besides, Carmen and I could use some help getting mom settled, tonight of all nights. Come to think of it, Victoria might have gotten someone else. She hasn't been over since you arrested Duz for killing her husband ... It might make her uncomfortable to be here. But she's reliable — I'm sure she'll send someone." Garrett nodded, the nod somehow satisfied.

"All right then. I understand that you want Victoria or someone to come on over, but I want you ..." He paused and cleared his throat, making his voice take in Carmen, Duz, Alma, and McCracken as well as Gritty. Everyone had started toward the house, Duz helping his mother, and they all turned to listen, their faces forbearing.

"Ms. Anderson tells me that it might be Victoria who comes to take care of Alma's nursing needs for the night. In the interest of police protocol, not to mention kindness and courtesy, please don't bring it up that we have arrested her daughter. Duz, maybe you could disappear for a while when she arrives, too. There will be a better time and place to give her the unfortunate information we have to deliver." There were tired nods and murmurs of assent.

Duz suddenly looked hopeful. "Then are you saying I'm for sure off the hook?" All eyes turned toward Garrett. In their compassion for Christa, the family had almost forgotten this bright aspect of the afternoon.

"It looks like it," Garrett said. "There's the D.A. to contend with, but ... well, let's just say you won't be going down to Riversmet tonight."

"Whoof!" Duz breathed out. "That sounds great! If you wanted me to, I would even hide with the rats in the cellar while Victoria's here, now that I know that!" A slight spring entered his step as he walked his mother to the house, Carmen leading them in.

Garrett leaned toward Gritty again. "It may be difficult for your mother to follow those instructions, especially since she's quite worn out. Please help her ... Victoria shouldn't have to be here too long."

Gritty looked resigned. "All right, Sheriff." She shook her head. "I still think Duval has an entrapment defense for Christa. But at least now I believe that is a good thing."

"Maybe." Garrett turned away, his eyes searching for McCracken. It took him a minute to home in on the homeboy. "Look, McCracken, run up to the clubhouse and get one of those Stoney City deputies. I want these cars out of here. Maybe it will be all right to park them up there. And bring our cruiser back. I want you here. We have ... paperwork."

Gritty looked at Duval's and Christa's cars. "I don't think those cars are a problem where they are."

"Victoria would ask ..."

"Oh. Yes, I suppose she would." She looked wearily up at the house. "Well, I'll go on in and help Alma get settled." She rolled her chair up the ramp as McCracken raced across the yard and then popped back, her quick movements comical in the baggy pants.

"No keys, Chief."

He grinned. "Hot wire 'em, Homeboy. And be quick about it." Then he followed the Weinant family into the house.

From where he sat at the table, he could see the highway both ways as well as the driveway entrance. He bent over his notebook and began to write diligently, glancing up to note that McCracken had successfully hot wired Christa's car and her little bald head could be seen above the seat, receding as she drove with all due speed toward the clubhouse. It looked like someone was with her, and suddenly he realized who the second person was that Hallie Flute had seen that night. It was the car seat itself, sticking up and not moving in the back seat of Christa's car. Someone had been with Christa that night after all: the little sleeping Eirene. He sighed and tapped his pencil on his paper.

Within a few minutes Carmen arrived at his elbow, carrying fresh coffee. "Cream?" she asked, wondering what was so urgent that he had to write it down here and now on this table. Probably nothing. "Sugar?" She suspected he was staying because he didn't trust her and Gritty to be discreet around Victoria. It irritated her.

"Black," he grinned, his hand casually covering the page from her eyes.

The cruiser came down and a Stoney City guy disembarked, raised the hood of Duval's car, and he and McCracken both bent over the engine. Only a minute passed and the car started. McCracken got back into the cruiser and pulled it into the space left by Christa's car as the other deputy took off in Duval's. Garrett looked at his watch. 6:25. Victoria was always very prompt. That's what both Alma and Gritty had told him. He lowered his eyes back to the notebook and thunked his pencil on it again.

McCracken came in, and he said to her, "I think Ms. Weinant has both coffee and lemonade. You probably need something after this afternoon. Why not slip out back with a cool glass of lemonade and put your feet up for a few minutes? Kind of crowded in here." She looked at him, a little shift of the eyebrows, the look immediately disappearing. Stone-faced cop, Garrett thought.

"Sure, Chief. No problem," she said, and Carmen, smiling, handed her the cold glass even as she turned around. "He doesn't always have to send you off. It's not that crowded."

"Oh, that's all right. The chief knows I like to get outside. Thanks, though. For the lemonade." McCracken ambled through the kitchen; Garrett would have sworn she was perfecting her shuffle.

He felt like he was in some sort of suspense film, waiting for a bomb to go off. Except for casting an occasional curious glance his way, the Weinants seemed to be contented to go ahead with their evening. Carmen was digging in a drawer, searching out a soft nightgown for Alma. Duz was making sounds about what might be kicking around to eat. Gritty started trying to help him find canned beans in the cupboard where she recalled she'd seen them on her last visit. McCracken appeared at the kitchen door in the back and snagged a cookie from a plate of cookies that had been set too temptingly on the cabinet.

Victoria pulled into the yard and entered the front door. Garrett acknowledged her entrance into the house with a nod. "My goodness! It looks like everyone is here," she said, looking around. Garrett let his eyes find the kitchen. It was empty. Not everyone, he thought.

Sighing, Gritty said, "Well, Carmen and I were going to eat with Alma, and Sheriff Garrett and Deputy McCracken had more questions to ask us, so we're just getting started ..."

Victoria glanced at Alma. Her face became subdued. "Oh, I'm so embarrassed ... so sorry about Duz. And even though ... well, this is an odd thing to say, but even though it was poor Reider ..." She stopped and swallowed, her eyes tearing. "I'm sorry. I just meant to say ... I can understand Duz's being horribly angry about the water." She wrung her hands. "Maybe I shouldn't have come tonight. Maybe you'd feel more comfortable just to ..." She looked searchingly at Alma, who returned her gaze with a look of curiosity. To be honest, Alma had forgotten why all these people were here.

Gritty glanced at Garrett, but he'd gone back to his notebook, writing busily. "Well, I ... no, you're here. After all, you must understand that *we* know Duz didn't do it ... didn't kill your husband. It's some kind of terrible mistake. So don't worry about that.

"We feel comfortable with you here. And Carmen and I need the help. I'm not used to all Alma's needs, and I'm getting a little behind on everything. I couldn't bathe her, last night, and there's her medicine, and Du ... do you know where she keeps all her canned goods? That will help."

Victoria smiled, the smile subdued, bitter-sweet. "Well, I do thank you. You're kind and understanding people. And I'm sure you're right about Duz. Surely he'll be free soon. Let's start with the canned goods." She took Gritty into the kitchen, and Garrett turned a page of his notebook.

Back in the living room, Victoria knelt by Alma. "How are you today, Dear? You look absolutely exhausted." She gave Alma's cheek a little tweak and smiled at her. "Been up to no good, have you? I think things will come out for the best, though, don't you? Things aren't always as bad as they seem ... they aren't always even *what* they seem, are they?" She paused, then added, "When we're tired."

Alma nodded and opened her mouth, but Gritty butted in strongly. "You're right. She's very tired tonight. I think going to the funeral yesterday tired her out. You must be exhausted, too—I'm sorry we didn't make arrangements for someone else to come tonight, considering what you've been going through."

Victoria cast a quick glance up at Gritty from where she knelt by Alma. "Well, yes, I'm exhausted, but the work keeps my mind off things. I actually appreciate the work. And Mary and Jeannie couldn't have come tonight anyhow." Garrett raised his eyes, lowered them back to the notebook, thought, 'Thanks, A-deet.'

"I didn't know that ..."

"Well, I have to confess. I did try to call them earlier," Victoria said shortly. "They had other priorities for tonight."

"Oh," Gritty said. She felt uncomfortable. "It is a tense time. Carmen and I can help ..." Victoria stood.

"Oh, please don't worry, Greta. I don't mind ..." She looked down at Alma, an odd expression crossing her face. "I really do not mind giving Alma the attention she needs."

Carmen, who had been listening and was feeling especially light-hearted, knowing Duz was free, said, "Well, let me draw the bath. Gritty can go ahead and cook up some supper, and you can do the nursey things you do best, like getting Alma her medication, especially those eye drops. I'm so clumsy, trying to put them in."

All three women began to bustle around. Victoria tipped Alma's head back for the eye drops, and from the kitchen Gritty called out, "If you don't mind, please fill Alma's pill boxes. I didn't get to that today, and I would like them done right."

"I don't mind at all," Victoria said, going around the corner into the bedroom where the medications were kept. Bath water could be heard splashing into the tub while Carmen hummed. Garrett thought she sounded way too happy for a woman whose husband was supposedly languishing in jail, but Victoria, seeming to catch the spirit, emerged from the bedroom humming, also, and carrying a plastic pill container.

"Pill boxes all full," she called cheerily toward the kitchen. "Here you go, Alma. Down the hatch." Her old hand shaky, Alma reached for the pills, her fingers closing around the container.

It was then that Garrett stood up. "Just a minute, Mrs. Weinant. From here, you know, that looks like quite a lot of pills." Victoria's head jerked toward him, the habitual sweet expression on her face soured. Swiftly she turned back and made a snatching motion toward the pill container, but Alma, her eyes large, held tight, and Garrett took the distance across the floor in two strides.

Before she could stop him, his large hand had closed on the plastic and he lifted it clear of Alma's startled grasp. "McCracken!" he barked. McCracken and another deputy appeared at the door.

"McCracken," Garrett repeated, opening his hand for a good look inside the container it enclosed, "Please arrest Ms. Victoria Beekermann for attempted homicide. Arrest her as well for homicide in the recent death of Reider Biedermann. Read her

her rights."

Victoria was staring at McCracken. "That isn't your deputy! That's the boy who delivered Alma's blackmail note to me last night." Her eyes went back to Garrett's face, and her creamy complexion flushed scarlet. "Oh, I see. While I was poisoning rats, I should have taken care of you as well as Reider, shouldn't I?"

35

What Did You Say Happened?

At That Chicken Shed?

Duz had been woolgathering on the back porch. Being in jail had given him a whole new perspective on the world. He'd thought then that the first thing he would do when he got out— he had never doubted he *would* get out—would be to put a better fence around the north slope, and set up a sprinkler system on that side. He had always wanted to try a sprinkler system, and sitting in jail, it occurred to him that, by golly, one only lives once, so why not get onto it? Also, he would contact Nancy Jane about their adjoining lower forty. The way that land set, he could see them going together on water to raise a good patch of drought-resistant red alfalfa. Could benefit them both.

He couldn't wait to tell Carmen; she'd be pleased with him. She would figure he had as many different takes on the focus of his own labors as she had on those fish she was always messing with. He sighed, smiled, closed his eyes, and stretched his feet forward in front of the porch swing where he sat. The funny-looking little deputy continued to fidget, but he ignored her and was almost to the point of a contented snore when he heard someone shout from within the house.

He jerked up, but the deputy had already shot into the house and someone he hadn't even known was there appeared from beside the porch, pushed past him, and ran into the house behind the deputy. What the hell?! Duz got onto his feet and hesitated for a minute, recalling that they were trying to spare Victoria's feelings by keeping his release from jail under wraps. Still, the sounds from within the house were tense. Maybe he was needed. Maybe the person by the porch was giving them trouble. Cautiously he stepped into the back door.

Gritty had parked her chair in the door between the kitchen and the living room, her back to him. Out of his view, he could hear Carmen saying, "My heaven! What in the world just went on here?" He stepped up behind Gritty, grabbed the handles of her wheelchair, and peered over her head into the living room. His mother was sitting where she always sat, looking around like a bastard calf in a bull fight, and Carmen had reached the window by the table. He heard the front door close to his right.

Looking up, Gritty said, "Hi Duz. You won't believe this! I ... they just arrested Victoria."

"Arrested Victoria? But why?" Duz gave Gritty a short push so that he could get past her into the room, then went to his mother. "You all right, Mom? I heard somebody holler ..."

"It was the sheriff hollering for the deputies," Gritty said, but at the same time Carmen said, "Everyone is coming."

"What do you mean, everyone is coming?" Gritty asked, pushing up to the window.

Carmen giggled. "Look! It's the whole neighborhood. And I can see that Pete and John ... Bud and Nancy, too—they have shotguns. But get a load of this: old Lew is packing a pitchfork! What in the world do they think they're doing?" It reminded her of the scene in Frankenstein when the mob came after the monster. Cars were pulling up along the road, people were getting out, and all of them were walking toward the house.

"I can't see," Gritty said, and she couldn't, because the east window took in the driveway entrance, but not the yard between the house and the shed, where apparently everyone was congregating.

"Well, what's going on?" Alma said. She'd struggled to her feet. As much to herself as to Alma, Gritty said, "Let's go see." She made for the door. Alma started thumping along behind her, and Duz got his hand under her non-cane elbow for support. Carmen stood impatiently, waiting for the traffic jam to clear.

Tapping her toe, she glanced down at the table. Garrett's much written-in notebook was there, wide open, and Carmen couldn't restrain her curiosity. Picking it up, she flipped through it. Page after page of rabbits, trees, flowers, deer, and bushes had been doodled right up to the margins, all embellished with an occasional spiral and the words, "hi dee ho dee hoo-dally ho." This was too much. Carmen laughed out loud, then laid the notebook down carefully where she had found it and followed through the now cleared doorway.

The sheriff's car, containing Victoria and the two deputies, was working its way through the crowd and out the driveway. Duz was edging toward a lawn chair with Alma, and Lew Harris was setting up another lawn chair beside it, gesturing with the pitchfork and seating Lucky. At least two dozen of their neighbors, women and men, were milling around the yard, their talk making a loud clacking buzz like blackbirds settling into a tree. Hallie was trotting authoritatively toward Alma, but no one had approached the sheriff.

Garrett was standing alone in his own pool of space, still holding the pill container, his eyes following the cruiser out the gate. The hard, angry expression on his face would have daunted any strong man.

The car finally attained the highway and moved on out. Abruptly, as if coming to himself, Garrett dropped his eyes to the people and looked around. "Well, well, well! And what might you all be doing here?"

Looking, perhaps, a little chagrined, Bill Brown stepped forward, his speech clipped and authoritative. "Hallie called us. She said that it looked like there might be trouble at Alma's again. She said she could see a lot of goings on over here."

Helpfully, Doreen Van Doran chipped in. "That's right, Sheriff. Hallie told us that this time she wasn't ..." Doreen hesitated, not sure she wanted to repeat Hallie's words in mixed company, then she forged bravely ahead. "She said that this time she wasn't going to be caught with her pants down."

Gangling John Michaelson, without tact, added, "Not a pretty sight."

Frieda Johnson used the broom she was clutching to push past John and impose her large body like an obstinate stump against the skyline. "Hallie said she saw police cars coming and going here all afternoon, and people in odd places around the yard, and she was afraid you might all be in trouble. We thought you might need help.

"But that was silly, I guess," she finished. "You seem to have everything under control?" This last sentence was a question, and Garrett smiled to himself. No one could keep their eyes from the main highway, down which a police car had just taken Victoria Biedermann, obviously under arrest, and their faces burned with the curiosity that good manners restrained them from expressing outright.

"Yeah, we do," he said.

Then he did one of those impulsive things that all his years of experience counseled against. Sometimes he wondered about himself, but these people felt like the kind of family one should confide in. Inwardly, he shrugged. As it had more than once on this case, intuition trumped training and reason.

Instead of keeping his own counsel and heading to the office of the prickly D.A., he took the more satisfying option. He held up the container of pills. "We did have a little problem, though. It seems that Victoria Biedermann was intent on poisoning Alma."

A gasp went through the group, with Agnes Michaelson saying, "Oh, my!" Then, realizing that he was going to continue speaking, they grew hushed.

"You see, Reider Biedermann did not die from a gunshot wound, as we believed at first. There was almost no blood from the wound, meaning that his heart had ceased to pump before the bullet ever hit him.

"Neither did he die from the blow to the head with the shovel that had Mr. Weinant's fingerprints. That blow caused bruising of the skin and some bleeding near the surface of the brain, but it wasn't so hard as to kill him. After he'd been struck by the shovel, he regained consciousness, got to his feet, entered the shed, and even located the particular box that he'd been planning to search through.

"It wasn't until all of the pathologist's results came in that we learned he had died from severe bleeding in the internal capsule of the brain, in the central portion, and that that bleeding was consistent with the fact that the laboratory found his body to be full of Coumadin. Such bleeding is an expected result of a Coumadin overdose."

"Coumadin?" several of the younger voices in the crowd

repeated, but Donna Caswell and others nodded knowingly. "Coumadin," she told the young and uninformed. "You take it for heart disease and stroke, to thin the blood. It's the stuff Alma takes."

Nancy Jane Barnswallowper crowed. She was delighted. "I never thought that Victoria Biedermann was what she put on. That stuff has another name besides Coumadin, doesn't it, Sheriff?"

Garrett nodded and spoke carefully. "Coumadin is a good medication for hearts, but it also goes by the name of Warfarin, which is rat poison. Warfarin kills rats by making their blood so thin that it won't coagulate, and they bleed to death, usually internally. A human who's being medicated can get too much, too. People who are on a prescription for Coumadin usually have their blood drawn at least once per month to monitor coagulation time. If it isn't coagulating rapidly enough, their doctor adjusts the dosage."

Frieda's eyes were on the pill container Garrett held. "So, what was going on? Did Victoria ... why did she try to kill Alma? Are you saying she gave ..."

Garrett pulled a chair away from the side of the shed and sat down. "Let's start at the beginning. I believe that the problem was just what we thought at first. It was the water deeds. See, Victoria was never Reider's wife. She was a mistress, and it was in that status that she had Mac and Christa. Then he just cut out on her and married a woman called Betsy Zakely. We're told that he married Betsy for the money; at any rate, they were married for some time, and he had a child by Betsy. The child was the Lindy Zakely that you all knew. The girl who stayed with Harris's."

"Biedermann was *her* father?"

"Biedermann was her father. But, according to sources, he continued to see Victoria, even during his marriage. He also had other, occasionally more adventurous, sexual liaisons."

Jilly Brown said, "Eeeooo, ukh! You mean ...?"

Garrett glanced mildly at her. "Probably," he said. "At any rate, he became infected with HIV several years ago, and he managed to infect the youngest daughter with the disease."

"AIDS," Jilly informed the group, a stage whisper.

The crowd murmured and shifted, moving forward. Garrett continued. "To make a long story short, it was Lindy's mother who shot Reider that night. It had to do with his treatment of her daughter, Lindy."

"Oh, my ..." the ripple ran through the group, "Oh, no ... couldn't blame her ..." Garrett ignored it all and continued.

"His other daughter, Christa, was the person who struck him with the shovel, before he was shot. That had to do with her fear for her own little daughter, Eirene. The blow appears to have been struck in self-defense."

Nancy Jane scowled. The sheriff was leaving out a lot, here. Before anyone could interject, however, he went on. "But it appears that there was a third woman who had problems with Reider Biedermann.

"As we have reconstructed the situation, we think Mr. Biedermann told Victoria about the coup he expected to pull off with respect to the ranch irrigation rights in this valley. He planned to convert those water rights to domestic rights and develop the whole Oozle area. The land would have lost its unique rural, agricultural properties. But broken up into housing tracts, it would have been worth millions.

"Victoria was thrilled, in part because at almost the same time she learned that Biedermann had AIDS. She expected to have him carry through the water scheme before he died, and she thought since she had at last won his heart, she would be the only beneficiary named in his will. Not only would the will have been a final, concrete testimony of his love, but in the end it would have been Victoria who gained by the water grab.

"Unfortunately for her, before she could fully prepare to celebrate this, apparently Reider mocked her, telling her he was interested in another woman. He told her that as soon as his real estate deal was set he planned to leave her. And he told her that he had changed his will in favor of the other woman." Garrett shifted on the chair, but the crowd, leaning on pitchforks, shovels, rakes, and rifles, stood still, mesmerized.

"Well," he continued, "They say there's no fury like that of a woman scorned. Victoria was a nurse, and she had a nurse's way of getting even. She may have tried to make Reider believe he shouldn't reject her, but however she went about it, what she did was to medicate him. From what we can gather, following up on prescription amounts that were 'lost' from the supplies of the elderly patients that she cared for, she accumulated massive doses of Coumadin, which she must have given to him under the guise of treatment for his AIDS."

"But didn't the pharmacists ... why did they keep refilling? People shouldn't keep getting extra rat poison ..." Donna Caswell was hugging Spit for comfort. She'd been one of those who were cared for by Victoria.

Garrett shrugged. "They didn't see a pattern. This is a peaceful area. People don't lock their cars. People don't poison other people. Usually it wasn't Victoria who called to request a replacement prescription. She took the drugs, but usually it was another caretaker who would find that not enough were available to fill drug cups. It was easy to think that a few pills had spilled, perhaps, or that a bottle had rolled under a couch."

"Wow," Jilly Brown said, her eyes huge. "This is a ... a terrible story." You could see that, for Jilly, it was "The Young and the Restless," come to a theater near her.

"From what we found when we searched her home the second time," Garrett continued, "It looked as if she was also dosing Biedermann with Tylenol and aspirin, as well as doses of herbal teas, such as Sweet Woodruff and Yellow Clover, all of which would intensify the effect of the Coumadin. Someone, possibly Victoria, had dumped boxes and bottles of the stuff in a hole in the back yard and buried them."

"I can just see it," Jilly breathed. "He suffers from the AIDS. The cocky bastard thinks he has her over a barrel. He believes she thinks he is the cat's meow, and he tells her his sob story, ouchy here, ouchy there—but she doses him up with ... with rat poison! Oh, wow! Can't you just hear him last Tuesday?"

Jilly's voice became mimicking. " 'Oh, Darling, I have such a headache,' he says, and she replies, " 'Never fear, Dearest. Just have this handful of aspirin and a double dose of rat poison. All will be well by evening.' " Jilly chortled happily, unaware that she was getting a very long look from Billy, not to mention shocked glances from some of the club women.

Donna, still clutching Spit, said, "But why Alma? Why did she try to poison *Alma*?"

Garrett met Gritty's eyes, his expression guilty. "We wanted ... well, we wanted a strong indication that the case we had put together, based on our detective work with the pharmacies, the autopsy, and so-on, wasn't an illusion. So we set a trap."

"Heh, heh, heh. A trap!" Lew Harris leaned forward on his pitchfork. "How about that, Lucky? They got 'er good."

Duz was leaning so far forward beside his mother's chair it looked as if he might topple. "But I wasn't in there. What happened?"

"Right," said Alma, who *had* been there. "What happened? I don't understand, Sheriff. What in the world was that all about in there? You say Victoria tried ... tried to *poison* me?"

"She thought you were going to blackmail her," Garrett said. "Remember the notes you wrote last night? We used those, Jenny and McCracken and I, to make one more note. We delivered a note to her that said you had seen her take your Coumadin bottle, and you intended to tell someone about it."

Alma drew herself up in her chair and her jaw firmed. "Shame on you, Lyle. Just shame on you. You should be able to do your job without lying. You almost got me killed!"

Everyone was quiet for a few minutes, trying to sort it all out, then Carmen said softly, "No, he didn't, Alma. Sheriff Garrett was there the full time, watching. Because of him and his good police work, our Duz is off the hook."

A murmur went through the crowd, but Garrett stood up and stretched, his eyes on Clint Harris, who in turn was looking at Duz Weinant, who was looking fondly at Carmen. Duz's gaze jumped back to the sheriff when Garrett said, "I suppose that's true, and yet I wonder ... what I've wondered all along. You see, I haven't been worried about the shovel that clubbed Biedermann. It had explanations. What has been puzzling me is the *other* shovel.

"Surely only a man with a lot on his mind would get so confused about his favorite tool. Maybe you'd like to tell us, Duz ... when you needed to help Alice get her vehicle going last Wednesday, why did you need *her* shovel? Where was your own shovel—I've never known a man in this neck of the woods who didn't keep his irrigating shovel right with him in the back of his pickup."

Duz's shoulders drooped and Clint Harris spoke for the first time since he had arrived in the yard. He said, "Oh, shit." The two men met each other's eyes, then Clint said, "Well, Weinant, you may as well tell him. You're the best talker."

What had passed for silence in the group before was as nothing compared to the quiet that occurred now. Patty's hand flew to her mouth, but Carmen's head turned toward Duz and, eyes narrowed, she nodded thoughtfully, an 'I just knew it' sort of nod. Duz cleared his throat.

"That night, last Tuesday night," he began, "I did go to the divider box after the water board meeting. And I did sit watching the water, worrying and thinking. But what happened then was, it hit me out of the blue where the quit claim deeds were. I remembered my mother being secretary of the board that year, and I remembered when Gritty's accident was. I even recalled Mom saying to Dad and me—Dad was alive then—she said, 'I'm going to put these deeds in this file before I go to help out with ... with my Greta Amelia.' That was what she said. But we were all stressed, then, and I guess they seemed safe there, so we all forgot about it.

"Anyhow, that night I remembered where they were. I went back to the house, thinking I would talk to Carmen, but she hadn't got home from the art show yet. I stewed around, kind of wanting some action, then I got out my truck and went over to see Clint.

"Clint was in the barn, fixing his tractor. We talked it over, and decided to drive up here to see if we could find the deeds. We figured that would resolve everything. Clint said Patty had got real mad and headed out somewhere, so he was feeling antsy, too.

"But anyhow, the thing was, when we got here, we saw a light in the shed. Neither one of us had brought a gun, and we were jumpy as hell, plus we both suspected it might be Biedermann.

"We drove by and parked a little ways down the road, then Clint dug around in his toolbox and came up with a claw hammer. I took my shovel, and we walked back up the road and came up to the shed, real quiet. I looked in there and I ... I looked in there and I ..." Duz's voice faded. He shook his head, trying to continue. "I don't quite remember." Clint, his eyes sympathetic, picked up the story.

"Weinant looked in there and saw Biedermann hunkered over his mother's boxes. It all hit him—the pure evil of the guy, sneaking into Alma's shed, going after those deeds like that. It all hit him. He just lost it.

"He got that shovel up and he was going to hit the guy. He was furious. I ain't ever seen him like that before. I saw, though, that something was wrong with Reider. I grabbed the shovel from behind Duz and pulled—I had to wrestle him to get it away, and I kept telling him that I thought somebody else had already done the guy in for us.

"I finally got him stopped, and then we did check Biedermann's pulse. We didn't much have to—he hadn't moved an inch in all the bangin' around we'd been doin' over that shovel. He was dead as a doornail."

Duz found his voice again. "This wouldn't have been such a problem, except we were so stirred up. We saw Mom movin' around there in the house, and we were sure she was okay, and we didn't want to stir her up, so we closed the shed door, got back in the truck, turned around down in the schoolyard, and started drivin' up the road.

"To be honest, Sheriff, in the state we were in, we didn't want to call about that body. We couldn't see why we should. The guy was dead. Not only was he finally harmless, but nobody could help him, either. We couldn't figure why we should get ourselves in the middle of the picture. I guess we just didn't foresee that it would be Mom that found the body, and all the fuss that would happen over it. We thought some drug dealer just shot 'im and Victoria would report 'im missin', and if he didn't turn up, then we could figure out a way to kinda 'find' him ourselves and report it then.

"So what we did, I dropped Clint off at the road and he went up by the back path. He managed to make Patty think he'd been workin' on the tractor all that time. Then I headed on home. I doubt if I fooled Carmen." Duz spread his hands, looked at his wife, who rewarded him with a stone face worthy of any cop in the business. He shrugged and managed to grin.

"Well, whatever. At any rate, I parked the truck, reached in and got that shovel, my good irrigatin' shovel, and looked at it for a long time. I contemplated how I had damn near killed somebody with it over a little water, and would have, except I was too late." He sighed, glanced at Alma. "Too late, as usual. I set that shovel down by the garage door. At the time—this is at the time, mind you, Sheriff Garrett—at the time, I thought I never wanted to see that damned irrigatin' shovel again."

About the Author

Karen Weinant Gallob is an anthropologist who taught for several years at Metropolitan State College, Denver, and at the University of Colorado. She is interested in the relationships among language, culture, and human perceptions of reality.

In addition to her Ph.D. thesis, *A Study of Humor in Mauritius* (complete with jokes), she has also published articles and reviews in her field, newspaper articles, and poetry. She wrote the "Carpe Diem in the Crawford Outback" series for the *North Fork Merchant Herald* from 2001 until 2005.

Although they are their own accomplishments, she is most boastful of her children, grandchildren, and great-grandchildren.

Karen lives on the family ranch south of Crawford, Colorado, where nary a summer day goes by that she doesn't hear her husband, Dave, say, "This place could really grow some hay if we only had a little more irrigatin' water."

All the Bad Stuff Comes in Threes

A Pat Garrett, Leigh McCracken Mystery

by Karen Weinant Gallob

Not your copy?

If you'd like to order your own copy of this book,
or get a gift for a friend,
please use the order form below.

ORDER FORM

Please send me _____ copies of *All the Bad Stuff Comes in Threes* by Karen Weinant Gallob.

Enclosed is my check or money order for $14.95 for each copy plus $3.00 shipping and handling (total $17.95 per book) *(Colorado residents please add* **43¢ state sales tax** *for each book ordered.)*

Name _____

Address _____

City, State, Zip _____

Send a photocopy (or clip out) of this order form to:
KAREN WEINANT GALLOB
2240 Clear Fork Road
Crawford, CO 81415